To Save a
World

Carolyn,
So nice to finally meet
you! Thank you so much
for your support. Yay us!
Enjoy the adventure!

HOLLIS JO McCOLLUM

PAGE PUBLISHING, INC.
New York, NY

First originally published by Page Publishing, Inc. 2017

ISBN 978-1-63568-857-3 (Paperback)
ISBN 978-1-63568-858-0 (Digital)

Printed in the United States of America

This book is dedicated to Ashley, without whom this story would not have been written. You are so much more than my best friend, you are my sister. I love and am thankful for you always.

CHAPTER ONE

*E*ithne's mother was calling. This was not unusual, and Eithne set aside her book on the table before going to answer her. Her mother, impatient, called again. She stepped a bit livelier into the small kitchen where her mother was stirring a pot of stew for supper.

"Finally, darling! What have you been doing alone in your room for over an hour?" Her mother inquired with a hint of impatience.

She was a tall, slender elf woman with a sweet and hasty manner about her. She was quite beautiful still and had many suitors in her youth. Her long reddish blond hair was knotted into a bun on the top of her head, and her brown eyes still held a sparkle of youth. Eithne's older sister, Rosalin, looked very much like their mother. Some people said that Eithne did as well, but she did not see it.

"I was reading a book," Eithne replied simply.

Her mother let out a practiced sigh of exasperation. "Why would you want to be inside reading on such a lovely day? Anyway, there are other much more desirable activities for young ladies to busy themselves with."

Eithne rolled her eyes at her mother's comment. It was the sort of thing she was often made to tolerate. "Was there something you wanted me to do, Mum?"

"Yes. Yes, there is, darling." She stopped stirring the pot, wiped her hands on her apron, and began sifting through a nearby drawer. "I would like you to stop by the baker's and buy a loaf of bread. While you are out, retrieve your sister for supper."

Her mother took some money and a dark-green ribbon from the drawer and walked over to her youngest daughter, who was standing in the doorway. Eithne pocketed the money and tried to turn away, but her mother stopped her and began to fuss over appearance.

"Honestly, Eithne, you're much prettier than this! Would it kill you to wear a more flattering dress and put a ribbon in your hair?"

"It doesn't matter, Mum. I think I look fine. Besides, I'm comfortable," she retorted with some pluck.

"Nonsense. You would be just as comfortable in something less plain." Her mother smoothed out Eithne's fiery red hair and tied it with the dark-green ribbon. Then she plucked at the wool shift dress Eithne wore as if straightening it out would somehow make it less plain. "Well, at least you're wearing green. It brings out those lovely eyes."

Eithne had inherited her father's eyes, which were a vibrant green, like the color of new spring grass.

"All right, may I go now? I don't understand why you always have to make such a fuss. I'm not like Rosalin anyway." Eithne resented that her mother always seemed to try to make her more like her older sister, who was apparently perfect.

Her mother sighed at her comment and nodded. Eithne turned and walked out through the front door of their house. Her family lived right off the main street of the village, so it would be a short errand. It would also be easy to find her sister. All she had to do was look for the adoring crowd of young suitors.

The village was solely inhabited by members of Eithne's tribe, the Aranni tribe. It was one of the many villages that all belonged to the same tribe as the Aranni were quite large in population. Once a year, all the villages would gather for a festival of several days that would celebrate a great many things at one time. All of its members were elves, like Eithne, who were characteristically tall and slender. People mostly lived in small wooden houses, each having a little garden to itself. Another well-known characteristic of her people was what marked the coming of age of each individual. Once a person passed adolescence, they would go to see a special shaman in the tribe, who would determine their spirit animal guide. Then the likeness of that animal would be permanently tattooed on the young elf's body in a place determined by the shaman. Eithne had always been quite proud of her animal guide because she knew that no one else in the entire tribe shared her same animal. A great phoenix had been tattooed on the left side of her body—its head beginning just beneath her left breast and ending with its tail feathers sailing down her thigh almost to her knee. Of course, no one ever saw the massive display of body art, as tribal elf women dressed quite modestly in long dresses covering their ankles. Eithne was quietly proud of her phoenix, nonetheless.

It had rained recently in the village, and the ground was still quite muddy. Eithne muddied the hem of her dress and her slippers in short time as she made her way. She first went to the baker's stall to buy the bread. There was not much to choose from. Even though the grain harvest was recent, crops were doing poorly. She did her best to purchase a loaf that seemed large enough to feed the family for dinner tonight and perhaps have some leftover for breakfast. Then she set off to locate her sister, Rosalin. After making a few inquiries to those who may have seen her, Eithne discovered that Rosalin was at the jewel shop with her friend, Gwendalyn. She should have known. The jewel shop was a favorite haunt for many young ladies and girls in the village, and Rosalin was no exception.

Rosalin was exactly there, exclaiming in an animated fashion over a gold and ruby pendant with Gwendalyn. Eithne, who was now impatient to get home for supper, wasted no time approaching them. When Rosalin saw her little sister, she smiled brightly.

"Eithne, isn't it beautiful? I wish it could be mine," exclaimed Rosalin as she gestured to the pendant.

Eithne glanced at the pendant passively. "Yes, it's lovely, but Mum wants us home for supper. I've already bought the bread." She held up the paper parcel with the small loaf of bread inside to further illustrate her statement.

"Don't be so serious all the time!" Rosalin chided in a very similar fashion to their mother. "Why do you always sit around, reading books, instead of coming out with Gwendalyn and me sometimes?"

Gwendalyn smiled a polite smile.

"I'm just not very interested in shopping, I suppose." That wasn't true. A part of Eithne desperately wanted to do all those silly girly things, but she also didn't want people to think that was all she was either.

"Well, you should be. I would love to see you in some new dresses and maybe some jewelry to match. I have even heard one of the boys saying that he fancied you." Rosalin gave Eithne a wink and placed her hands on her hips.

Eithne sighed internally. Her sister simply did not understand. "Rosalin, you know I don't care to talk about things like that. Besides, I don't have to worry about it until you're married off. Now, Mum has supper ready, and I'm hungry. Are you ready to go?"

Rosalin gave her a suspicious look for a moment but did concede to leave. She said good-bye to Gwendalyn with a shared cheek kiss then hooked her arm with Eithne's as they walked out. Eithne noticed the clerk noticing Rosalin as they left. It was nothing out of the ordinary. She had always thought that her older sister was more beautiful than she, and though she hated to admit it to herself, she was secretly quite jealous. Rosalin was practically the picture of their mother in her youth. She also had long, wavy reddish blond hair that fell gracefully down her back and sparkling brown eyes. She was slightly taller and a bit more robust than Eithne, and she smiled a lot. Rosalin had more suitors than any other elf maiden in the village. Eithne had none.

As they walked back through the busy streets, Rosalin chatted to Eithne about her day and whatever other thoughts passed through her mind at the time. Eithne's attention wavered in and out, depending on her sister's discussion topic. It was during one of her episodes of not paying much attention that she found that they had stopped walking. Eithne looked up to see a male elf standing in front of them. His name was Darian MacAllow. Eithne and Rosalin knew him from childhood, though the sisters did not know him so well as an adult. Darian was very accomplished for his age. He had already risen to the rank of captain of the guard for the small military force in their village. Everyone knew that he had much greater ambitions, however. He had sleek black hair that was pulled back and tied with a leather thong at the nape of his neck, as was the fashion for men in their tribe. His eyes were a piercing steely blue, and his skin was tanned from practicing outside with a sword regularly.

"Good evening, Rosalin, Eithne." Darian bent low and kissed Rosalin's hand then politely inclined his head toward Eithne.

Eithne returned his nod, only a bit more curtly. Rosalin flushed with pleasure as he greeted them.

"Where are you ladies going?" Darian asked.

"We were just on our way home for supper," Rosalin replied. "Are you off to your home for the same?"

"Yes, in fact, I am." He seemed somewhat awkward and at a loss for words, but Darian still wished to chat idly.

Eithne rolled her eyes from impatience. How long was this going to last? She just wanted to eat. The deficient conversation continued for several moments as Rosalin blushed and smiled prettily for him. Occasionally, Darian glanced at Eithne and gave her a small smile in order to give her the impression of being included in the conversation. She would smile or nod back and then look at her sister to see when the painful display would end.

When they threatened to move on to an even more menial subject than the weather, Eithne interrupted, "Well, I'm really very hungry, dear sister. Perhaps we should get going and you two can continue your conversation another time?"

Darian looked a bit embarrassed but gave his accord to Eithne's suggestion. He bade them both a good evening and stepped aside so they could walk past. He stood and watched the pair of sisters walk down the street. Eithne looked back as they went and made eye contact with Darian. He quickly turned away. She thought there was no need for him to be embarrassed. Lots of men watched her sister as she passed.

For the rest of the evening, Eithne heard about nothing but Darian MacAllow. Firstly, on the rest of the walk home with her sister, which was mercifully short. Then as soon as Rosalin mentioned his name and the encounter to their parents, they became too excited and would not stop talking about him either. Of course, his good looks were the foremost topic discussed. Even though Eithne was annoyed with the conversation, there was no denying that Darian was a very handsome elf with his straight, chiseled features. Next, her parents went on and on about his accomplishments as the captain of the guard at such a young age. It was also true. That discussion only led to the topic of Darian's most distinguished military lineage. Both his father and grandfather had been high-ranking officers who held much respect in the tribal elf communities. Even Darian's mother had been a nurse to injured soldiers in times of war.

Eithne managed to suppress a yawn. She wondered when she could be excused from the table, and her mind wandered to more entertaining thoughts. Her musings were interrupted when she realized that she was expected to participate in the monologue of Darian.

"Darling, are you even listening?" her mother chided. "Rosalin was just saying that Darian had expressed a desire to court her for marriage yesterday! Isn't that exciting?"

Eithne should have been more excited, and she would have been if a new man didn't express his desire to marry her sister every week or so—though Darian was probably the best option so far, not only for Rosalin, but also as a brother-in-law.

"Yes, very exciting, indeed. He seems like he would be a good husband," Eithne said sweetly. There was genuine warmth in her voice. "I mean, he certainly has an even temper and doesn't get angry easily."

"Why would you say that?" her father asked, curious of his youngest daughter's insight.

Eithne was just on the spot and could only blame herself. She had said too much. She knew this about Darian because he had good reason once to be very angry with her in the recent past. He had found her practicing with a sword, which was strictly forbidden of elf women in the tribe. Women were not allowed to learn any fighting skills or how to be a blacksmith. It was considered to be quite the egregious offense, and any elf woman caught doing such things met with harsh punishment. Eithne had been just such a lawbreaker for many years now. She would sneak off to the training fields to watch the men practice, trying to learn the proper techniques. She had also stolen a sword from the weapons chest at the training fields—another horrible offense—and had been using it for a long time. Eithne had always found a secluded place to practice. Only a few short weeks ago, she thought she had found a new, perfectly safe spot—a pristine little meadow that was not far from her home. Little did she know that Darian also thought the meadow to be an excellent place for sword practice. Eithne had been in the middle of figuring some new maneuver when she turned to be confronted with the dark, glaring gaze of those steel-blue eyes. He did not say anything for what felt like forever, and Eithne had never been so terrified, her heart beating wildly in her chest. He had every right to explode in a rage and drag her in front of the tribe's elders by her fiery hair right that second, but he did not. He thrust his hand out and briskly demanded her sword. She gave it quickly. Then he told her to go home and never come back. Again, she did exactly as he ordered. Darian was good at giving orders. She had never spoken of it, and he, to Eithne's great and profound relief, never breathed a word of the encounter to anyone. He also continued to treat her normally. Eithne would be forever in his debt, for it was no small gesture on his part. If anyone ever found out that the captain of the guard had allowed her to get away with such prohibited behavior, he would be in just as much trouble as she.

"Well, darling?" her mother prompted, and Eithne realized she had taken far too long to answer her father's query.

"I've just never once seen him lose his temper. That's all." Then Eithne attempted to deflect the attention from herself, "You know, all part of being a good leader. Darian is quite the natural, don't you think?"

"Yes, he is," Rosalin answered dreamily.

"You two would make a smart match, sweetheart," her father said affectionately, and the conversation lapsed back into all things Darian MacAllow.

Eithne breathed a sigh of relief. She waited a few more minutes before excusing herself from the table and going to her room.

CHAPTER TWO

❧
---

*E*ITHNE COULD NOT stop thinking about the poster outside of the village hall—or, more precisely, the information on the poster. She had always been discontented with her place in the village. No one living in the village would ever understand why, of course. She came from a respected and loving family, and though Eithne had no suitors presently, it would not be difficult to find one, given her family's status. Everyone thought she was a bit odd in personality, but most simply assumed it was a case of extreme shyness on her part. The poster seemed to offer an avenue out of her boring, dissatisfying existence, which she found herself desperate to escape. The poster stated that the captain of the guard would be selecting a group of warriors to go with him on an important mission that would take at least two months. Those who wished to be considered for the mission were to meet at the training fields tomorrow at sunrise.

Eithne felt that she had to be good enough with a sword to be selected, but as a female, she wasn't even allowed on the training fields—let alone trying out for the mission. To Eithne, the solution to her problem seemed obvious. She needed to disguise herself as a man. She could only hope to pass as an adolescent male elf who was barely old enough to try out, but that was all she needed. Besides, she was certain that a good number of young boys would be trying out. Adolescent boys are always looking for ways to prove themselves. Eithne was trying out for several reasons, and she did have to admit that proving herself was among them. However, the more persistent reason was her ever-growing need to leave the village. This seemed the perfect opportunity to do so to her. There was safety in numbers, and after she became comfortable with her own fighting skills, it would be simple to sneak away from the rest while on the trail so that she could start her own life.

Eithne had already prepared her disguise: just some of her father's old clothing that he wouldn't think to miss, a pair of beaten-up work boots, and a hat that flopped over her eyes. She would rub some dirt on her face to give the appearance of immature male stubble, tie her red hair back in the fashion of the men, and wrap her chest to flatten her breasts. She was still terrified of being discovered. If she were, the punishment was sure to be severe, but she had never heard of this particular crime being committed and had no idea what the punishment would be. Perhaps the tribe's elders simply would not know what to do with her. Eithne did not want to find out.

Tomorrow morning, she would sneak out early for the tryout. Her stomach was certain to be in knots all night. At least, she would not have trouble waking up on time.

The early autumn morning had a damp and bitter chill to the air. Though Eithne shivered beneath her wool shirt, she was in a cold sweat. She was one of the first to arrive at the fields. Darian had been there before anyone else, of course. He casually paced the fields while he let the crowd of hopefuls gather. He looked impressive with his easy gait and sword in hand. His eyes drifted over those gathering now and then, and Eithne could tell that he was sizing them all up— predetermining whether or not he thought they had what it takes for the quest. Eithne swallowed hard as his judgmental gaze passed over her. The way Darian looked at her made her feel like an insect pinned down, wriggling frantically but to no avail. It felt wrong and uncomfortable, like he were staring the longest at her. What if he was? Was Darian taking a closer look at her than anyone else? Her heart leaped into her throat and beat wildly. Did he recognize her? Eithne looked away and stiffly swung her sword a bit. She told herself that he didn't recognize her, that she was just being overly nervous and paranoid. No one else was giving her a strange look. They all accepted her disguise. She ventured another glance at Darian. To her great relief, his scrutinizing eyes had moved on to other prey. He must not have recognized her after all.

After some time, and more participants had arrived, it was time to begin the tryouts. Darian stepped forward and commanded that all present form a shoulder-to-shoulder line in front of him. Many had shown up to participate. Eithne guessed at least fifty. Darian paced once up and down the line, looking at each of them.

"Anyone under the age of eighty, leave now. I won't have mothers crying over those of you who still smell of milk," Darian ordered plainly.

As elves were a very long-lived race with an average life span of roughly seven hundred years, those under the age of eighty were still considered to be adolescent and not grown enough for adult matters. Darian himself was aged 130 years, which could be roughly equated to someone in their twenties by human standards.

Several of the younger boys kicked at the dirt and hung their heads as they left, disappointed. Eithne probably looked so young in her disguise, but the truth was that she was 123 years old, and she was staying. She thought she imagined the steely blue flash of Darian's eyes at her, but she told herself not to be so paranoid. Once the younger ones had cleared out, Darian pointed at a few others and told them to leave for various reasons: too old, still too young, handicaps, and one or two because Darian knew they had just been married or started a family. Eithne held her breath with each person he eliminated. She thought that she would be next for certain, but he did not dismiss her. It was time for the tryouts to truly begin.

First, he began pairing people up in twos to fight each other. Eithne found herself paired with a tall, skinny elf, who probably weighed about as much as she but with a much better reach. She would have to close the distance on him if she wanted to win. She had never sparred with a partner before, and though she logically and practically knew what she should do to win, she was only all the more terrified of the situation. What if she was actually terrible with a sword? What if she was just fooling herself that she could do this? Eithne had picked one hell of a way to find out.

Darian shouted for those who selected to begin.

The tall elf swung at Eithne in a wild arch with his two-handed sword. She barely managed to recover from the shock and leap to the side in time. Her opponent had surprised her already. She could see by the smug look on his face that he thought he was going to win. Eithne was determined to prove him wrong. He made several other swings at her. They were aggressive but sloppy. Eithne could work with that. She continued to dodge them while she worked out how to close the distance. A few swings and parries later, and she saw her opportunity. He swung his sword in a high arc again over his head, leaving his body exposed. Eithne rushed forward, kicking dust up under her feet. She slipped in underneath his sword and thrust the butt of her sword up hard into his chest, just below the rib cage. She knocked the wind cleanly out of him. He froze with his sword still above his head and made a little wheezing sound. He dropped his weapon, and it fell to the ground behind him, before he went staggering to the ground, desperately trying to retrieve his breath. Eithne took her chance to calmly walk up to him and put the tip of her sword to his throat. Darian came over and curtly declared her the winner of the match. It took a moment for the overwhelming feeling of the pride to seep in. She had won! She had won well! Maybe she wasn't half bad with a sword after all.

The other matches began to wind down as well. One by one, Darian waited for the finish of each match and declared the winner. It seemed to Eithne that he kept glancing her way, and she felt the icy fear and paranoia grip her again. Did he suspect? She turned her face away from him once again and prayed that it was just her imagination.

Darian set up the matches again. This time, Eithne was more intimidated by her opponent. He was a bit shorter than the other one but still taller than she. Also, he was much broader and more thickly muscled. She glanced around at other matches and couldn't help but notice that hers seemed the most unfair. She risked a glance at Darian. To her surprise, he was looking right back at her and even seemed to have a smile on his lips. He shouted for the matches to begin. Her opponent had a different and much more effective fighting style. He closed the distance between them quickly and swung at her hard with his weapon. She managed to parry, but the force of his blow caused her to slide backward. He was strong, much stronger than she. He came at her again like a charging bull. Eithne leaped out of the way in the nick of time, but he diverted his course just as fast. He was too quick! He just kept coming, no matter how she tried to evade him. She barely had time to think about getting out of his way, let alone figure out how to best him. Eithne did not know how to fight this elf and win. Obviously, she faced a skilled and experienced fighter. She darted away from another one of his advances. He followed and swung at her again. She managed to block the bone-crushing blow but found herself gritting her teeth with the effort. She tried to advance on him. To her dismay, he seemed to welcome the challenge and dispatched her all too quickly. Eithne was getting very hot, tired, and frustrated. This swift brute was standing between her and her chance at freedom, and it looked like he was going to win. Even worse, she was going to lose. She realized that she had one chance at beating him, and that was to get creative. A little dumb luck wouldn't hurt either. Eithne wasn't particularly proud of her plan, but she had to win. She had to! She waited for him to charge her again, and then she took the chance of her life. Eithne propelled herself downward and, using his forward momentum, easily skidded toward him, creating a cloud of dust in her wake. Everything seemed to happen in slow motion to her as she slid at him and swept his legs out from under him. Basically, she tripped him, and she wasn't proud of it, but it seemed to do the trick. Her opponent was genuinely shocked by the technique—his eyes wide in disbelief as he comprehended what she had done. Eithne looked at his face as he sailed through the air above her. He landed on his face; he had been stunned, but he did not lose his grip on his sword. Eithne scrambled to her feet as soon as the space above her head was clear. He would recover quickly. She practically leaped through the air herself to close the distance so she could put her sword to his neck before he got up. She was nearly upon him, her victory within her grasp, when there was an interruption.

"That's not how you win a match." It was none other than the authoritative voice and steely blue glare of Darian MacAllow.

Eithne froze where she stood, sword in hand, like a doe come upon suddenly in the forest. Her opponent also remained still. Her heart thudded rapidly in her chest; her eyes had gone wide with horror. Darian looked angry, and his tone was none too pleased. She locked eyes with him and saw everything then. He had recognized her. That's why he had put her up against someone obviously superior in skill and strength: to get her off the field as soon as possible. But she had ruined his plan when she pulled her little stunt. Now she was in trouble.

"I guess pretty boys don't think they have to fight fair," one of the other fighters sniggered to his friend.

Eithne's heart dropped to her feet when she realized that her hat had come off when she dropped down to trip her opponent. How couldn't Darian recognize her now?

Darian continued to stare at her for what felt like an eternity. She had been caught in her great lie, and now he was going to report her to the tribal council, and she would be dealt a punishment too horrible to imagine.

Once again, Darian surprised her. He drew his sword and gestured sharply for her to go over to him. He meant to have a match with her. Eithne gulped down hard, still frozen in place. She couldn't believe this was happening. Darian had just challenged her to a match! She knew she would lose against him. Darian was an excellent swordsman, with total superiority not only over her but all other warriors in the village. He gestured again, annoyed with her dallying. With a great effort, Eithne somehow began to move her feet toward him and stiffly ready her sword. Vaguely, she was aware of her former opponent getting to his feet and the rest of the fighters present gathering around the two of them in a wide circle. Somehow, she found her way over to stand in front of Darian with her sword poised. She very much doubted her ability to move, however. Frozen with fear, she probably wouldn't even react to his attacks. At least, it would be over quickly.

"The conditions, *boy*," Darian put sarcastic emphasis on the last word. "If you can beat me in a fair match, then you will be recruited for the mission. Understood?"

All the blood rushed to Eithne's face. Was he serious? Of course, he knew as well as she that he was going to win, but to make such an offer was still a huge shock. There was still that smallest of chances that Eithne actually might best him, and he was willing to take that risk. All knew Darian to be a man of his word. If, by some miracle, Eithne did win, she would get out of the village. She knew that he recognized her. Why didn't he just tell her to leave? Eithne managed a nod to show that she understood. Her grip on her sword tightened, and every muscle in her body tensed. She had to try her best just in case luck was with her today—a lot of luck.

Darian did not rush at her as the other two had done. No, he bid his time and circled for a few moments before closing the distance between them. It seemed that he was a calculating and methodical fighter. When he did come at her, he was so swift that Eithne could have blinked and missed it! Their swords clashed in a series of parries. Eithne got the feeling that he wanted to see what she could do before disarming her. She felt like an insect again, an insect being toyed with by a cruel cat. She was certain that, even though she could barely keep up with his blows, he was only casually testing her abilities. Why was he fighting her, knowing who she was? Eithne could not banish the question from her mind. It distracted her from concentrating on the fight. A moment later, it no longer mattered whether or not she could concentrate at all. After a few more blows were traded, Darian reached out his hand with lightning speed and painfully gripped the wrist of her sword arm. He gave it a little twist, and Eithne dropped the weapon. She just managed not to yelp from the sudden pain. She couldn't do that. Not in front of Darian. Not now. Then he jerked her in close to his chest. She practically stumbled into him as she had been thrown off balance by the sudden movement.

"Eithne, this is not your place," Darian whispered to her in low, cold tones. "Leave your sword where it lies, and go home now. You are lucky that I am not reporting you to the council for the second time. However, if I see you with a sword again, I will not be silent any longer. Do I make myself clear?"

Eithne wanted to sob, and she could almost feel her lip quivering. She couldn't allow for such weakness to be seen, especially not at this moment. Darian's words cut her deeply, but at the same time, she owed him much gratitude. She managed to keep the choking out of her voice as she whispered back that she understood him. He released her once he had his answer. She did as he bade her and left her sword on the ground. Darian was very good at giving orders. She hung her head and left as quickly as she could without breaking into a run. Several elves in the crowd jeered at her as she left. They called her "pretty boy" and told her to fight fair next time. Eithne didn't care what they said, and she didn't look back at any of them either. She needed to get off the training field and be alone for a while so she could cry away the utter humiliation.

Darian's eyes followed Eithne as she left. He probably shouldn't have let it go so far. Honestly, he had not expected her to make it past the first match. He ought to have dismissed her at the beginning with the others, but he was too curious. There was a part of him that simply wanted, or needed, to know if she could actually do it—stand up against male fighters. Eithne had not only stood up against them but had actually fought impressively. Darian would never admit it out loud, but he was really quite taken with her tripping maneuver. It was creative, practical, and a complete success against one of the best fighters in the village.

CHAPTER THREE

*D*EFEAT WAS NOT an option, nor was mediocrity. It no longer mattered whether or not Eithne had been chosen for the quest. There had been no chance of that from the beginning. She knew that now. Darian knew who she was from the start of the tryouts, and he had humiliated her in front of everyone for reasons she did not understand. It no longer mattered, however. After that awful morning, Eithne had realized that she did not need to leave under some justification but could do it of her own accord. She did not need anyone's permission or approval to start her own life. Still, Eithne feared venturing out into the world on her own. She may have been stubborn and determined, but she was not a fool. She knew she could handle herself in a one-on-one, controlled match, but she was still untested in the field of battle and had never taken a life. Eithne didn't know if she was ready for that.

Once again, Eithne was not particularly proud of her plan, but she knew it would work. She would follow the group selected to the quest out of town tomorrow morning and stick relatively close to the group until she was at a point to venture out on her own. If she were to be discovered by Darian and his men, then they were sure to drag her before the council, but they would already be out of the village by then. The worst-case scenario would be that she would be held as a prisoner until they returned to the village, which should give her plenty of time to figure out an escape plan. Eithne had already packed a bag with some clothing, food, flint and steel, a compass stolen from her father, and the sword she had stolen from the training fields chest for a third time. She also packed some medicinal herbs. Eithne had always been interested in the healing powers of plants since she was a child and had a knack for it. Her interest in medicinal herbs was one of her few hobbies that she did not have to hide from anyone. She was as ready as she could be. Her plan was to sneak out of her house before sunrise, take her father's horse, and wait in the forest just outside of the village for Darian's party to leave. Once they had passed by her, she would follow from a safe distance.

There would be a display as those leaving for the quest exited. It was tradition that when a group was leaving for a quest, or to go to war, the villagers would line the streets and throw flowers at the feet of the warriors' horses as they rode through the village. It was all part of a proper and honorable send-off for the warriors so that they knew the people they protected appreciated their efforts. It occurred to Eithne that Darian had never actually mentioned what the quest was about, or where they were going. He had said that it was a very important mission, meant only for the best fighters, but had never said why or what they were looking for. Eithne did not question Darian's motives, for he had proven himself to be honorable and valorous. Still, she was curious. Why all the secrecy? What was he after that was so important that he couldn't even tell anyone where they were going? She suspected that he must have told the ten elves he had selected to accompany him, at least, but they were saying nothing of the goal either. Eithne mused that was another reason she had chosen to follow Darian's party. She was very curious to know what they were searching for.

It was the night before Eithne would leave her home, and she had been awake in her room for hours. The rest of her family were dozing peacefully in their beds, completely unaware of their youngest daughter's plan for flight the next morning. During the week preceding the tryouts, Eithne had been making more of an effort to spend time with her family. She felt very guilty about leaving them this way; they did not deserve such harsh treatment, but Eithne could not stay. They would never allow her to leave otherwise. Unfortunately, this was her only avenue of escape. Eithne had written letters of goodbye for each of them. Of course, there was no mention of where she went, but she did say why and that she would miss each of them very much. She had been crying on and off all night. She was leaving all that she knew and hurting the people she loved in the process, though she could not stay in the village. If she did, for the rest of her life she would lead the miserable existence of a bird in a gilded cage. No, she could never live that way. Something in her soul was screaming to get out and have so much more in life. So she would leave. It would be a hard and possibly short-lived existence, but at least she would be free to make her own choices. It was worth the pain. Eithne would leave the three letters to her family on the kitchen table when she would leave, each labeled with the name of the proper recipient. It was the least she could do to offer some explanation for her actions. They would probably send out a search party for her, which was another advantage to sticking close to Darian's party. They wouldn't expect her to be with them, and her tracks would blend with those of the party. She would be extremely difficult to find.

It was surprising how easy it was to sneak away. Eithne still felt quite guilty and sad leaving her family behind, but she was able to go through the motions of her plan easily enough during the early hours of the morning. Her small pack filled with travel supplies and sword was all she carried. She once again donned her father's old clothes, which were ill fitting on her lithe feminine form, but did not attempt to disguise herself as male. Her father's horse went to her happily when she came to take him away. He was a beautiful animal, who was mostly used for pleasure and occasionally pulling a carriage, certainly not a warhorse, though he was very healthy and well tempered. Eithne would need a mount if she meant to keep up with the party. Everything went according to her plan, and she was well hidden in the woods just outside of the village by the time Darian's party began parading down the streets to start their journey.

Eithne thought that she would probably say a prayer to one of the gods, if there were any left to listen. Just over sixty years ago, when Eithne was still a small child, there were many gods that dwelled in the heavens and were worshipped throughout the world of Raashan. For most of her early childhood, Eithne had been taught by her parents to pray at the small altar above the fireplace once every morning. The elves of Eithne's tribe traditionally worshipped Jeilei, the highest of the gods of light, as well as Myla, goddess of the forests and nature. Both had once been represented in her childhood home by beautifully carved wooden figures on the altar in the sitting room. Her mother would take great care in dusting and polishing the figures. Eithne and Rosalin were to be very practiced and respectful in their prayers to the gods as their parents were. Her family, as all the elves of the Aranni tribe, had once been reverent and loyal to the gods.

Then the Heavenly Wars happened. The gods, who had always been known to bicker among themselves, began a holy war. Gin, the highest god of darkness from the underworld, tried to usurp Jeilei from his thrown of light and rule over all Raashan unchallenged. Terrible divine battles ensued, and the heavens were not the only place the gods fought their war. Raashan was also subjected to the destruction. The planet all the gods had created together, many eons before, and all those who inhabited Raashan could do nothing but stand by helplessly as the gods raged above and below. It stormed ruthlessly for so long that many areas flooded and were destroyed. Climates of other places would suddenly change without warning. Eithne had even read that an entire continent, which had once been green and lush, was turned into a desert wasteland in less than a month! In other places of the world, mountain ranges violently thrust out of the earth overnight, and islands were drowned by the sea, never to be seen again. It was a terrible cataclysm in which a great many inhabitants of Raashan needlessly lost their lives. The terrorized people prayed and begged the gods to stop their fighting, for their wars were destroying the very prize that they fought over! But the gods were no longer listening. They had become completely consumed by the Heavenly Wars and lost sight of why they started fighting in the first place. Even those mortals that were most devout began to turn bitter. Now, there were no longer any gods to pray to or curse. The gods had destroyed each other long ago, leaving the world in turmoil. Weather patterns were unpredictable, and it became harder and harder to have a good harvest. Raashan was slowly dying without its creators to maintain it. Those who survived the cataclysm could do nothing but watch the world slowly die around them, sadly knowing that one day, nothing would be left.

Eithne's people had been among the luckier ones. The climate in the area of the world that they lived had cooled slightly but remained relatively the same—though times were still difficult. Crops were failing, and hunting was much scarcer. Eithne suspected that Darian's quest might have something to do with helping to pull their people out of an increasingly dire situation.

The clomping of horse's hooves on the packed dirt road got closer. Eithne ducked deeper into the underbrush as the party rode by. There was very little chance of her being seen. No one would even think to look for someone hiding in the forest just outside of the village. Still, she held her breath and kept very still as they passed.

Eithne let them get a little further ahead before she began to follow. There was a moment of hesitation before Eithne began to move. Once she took that step, there would be no turning back. It was her point of no return. If she chose to turn around and go home, she would continue on in her safe, yet stifling, existence. She would be cared for the rest of her life, but she would be unhappy.

Eithne stepped forward, toward the road.

CHAPTER FOUR

*T*HE FIRST DAY on the trail was pleasant enough. Nothing much happened, and it was easygoing. The weather had suddenly changed from cold and damp to hot and sunny. These sorts of shifts in the weather were commonplace these days, so none on the road gave it a second thought. Eithne kept pace with the group but kept out of sight. She simply followed the tracks left by their horses. The next three days were not so pleasant as the first. The sky became dark and poured down heavy rain day and night. It was cold, miserable, and increasingly harder to keep up with the party. She was forced to follow more closely in order to stay with them and hoped that the constant downpour kept her from being detected.

The afternoon of the fifth day, it stopped raining, and that night, Eithne was keen to build a fire to warm herself after being chilled to the bone. Building a fire proved to be very difficult. The only kindling she could find was damp, but after at least an hour-long effort, she managed a small fire. Eithne sat close to her fire, warming her toes and chewing some dried meat when she noticed some other orange lights in the forest not far from her. It was Darian's camp, and she was far too close for comfort! She had no idea how closely she had been trailing them in the rain. Her first instinct was to douse her fire and let them get a little further ahead in the morning, but it was a difficult thing to dash out the little flame she had worked so hard to spark. Maybe no one in the other camp would notice. They all must be just as tired as she was from the days of traveling in the rain, and they may very well assume that her fire was just another traveler on the road. Her gut told her to douse her flame, but Eithne had rationalized way to keep it burning, and so she would.

It did not take long for this folly to catch up with Eithne. She sat happily musing on her own thoughts when there was a tap on her shoulder.

"I thought I told you that I never wanted to see you with a sword again. What the hell are you doing here, Eithne?"

She knew exactly who it was from the blunt tap on her shoulder. Darian had found her, and he sounded angry.

At first, she did not turn to see him. She was frozen by the shock of being discovered by him so easily. Then something occurred to her: she had left the village and didn't mean to go back. Eithne no longer answered to that authority. This realization gave her courage she didn't know she had.

Eithne stiffly stood to her full height, which was still about a head shorter than Darian, and turned to face him squarely. "What do you care where I go and what I do?"

Darian wasn't prepared for her to retort in such a feisty manner. In their two previous encounters that dealt with this issue, she had responded quite positively to his angry, authoritative voice. This reaction was new and unexpected.

"I care what you do because I know your family," he returned in his most authoritative tone. "They must be beside themselves with grief, not knowing where you are. Return home immediately!"

"You only care what happens to me because you want to marry my sister. Well, my family doesn't know that you know where I am. So when you get back, you can just join them in their grieving process as if you never saw me. We are not in the village anymore, Darian, and I'm not going back."

Eithne immediately felt that she was being a little harsh, but she had decided to give Darian a fight, and she was getting a little carried away with her newfound attitude.

Surprised and frustrated with her, Darian took a step forward and gripped her arm firmly. He did not like what she said about him only caring because he wanted to marry Rosalin. She didn't know what she was talking about. Eithne winced a bit, not from pain but simply from the contact. She wasn't used to being touched by men.

"Why are you doing this, Eithne? Why are you following my party? You don't even know where we are going."

Eithne was silent for a moment as she stared back at him with defiance. She told him the truth: "I don't care where you're going. I'm following you because it's safer than running away into the forest alone, and I'm running away because I can't stay in the village anymore, living a false existence."

Darian knew that she was telling him the truth. A part of him felt bad for her. She was so determined to get away from her life. Her family must be devastated at finding her gone for almost a week. The trail was not dangerous for her to go back alone. They were still within their tribe's boundaries. By the end of tomorrow, however, they would be outside that net of safety. Eithne did not know that and would be completely unprepared for the dangers ahead. She had done well in controlled matches, but that was completely different from being surprised by a demon on the road. No, she had to go back. She would want to, anyway, after she had a real taste of life outside the village, Darian assumed. Also, Darian felt responsible for her. It was true, in part, that he was telling her to go back because he wanted to marry into her family, but he respected them beyond that. What Eithne was doing wasn't right by them. Darian suspected she already felt a good deal of guilt about it. Though he wasn't sure at all what she meant when she said she led a "false existence" back in the village. He knew that she had always felt like an outcast, but that was no reason to discount her entire life.

"Eithne, go back, or I will take you back there myself even if I have to drag you behind my horse the entire way." Darian's threat did seem to daunt her a bit, which pleased him.

The threat had given Eithne pause, but she had come too far just to be dragged back to the village in shame.

"You don't have the time to do that. We are almost a week outside the village, and the rain caused you to move slower than you would have liked already. You can't make me go back because you can't afford to lose any more time. I've noticed that, wherever you're headed, you're in a hurry to get there."

Eithne was almost smug and somewhat proud as she spoke. This made Darian even angrier. It was even worse that she was right, and they both knew it. He couldn't lose the time it would take to drag her back to the village, and he couldn't afford to send one of his men with her either. He would need every one of them. Besides, the way she was behaving, Darian didn't trust anyone but himself to be able to take her back without her getting away from them. Eithne may be a woman, but she was clever and knew how to use a weapon. The other men didn't know of her disregard for the laws as Darian did. Neither was anyone else so aware of her feisty disposition. Darian was most familiar with Eithne, and even he had to admit that this conversation was bringing to light whole other facets of her personality that he did not know about. She was a handful, to be sure.

"You can't come with us, Eithne. It's against the laws of our people, and you would only slow us down, anyway." Darian didn't really think that she would slow them down, but he needed excuses to offer her.

"I've kept up with you well enough so far," she shot back, unmoved.

"Go home."

"I won't!"

"I can't be responsible for you!"

"You don't have to be! I can take care of myself!"

"Then why did you even bother following me then?"

They had escalated to yelling. Darian was unhappy that Eithne managed to get him so emotional. He was usually in perfect control of his emotions. Fortunately, his last question had given her pause again. He knew as well as she did that she was sticking close to him for both comfort and safety. She could not deny that. It was more difficult for her to rebuke that argument, and she wasn't sure how to respond. So Eithne simply stared back at him defiantly.

Darian still held her arm. His grip tightened. As she stared into his face, she watched him clench and unclench his jaw muscles. The cold blue of his eyes even seemed to be giving off chills that shivered down her spine as he held her gaze. He was waiting for her to answer him, and that she hadn't answered almost seemed to make him more frustrated with her. Though Eithne now felt that she need not say anything. No matter what her motives, she had made herself clear that she wasn't going anywhere.

After what seemed like an eternity of staring daggers at each other, finally Darian turned on his heel and strode away. He could say nothing to the stubborn Eithne to make her go back. It was infuriating. At that moment, he ceased to care whether she went back or not. For that moment, she was none of his concern, which seemed to be exactly what she wanted.

Eithne continued to follow Darian's party as they traveled along the road. She no longer tried to stay hidden and followed more closely. She still did not know where they were going but knew that they would have to stop in a town or village eventually. Perhaps, that place would be the where Eithne could leave the party and strike out on her own, though she was still very curious as to where Darian was headed, and being around him helped her to feel safe. She couldn't explain it, but Darian had always made Eithne feel safe and secure. She supposed that he had that effect on most people, being such a strong warrior who always seemed to be in control. Not to mention his code of honor. Regardless of how angry he might be with her, Darian would never allow harm to come to a woman. Uneventful days had passed on the road. The weather grew even colder. Gloomy skies continuously threatened more rain, but thankfully, it did not rain. The distinct chill of winter was biting early, and Eithne was sorry that she had not waited until spring to run away.

When the party stopped in the evenings, Eithne still camped out of sight, but close enough to see the fires twinkling through the trees. She knew the entire party was now aware of her presence, but they generally ignored her, most likely by Darian's command. One night, three days after she and Darian had argued, some of the men from the party came upon her while they were gathering firewood. They had given her a good scowl and stalked off but did not bother her otherwise. Eithne was defying many basic principles of their culture by doing what she was doing, so she well understood their contempt toward her. Though if some of the party felt angry enough, things might become dangerous. Eithne did not fear rape. Elves were not known for such vulgarity as some other races were, but the idea of her being tied to a tree in the middle of nowhere and left for dead was unpleasant, to say the least. It was also because of this, perhaps irrational, fear that Eithne wished to remain near Darian. She instinctively knew that he would protect her.

Two days after the men of the party had scowled at her, they arrived at a somewhat large port town called Tomak. Even though it was not very large compared to a major city, it was the biggest place Eithne had ever seen! The buildings all seemed so tall and close together. The paved streets looked so congested with people, carts, livestock, and merchants peddling their wares. Tomak was predominantly populated by elves. Eithne saw members of her own tribe from other villages mingling on the streets with elves from other tribes. She also noticed several city elves, who were characteristically much darker in coloring than their tribal cousins. However, the individuals that stood out the most to Eithne were the few humans, as well as some cloaked figures who kept their visages so well hidden that it was impossible to tell who or what they were. She had only ever seen other elves up to this point in her life, and she found it fascinating to look upon humans in real life. Eithne found humans to be a bit stocky and unattractive. They were shorter than most elves, appeared to carry more weight on their bodies, and even moved with an awkward clumsiness to her eyes. She had read that elves were considered to be among the most physically attractive and graceful races, but she had never had a true basis for comparison until now. Eithne smiled to herself as she felt a sudden surge of pride for her race.

There was certainly no lack of stimuli for Eithne in Tomak. Aside from the bustling people, there were the merchants' colorful wares of all varieties as well as the paved cobblestone streets and large stone buildings. She surmised that is was all about commerce here and the mingling of cultures. In fact, Eithne realized, after a while of wading through the streets, that most people barely gave her a second glance. If a woman had openly walked down the street dressed in men's clothing with a sword on her hip in her village, everyone would be aghast and very offended. Even if the woman was not of their tribe, it would be completely unacceptable. A few elves, mostly of the woodland tribes, did make an expression of distaste or offense when they saw her; but generally, she was accepted here just as she was. This gave her yet another surge of pride and pleasure. No longer would she have to pretend to be something she was not. She felt a sense of being personally complete in this moment. Eithne decided that she loved being in the city with its gray cobblestone streets, tall white-washed stone buildings, and all the hustle and bustle that went with it. There was also an unfamiliar scent to the air that smelled heavily of salt. It must be the smell of the sea, she realized. Tomak was a port town, located on the Straights of Gibson between the Northern and Southern Continents. There was much trade that happened here, though many people simply passed through and did not stay in town. Therefore, Tomak had never grown to be as large as many other port cities.

Eithne glimpsed Darian and his party in the crowd and wondered why he had come here. Most likely, he meant to charter a ship to the Southern Continent, she reasoned, but where exactly? She was too curious about the quest now to let it go. She had decided to go with them. The men may despise her, and Darian would be absolutely offended at the suggestion, but her mind was made up. Besides, she had already proven that she wouldn't be a burden and that she could handle a weapon. She would have to get Darian alone for a moment and try to present her going with them in a way that wasn't completely absurd to him. Eithne pushed through the crowd of people in order to catch up with Darian's party. She was focused on a goal, and the distractions of Tomak blurred around her.

The men of Darian's party were quite taken with the sights that Tomak offered. Many of them had never been outside the village before, and their new surroundings captured their fascination. They pointed at the different races and exclaimed over the beautiful women who walked by. Overall, their mood was quite upbeat, considering the slow getting here through the abysmal weather. One of the men pointed out, in shock, at a human woman who was dressed as a mercenary. Several of the others looked and let their distaste be known.

"That ridiculous thing that's been following us should just stay here," Proithon stated with bitterness. "She would fit right in with the other freakish women."

Some of the others grunted their agreement. Darian chose to ignore the statement but found just hearing it left a bad taste in his mouth. Despite her rebellious ways, Eithne did not deserve cruel comments from others. Thinking of her, he scanned the crowd to see if she was still following his group now that they were inside the walls of Tomak. He half-expected not to see her, for there were many things to distract her here, but the bright shock of fiery red hair gave her away easily. Her attention was on the crowd around her, and the town—not Darian or his party—so she wasn't necessarily following them anymore. She could just be coincidentally wandering in the same direction. Darian could not be sure. She looked well and was seemingly staying out of trouble. So he shrugged and continued leading his men through the streets to the Dragon's Belly Inn.

Darian had stayed at the Dragon's Belly Inn before while on route for past journeys, and he had an accord with the innkeeper. It wouldn't be difficult to acquire lodging for one night for him and his party. They left their horses at the stables and tipped the stable boy. Darian strode into the inn first and was greeted heartily by the innkeeper as the rest of his men filed in behind him. The innkeeper was a rotund human named Fredrick. Darian had actually known his father before him as well and seen Fredrick as a child. Since humans lived such short life spans in comparison to elves, Darian had been giving the family good business for generations, though he was still considered to be quite young by elvish standards.

"Captain Darian! Excellent to see you again, sir!" Fredrick greeted happily as he shook Darian's hand. Darian grinned at him warmly. "And I see you have brought your men with you this time." Fredrick peered past Darian and made a mental note of how many beds would be needed.

"Good to see you too, my friend," Darian responded heartily. "We are only in town for one night but would be very grateful of your hospitality if you have the space."

He had originally hoped to be in Tomak for a couple of days to allow his men to rest and gather supplies before setting sail, but the rain delay had put them behind schedule.

"Of course! Of course! There is room enough for all of you, though your men will have to share rooms."

"That is not a problem at all." Darian looked about the room and saw that food was being served, and a fire was roaring in an inviting fashion in the large fireplace located at the center of the dining area. "Shall we settle ourselves down here while you ready our accommodations?"

"Yes, please do." Fredrick gestured for the men to make themselves comfortable and called over the barmaid to take care of them right away. Then he hustled up the stairs to ready the rooms.

Darian ordered a round of ale for all his men and then told them to order food if they were hungry. Most of them were very hungry. Given the large order, the barmaid was quite efficient in bringing everything out, which pleased them all greatly. A few of the men even made sport of innocently flirting with her, which excited the barmaid very much, coming from handsome elf men. The barmaid was a homely human girl with hair like yellow straw and a very plump bottom. Flirtation from attractive men, who weren't drunk, was rare for her.

The Dragon's Belly Inn had been long established in Tomak and was among one of the more popular places to stay because of its reputation and good food. It was right off to the main street near the harbor and had an abundance of comfortable rooms. Outside, it looked like an average place, except that the stoop was always cleanly swept and its stone walls always seemed freshly washed. Even the paint on the hanging wooden sign was continuously renewed, so that the fat, happy dragon that resided on it always shone vibrant green and yellow. Inside, the place was just as clean and well kept. There was a huge stone fireplace that jutted through the center of the dining area, surrounded by oak tables and chairs that were heavily used but very sturdy. The bar at the far right side upon entering was as long as the wall and polished to a reflective shine. Fredrick and his family took great pride in their family business and were rewarded with many loyal customers.

Darian had made sure that his party went to the inn first to be sure that there were enough rooms available. About half an hour after they had arrived, many more patrons began coming in looking for lodging and food. Darian was in no mood for crowds tonight, so he left his men to enjoy themselves and brought his things up to his room. Darian was thankful that Fredrick had enough space to allow him a private room. He was the sort of person who liked having his own space. Once he had stripped off his leather armor and washed up a bit using the bowl and pitcher prepared in his room, he felt more refreshed.

The room was small, but like everything at the Dragon's Belly, it was clean and comfortable. Darian sorted around the little room a few moments more before he decided to leave the inn for a while. After all, the fresh sea air would be nice, and Darian wanted to take a look at the ship they would be setting sail on tomorrow morning. Grabbing a clean shirt from his pack and tugging it over his head, Darian left the room and continued down the stairs toward the exit. Several of his men toasted their mugs to him as Darian walked through the dining area. Some of them might have a difficult time getting out of bed in the morning at the rate they were drinking. He inclined his head and smiled, to indicate his appreciation for the toast, and continued to walk through the door.

Once outside, Darian found himself in the crowded streets again. He knew his way and did not have to suffer long with the crowd. He made his way to the harbor, which was not far from the inn. He located the ship that he and his men would be taking across the Straights of Gibson in the morning. Some of the sailors were loading supplies unto the vessel for the short journey, so Darian asked if they minded him inspecting the ship. The sailors dismissively grunted their consent, and Darian was pleased to inspect the vessel to his satisfaction. He found that he was rarely questioned.

Darian was just walking off the ship and stepping unto the dock when he was confronted with a somewhat unwelcome sight.

"What are you doing here, Eithne?" he asked through gritted teeth.

Eithne was standing in front of him with her father's horse as though she had been waiting patiently for him to approach. She seemed to be in good spirits, despite Darian's obvious dislike for her being there. She smiled at him sweetly. There was mud from the trail still covering her and the horse, but she still seemed to be aglow. Perhaps it was the new environment. *Or perhaps*, Darian thought, *that fiery red hair of hers just made her look brighter than the rest.*

"I was waiting for you, as you can probably see," Eithne replied politely. "I want to talk to you."

Darian crossed his arms across his chest. He remembered how their last conversation had gone, and he feared that she would rile him again.

"We don't have anything to talk about," he coolly responded.

Eithne giggled a little, which annoyed him since he did not know why.

"You don't even know what I want to talk about. Maybe I just need to ask where the most respectable places in town are so I don't get taken advantage of."

Darian remained stoic to her girlish smiles. "That's not what you want to talk to me about."

Eithne let out an exasperated sigh. "Fine, it's not about that, but I'm just going to follow you around until you at least hear me out. So you might as well listen to me now and get it over with."

Her horse shook its head as if the animal agreed, and Eithne absentmindedly smiled and patted its neck before looking back to Darian for an answer. After taking a few seconds to think it over, he uncrossed his arms and gestured for her to follow him. He walked to an area of the dock where there weren't sailors carrying crates that could eavesdrop. Whatever she was about to say, he was fairly certain that he didn't want others listening to it. Eithne beamed and practically hopped into step behind him. She didn't expect him to listen to her that easily! She was very pleased.

Once at a sufficiently quiet spot, Darian turned to face her and crossed his arms again. "I'm listening."

"I want to come with you on the mission," Eithne said bluntly.

She had decided that being open and direct would probably be the best approach. She had noticed how forthright Darian was and assumed he respected the same quality in others.

"No," he answered flatly and began to walk away.

Eithne moved to block his exit. The horse with her really helped to block his avenue of escape.

"You said you would at least hear me out," she stated firmly.

Darian looked down at her, considering whether or not it would be better or worse to turn her down now or let her talk, get her hopes up, and be turned down later. Eithne was looking back at him with fierce determination in her grass-green eyes. She wanted very much for him to listen to her. Ultimately, Darian reasoned that she would be more hurt if he never even listened in the first place. Also, if he got that part over with now, it would prevent her from trying to persuade him again in the future. He indicated with his head that she could continue.

Eithne relaxed visibly and collected her thoughts for a second before speaking again. "As I said, I want to come with you, and I know there are reasons that you don't think I should come. I am well aware of your feelings on the matter. However, have you considered that I could be an asset to you on your journey?"

Darian did not respond verbally but cocked an eyebrow at her, intrigued to see where she was going with this.

Eithne took this nonverbal encouragement as a positive sign. "As a woman, I have certain skills that men don't. I can dress wounds and mix healing herbs. I'm really great with healing herbs. I'm sure I'm better at stitching wounds closed than any of the men in your party too. I know you're thinking that you have all survived before without a woman to mend you, and probably you have your own ways of dealing with injuries, but you and your party would be better off with my help. Also, I know how to fight."

Darian uncrossed his arms, placed his hands on his hips, and looked at the dock that he stood upon with a tired sigh. He didn't see her last point as a valid argument. She was better off sticking with her medicinal skills.

Eithne saw him doubting her last statement, and it worried her. It also made her mad.

"I can fight!" she said too loudly and indignantly. "I may not be experienced, or quite as good as some of the other men in your party, but I feel that I'm good at fighting and can protect myself. I'm not afraid to stand up for myself in the real world, Darian, and I'll only get better. Besides, it's one more sword added to your party against whatever attacks us. The only reason you refuse to see me as a legitimate fighter is because I'm not male!"

"Eithne," Darian began in a tired tone that a parent would use to explain something to a child, "our culture has certain practices and laws. You know what they are and why it does, in fact, matter what your sex is. You seem to be the only person who can't abide by these laws that have kept our people stable and happy for many generations."

"The laws are prejudice, ridiculous, and wrong, and the ones in which you and I are speaking of have had no bearing on how happy our people have been. I'm not happy, and many might argue, unstable as well," Eithne returned heatedly.

Darian might have argued for the "unstable" part, but it panged him when she said that she was unhappy. Is that why she was doing this? She thought it would make her happy?

"I don't want to argue with you, Eithne. So if you have said all you wanted to say, then I will be going." He gave a resolved look and politely waited or her to reply.

Eithne pressed her lips together and looked up at the dimming sky. She was feeling very frustrated and decided to resort to something she did not want to say before. It involved a white lie, but if he ever found out about it, it would be too late for him to change his mind. She would probably feel guilty about saying it in the first place, but she would most likely get her way. Eithne was indeed headstrong . . . She could deal with a little guilt. She couldn't quite explain it, but Eithne felt the need to stay with Darian and go on the mission. It was just something she had to do.

Darian felt that he had given her enough time to respond. He gave her a nod, indicating that they were finished, and began to move past her. This time, she did not try to block his path, but he did not get far.

"Do you love my sister?" Eithne voiced the question just as Darian took his third step. He stopped but did not turn.

"I don't see how that is any of your business," he answered curtly.

"It is my business. Rosalin is my sister, and whomever she marries is going to become a part of our family. So tell me, Darian, do you want to marry my sister out of love?"

Darian turned around and fixed his eyes with hers. "Why do you need to know?"

Eithne held his cold blue eyes. It was no small task. That steely stare could be difficult to take without showing submission, but Eithne was determined not to.

"Because if you really do love her, then you would want to know about the other men who have also proposed to court her for marriage."

"Rosalin is lovely and popular. I am well aware that she has other suitors," Darian returned plainly.

"Yes, but she is actually seriously considering more than one candidate for her husband. All of which are quite accomplished, and one of them, not you, is a favorite of my parents. If you wish to sway my family in your favor, you're going to need leverage." Eithne mustered as much confidence she could as she spoke to appear convincing.

"Whatever you're getting at? Spit it out. Now." He was being direct again.

"I'm talking about me," Eithne replied calmly. "I would be your leverage."

Darian's brow furrowed. He understood her exactly. If he went along with this, then he would have to have her along on the mission. The men wouldn't like that. Of course, it also meant that Eithne was agreeing to return to the village after it was all over. She really was clever, and a little sneaky. This way, he could ensure her safety while on the road and be a hero to her family for returning their beloved daughter to them. His place as Rosalin's future husband would be secure. It was still giving Eithne exactly what she wanted, though, and he had no doubts that she would be anxious to join in the fray of the fight.

Darian inspected her physique. She was lithe, willowy, and didn't look like she would be able to take a hit at the first glance, but there was strength and lean muscle there. She was a bit thin, but it was easy for a warrior to see that she did have muscle on her bones. She wouldn't break as easily as some might think. And she possessed a strong determination with a competitive edge. Those are two good qualities for a fighter to have, although Darian could not help but think of how her proposal smacked too much of blackmail.

Basically, she was telling him to take her with him, or he wasn't going to marry Rosalin. He wasn't even sure that she was telling him the whole truth about the other suitors. He felt fairly confident that Rosalin liked him the best, but it was her parents who had the ultimate word on the matter. If they favored someone else, then he could have good reason to be nervous.

"Well?" Eithne prompted. She felt uncomfortable letting him think this through too much. Darian was too smart to be allowed enough time to fully analyze her proposal.

"You're very impatient," Darian muttered at her.

"It's a quality I've come to accept about myself. What is your decision?" she snapped back.

"I know what you're up to, Eithne. I'm not blind. How do I know I can trust what you say about the other suitors?" he replied skeptically. He didn't like her attitude.

Eithne sighed. "Honestly, Darian, you know how many suitors there are after Rosalin. She's beautiful, friendly, traditional, intelligent, and comes from a very well-respected family. Almost every eligible bachelor in the village is trying to court her. I'm not just telling you this so that I can come along on the mission. It's part of it, yes, but another reason is that of all my sister's suitors, you are the most tolerable. I would like you best as a brother-in-law, and I think that you would be good to Rosalin. So what do you say?" She thought that some flattery couldn't hurt her case. Anyway, it was true.

Darian took a moment to study Eithne's face in the early evening light. She appeared to be looking back at him in earnest. Also, he couldn't pretend that he wasn't flattered by what she said about him. He had never really been sure what Eithne thought of him before now, but had always wanted to know.

"All right, fine," Darian finally conceded. "But only on my conditions. If you don't obey my orders, you're out. Understood?"

Eithne could not disguise her excitement as she gave a vigorous nod to show that she did understand his terms. She could have hugged him in that moment, but she knew better. She was just so pleased that he had agreed to allow her to go with him! Quietly, Eithne mentally noted to keep her word and listen to Darian's orders, even if it was something she didn't like hearing.

"The first condition," Darian began, assuming his authoritative voice, "is that you give me your sword."

Eithne's mouth immediately opened to argue the point, but then she remembered what she had just promised to him less than a minute ago. Instead, she shut her mouth and unbuckled her sword belt to hand it to him.

"May I ask why you are disarming me?"

"You'll get it back tomorrow," he stated curtly as he took the weapon.

Glancing at the hilt, Darian noticed it had the stamp of a training weapon on it. He should have known where that missing sword had gone from the training field's chest.

"I'm not going to tell the men about this until we are on the ship headed to the Southern Continent. That way, they won't be able to insist that I just leave you in Tomak. My men and I are staying at the Dragon's Belly Inn, not far from here. You're on your own for accommodation tonight, but stay on the east side of town. It's safer. Be at this dock, ready to leave, at sunrise tomorrow morning."

With that said, Darian did not wait to see if she had any questions. He turned about sharply and walked off in the direction of the main street.

Eithne was still in shock. She was going with them on the mission! Questions flooded her mind, and she wanted nothing more than to chase after him and ask every one. Of course, that would be a bad idea. She had pushed her luck enough for one day. A few seconds later, a burst of adrenaline coursed through her body. Eithne could not contain her excitement and gave a whoop of joy accompanied by a hop. Some of the sailors on the dock stopped to look at her. She wasn't even embarrassed about her sudden outburst. She was going on the mission! She was about to have her first real adventure!

Chapter Five

❧

*I*T WAS A long night for Darian. He had agreed to have Eithne along on the mission and was already regretting his decision. The men would disapprove, and he could possibly lose some respect from them; though deep down, he couldn't help feeling that it was the right thing to do. Eithne had been so overjoyed when he said she could come, and he even thought he heard a happy "whoop" as he left the docks. Darian hoped that she would be as valuable an addition to his party as she seemed to think she would. He smiled to himself, thinking of her stalwart determination. With that kind of attitude, she would make herself useful if it killed her. He also liked the idea of being able to keep an eye on her and bring her back home. The mission they were on was dangerous. Darian was certain that they were not the only ones after what he was looking for. His main concern was getting to it quickly and hopefully retrieving the item before anyone else managed to get to it.

Darian sat for a long while on the bed in his room, thinking things through. The sword that Eithne had stolen from the training fields rested on his lap. He ran his thumb down the edge of the blade. It was very worn and dull, not at all something a warrior should be carrying. Eithne probably didn't even realize that the blade was practically useless in a fight. She would do better using it as a club. He was glad that he had taken it from her. Darian gave a heavy sigh and stood from his bed. Then he went to his pack, got out his sword-sharpening stone, and went to work on Eithne's blade. She would, at least, need a decent weapon if she were ever going to hold her own out there.

Eithne was waiting at the dock before sunrise. The air was much damper by the sea, and she felt the cold chill more acutely. She rubbed her arms vigorously to warm herself. She had been glad when Darian mentioned the Southern Continent yesterday, for it meant they would be traveling into a milder climate, at least in theory. Nothing was guaranteed anymore when it came to the weather patterns of Raashan. Eithne had not slept very well the night before and had arrived early as a function of that. She had found some very cheap accommodation at a boarding house on the east side of Tomak. It had not been a pleasant experience. The room she stayed in had been crammed full of beds and people. There was barely any space to breathe. She had felt very uncomfortable on the old, lumpy mattress and slept holding her belongings close to her chest. Eithne would not stay in such a place again if she could help it. She had also felt completely exposed without a weapon. She still did not understand why Darian had asked for her sword, but she knew he must have had a good reason.

At last, the morning sun began to rise, exposing a grayish morning mist over the docks. After a few moments, sailors and other dock workers arrived to start their day of work. Eithne knew that she must look very out of place. There she was, an elf woman dressed as a man, just standing around on the dock with a horse in the early hours of the morning. Nonetheless, the workers didn't even seem to take notice of her presence and went about their business as usual. Eithne was feeling anxious about the journey. The sun had only just begun to rise, but doubts were streaming through her mind. What if Darian wasn't going to show? What if he and his party had already departed and were now laughing over leaving her waiting here like a fool? Eithne shook her head to clear it. Those were ridiculous notions. The ship Darian had chartered was clearly present, and he would not be so cruel. No matter what he thought of her, he was a man of his word. She took a deep breath of cold air into her lungs and exhaled it slowly. She closed her eyes and had a small moment of soothing, personal meditation to quiet her nerves.

"Not much of a morning person, are you?"

Eithne's eyes flew open to find Darian standing in front of her. The rest of the party was not with him, and it seemed there was something different about his demeanor this morning. There was a little smile on his lips. He actually looked happy to see her. Even his remark was almost playful. She found this change in him welcome and decided to go with it.

"You're unusually happy in the morning," Eithne returned, smiling back at him.

Darian looked perplexed. "Am I not usually happy?"

Eithne laughed. "Not really. It's just that whenever I see you, you seem so serious and in charge. I'm not used to this side of you."

He answered her with a thoughtful, "Hmmmm," and studied her for a few seconds. "Are you ready to leave?" Darian resumed his authoritative tone, and his smile faded.

Eithne nodded and held up her small pack. She was sad that his playfulness was short-lived.

"Then let's get you onboard the ship. The rest of the party will be here soon."

Darian went past her and walked up the ramp to the ship. Eithne fell into step behind him and led her horse up with her. She was outwardly calm, but her stomach as all fluttering with butterflies. She could barely contain her excitement. Eithne wondered if Darian noticed that she was so nervous. If he did, he didn't acknowledge it but simply led her onward silently. Darian took her below deck into an area where horses and other animals were kept. There, she tethered her horse in the far corner where it wouldn't be easily seen. Darian turned and walked again, expecting her to obediently follow. She did. He took her to the cargo haul. It was dark and full of crates, barrels, and other various things, and it felt cramped—though it wasn't terrible. The cargo haul seemed relatively clean and didn't smell as badly as some places onboard probably did.

"This is where you will stay until I come and get you," Darian stated shortly and started to leave.

"Should I hide anywhere in particular?" Eithne called after him irritably. She was annoyed with his shortness.

Darian could not help but to smirk at her attitude as he turned to look back at her. Eithne might become a fair fighter, but she would always have that feisty disposition.

"Just make yourself comfortable. If you hear anyone coming, then get out of sight." He was about to walk away again when he remembered something. "I almost forgot." Darian unbuckled a sword from his belt and held it out to her, hilt first. "Your sword, as I promised."

Eithne stepped forward and took her weapon gladly. "Thank you."

"I cleaned and sharpened it for you. It was so dull that it was nearly useless. It will serve you much better now."

Eithne was filled with gratitude. She didn't know what to say to him. She had no idea that her sword was in desperate need of cleaning and sharpening. She supposed that was her utter lack of experience coming through. He had probably glanced at the sword once and realized how lame it was. "I . . . um . . . thank you. That was very kind of you," she stammered.

Darian smiled and nodded. "I'm supposed to return you alive and healthy, right? From now on, keeping your weapon fit for combat is your responsibility."

He turned and left Eithne in the dark cargo haul clutching her sword. She very much wanted to look at the newly cleaned and sharpened weapon in the light. She had known that her sword was not in the best condition but had no idea how bad it really was. Once again, she found herself in Darian's debt. Eithne wondered if she would ever be able to repay him for all his kindness. She made herself as comfortable as she could on one of the larger crates and decided to try and get some more sleep. She purposefully lay down on a place that she would not be seen from the entrance to the haul.

Eithne was not dozing long when she was awakened by muffled voices and the boards creaking above her. The party must be boarding the ship. She wondered how long it would be before Darian told them that she was now going with them on the mission. They would not take it well. Darian would probably wait until they were well on the way before telling the party—at least, far enough along so that no one could demand that they turn back and leave her in Tomak. She would probably be down in the cargo haul for hours.

Eithne wondered if the ship's crew was aware of her presence. She suspected that they did know. Darian probably asked the captain's permission to have her down here. Still, it was probably best not to show herself to anyone but Darian. With that in mind, Eithne looked around to make sure she was in the most inconspicuous place. She moved deeper into the cargo haul behind some of the larger crates and lay down using her pack as a pillow. She allowed herself to drift off to sleep, ushered by the rhythmic rocking of the ship.

CHAPTER SIX

*T*HE MEN WERE unhappy. Very unhappy. Darian had just told them that Eithne was coming with them on the mission. At first, they only gave him hard, disgruntled stares. It was an awful feeling. No one had ever looked at him like that before, especially his men. They just kept staring for what seemed like an eternity. Outwardly, Darian did his best to stand proudly with his shoulders back and his head high, but he wondered if they saw the nervous clenching of his jaw muscle as he waited for one of them to speak.

Finally, Proithen broke the silence, "Sir, I have never questioned a decision you have made, or one of your orders, before now. So I know there must be a good reason why you would allow that freakish woman to come along. I would like to know that reason, sir."

Darian relaxed and breathed an internal sigh of relief but still maintained his outward stoic demeanor. This was the reaction he had been hoping for. He was also glad to hear it voiced from Proithen, who was one of the most experienced soldiers in the group. They had gone on many campaigns together in the past. The rest of the party was likely to follow Proithen's lead on this matter. He scanned the rest of the men before responding. Most were patiently waiting to hear his reason before passing judgment. However, Finnis and Dal seemed to be less inclined to listen. Darian didn't think anything of it. Perhaps they would be swayed after hearing what he had to say.

Darian had his answer prepared, "The Lady Eithne is trying to run away from home. I greatly respect her family and believe they deserve to have their youngest daughter returned to them. I feel responsible for her welfare. I do not condone her running away and following us. I tried to dissuade her on several occasions. She is quite stubborn, to say the least. Her family is unaware of her whereabouts and probably extremely distraught by her absence. My intention in allowing her to travel with us is to be certain of her returning home safely, nothing more. She is under my protection in the meantime."

The men grumbled among themselves for a moment. It was a perfectly rational answer, but none of them liked the idea of having a female traveling with them.

"Will she be allowed to carry a weapon?" one of the men asked.

Darian nodded affirmatively.

This answer caused a bit of an uproar. Several of them spoke out at once against Eithne being allowed a weapon. It was against the ancient laws of their culture! Tribal elf women had never wielded weapons in all their known history. Besides, they did not realize that Eithne actually knew how to use a sword. The men all presumed that she had no idea how to fight in the first place; therefore, it was ridiculous for her to have a weapon, anyway.

Darian held up his hand for silence, and the men quieted.

"As I stated before, my goal is to keep her safe until I can return her to her family. In the event that we are attacked, I cannot be certain of my ability to stay between her and possible danger. I will not have her defenseless against an enemy."

"She probably doesn't even know how to hold a sword!" Finnis grumbled loudly. He wanted everyone to hear him.

Darian spoke with more force in response to the chide, "Do not make the mistake of assuming that Eithne is a witless female who doesn't know the sharp end of a blade. She has made it this far on her own and will pull her weight on the journey. She is skilled with medicinal herbs and ways of healing. I have instructed her to only use her weapon in self-defense as needed."

He looked at his men and gauged their reaction. They were quiet, somber, and stiff. Some of them still looked angry. Darian decided to try and lighten the mood.

"Besides, why should any of you be concerned that she's carrying a sword? I can't believe that any of you are worried about her using on you."

A few of the men chuckled at the notion of Eithne successfully using a sword against them. Others seemed to become less tense, but there were no smiles. Darian wasn't expecting anyone to smile, but it would have been nice if they had. At least, he managed to alleviate some of the tension. Now might be the best time to retrieve Eithne from the cargo haul. He was about to go and get her when another one of the men spoke up.

"What if we are simply unwilling to travel with a lawbreaker?" It was Croel who voiced the concern.

He was a little older than the others and very pig-headed but a good warrior. A few of the other men mumbled in agreement, which concerned Darian. He had hoped to avoid this particular conflict by making it seemingly impossible to turn back. They couldn't even see Tomak anymore. The coast of the Northern Continent was a hazy dark line on the horizon.

"This is not your decision, it is mine. I bear the responsibility for Eithne's presence," Darian returned firmly. He hoped that by taking full responsibility, he could avoid further argument.

"No matter whose decision it is, we're still being forced to travel with some crazy she-elf who thinks she's a man!" Croel shot back. He was getting angrier. Several of the other men grumbled in support of him.

Darian drew himself up to his full height and fixed Croel with a hard look. "You don't have to acknowledge her presence if you don't want to, but my decision is final. Eithne stays with me until she is safely home."

Croel and Darian exchanged glares for a long moment. Neither of them was the sort to give in, but Croel was at a distinct disadvantage since Darian outranked him.

Finally, Croel broke the silence, but not the stare, "Fine then. I'll just be returning home. Anyone else who can't stand this absolute heresy is welcome to come with me. I won't travel with some insolent female who's just going to get herself, or one of us, killed!" That said, Croel turned on his heel and stomped off.

He had made his own decision. After a few seconds pause, one of the other men got up and followed him. Darian had just lost two good fighters. It stung him deeply. He had never had a problem with dissention in the ranks before now.

Trying his best not to show his own upset, Darian scanned the remaining members of his party.

"Anyone else want to leave in light of the new development?" His question rang out clearly. His tone made it clear that now was the time for them to make their final determination.

No one moved.

"All right then. We will be at the Southern Continent by early tomorrow morning. I would suggest the rest of you use this time wisely. So see to your weapons, and get some sleep." Darian did not offer any further time for argument. He turned and stormed off below deck.

The men stood on the rocking deck of the ship for several moments, unsure of how to proceed after such a scene. Eventually, Proithen heaved a sigh and mumbled that he was going to go sharpen his blade. The rest of them dispensed from there to do similar tasks.

Eithne found herself being gruffly shaken awake. She opened her eyes to see the rather unpleasant sight of Darian's angry face. It was frightening, and just for a second, she thought he might strike her.

"You just cost me two good warriors," he stated darkly.

Eithne sat up slowly as she woke up and digested his statement. How could she have done anything? She had been asleep here the whole time, doing as she had been instructed. She was confused and still groggy.

"What do you mean, I cost you two warriors?"

"Exactly what I said," Darian snapped back. "Now, come up to the deck."

He turned and left without waiting for her. Eithne scrambled to her feet and clumsily grabbed her pack, hurrying after him. She hated that he was in such a sour mood. He had been so pleasant this morning. The men must have taken the news badly.

In her haste to catch up with Darian, Eithne practically stumbled out onto the main deck. Everyone immediately stared at her, and it wasn't at all friendly. As if on cue, a cold sea breeze blew over the ship, causing the chill in the air to be felt more acutely. Eithne stared back for a moment and took in all the dread. This was not going to be as nice as she had hoped. Darian was the only one who wasn't staring. His broad back was facing her. It felt worse to see his back than the other's eyes. Eithne managed to drop her gaze and tried to make herself as inconspicuous as possible. She tried to shuffle off to a corner somewhere, but they all followed her steadily with their glaring eyes.

It was the most awful feeling she had ever felt. It only made it worse that it was her actions that caused the feeling in the first place. There was nothing she could say or do to make it better, and Darian was angry at her. He could offer no small expression of comfort. Only his back.

Eithne went to sit by some barrels and brought her knees up to her chest, trying to make herself as small and invisible as she could. It was going to be a very long rest of the day. She was glad to have napped through the first half of it.

Eithne did not move from her hiding place for some time. She did not know what else to do. There was no work for her to do, and certainly no one wanted to talk with her, so she just sat. Even the excitement of being on a ship for the first time was doused by everyone's disgust over her. Under other circumstances, she would have sought out Darian, but that would only serve to make things worse right now. So she sat there for the rest of the day, looking through the railing posts at the sea churning as the ship cut through it. It was peaceful and very nice to look at something that didn't scowl back at her. Her body was numb to the freezing wind and sea spray that washed over her.

When darkness began to fall, the wind became more persistent and colder. Eithne realized through her haze of self-loathing that she needed to go below deck to sleep if she didn't want to freeze to death. She did not want to be in the same space as the rest of the party. They might not even allow it. She thought it would be best if she secluded herself in the cargo haul for the night. Crates and barrels didn't hold grudges, at least. Eithne stood up and found that her limbs were chilled stiff and stung from the movement. She had been exposed too long already. It was hard to believe that, according to the calendar, it was supposed to be late summer or early autumn. It felt like the dead of winter. She made her way below deck and headed for the cargo haul. To her surprise, she found Darian standing at the entrance with his arms crossed in an imposing fashion. He still looked mad.

"I thought you might try to hide in here again," Darian stated bitterly. "If you want to be a part of the group, then you need to stay with the group."

That said, Darian grabbed Eithne's arm roughly and escorted her to the sleeping quarters. Every instinct told her to run as he dragged her into the sleeping quarters. She could see that the men did not want her there, but no one would challenge Darian's authority. He yanked her to stand next to one of the available hammocks by the wall. Then Darian claimed the hammock next to hers and began getting ready to sleep. Eithne was still as stone, clutching her pack and sword to her chest while the eyes of everyone in the room bore into her. It was terrifying. She shook her head to come out of her daze and quickly, if not clumsily, climbed into her hammock, trying to ignore the stares. She realized with resignation that she wouldn't get much sleep tonight either.

CHAPTER SEVEN

*T*HE SOUTHERN CONTINENT was not much warmer, as Eithne had hoped it would be, though the icy wind died down as they got further away from the coast. The party had been traveling for seven days since getting off the ship. Croel and one other had chosen to return with the ship to Tomak. There were now only eight left in the party, ten if Eithne counted Darian and herself. Even though it had been a week, still no one spoke to her except Darian. The most she could get out of anyone else was an annoyed grunt or disapproving look. Of course, Eithne was not trying all that hard to make conversation. She completely understood why they did not want to speak to her, and she didn't know what they would say to each other, anyway. The days had been uneventful and quiet. None of the party was happy. However, Eithne suspected that Darian's temper had subsided, at least, which made her feel better.

The eighth day seemed as if it would be more of the same. They awoke in the early morning and set out on the trail. Things changed abruptly around midmorning. As the party was coming around a bend in the trail, a large horned demon stepped out in front of them. It held a hefty club that it was suggestively slapping into its big palm. The demon's ugly yellow face sneered at them maliciously. Darian reined his horse to a halt and motioned for the rest of the party to stop behind him. There was a rustle behind them. Eithne turned around in her saddle to see three other demons step out of the forest. They were surrounded. Eithne had never seen a demon before but knew enough about them from her reading to know that it was not a fair match. Even though they outnumbered the demons by six, the demons had the upper hand. Each demon stood at least seven feet tall and brandished a wicked-looking weapon. It was well known that demons were at least twice as strong as an elf, not to mention that they innately possessed special abilities that generally gave them the advantage in a fight. Eithne had read a lot about demons, and she had learned that some of them could even spit acid or had sharp needles that shot out of their skin. It was frightening. This was going to be Eithne's first real fight, and it was very likely that she was going to die. Her heart began beating frantically, and she swallowed hard.

"Give us your valuables, and we will let you pass unharmed," the big yellow leader stated boldly in rough common tongue.

Darian waited a few seconds before responding. "What if we refuse?" he spoke in the common tongue. The demon clearly did not speak elvish.

The sallow demon grinned, exposing black pointed teeth. "Then we take the valuables by force." Its eyes drifted to Eithne. "And probably have one of you for dinner."

Eithne felt her stomach turn over. She had very strong feelings about becoming dinner. She was firmly against it.

Darian slowly drew his blade and held it at the ready. The rest of the party did the same. Eithne tried not to shake as she drew her sword out of its sheath. She had never felt so terrified. It felt like she was going to be sick and was certain that her bottom lip was quivering.

"Keep control of your mount. He's going to spook when they come at us," Darian whispered to Eithne. He could see how nervous and upset she was, and he needed her thinking clearly in order to survive this. "Stay close to me, and remain focused. You'll get through this."

Eithne wanted to thank him for that small comfort but was not granted the opportunity. The demons rushed in on the party. The big yellow one came straight for Darian with its giant club. Darian reared his horse up on its hind legs and pummeled the demon back with its hooves. While the demon tried to evade the pummeling hooves, Darian used his sword to slash at its throat. His opponent stepped back so that the blade only scratched its chest. Darian pressed his advantage and urged his horse forward.

At first, Eithne's horse gave a shriek of panic and tried to rear. She was able to restrain the horse with great effort, then she got her bearing of the scene around her. None of the demons had gone immediately for her. They targeted the most formidable-looking fighters first, so Eithne was able to assess her surroundings. It seemed almost calm at first. All around, everyone else was engaged in battle, but no one was attacking her. Suddenly, a demon with reddish brown skin and long, sharp talons on its fingers grabbed her thigh and tried to drag her from her horse. Eithne reacted quickly and brought her blade down hard on the demon's wrist. Such a blow would have severed the hand of an elf or human, but demon bones were much thicker and harder. It cut into the bone, which was enough to make it let go. As soon as it did, Eithne turned her horse and tried to get to Darian's side. Her attacker found a new target within seconds.

Darian was still battling the yellow leader, and he was doing well. It looked as though he was about to win when the demon brought its club hard on his horse's forehead, right between its eyes. The animal was dead instantly and fell limp, taking Darian down with it. His leg was pinned beneath the dead beast, and for a moment, Darian was trapped. His opponent grinned its black pointed grin with vicious pleasure as the demon advanced with the intention of smashing Darian's head in. The demon leader was practically salivating at the prospect of the kill. Eithne rushed up behind the demon, who was oblivious to her presence, and made a wild stab at the back of its neck. Her sword jutted out the front of the demon's neck, and she looked on in horror as blue blood spurted from the wound. The yellow demon gurgled with shock and fell to the ground dead.

In the meantime, Darian struggled out from under his dead horse.

Before Eithne had even realized what she had done, he had dislodged her sword for her, wiped the blood from the blade, and held it out for her to take, but she was too stunned to take her weapon. The fight was over. They had won, though not without a cost. Two of their men were dead, and another was seriously injured. Eithne was still in a state of shock for more than one reason. She had just survived her first fight, killed for the first time, and now she was seeing death in battle for the first time. Nothing she had ever read could have prepared her for the overwhelming despair that gripped her heart. She wanted to look away from the blank, lifeless faces of people she used to know, but it was difficult. Then she felt her horse move beneath her. Darian had taken the reins and was leading her horse to where Proithen knelt over the injured Elrick.

"How bad is he?" Darian asked.

Proithen looked up and shook his head. Eithne came out of her daze and leaned over to get a better view of Elrick's injury. He had been stabbed in the side and was sweating feverishly. There must have been poison on the blade that stabbed him. She forgot her shock and started thinking like a healer. She dismounted to help him, but as Eithne tried to stand, her right leg gave out. Darian caught her as she fell and frowned as he looked at her leg.

"You need attention too," Darian said matter-of-factly.

Eithne looked down at her leg and saw three deep gashes above her knee where the demon had grabbed her. It must have been its sharp talons that caused the gashes. She wondered why she had not felt it before. Now that Eithne saw it, she felt the sting of pain but chose to ignore it.

"I'll take care of that later. Right now, I might be able to help Elrick," Eithne said and hoped that none of them heard the slight quiver in her voice.

She really had no idea if she could help Elrick at all, but she had to try. She leaned on Darian's arm as she knelt down to attend Elrick.

Proithen looked to Darian for approval. Darian nodded and handed down Eithne's pack. She took out her waterskin and put it to Elrick's lips. Then she poured some water over his wound. Whatever the poison was, it was moving fast through his body. She needed to work quickly to try and combat the effects. The cut was clean, at least. It would be easy to stitch closed. Eithne asked one of the other men nearby to search the dead demons for an antidote. If one of them carried a poison blade, then it only stood to reason that they would have an antidote in case of an accident. It was worth trying. She began preparing the needle and thread to close the wound. She was about to begin stitching when Proithen put his hand on hers to stop her. Eithne looked at Elrick and realized that he had stopped breathing. Elrick was dead. Eithne pressed her lips and looked away to keep from crying. Proithen closed Elrick's eyes and walked away.

Darian helped Eithne stand. "Come on, let's take care of you next."

Eithne nodded dumbly and allowed him to lead her over to a good sitting place. Darian told her to stretch her leg out straight, and then he used a knife to rip open her trousers around the gashes. If she were a man, he might have had her remove her breeches in order to get a better look at the wound, but that was out of the question. This sort of contact made Eithne slightly uncomfortable. A man had never seen her bare legs, or touched them, before, but there was nothing sexual about the contact. He took out his water skin and doused the gashes to wash away the blood. There was a lot more blood than Eithne thought there should be. After inspecting the cuts, he decided to stitch it closed. He gingerly took the needle and thread she still held in her hand to use on her wound. All was quiet while Darian concentrated on mending. The stitches pinched as he worked, but it was tolerable. Eithne watched what the others were doing while he worked. The rest of the men were rounding up the horses and dragging the dead bodies off the trail as well as taking care of their own minor injuries. Darian's horse was too heavy to move, but they collected his belongings from the dead animal and began loading them onto one of the horses whose previous master was now dead. The whole scene seemed rather mechanical and very depressing. She noticed that after other things were taken care of, the men started using their swords to dig out graves for their fallen comrades.

"Is it always like this?" Eithne asked in a small, almost-childlike voice.

"This was a bad raid on us," Darian answered without looking up or pausing in his work. "Those demons were tough. I'm actually glad that we only lost three. It doesn't dull the pain of losing them, however. I wish it did. Elrick wanted to marry when we returned . . ." his voice trailed off.

Darian finished stitching the second gash and began work on the third. Eithne was surprised that it didn't hurt more. Perhaps her body was simply numb.

"I owe you, thanks," Darian said after a quiet moment.

Eithne blinked at him. She didn't know what he meant.

"You managed to save my life back there. Thank you," he clarified.

Eithne was taken aback. She had not realized what she had done, but as she replayed the scene in her mind, she saw that it was true! It had been completely by chance. Of course, she was trying to help him, but she had not been sure of exactly what she was doing in the moment at all. It had been a lucky blow.

She gave a nervous laugh. "Well, neither one of us imagined that would happen. Anyway, after all you have risked for me, thanks is hardly in order." Eithne was pleased with herself but also embarrassed. So she tried to make light of the situation.

"You saved my life, Eithne. Don't dismiss the nobility of your actions. You have earned respect from more than just me this day."

Darian's words caused her to blush. She looked down at her hands clutched in her lap while he finished mending the gashes on her thigh.

After the burial of their three comrades, the party continued along the trail. The mood was silent and still, but Eithne noticed a change in the way the men acted toward her. They no longer ignored her or gave her hard looks. It seemed that they were coming to accept her presence now that she had proven herself to a degree to be worthy of traveling with them. Some of them may have regarded her survival of the fight as sheer luck—even Eithne thought that was partially true—but she had saved Darian's life. No matter how lucky she may be, the men no longer doubted her spirit, and that is what really mattered.

The eleventh day of their journey into the Southern Continent was horribly unpleasant. A freezing drizzle fell on the party and slowly soaked into their skin. Everyone was miserable. The mood of the group was dark and grumpy. Eithne found nothing better to do than to mull over her own thoughts to distract herself from the icy cold. In her pondering, she came upon an unanswered question: Just where were they going anyway? Darian still had not told her, and she believed she had the right to know. Eithne kicked her horse forward and came up beside Darian. He nodded at her as she approached but said nothing.

"Where are we going?" Eithne asked in low tones.

It was obvious to her that the question startled him, but he maintained his composure. "To the center of the Southern Continent," he replied frankly.

"What's there?" She pressed.

"A network of caves. At least, that's what I'm told."

Eithne was getting tired of his game. "Darian, what is the point of this mission? I need to know, and you're being indirect," she said with a hint of impatience.

Darian eyed her with annoyance. "And you're unruly, but I suppose you deserve more information."

He paused while he thought on how open he should be with her about the mission. He decided to tell her everything. Darian didn't know why he felt such compulsion to communicate so openly with Eithne, but he wanted to confide in her. Despite her feisty attitude, he knew that she could be trusted. He took a quick look at the others to be sure that no one else was listening.

"Have you ever heard of the Stone of Elissiyus?"

"I've heard the legend. Do you think it exists?"

Eithne was surprised. Most people thought the legend was just that and that the Stone of Elissiyus did not exist. It was said that, long before the Heavenly Wars, there lived an extremely powerful wizard named Elissiyus. He had foreseen the death of the gods, and so he imbued a large quartz gemstone with all his powers in hopes that it could be used to ease the suffering of the world. It was said that whomever possessed the stone could do or have anything they wanted, even have the power to become a god themselves! Of course, in the wrong hands, the stone could create great evil. To combat this problem, the great wizard placed a charm on it wherein no one with evil intent toward the world or others, nor could any single person alone, find it. There had been many stories of the stone's location before, but since the world had changed so much, even those who believed that the Stone of Elissiyus existed considered it to be lost.

"I have heard that the Stone of Elissiyus does exist and that it is hidden in the caves at the center of this continent," Darian stated plainly.

Eithne noticed that he kept his voice very low and looked around to see if anyone else was listening to the conversation. The rest of the party seemed to be absorbed in their own thoughts, not paying any attention to them.

"But no one has ever seen the Stone of Elissiyus. Its existence was never confirmed. People aren't even certain that Elissiyus himself existed," Eithne couldn't suppress her feeling that this mission might be all for nothing.

"Times are hard, Eithne. Crops are failing everywhere, and people are dying. There isn't much left to believe in, but the stone has the potential to save us all. I have chosen to believe in it because something good has to be out there," Darian spoke with soft conviction.

"You're trying to save the world?!" Eithne exclaimed in a whisper.

Darian turned his head and met her eyes. "Somebody has to do something. I'm not the sort to sit idly by while everything around me slowly dies."

Eithne felt admiration for him swell up inside her. She never knew how nobly ambitious and kind Darian was before this moment. She thought that he might be the best person she had ever known, or would ever know.

"Do the others know what we are looking for?" she asked.

"I have told them we are looking for an ancient artifact that may help our people, but I have not mentioned the Stone of Elissiyus specifically. I would appreciate it if you did not tell them either," Darian answered.

Eithne nodded her assent. She had no intention of saying anything to the rest of the party. She understood why Darian would want to keep that information secret. It could make their captain seem like a desperate person—though these were desperate times.

They rode for a while in silence. Neither of them wished to continue discussing the subject in the company of others. Eithne longed to learn more about the mission. She wanted to know if there was more to the legend and how Darian had acquired his information.

Eithne was about the broach a new topic of conversation when they came upon another traveler. The traveler wore a black hooded cloak and was about the size of an elf or human, but they could not be sure what this traveler was. Demons came in all shapes and sizes. The traveler walked alone and paid them no mind even though they must have heard the group of seven riders coming up behind them. Darian motioned for the party to stop. He rode up to the stranger on his own to see if they posed any threat to the group.

"Traveling alone is dangerous these days," Darian stated in the common tongue as he approached and reined up his horse beside the traveler.

The traveler turned toward Darian, exposing his identity. He was an elf man with black hair and brown eyes. He had the look of a city elf, but Darian guessed that he had not lived in a city for a long while. His skin was tanned, and his clothing was that of a nomad.

"I've learned to handle myself well enough," the traveler responded in elvish.

"My name is Darian. My party and I are headed south. What is your name, friend?" Darian switched to speaking in elvish as well.

"I am called Aram. I am also headed south, but I do not wish to reveal my business."

Darian nodded with understanding. He did not wish to reveal his business either. He liked Aram and instinctively felt that he could be trusted. City elves and tribal elves rarely socialized, but there was no feud between them.

"Why don't you travel with us until our paths part? There is safety in numbers, and we would be glad for the fresh company," Darian offered with a smile. "We even have a spare horse that you could ride."

Aram was quite surprised at Darian's offer. No one had ever shown him this courtesy before. He was pleased by the invitation and agreed to travel with Darian and his party for a while.

Darian called to have a horse brought over to Aram. Oddly, the animal seemed to spook a bit when Aram mounted up. The horse was definitely uneasy about its new rider. No one said anything, but Aram felt their confusion. Elves of all backgrounds were renowned for their ways with animals. Aram looked embarrassed and made an excuse about never having a gift with horses. The party accepted this well enough for the moment, and they all continued on the trail south together.

CHAPTER EIGHT

*E*ITHNE LIKED ARAM. He was very quiet, but that meant he didn't say anything unpleasant either. Also, she found him to be very handsome. His features were straight and delicate with deep brown eyes lined with thick lashes. His hair was a lustrous black that fell about his face in an unruly fashion and curled slightly at the ends. Aram was tall, with a warrior's build. Eithne guessed that he was a talented fighter and wanted to ask him all sorts of questions about fighting techniques. When she did ask, Aram would humor her to an extent but didn't seem to like talking about himself and would always cut the conversation short to avoid doing so. Still, he was willing to enlighten her more about combat than the rest of the men, and it pleased Eithne greatly. It seemed that city elves did not have the same social rules for women that tribal elves did.

Darian liked Aram as well. He wasn't as chatty about it as Eithne, but he found himself enjoying the newcomer's company and that they had certain things in common. Also, Darian couldn't quite explain it, but he felt a kinship with Aram. He suspected that the feeling was mutual, though Darian also sensed something else in his new friend. Aram was obviously a formidable fighter. He did not flaunt it, but it was clear. It was also obvious that he was keeping a great many secrets. This did not make Darian mistrust him, but all the same, he was hiding something. The horse they lent him never warmed to him, even after several days. The other horses shied away when Aram was close too. Darian could not put his finger on it, but there was something darkly different about him.

The men had mixed feelings about their new companion. They accepted him into the group willingly enough but didn't seem to like his quiet attitude. They wanted to know more about who they were traveling with and would even prod Aram with questions when the opportunity presented itself. The most any of them could get out of him was that he was 128 years old and had been raised in the elven city of Amara but had been living on the road for sometime now. As far as anyone knew, the City of Amara had escaped devastation after the death of the gods, and so Aram's reasons for leaving must have been of a personal nature. Some of the men even suspected that he was a fugitive who lived his life on the run, but Aram would nothing to confirm or deny this notion.

One night, after Aram had been traveling with the party for a week, Eithne lay awake in her bedroll. Darian appeared to be asleep only a few feet from her. Almost everyone else in the party was awake. She could not see where Aram had gone but knew he wasn't close by, as the others were talking about him.

"I still think we should voice our concerns to Captain Darian," said Finnis. "I just can't trust him, and I don't know why the captain trusts that pretty boy either!"

Eithne smirked at the term "pretty boy," remembering how she had been called that when she had disguised herself as a boy for the tryouts.

"I agree he can't be trusted, but he has to be leaving soon. He's only supposed to travel with us for as long as we are going in the same direction. It's absurd to think he would be going to the same place that we are. Let's just wait for him to leave," Proithen urged. He did not like Aram either but also had complete trust in Captain Darian.

"Is it so absurd to think that he's going to the same place?" countered Finnis. "What if he's after the same artifact? Just because our mission is secret doesn't mean that others aren't after the same thing. I think we should tell him to bugger off before he steals the artifact from us!"

"I agree with Finnis. I don't think that Captain Darian has been himself lately, and we need to talk some sense into him. Look at us! He already has us traveling with a woman who thinks she's a man, and now this stranger! Something is wrong with him," Dal said in a heated whisper.

They were all keeping their voices down so as not to wake the others that were sleeping.

It hurt Eithne to hear the men talk about Darian that way. She had always known Darian to command the utmost respect from his men. That they doubted him was quite a blow. She glanced at Darian again to see if he really were asleep. He was lying on his side, facing her, and he did not betray any signs of wakefulness. Eithne was glad. It would hurt him to hear what they were saying about him. She pretended to roll over in her sleep to see if she could locate Aram. The men paused in their conversation as she moved, but resumed quickly. Eithne still could not find Aram. His bedroll was laid out, but he was not in it. She was tempted to get up and find him, but perhaps he was seeking solitude. Besides, she didn't want the others to know that she heard their conversation. Eithne closed her eyes and tried to sleep.

Aram was not far from the camp. He sat on a boulder, looking up through an opening in the treetops. It was a clear and starry night, and he liked feeling the fresh, cold air in his lungs. He could hear every word of conversation between Dal, Finnis, and Proithen and was not in the least bit surprised by what they said.

Aram was not used to being made welcome. His secretive nature put off most people, and if he were honest with himself, he had begun making a habit of putting them off anyway. It had been years since he had been invited to travel with anyone, and his first instinct had been to reject the offer, but there was something about Darian that made him accept. Aram felt that they had some common connection somehow, and even felt trust. If Aram's circumstances had been different, he would have considered himself to have found a friend. He liked Eithne as well. She was very odd for a tribal elf woman, but clever and personable. He also felt that she didn't judge him. Perhaps it was because she was a bit of an outcast herself, but it was a good feeling not to be looked upon with judgment. It had been a long time since he had allowed himself companionship of other elves and truly enjoyed the company, but he would part ways with them tomorrow morning. He could not stay. It was obvious that Aram was not wanted by the rest of the party. Also, he feared that

Finnis was correct about them all being after the same thing. Aram had to admit that he had also expected to part ways before this and found it uncanny that Darian also seemed to be headed for the caves. Aram could not be sure just how many had heard the rumor about the Stone of Elissiyus. He sighed and stared up at the nearly full moon, listening to the men's faint conversation back at the camp. He wondered if Darian was awake to hear it.

The next morning, Aram packed his gear and told Darian that he was leaving. Darian was disappointed.

"You know, you don't have to leave on account of those three," Darian offered in low tones. "You're more than welcome to continue with us if it suits you."

Aram found himself smiling, which he rarely did. "Thank you, but I must head west from here."

"Well then, I wish you the best of luck. I hope our paths cross again someday, my friend." Darian held out his hand.

Aram gripped his hand with gratitude. "I truly hope we meet again as well. Thank you."

Aram said a brief good-bye to Eithne, who was equally sorry to see him go. He did not bother with the rest of the party, as they were happy to be rid of him. At least they wouldn't be staging a mutiny because of him now. Aram headed west out of sight then resumed his course south, through the forest. He would stay off the trail from now on to avoid meeting Darian's group again.

Aram traveled alone for two days and found a decent spot to camp on the second night. He would be at the caves by midmorning tomorrow and hoped to get a good night's rest before then. He had no idea what could be lurking in the caves. He also hoped to get an early start. It was possible that Darian could reach the Stone of Elissiyus before him, and Aram did not want that to happen. He needed the stone for something very important to him. Something that would change his entire existence, make it better. However, Aram mused that after his need of the stone had been fulfilled, he would give it to Darian. Aram only wanted one thing and was not the type who wished to be beholden of great power. He preferred a quiet life.

Aram heard a twig snap underfoot. Someone was near his campsite. Aram did not douse his fire, as whoever it was would have already seen it. Dousing it would only let them know that he had detected their presence. Instead, he slowly rose from his position, drew one of his daggers, and stealthily began tracking the noise. About thirty feet out, he came up behind the figure of a short humanoid female. He wasn't sure if she was trying to sneak up on him or sneak past him. Either way, he wasn't going to wait to find out. Aram rushed up behind her silently and put his dagger to her throat.

"Why hello there, Wolfie!" she said in a womanly voice. "I guess I should have known you would get the drop on me."

Aram was startled by her reaction. It was actually friendly and charming—except for the "Wolfie" part. He didn't appreciate that at all. He wasn't even sure what to do with her for a moment; he was so taken aback. Who in their right mind responds that way to a stranger who just put a dagger to your throat? Aram decided to take her back to his camp for interrogation and security. He could tell that she as neither elf nor human. He could smell what she was: a demon. Aram began roughly escorting her in the proper direction.

"You know, there's no need to be like this. I don't have any plans to hurt you. I was just hoping for a little company, is all," the she-demon protested verbally, but she made no attempt to get away or reach for her sword, which gave some credit to her words.

Still, Aram made a habit of not trusting strangers who try to sneak up on you in the middle of the night.

Once at his camp, Aram took away all her weapons and bound her wrists and ankles. He realized that she was actually rather beautiful once he could see her face. The only clues to her demon heritage were a pair of black curling horns emerging from a thick mane of violet hair. Other than those features, one could swear that she was a city elf by her appearance. She had deep blue eyes that were almond shaped, a small button nose, full lips, and sun-kissed skin. Her body was also quite alluring. She was petite and curvy with full breasts, which her low-cut blouse only accentuated. Aram had to keep himself from staring.

"Wolfie, stop staring! You're making me blush," she said coyly and smiled at him.

Aram wondered if this was her true form or just an illusion.

"Stop calling me Wolfie. Now, who are you, and what were you doing sneaking around my camp?" Aram demanded.

"Well, even though you're being a little rude, I will answer because it's what polite people do. My name is Yocelin, and I already told you that I was just looking for some company. I thought that since we are both sort of outcasts, it would be a welcome idea. I guess I was wrong." She smiled politely back at him, as if she were having a civil conversation in a sitting parlor, not tied up in the middle of the forest. "What is your name, if you don't want me to call you Wolfie?"

"Why so anxious for company? Also, is that your true face?" Aram ignored her inquiry for his name.

Yocelin rolled her eyes and made a little sigh. She was getting frustrated with him.

"Well, nobody likes to be alone all the time, do they? Besides, I will need a companion for tomorrow and thought you might need me too." She smiled enticingly. "Oh, and of course, this is my true form! Don't you think I would have gotten rid of the horns other-wise? I know that you can smell what I am just as much as I can smell what you are."

"Why should I need your help tomorrow? How long have you been following me?" Aram did not like the idea that she had possibly been tracking him for some time without him realizing it.

"I'm not answering another question until I know your name," Yocelin stated plainly and stuck her chin out sharply.

Aram did not want to tell her his name out of principle, but what harm would it do? It wasn't as if he were known anywhere, or wanted for anything. He always did his best to go unnoticed and had become quite successful at it.

"You may call me Aram," he conceded in a stubborn tone. "Now answer my questions."

Yocelin smiled brightly at him. "Aram, it's nice to meet you. Regarding why we would need each other tomorrow, I assume that you are also seeking what is hidden in those caves. Well, the legend says that no individual person can find it, you have to have a companion. Seeing as we are both alone, I thought we could help each other out. I only need one thing, and then the stone is yours," she kept smiling as she spoke in a very persuasive way.

Aram had forgotten about that part of the legend until she mentioned it. There was no way to know if it were really necessary to have a companion, but it was better to be safe than sorry, he supposed. He studied her more closely as he blinked at him, waiting for his reply. She didn't look like much, but she was still a demon, and that meant that she was probably full of surprises. Aram knew that he was stronger than her physically, but that didn't merit taking undue risks. Also, Yocelin appeared to be cunning. Who knew what else she might be planning? Aram decided on his course of action.

"All right, we will go into the caves together tomorrow," he said.

"That's a relief!" Yocelin beamed. Then she realized that he made no move to untie her. "Well, what are you waiting for?"

"I didn't say I would untie you. We can go into the caves together with you as my prisoner," Aram said matter-of-factly.

Yocelin made a little huffing sound. "I'll just wriggle out of these ropes. You don't think that I haven't been tied up before, do you? Elves and humans alike hate me because my horns give away my heritage, and other demons hate me because I look like an elf. People have been tying me up to take me prisoner or kill me for most of my life, and well, I've gotten away every time, obviously. So you should just save me the trouble and untie me now. I promise to be very good. I won't go anywhere, and we both know that you're stronger than me." She looked at him expectantly.

"You talk too much," Aram responded flatly and laid out his bedroll to get some sleep.

Yocelin made a frustrated groan. So that's how it was going to be. She had truly been hoping for some companionship and friendly conversation. It looked like she was just getting an uncomfortable night and the silent treatment.

Aram came over and checked the ropes to be sure that they were still intact. He even added some extra knots to be safe. Yocelin followed his movements with her eyes, looking peeved. He ignored her expression and went to his bedroll, lay down, and went to sleep.

He was just drifting off when Yocelin loudly announced, "I'm cold."

Aram sat up and glared at her.

"I can't believe that you would treat me like this!" she continued. "You must know what it feels like to have no one want you because of what you are, even though you're a perfectly nice person! It's horrible that you can do these things to me without even thinking twice about it. Even though you must know exactly how terrible it feels!" Yocelin very much disliked this particular injustice that she was being dealt.

"You said you could get out of them, anyway. So why don't you fix your own problem?" Aram responded shortly, though he did know how it felt to be treated that way, and it was terrible. Still, he wasn't sure if he could trust her. Something told him that he probably could trust her, but he wasn't in the mood to take chances.

"It's not that I can't do it, but the principle of the matter, you need to have a little bit of trust in me if we are going to find the stone together," Yocelin appealed.

Now that was a valid point, Aram had to admit. He stood and went over to her. He knelt beside her and looked her in the eye. Yocelin looked back and did not waver. After a moment, Aram took out his dagger and cut her bonds.

Yocelin smiled and leaned into him with a slight giggle. "I'm adopting you," she said and touched the tip of his nose with her finger.

Aram jerked his head back. "Did I just untie a crazy person?"

Yocelin laughed. "Of course, I'm not crazy! It's just something I do when I decide that I like someone enough to be their friend. When I said that I'm adopting you, I mean that I will now take care of you as my friend." She kept smiling.

"It's still a bit loony," Aram said and went back to his bedroll. She had thrown him off, and it was obvious. She was a strange woman. "Just go to sleep now." He rolled over and tried to rest.

70

Yocelin didn't care what he thought. She got her things prepared for the night and went to sleep.

When Aram woke the next morning, Yocelin was gone. He had no idea when she had snuck away, but he was very irritated about it. He had actually trusted her to stay after her pretty speech last night. He was a fool for thinking that she would keep her word—though, Aram supposed, it didn't really matter. He could very well find the stone by himself, without her. Aram quickly packed up his belongings and headed for the caves, trying very hard not to think about the part of the legend that said that no single person alone could find the Stone of Elissiyus.

Aram was not far from the campsite when he came upon something curious. There was a small package wrapped in a piece of black cloth and tied with a blue ribbon. It was very odd, but unthreatening. Perhaps some other traveler had dropped it, perhaps Yocelin. The little parcel did remind him of her somehow. Aram bent and picked it up. There was something solid inside. He shrugged and pulled the ribbon loose. The package contained a dead sparrow. Its neck had very recently been snapped. He wrinkled his nose at it, confused and a little appalled. Dead things didn't bother him, but it was very queer to find a dead bird gift-wrapped in the middle of the forest. Aram dropped the sparrow where he found it and continued on his way.

As he continued to the caves, Aram found several more black cloth packages, all containing similar "gifts." A dead squirrel, dead chipmunk, more dead birds, etc. . . . Another person may have been deeply disturbed by this morbid bread-crumb trail, but Aram was simply annoyed. He had a very good idea who was leaving presents for him.

There was no sign of Yocelin when Aram got to the caves, but he could smell that she was close. He approached cautiously and drew his sword as he walked. If Yocelin had wanted him dead, she had had opportunity enough, but he didn't know just how crazy she really was. She could be the sort who enjoyed playing with her food before devouring it. Just as Aram was about to enter the caves, he saw something move off to his right. He turned slowly and started to look around a large boulder. Yocelin stood from her hiding place and faced him with a smile.

"I shouldn't even try to hide from you," she said in her charming voice. "Did you like your presents?"

Aram studied her for any sign of aggression. She was relaxed with an open and friendly demeanor. Her sword was at her hip, but she showed no indication of using it.

"Why did you leave without me this morning?" Aram asked irritably.

"So that I could leave you the presents, of course! I thought it would be nice to have lunch together once you caught up with me," Yocelin answered as if her intentions were obvious.

"Lunch?" Aram was perplexed.

Yocelin held up a freshly killed squirrel by its tail. "I'm a demon. What do you expect me to eat? I thought that you might like to eat the same things, given your situation."

Aram understood now. Demons were carnivores that generally preferred their meals raw, so it made sense that Yocelin would view dead birds and rodents as tasty morsels. He still thought that she was probably a little crazy, but sweet in a way, and not a real danger to him. In fact, it seemed that she was trying her best to befriend him. It was odd.

"I don't eat like that," Aram returned plainly.

His response sounded a little rude to Yocelin, and she pouted, "So you didn't like your presents?"

"No." Aram was not overly concerned with her feelings.

Yocelin sighed and looked crestfallen for a few seconds. Then she brightened again, smiled at him, and shrugged as if to redeem herself from the disappointment. She took a seat on the ground and began getting some items out of her pack. Aram watched her with curiosity as she took out a knife, fork, napkin, and flat, smooth piece of wood. She placed the squirrel carcass on the piece of wood and arranged all the items in front of her for dining. She looked up expectantly at Aram.

He looked back at her with confusion. "What?"

"Aren't we going to have lunch? I don't want to go looking for the stone on an empty stomach." Yocelin continued to look at him with pleasant expectation.

Aram considered being stubborn about sitting to have a meal with her, for it was his inclination. However, there was nothing to be gained by being stubborn in this instance. It wasn't as if she were forcing him to eat the dead things she had left along the way for him. It seemed that she was genuine about wanting to enjoy a meal together. Aram resigned himself to the situation and slowly sat down across from Yocelin.

They sort of stared at each other for a moment, not sure what the other was going to do next. Then Yocelin laid her napkin across her lap, picked up the knife and fork, and began cutting small pieces from the squirrel carcass and politely eating them. Aram went into his pack and took out some dried meat. They sat in silence for a while, each doing a visual study of the other. Aram did find Yocelin to be very strange, but intriguing. It was no surprise for a demon to be eating raw meat. It was simply the usual diet for demons, but it was the way she ate that intrigued him. Most demons made a disgusting display by eating their meals alive, ripping into them with bare hands and blood squirting out. Yocelin had given the squirrel a quick and humane death by breaking its neck before eating it. Then she ate her meal with surprising etiquette. She was polite and even dainty, cutting her food and taking small bites. Perhaps she was not a full-blooded demon. Such offspring were extremely rare and usually only a product of rape. Demons and other humanoids weren't generally attracted to each other. It was very strange for a demon to find an elf or human physically attractive, so any kind of sexual contact that might occur was almost always out of cruelty or anger.

Yocelin looked up at him and smiled. "Aren't you going to eat, or do you enjoy watching others more?"

Suddenly, Aram remembered the dried meat in his hand. He began to eat without speaking and looked away from her. He must have been staring again.

Yocelin tried her best to draw Aram into conversation during the rest of lunch, but he would have none of it. She got the feeling that she confused him, and until he was certain about her in some way, he would remain a generally silent companion. Yocelin was not deterred by his coldness. On the contrary, it almost endeared him to her. She viewed him as someone in desperate need of a friend, though he would never admit to such an emotion, and Yocelin saw him as a wonderful candidate for her friendship. It appeared that he was a loner by choice. She was a loner too, but out of rejection. She was of an extremely sociable nature and craved the company of others. She was determined to make a new friend in Aram, and she suspected he needed one.

After eating, which did not take long, the pair of them continued on into the caves. It was a dangerous place, so both entered with weapons drawn and senses alert. They had no idea who or what may be lurking in the darkness.

CHAPTER NINE

*E*ITHNE'S MOTHER'S HANDS shook as she stared sorrowfully down at the letter her youngest daughter had written. She had read it over at least twenty times since she found it. The paper was becoming worn, and the ink smudged with tears. The tone of the letter was remorseful and loving, but her child had still gone away. Why did she have to leave at all?

Eithne had written that she could not abide by the rules of their society and be happy. Her mother did not understand, could not bring herself to comprehend, why life in the village was so suffocating to Eithne. She had always known that Eithne was different from the other girls. She was bright and beautiful and could have been popular if she wanted to be, but she did not. Eithne preferred shutting herself inside her room and reading books for hours. Sometimes, when her mother went to check on her, she would find Eithne missing and the window in her bedroom open. Her mother would panic and send her father out to find her, but then later, she would find her sitting in her room, reading again as if she had never left. Her mother would question her incessantly about where she went without saying anything. Sometimes, Eithne would claim that she had never left her room. Other times, she would say that she went out for a walk because it was a nice day, never saying why she didn't exit through the front door. Her mother always suspected that Eithne was up to something, but she could not imagine what. In her highest hopes, she had thought that Eithne may have a friend that she was being secretive about, but that was not the reason. Eithne had explained her absences in the letter.

The real reason was that she had taught herself how to use a sword, and she was sneaking off to practice. Her mother was not angry when she read the explanation; she was terrified. What would the tribal council do to her beloved daughter if they found out? Knowing that Eithne learned to fight with a weapon tainted the idea of her return, for if she ever came back, she would be found guilty of horrible crimes, and then what would come of her? Her mother felt a new batch of tears welling up in her eyes and wept openly. She had been crying ever since she found her daughter missing. Eithne's father and Rosalin had been crying too. Their once-happy household was now in mourning for their lost daughter.

"Mum! Mum! A letter arrived from Captain Darian! You have to read it, Mum!" Rosalin burst into the room, clutching a letter in her hands. Her father was not far behind her, looking equally anxious.

"Rosalin, I love you, but I cannot read a letter from your suitor. I'm sure it's wonderful, but I just can't right now," her mother replied.

She did not bother to wipe the tears from her face. She had cried so much the past couple of weeks that she no longer cared how she looked. Her reddish blond hair was pulled back in a disheveled bun, and her dress haphazardly put on. She used to take such great care in her appearance. It didn't matter anymore.

"You should read the letter, dear," her father prompted gently.

Seeing his beloved wife in such pain hurt him. He did not show it, but he was perhaps in the most pain over Eithne running away. He mourned his youngest daughter and mourned what it did to his wife and oldest daughter. His grass-green eyes were hollow and worn with worry, and he barely slept, but he suffered in silence. He could not burden his wife and oldest daughter with his emotions. They needed him to be their strength.

The mother gazed at her family blankly.

"I'll read it to you!" Rosalin offered hastily. "You need to hear what it says, Mum."

Her other nodded dumbly. Perhaps a letter from Rosalin's suitor would cheer her up.

Rosalin, who had also done her fair share a crying for her sister recently, sat on the bed and cleared her throat before reading the letter:

> Dear Alfrey Family, I must write to inform you that your daughter, Eithne, has followed my party and me to the town of Tomak. I have tried to reason with her and persuade her to go home, but she will not. So I have taken the responsibility of caring for her. I cannot send her back with one of my men, for she will certainly get away from them easily, nor can I defer from my mission. Therefore, Eithne is coming with my party to the Southern Continent. Please know that I will do all in my power to keep your daughter safe and return her to you. For now, Eithne is in excellent health and doing well. I will continue to write you letters to keep you updated. I promise to protect her. Kindest regards, Captain Darian MacAllow.

Rosalin sniffed as she read the letter and did her best to keep herself from crying again. She looked at her mother with hope.

"Did you hear that, Mum? Captain Darian is with her and caring for her. Eithne will be all right. We even know where she is! Eithne will come home to us soon!"

Their mother burst into tears all over again, but this time, they were tears of relief. Her daughter was alive and being protected by a trusted friend. She could allow herself to hope that Eithne would be returned to her safely. She would be able to kiss her daughter again someday.

CHAPTER TEN

⚜

*I*T WAS EARLY morning when Darian and his party approached the cave entrance. It was just before sunrise; the light was dim and dusty. Darian had arrived as he wanted to and was pleased with the progress. He had no idea where in the caves the Stone of Elissiyus may lie and hoped that they would have luck enough to find it before nightfall. He did not wish to spend a night in the caves. It was a very dangerous place where one always had to be on guard.

Before entering the caves, everyone dismounted, unsaddled, and tethered their horses. The caves were no place for the animals. The horses were left with long tethers so they had the opportunity to graze about and feel somewhat unrestricted. The cave network wasn't so large that they would be gone for more than a day or so. After the horses were cared for, the men went about lighting the torches they had made yesterday. Elves had better night vision than humans but still required light in order to see clearly. The rays of the sun were just beginning to pierce through the dawn as the party entered the inky darkness of the caves. Eithne followed close behind Darian and remained quiet. There was a silent tension in the air. The party walked for a while with no consequence, and everyone became more relaxed in the new environment.

After some time had passed, Proithen approached Darian and spoke to him in hushed tones, "Those two are up to something."

Darian nodded. "You mean, Dal and Finnis? I've noticed."

"Sir, I'm worried about their intentions. They might try and take the artifact for themselves!" Proithen whispered urgently.

"It's probable. They are both greedy and power hungry. Luckily, they don't know what artifact we are looking for in here," Darian responded nonchalantly.

"Well, none of us know exactly what the artifact is except for you, sir, but we all know it must be powerful. Don't you think that's enough?"

Darian nodded slowly. Proithen was honorable and intelligent. He liked that about him very much. In fact, Darian fully intended to make him an officer in his guard once they returned.

"I appreciate your concern, Proithen, but there is little to do about it right now. We will keep a sharp eye on Dal and Finnis for the time being."

Proithen nodded his concurrence with the captain's decision and glanced back at Dal and Finnis. They were whispering to each other again. The other men probably took it as innocent conversation, but Proithen felt that they were plotting something.

Darian stopped and held up his hand in a military fashion for everyone to halt. The party obeyed silently. He drew his sword and crept forward to look around the corner. He thought he had heard a sort of rustling and didn't want to walk blindly into a monster. A monster was indeed what he saw when Darian rounded the corner. There was a cave worm just around the bend, and that wasn't good. Cave worms were massive beasts with lumpy tubular bodies of a dark-brown color. The head, if you could call it a head, erupted into a plumage of rubbery-feeling antennae with a circular mouth filled with sharp rows of teeth at the center of the mass. They had no eyes, for cave worms relied on touch and sound alone. In fact, it was lucky that it had not heard the party approach. The worm seemed to be concentrated on devouring whatever it had just killed. Darian was thankful for the creature's distraction. Cave worms had a nasty reputation for being ravenous and very aggressive. It would be foolish to try to go around it. Darian came back and motioned for the party to follow him back the way they had come. He also gestured with a finger to his lips to keep quiet. All obeyed and followed him silently. Darian backtracked to a tunnel they had passed earlier and took it instead. He made a mental note of which way they went and hoped that the rest of the party tried to do the same. He had no idea where the Stone of Elissiyus was hidden in the caves, so it didn't really matter which direction they traveled so long as they generally headed toward the center of the cave network. Darian made the assumption that when Elissiyus had hidden his stone, he had put it at the center, where it would be most difficult to find. There was a great fear of getting lost in the caves, but Darian had to push that fear out of his mind and be a confident leader.

More time passed as they wandered through the caves, and the party was beginning to get nervous. They needed a better course of action, and Darian didn't have one. He had approached the village soothsayer several times before embarking on the mission in hopes of gaining some magical means of locating the stone, but none could be found. Magic, like the rest of the world, was declining and not nearly as potent as it once was. Since the death of the gods, those who relied on magic found themselves struggling. So Darian had been forced to go into the caves with no real direction. He hated the feeling, but there was nothing to be done except to keep searching.

"Sir?" Dal inquired. "Haven't we been in this tunnel before?"

Darian grit his teeth at the snide question. Even though they were wandering, he had been trying to do so in a systematic manner and was quite certain that they were not going in circles. "No, we have not," he replied plainly. "I am keeping track of where we have been."

"Sir, I can't help but notice that you have no map. So forgive me, I can't help but be nervous down here," Dal continued, trying to sound subordinate and helpful, but Darian knew exactly what he was getting at. Dal was going to suggest the party split up and search separately for the artifact. That way, he and Finnis could easily get away from the group to carry out whatever they had planned.

"No one knows exactly where in these caves the artifact is hidden. Therefore, there would be no map. I am taking a systematic approach to exploring the caves, so don't worry. We are safe as long as we are together as a group."

Darian did not enjoy explaining himself, but he felt that he needed to in order to cut Dal off. As much as he knew, it would be folly to separate. The rest of the men may be too anxious and support the proposition to split up.

Dal became quiet but continued to exchange looks with Finnis that Darian did not like. They were still thinking of separating from the group somehow. He wondered if they had figured out that they were looking for the Stone of Elissiyus. It wasn't so far-fetched that they could deduce what the artifact was since anyone who bothered to inquire could have heard the same rumors about the stone.

A moment later, Eithne stepped up beside Darian. "I think we are going the right way," she said with confidence.

Darian cocked an eyebrow at her perplexed by her statement. "Oh? Why is that?"

She shrugged. "It may sound stupid, but I actually feel that we are headed in the right direction now. We weren't when we first entered, but after we backtracked and took the other tunnel to avoid the worm, I've felt very good about our direction."

Darian allowed himself a small musing smile. Her support was comforting. "Woman's intuition?"

Eithne smiled and cocked her head to the side as she looked up at him. "Maybe."

Eithne and Darain continued walking next to each other in comfortable silence, each happy with the positive feeling their small conversation had invoked.

Suddenly, a large cave worm emerged from a tributary tunnel only mere feet in front of the party! They all immediately halted, and Darian held up his hand for silence. If the worm did not hear them, perhaps it would turn away and they could avoid a conflict. All were stone-still as the worm hesitated, half out of the tunnel. It was huge and bulky, taking up almost the entire width of the tunnel with its girth. They could not yet see how long it was, but Darian guessed it to be at least twenty feet in length.

The worm had sensed movement as it emerged from the tunnel, and it was certain that prey was nearby; but whatever it was, the prey was keeping still and silent, not letting its presence be known. The worm could be patient, for it was a skilled hunter. It was also very hungry. Food was difficult to come by in this environment, so the worm hesitated, its feelers wriggling in anticipation of movement.

Darian knew that they were probably going to have to fight the beast now. It was not aware of the party's present position, but the animal clearly knew that they were nearby. It was simply waiting on a sign of their presence. He would have to do something, but what? Darian's entire body tensed as he tried to think about what course of action would be best. They could charge the beast and try to gain the upper hand. It was still only about halfway through the tunnel, so it would be at a disadvantage. His other options were to run further down the tunnel, let the worm gain some ground, then turn and fight, which was ridiculous. They could also try to just run away, but the chances of outrunning it were slim to none. Darian had never fought a cave worm before, but he had heard that they were much faster than their cumbersome-looking bodies suggested. Running would do no good. They were going to have to charge. It was the best option. The horrible part was that Darian was not sure how to kill it. It was too thick to slice through, had no head to chop off, and any vital organs were probably protected by a thick hide and fat. They were simply going to have to stab at the worm until it bled out . . . hopefully.

Darian was about to give the signal to charge when he noticed Eithne bending down slowly next to him. The worm wriggled its feelers in her direction, but she moved too slowly and soundlessly to merit a real reaction. She picked up a rock the size of her fist and threw it down one of the adjourning tunnels. The clattering of the rock against stone walls distracted the beast immediately! It bolted after the source of the sound with surprising speed. Eithne heaved a deep breath of relief. Darian grinned at her cleverness.

Roth, one of the party, was so thrilled with the tactic that he cried out, "Excellent work, girl!"

It was a warmly meant gesture that brought the worm zooming back to them.

"Dammit, Roth!" Darian yelled as he simultaneously drew his sword and pushed Eithne behind him.

The worm was huge and aggressive. It attacked with a roar as it thrust its disgusting head at the party and tried to snap its mouth of razor sharp teeth around Darian. He stabbed into the mass of antennae with his sword, and the worm reared back more in shock than pain. It lashed back just as quickly by using its bulky body like a club and slamming itself down upon the party. Roth paid a heavy price for his exclamation as he was crushed beneath the worm's body. Roth died instantly. The rest of the party managed to scramble out of the way in time but had to keep moving as the enraged worm continued to use its body again and again to club the party. As the beast employed its tactic, the party continued to dodge and tried to stab at it with their weapons. It was extremely tiresome for the opponents, but neither side would give up. The worm would not stop until all of them, or it, was dead. There was no choice but to keep on fighting and stabbing at the beast. Darian tried to make Eithne back away from the fray for her own safety, but she would not. He wished he had the opportunity to tell her to stay out of the fight, that it was for her own protection, but everything was happening too quickly and there was no time for words. Thankfully, she was quick, agile, and exercised extreme caution. At least, she wasn't the type to try to claim glory. Darian could do nothing else but to try and stay close to her so that he could protect her as best as he was able.

The fight was long and hectic, but finally, the party was able to injure the worm badly enough so that it bled out. The huge creature let out a strangled moan and slumped onto the ground. The party stood for a long moment, swords at the ready and panting from exhaustion to be sure it wouldn't rise up again to try and pummel them. The worm was still. Several of them stabbed it several more times for good measure, then they relaxed.

"Is everyone all right?" Darian's voice rang out clearly.

"Bruised and tired, sir, but I think we made it through just fine," Clemen answered. The other men all grunted in agreement with his words.

"Eithne?" Darian turned to see if she was unharmed.

She stood, covered in sticky worm blood like the rest of them, sword still in hand with her head down and shoulders slumped. She looked upset.

"What's wrong? Are you hurt?"

Eithne shook her head and looked up at him with sadness in her eyes. "Roth isn't all right," she said simply.

Darian felt a sudden shock of loss as the realization hit him that Roth had died in the fight, crushed beneath the worm's massive body. He glanced over at his remains. It was not a pretty sight. Roth's body had been smashed flat; his face was no longer recognizable, and there was a pool of thick blood and guts around his flattened corpse. Darian was thankful for the darkness of the caves, so they did not have to see every detail.

"He was kind and supportive of me." Eithne said quietly. "Because he was trying to be nice to me, he got killed . . ." She looked as though she were on the verge of tears. She was staring at Roth's body.

Darian walked over to her and gripped her shoulders. "Eithne, look at me," he commanded. He did not want her staring at the body. She met his gaze. "It's not your fault that Roth is dead. Yes, he did something nice for you, but he shouldn't have shouted. He knew better. You can't blame yourself for these things. If you start blaming yourself, the burden will become too heavy to bear. Honor and respect those who have fallen, but never blame yourself."

Eithne seemed to understand him, for he saw something in her face change, and she nodded firmly.

"Sir!" Proithen's alarmed voice cut through the moment. "Dal and Finnis are missing!"

Darian released Eithne and whirled around to survey what was left of their party. The only body on the ground was Roth. Dal and Finnis were not among those left standing. They had run off sometime during the fight in order to seek the stone on their own! Darian swore under his breath. How could they desert their comrades in the middle of a fight for their own selfish greed? It felt like everything was falling apart.

Aram and Yocelin had been investigating the caves for several hours in silence, and Yocelin was tired of it. They had managed to avoid any dangers in the caves so far, which was good, but it was also boring. She needed more stimulation. Aram might enjoy the quiet, but Yocelin did not, and she felt that there had been enough of it.

"So do you have any idea where we are going? Because I've just been following my instincts," Yocelin thought the question would be a good conversation starter.

Aram shrugged. "To be honest, I've been trying to get to the center of the cave network. That seems like the most logical place that Elissiyus would have hidden the stone."

His tone had a sort of finality to it that meant that he didn't wish to continue talking. Yocelin would have none of that.

"Well, I have no idea how close we are to the center of this place, but I feel good about our direction so far," she said in a very cheerful voice. "Don't you agree?"

Aram grunted in reply, which was a passive attempt at silencing her, but he would have no luck there.

"So," Yocelin continued undaunted, "do you think there's anyone else in here looking for the stone?"

"Yes."

Yocelin stopped walking abruptly. She was surprised by the strong confirmation in his voice. "You know there's someone else in here looking for the stone right now?"

"Yes," Aram answered simply and continued walking on ahead.

"Now, just hold on a second!" Yocelin commanded firmly.

Aram did not stop walking. She caught up and came up next to him.

"How do you know that, and why didn't you tell me before now?"

"It wasn't important. It's not as if their presence makes a difference." Aram did not look at her and did not break his stride.

"Well, what if we run into them, or they get to the stone before us? Just how many other people are in here anyway?" she retorted, flustered by how calm he was about the situation and that he had kept the information from her.

Aram could tell that she wasn't going to let this go, and he wished he had never answered her question in the first place. He resigned himself to have this conversation. He would try to make it as short as possible.

"I met a group of elves on my way here, and it was obvious to me that they were also seeking the Stone of Elissiyus, though we never spoke of where either of us was going. They probably entered the caves around the same time we did, only a little further to the east."

Yocelin crossed her arms and gave him a firm look. Aram had possibly jeopardized their search! Well, she supposed, not really. He had not divulged any details to the other group, and it really was a game of chance finding the stone. Now it just seemed more like a race. She didn't particularly like the competition, so Yocelin decided to think on what they would do if they encountered the other group.

Aram didn't know how it happened, but Yocelin was quiet again. He was thankful.

After a couple more hours of wandering, Aram was becoming frustrated with their lack of progress. He and Yocelin had managed to evade several cave worms, and other possible threats, but no stone. They had not seen any others who were searching for the stone. Yocelin faded in between being talkative and being silent. Her periods of silence were generally brought about by Aram's lack of participation in the conversation. He felt as though they were getting nowhere fast, and he did not like it. In fact, he was getting frustrated and worried that they had been beaten to the prize. He let out a sigh of frustration, which made Yocelin give him a quizzical look.

"What's wrong?" she inquired. "Are you getting upset that we haven't found the stone yet?"

Aram shot her an annoyed look that she had grown quite used to over their time together and was therefore unfazed.

"If you talk to me, you would probably feel better," Yocelin coaxed sweetly.

Aram didn't feel like confiding in anyone but knew she wouldn't leave him alone until he talked. "I'm just frustrated about the stone, and I'm beginning to think we are lost."

"That's what I thought," she replied, too cheerfully. "But we can't be that lost as we are getting closer to an exit. Can't you smell the fresh air?"

Aram had not noticed it before, but now that she mentioned it, he could smell fresh air wafting in their direction—which, of course, meant that they were headed for an exit from the cave network. He saw this as bad news and could not understand why Yocelin seemed so happy about it. They needed to get to the center of the network to find the stone.

"We need to take another direction," he said with authority.

"Nope," Yocelin answered.

"Are you giving up?" Aram was confused. She was a confounding person.

"Nope." This time, she gave him an infuriating smile and put some extra bounce in her step.

"Then why don't you want to change direction?" Aram demanded coldly. He was getting angrier by the second, and she was only provoking him.

"Because I think that we are already going the right way to find the stone." Yocelin continued to smile and bounce like it was a child's game.

"How can we be headed in the right direction? Would you have hidden the stone in an easy-to-find location?" Aram spoke at a raised volume.

"Nope," Yocelin answered with a grin.

Now Aram was furious with her and felt the animal within him begin to boil up to the surface. Aram was usually in excellent control of his inner wolf, but somehow, Yocelin brought it out in him.

"Did you just growl at me?" Yocelin exclaimed, but she wasn't afraid; she was amused. To make matters worse, she laughed.

In a fury, Aram grabbed her by the arms with lightning speed and slammed her up against the cave wall.

"I demand that you explain yourself immediately." He growled through gritted teeth. Aram did not like playing games.

"My, my, such a temper!" Yocelin started to be playful but quickly decided to explain when his grip tightened. "All right, calm down. The reason I think we're headed in the correct direction is because I just have this inexplicable feeling that we are. I know it doesn't make a lot of sense, but it's almost like I can sense the stone's power and am drawn to it."

She looked into his eyes and could see that this explanation did not satisfy him. That, and he did not release her or loosen his grip. She sighed and decided to give a more rational explanation, even though she had already given her reasons.

"Also, from a rational viewpoint, you and I may have hidden the stone at the center of these caves, but would Elissiyus have done that? He was a wizard and a scholar, not a warrior. Why should he put himself in undue danger by traipsing all over these caves when he could just throw some extra enchantments on his precious stone and leave it not far from where he entered the network? Not to mention, pretty much anyone looking for the stone would assume it's at the center. Hardly anyone would think to look near the exit."

Aram stared at her hard for a moment and then released her slowly. "Fine. We will keep going this way for now. I suppose we can just turn around if the stone isn't where you 'feel' it to be."

"Wonderful!" Yocelin said with a confident smile as she brushed past him, flipping her purple hair. She was completely unfazed by being cornered by a werewolf mere seconds ago.

Aram fell into step beside her again. "And stop doing that annoying thing that you do," he grumbled.

"You know, you're kind of cute when you think you're in charge," Yocelin responded flirtatiously.

"That. That's what needs to stop."

Yocelin was pleased with herself and grinned as she walked with her cheerful bounce while Aram brooded next to her. She was just about to make a happy comment when another noise sounded in the tunnel. It sounded like a man crying out in pain far ahead in the tunnel. Had Yocelin not been a demon and Aram not been a werewolf, neither would have been able to hear it, but they did. They did not need to communicate what to do next. Without even looking at each other, they broke into a run. Both had a very bad feeling that someone had just beaten them to the Stone of Elissiyus!

Darian thought that things were not going well. Dal and Finnis had deserted; Roth was dead, and he had the feeling that they were nowhere near the center of the cave network, which is where he thought he wanted to be. Proithen had suggested that they track Dal and Finnis down before continuing their search for the artifact, but the stone was Darian's first priority. He did not feel like wasting time on greedy fools. It stung him deeply that they deserted the way they did, just leaving their comrades during a fight. It was cowardly and wrong. Darian would not forgive them if he ever found either one of them. At least, he could feel secure about the loyalty of Proithen, Clemen, and Eithne. They were all that remained of his party now. The mission was beginning to feel like a disaster.

"Darian?" Eithne's soft voice interrupted his dark thoughts. He turned his face toward her to show that he was listening. "This may sound silly, but if it doesn't make any difference to you, could we take that next tunnel?" Eithne requested.

Darian raised his eyebrows at her intrigued by the request. "Why?"

Eithne shrugged and looked a little embarrassed. "I just think that it's the right way. I guess you could call it women's intuition."

Darian gave her a concentrated look, which she may have mistaken as scrutiny, for she seemed to shrink back from him. After a few seconds of thought, Darian had decided.

"Well, there would be no harm in following your intuition, I suppose. One way is as good as another right now."

Eithne beamed back at him, and it made Darian feel warm inside. Some of the negative emotions he had been harboring seemed to wash away. He smiled back at her, and they turned down the tunnel that she had suggested.

Proithen watched the exchange between the captain and Eithne. He was beginning to understand why Captain Darian had allowed her to come along on the mission. He seemed to have a soft spot for the girl. Proithen knew that Darian had interest in marrying Eithne's sister, so he reasoned that perhaps Darian felt a sort of "big brother" affection for her. Either way, Proithen had to admit that the journey had been more entertaining with her along. She seemed to brighten the mood, even though all else was going so poorly. However, Proithen couldn't shake the feeling that Dal and Finnis should be pursued. Maybe he just wanted some vengeance, but what they did went against everything he believed in. An honorable warrior should never desert his comrades. It was cowardly and wrong. He felt that they needed to be brought to justice.

Suddenly, a shout pierced through the silence! It sounded like a man who was in pain or fighting for something. It immediately occurred to all of them that Dal and Finnis had found the artifact and were now fighting over it. That, or perhaps there was a supernatural guardian they were fighting. There was another shout this time, from a different man. The party began running down the tunnel as fast as they could toward the source.

As they got closer, Eithne found that she was feeling as if they were getting closer to the stone. It felt like she was playing the "getting warmer" game she and her sister would play as children. There was a sort of warmth inside of her glowing brighter and brighter the further she ran in this direction. There was more shouting. It sounded much clearer now, and Eithne thought she recognized the voices of Finnis and Dal. She pushed herself to move faster. Those greedy cowards had the stone and were probably fighting over it right now. They were closing in on the source of the noise when the shouting suddenly ceased.

Moments later, the party burst into a cavern and found Darian's worst fear: an empty altar where the Stone of Elissiyus had been resting shortly before. Dal and Finnis had managed to break through whatever defenses had been in place and steal the stone away. Darian cursed under his breath and began looking for a sign to see which way they had gone. There were three other tunnels that branched off from the chamber. It was almost impossible to know which one they had taken.

Just then, two figures came running through one of the other tunnels and skidded to a halt just inside the chamber.

"You're friends, I presume?" said a purple-haired she-demon in a cordial voice.

Her companion, who ignored her comment, was none other than Aram.

Tense seconds ticked by while each group stared at one another. Neither knew what to do or say at first.

Then Aram spoke, "Who took the stone?"

Aram directed the question to Darian, who was regarding him with a confused mixture of gladness and distrust. The distrust, Aram was well familiar with; it was the gladness that made Aram realize he was also very glad to see Darian again, even under the awkward circumstances.

"Aram!" Eithne cried out. "What are you doing here?" her tone was that of greeting someone on the street casually. It made Aram feel good not to be looked upon negatively, but he maintained his outward stoicism.

"Isn't it obvious?" Aram replied. "We were all after the same thing, and it appears that we were all beaten to it."

"Oh . . ." Eithne replied meekly and looked down at her feet.

"Who is your companion?" Darian's expression was dark as he regarded the she-demon. It was blatant that he did not approve of Aram's new friend.

"Hello, my name is Yocelin," the she-demon replied. She was pleased to be noticed. "Aram and I ran into each other the other day and decided to look for the Stone of Elissiyus together. We're very good friends now." She punctuated her statement with a radiant smile.

"We're not friends." Aram growled at her. "This is a temporary business agreement."

Yocelin used her hand to block her mouth from Aram's view and mouthed the words, "Best friends," at Darian and his party.

Aram ignored her, as did Darian.

"Strange to find you in the company of a demon," Darian stated suspiciously.

It was a hurtful statement, and Aram could not blame him for it. He did not know how to respond either. A tension-filled silence began to build between the two groups.

Eithne hated the feeling growing in the chamber, and she did not like the way that Darian was treating Aram. She regarded Yocelin. Yes, Yocelin was a demon, but she really didn't seem bad at all. In fact, she looked like an elf—except for her horns—and seemed very pleasant. Eithne looked at Proithen and Clemen. They were glaring suspiciously at Aram and Yocelin. She decided that the silence needed to be broken.

"Hi, Yocelin, I'm Eithne," Eithne said as cheerfully as she could without sounding false. "It's nice to meet you, and it's good to see you too, Aram."

Everyone else in the chamber was so surprised by her outburst that they all faltered a bit and lowered their weapons slightly.

Yocelin was the only one not taken aback. She was eager to exchange pleasantries. "Thank you, Eithne! I think I like you very much."

Eithne beamed at the open and friendly words. She was about to respond when she felt Darian's iron grip on her arm and was somewhat violently jerked closer to him.

"Eithne," Darian said in low tones through gritted teeth, "what are you doing?" He was giving her his hard, steely glare, which did intimidate Eithne fairly well.

She gave him a sheepish grin and did her best to keep eye contact. "Um . . . being friendly."

"And why are you being friendly to a demon?"

"Well, she seems perfectly nice, and she can't be all bad if Aram agreed to travel with her."

Eithne swallowed and continued to suffer under his glare while he scrutinized her answer. Then the rebellious side of her found some reckless courage. After all, she was already in trouble, so why not take it all the way.

"Also, I don't think you should be acting so coldly toward Aram. He's a friend and deserves a warm welcome, not your scrutiny. Besides, I've read a lot about demons, and they are just like any other humanoid race on Raashan. Their cultural practices may be different from ours, but that doesn't make all demons evil."

Darian's grip on her tightened, and the furrow in his brow deepened. Why would she choose now to be such a brat? He did not understand her reasoning at all. This was a delicate situation, and she was making small talk, like it was nothing! Proithen cleared his throat out of awkwardness. Neither he nor Clemen could believe that Eithne was speaking to Captain Darian that way.

"If I may," Yocelin's voice rang out, "while all of you are standing around judging me and rebuking Eithne, whoever took the stone is getting away."

Aram was so preoccupied in the moment that he didn't realize that they had been losing precious time! He stood straight, surveyed the chamber, trying to decipher which way the culprits had gone. He sensed that they had run through the tunnel to his right. Aram gave Darian a nod of acknowledgement and took off after those that stole the stone. Not missing a beat, Yocelin gave a cheerful wave and ran after him.

Darian understood Aram's meaning and did not waste time. He immediately released Eithne and pursued Aram and Yocelin down the tunnel. Eithne, Proithen, and Clemen all followed instantly.

It wasn't long before they all emerged from the caves into the forest outside. The sudden flash of sunlight blinded them. It seemed to be late afternoon. They had been exploring the caves for most of the day. Aram did not take time to speak with anyone as their eyes adjusted to the light. He quickly assessed the appropriate direction and continued his pursuit, not bothering to notice if the others were following him.

Eithne and Darian were right behind Yocelin and Aram in the race with Proithen and Clemen coming up the rear. Eithne ran beside Darian, keeping up with his fevered pace. She looked at him, wondering exactly what he was planning on doing if they caught Dal or Finnis. Aram was in the lead, so chances were he would catch them first, and it wouldn't be Darian's decision at all. Darian would not like that. It was very strange day.

"So," Eithne inquired between breathes as they ran, "what happens if we actually catch them?"

Darian shot her an angry look. He had had quite enough of her today. "You're being uppity today."

"And you're more of an intolerant bigot than I thought!" Eithne decided that she feeling very uppity, actually. Besides, she had the recent realization that Darian would not really punish her beyond a firm grip and harsh words. That they were chasing after Dal and Finnis only made her feel her adrenaline more. She was in a reckless sort of mood anyway.

"What did you just say to me? Did you just call me a bigot?" Darian's tone was low and angry; his chiseled features became harder. Why was she doing this to him right now? He was angry about so many things, and it was as if she was doing her best to bring it all to the surface.

Eithne saw how angry Darian was becoming, and she was still a little scared of him despite her mood, so she looked away for a few seconds—though she had gone too far already. Darian was giving her a glacial glare. She had pushed this argument, and now they were going to have it, no matter how inappropriate the situation might be. Though they were speeding through the forest, neither of them broke their pace for the quarrel.

"Okay, fine," Eithne conceded, "I didn't like the way you treated Aram and his new companion. You acted like the two of you never had any sort of good relationship! It was very hurtful how you treated him."

"Let's get a couple things straight," Darian said with harsh condescension and great authority. "First of all, you have no right to reprimand me. I am your superior, and you will obey my orders without question as we agreed. Second, the exchange that took place in there was extremely brief. I was shocked to find Aram in the company of a demon. I had thought better of him. Be grateful you are here at all, and know your place."

Half of Eithne wanted nothing better than to retort with the full force of her anger, just throw everything she could think of right back in his face, whether it was valid or not. The other half knew better. It killed her to admit it, but Darian was right. It wasn't her place to tell him how to treat Aram. She knew she would come to regret it if she pushed him any further, so she told her feisty side that she was too out of breath to keep talking and running at the same time and swallowed the urge to talk back to him. It was difficult, but to say anything now would only serve to make him more upset, and now was not the time. She turned her face forward and concentrated on the chase.

Darian could see from her defiant expression that Eithne had not been cowed into subordination. Her cheeks were flushed pink, and her full lips were set in a hard line. It was the fiery anger in her bright-green eyes that said it all, though. He knew this wasn't over. It was only a brief respite from the fight. She would bring it up again. Darian realized that the problem with Eithne was her temper. She was easily riled when it came to people she liked or respected, and he knew that Eithne had come to like Aram very much in the short time they had spent together. She might even have a crush on him. The notion that Eithne might have a crush on Aram panged Darian a little, but he ignored the emotion. Right now, he was still too mad at her to think about that. He turned his mind to the business at hand: retrieving the Stone of Elissiyus from the traitors. Then Darian felt himself become even angrier with Eithne when he realized that her question of what would happen if they actually caught up with Dal and Finnis was valid. He wouldn't be speaking with her for a while.

Aram came to a sudden stop. The sun had dipped below the horizon quickly, as it sometimes did unexpectedly these days, and it was already dark. As the others all stopped behind him, the darkness made it difficult for them to see why Aram halted.

"Well, he's dead," Yocelin made the matter-of-fact remark as she looked at the body at Arams's feet. "Friend of yours?" Yocelin asked Darian as he tried to see what she was talking about.

"It's Dal," Aram stated plainly and stepped aside for the others to see.

Dal had been bludgeoned in the back of his head. His expression was blankly stunned. Finnis must have carried on with the stone after taking out his immediate competition. Darian was very angry and saddened at the same time. It upset him greatly that Finnis would allow greed to degenerate him so much to kill his friend. They all stood around, looking at the corpse, for a quiet moment. Eithne had to look away after a bit to keep herself from crying. So much had happened today, and Dal's murder was a lot to manage on top of everything else. Proithen and Clemen stood in silence, processing mentally just how many of their comrades had died on this mission. Darian bent down and shut Dal's eyes.

Aram allowed enough time to pass before saying what was on his mind. When he felt it was appropriate, he motioned to Darian that he wanted to speak with him privately. Darian nodded, and the two of them stepped away from the group.

"Forgive me if this sounds cross, but we are never going to retrieve the Stone of Elissiyus this way. He has too much of a head start at this point," Aram said.

Darian nodded in agreement. "And we have all confirmed that we are after the same thing, so what are we going to do about it? I don't wish to work against you."

"Nor I against you," Aram responded. He was relieved to hear that Darian felt that way. "Perhaps we could team up for the time being to retrieve the stone? Then we could all take turns with our use of it once we have found it."

Darian liked the idea of joining forces. The concept of sharing was simple, but adults rarely considered it under such circumstances. Greed and selfishness usually won, but Darian was not that sort of person, and he did not think that Aram was either. He trusted Aram to keep his word, but he did not trust the she-demon at all.

"What about your new companion?"

Aram shook his head.

"She will do whatever pleases her. If she wants to tag along, there is no stopping her. To her credit, she doesn't mean any of us harm and is honest enough. Yocelin does not exhibit the bloodlust that some other demons demonstrate. In fact, she had done nothing but be nice and try to befriend me ever since we met. It gets tiresome."

"That sounds like a fair assessment." Darian's voice trailed off.

He did have to try to be evenhanded about this arrangement, but demons always left a bad taste in his mouth. Almost everything he knew about demons was bad. He looked over at Yocelin and wasn't sure that he liked what he saw. Eithne was talking quietly with her. The she-demon even seemed to be comforting her. Clemen and Proithen stood apart from the women, clearly unhappy with Yocelin's presence.

"Will your men be agreeable to joining forces? The only person left that they seem to have any respect for is you." Aram's observation was true.

Darian breathed out and shrugged. "They have dealt with so many losses and surprises on this mission, and I have no idea how they will take the idea of working together. I will not insist that they come along. It needs to be their choice."

"Do you think they are ready to give up and go home?"

"I honestly don't know what they want. The least I can do is to let them choose for themselves." Darian's eyes did not leave Eithne as he spoke. "Eithne will come with us, though. It's the only way I can be certain of her safety. She does not want to go home, anyway."

Aram nodded. "So we are in agreement about joining together to find the stone?"

"Yes, we have an accord."

Darian held his hand out to shake on the agreement. Aram took it firmly, and they shook on their new partnership.

Chapter Eleven

IT WAS DECIDED to give Dal a proper burial despite his betrayal. He did not deserve to be murdered, nor for his body to be left for the scavengers of the forest. All present helped to dig the grave, even Aram and Yocelin. Darian and Eithne accepted their help willingly, but Proithen and Clemen did not approve.

"That one is probably just waiting for us to turn our backs so she can tear into his flesh," Clemen said under his breath to Proithen, unaware that both Aram and Yocelin could hear him quite clearly.

"Aye," Proithen agreed, eying Yocelin. "Why are they even here? Shouldn't they be going on their own way?" He shoveled more dirt into the grave. "I don't like this."

"What are we going to do? Do you think the captain agreed to travel with that filth? The crazy elf woman I can handle, but I won't tolerate flesh-eating demons. That Aram character isn't right either. Elf or no, I don't trust him," Clemen quietly fumed.

Proithen nodded darkly. "I won't be caught traveling with either of them."

Neither Aram nor Yocelin made any indication of hearing the conversation. They were both well accustomed to such treatment. Besides, it was better that Proithen and Clemen thought that their conversation remained private.

After Dal had been properly buried and a respectful silence had been observed, it was time for Darian to present the choice to his remaining men. In his classic fashion, he decided to be direct. Darian was never one for frivolous words.

"When Aram and I spoke before, we came to an agreement to join together in search of the Stone of Elissiyus. However, this is an agreement between Aram and myself, no one else. I do not expect either of you to feel obligated to continue with us. This mission has been hard on all of us, and you are free to make whatever decision you feel is best for you."

Darian surveyed their faces as he finished. They looked relieved to know that they had a choice.

"I'm staying with you," Eithne replied promptly. She had no need to think it over.

Darian paid no mind to her. He knew that would be her decision. Anyway, he would not allow anything else in her case.

Proithen looked Darian straight in the eyes. "You say that this deal is between you and Aram, but what about the demon?"

"I have made no agreement with her, and I am not in charge of her. I cannot deny that she will probably be along," Darian responded evenly.

"You are willing to allow that?" Clemen asked angrily.

Darian turned his steady gaze on him. "I can't control what she does. Aram believes that she will follow us of her own accord. He also assures me that she means us no harm."

"Why not just kill her?" Proithen spat.

Darian's brow furrowed, and his expression became sterner. As much as he did not care for the she-demon, he still believed in acting with honor. The demon had done nothing to provoke a fight, or merit being killed. He was about to respond harshly, but Eithne beat him to it.

"How dare you suggest something like that! Yocelin has done nothing to you! She even helped us bury Dal! Being a demon doesn't make her evil!" Eithne was too loud, and her cheeks were pink with anger.

Darian was still mad at her for the words they exchanged during the chase, and he did not enjoy her pluck at this time. "Eithne," he addressed her in a warning tone, "you have stated your intention, and I do not require any further input from you at this time."

The fire flashed in her eyes, but she said no more. Eithne jutted her chin out in defiance and strode away to stand with Yocelin, who accepted her company gladly.

Darian turned his attention back to Proithen, who looked more confident since Darian scolded Eithne for defending the demon. He would soon find that he was mistaken in his confidence.

"As for you," Darian looked at Proithen with the full force of his steel blue glare, "we are not killers, and I am very disappointed that you would suggest such a thing. You may either come with us or go home. Make your decision."

"I think I've had enough of this mission. It only gets stranger, and the company is distasteful," Proithen answered with disdain.

"I must agree," stated Clemen. "I have no wish to travel in such company."

"Very well." Darian took some coins from his belt and gave them to Proithen. Then he pointed to the northeast. "If you follow that way, you should be able to find your way back to the horses and the road easily enough." He then turned away and walked over to where Aram, Yocelin, and Eithne stood.

Proithen already felt regret for his words. The captain did not deserve to be spoken to so harshly, but it was too late to take it back now. He had made the right decision for himself. Proithen and Clemen gathered their things and called out, "Thank you, sir," to Darian who acknowledged them with a curt nod. The pair turned and walked northeast.

"So now what?" Eithne asked Aram. She was too upset with Darian to address him.

"We continue to track the one who stole the stone. Am I correct in assuming that it was Finnis?" Aram answered.

Both Eithne and Darian nodded affirmatively. There was an awkward moment as they all tried to think about what to say next.

Yocelin spoke first, "Well, it certainly has gotten late all of a sudden. I don't know about the rest of you, but I'm really tired. I'd wager that this Finnis person is going stop for the night too. I say that we make camp and get some rest, then wake up early tomorrow morning to track him."

She was right. The stars had already come out, and they had all spent an exhausting day roaming the cave network. There was the concern that Finnis would get too far ahead of them, but none of them were in any condition to properly track him at night. It was best to start fresh in the morning.

"I agree with Yocelin. We should sleep now and get an early start tomorrow," Eithne agreed.

The two women smiled at each other.

Darian and Aram also exchanged a thoughtful look. They were concerned with losing the trail, but Finnis probably would not be able to get very far without stopping. There was even a chance that he had been injured in his fight with Dal to slow him further.

"All right," Darian stated in a commanding tone, "we will camp here for the night."

The four of them set about making camp. Eithne insisted on cleaning herself as she still had dried worm blood on her from the battle in the cave. She suggested that Darian do the same as he was in the same state. The two of them found a nearby stream and washed as best they could without disrobing. It was far too cold to bath fully, but they both felt much better for it.

When they came back to camp, they found the Aram and Yocelin had gotten a fire going and were already cooking a rabbit over it. Yocelin had a dead bird next to her on a flat piece of wood, but it appeared that she was waiting for the rabbit to be ready so that they could all eat together. They all sat around the fire, waiting for their meal to be cooked in silence. Aram generally preferred the quiet. Darian was too frustrated to speak to anyone, especially Eithne or Yocelin. Eithne was still pondering on her argument with Darian and realizing that she was still fairly mad, so no one really felt like talking—except for Yocelin. She was feeling quite chatty, and ecstatic, that she not only had one but three new companions to converse with! She especially liked Eithne, who seemed very personable and open to new friendships.

"So, Eithne, how did you end up on this journey?" Yocelin inquired cheerfully. She was ready to learn about her new friend.

Eithne started at the breach of silence but found that she was grateful to be spoken to. Besides, she was rather curious to know more about Yocelin.

"Actually, I ran away from home and sort of forced Darian to take me on his mission."

Darian flashed an angry look at her. Eithne ignored him.

"If I may," Eithne continued politely, "are you a full-blooded demon? I mean, if it weren't for your horns, I would have taken you for an elf—a very petite elf."

Yocelin giggled. "Yes, I am pretty unusual-looking for my race, and I'm pretty short, but I'm a full-blooded demon, as far as I know. I can't be totally sure, though."

Eithne wanted more information, so she pried further, "Also, your elvish is perfect. You sound like a native city elf."

"It should sound good. It's my first language."

That was an interesting reply. Even Darian and Aram showed some interest in the conversation.

"How can that be?" Eithne asked, intrigued. "Are there demons that speak elvish?"

"No, no," Yocelin laughed. "I was raised by elves. You see, these horns didn't come in until I hit puberty. As far as I can figure, my demon mother must have abandoned me outside of the elven city of Gwyn, and I was found by the people that raised me."

The rest of them stared at Yocelin. Her story was becoming very interesting.

"So you grew up believing yourself to be an elf, knowing nothing of your demon heritage?" Aram asked.

It pleased Yocelin greatly that he wanted to know more about her.

"Basically, but I always knew I was different. I never liked the taste of anything but meat, seemed to grow a little faster than the other children, and I just had certain tendencies that didn't fit in. My parents always saw that I was strange but accepted me for most of my childhood. That is, until these started coming in." She reached up and touched the tip of one of her curling black horns. "At first, my parents were just confused by what was growing out of my head, but when my horns became too long to be covered by my hair, they took me to a medicine man. The medicine man recognized almost immediately what I was and why I had horns. My parents were shocked, to say the least, and ultimately, their reaction was pretty horrible. I ended up having to leave my home soon after I learned of my heritage." Yocelin's cheerful tone turned serious as she told her story. She was quiet and did not look at any of them for a moment.

"That sounds very sad," Eithne said quietly.

Yocelin put on her smile again. "It was a long time ago. I've learned a lot since then. I don't really hold a grudge. I used to, but not anymore. Elves tend to be racist and judgmental toward other races. I was raised to think that way myself."

"You are very open about your past," Darian commented suspiciously.

Yocelin made eye contact with him and nodded. "Sure, I am. I have nothing to hide, and I'm not embarrassed of my past. It just makes me a little sad." She then turned her attention to Eithne. "Pardon my asking, Eithne, but why are you so open to other races?"

Eithne took the question as a compliment and was pleased by it. It made her like Yocelin more. "Well, I guess I've just always been an outcast among my own people. I just don't feel right about passing judgment on others. I know what it feels like to be looked at like you're some kind of freak. Also, I always was fascinated by life outside of my village. So I would read all sorts of books about the outside world and all the different races that populated it."

Yocelin gave a chiming laugh. "Aren't we just a fine bunch of outcasts?" she said with glee and looked at her three companions.

Eithne giggled too and found that it felt good to lighten the mood. Then she found she was curious about another member of their group.

"Why are you an outcast, Aram?"

"I never said that I was one," Aram responded grumpily.

"I'm sure it had to do with his cranky attitude," Yocelin teased in a loud whisper to Eithne, and the two women laughed at the joke.

Aram ignored them and ate his portion of the rabbit.

"Oh, wait!" Eithne exclaimed. "Darian isn't an outcast at all! He's considered to be among the most upstanding of citizens in our little community."

"I should have known. No wonder he's looking so tense and uncomfortable with us," Yocelin chortled.

"Don't include me in your conversation," Darian said coldly and gave the two women a hard glare of disapproval.

Eithne rolled her eyes at him but then remembered that she was still mad at him and wished that she hadn't tried to include him at all. She was having fun with Yocelin, and she didn't want Darian spoiling it.

"We don't need them and their sourness, anyway," Yocelin said dismissively.

The two women continued to talk and bond over the evening meal. This irritated both Darian and Aram, especially Darian. He very much disapproved of Eithne socializing with a demon. He had no idea how she was able to put aside all that she had been taught about demons in their society. Even after they had been attacked by demons on the journey to the caves, Eithne still did not appear to have any prejudice. He could tell that Yocelin meant them no harm. Aram's judgment of her was solid, but Darian did not see that as good enough reason to be so open and friendly with a race that elves were traditionally at odds with. It just didn't seem right to him. Then again, nothing on this trip had gone right so far.

Aram sat quietly while the women chattered and Darian seethed. He did not wish to engage in any sort of conversation. The only person he would have considered talking to was far too bitter at the moment. So Aram decided to get some sleep. He set out his bedroll, lay down, and tried to fall asleep.

Darian took note of Aram's actions and thought it was a good plan, though he was not in the mood to sleep. He interrupted the girls to tell them he would take the first watch and that they should try to get some rest. Eithne and Yocelin decided to listen and soon took to their bedrolls. After all, it was going to be another long day tomorrow.

They all woke just before the sunrise and set to work, tracking Finnis. Unfortunately, soon after finding his trail, a freezing rain fell hard from the sky. You could have barely known that the sun had risen at all that day. It was dim, gray, and raining from morning to night. The unlikely foursome was cold, wet, and miserable. Even Yocelin's mood had been dampened. They lost the trail due to the weather, and not even Aram could sniff out Finnis's scent.

It continued to pour rain upon them until midmorning the next day. The sky remained gray, but to have a reprieve from the chilly downpour was welcomed by the group. They barely spoke at all while it was raining, so it seemed odd when Eithne broke the silence.

"So what are we doing now? We've lost his trail, right?"

"We have," grunted Darian. "But it's reasonable to assume that he is headed for Eylme." He was intentionally gruff, but he had gotten past shunning her entirely at this point.

Eithne was pleased and encouraged by his response to her question. "Is Eylme a big city? How far is it?"

Darian would have answered, but Yocelin was starved for conversation and quickly answered for him, "Eylme is one the larger port cities on the western coast of the Southern Continent. Luckily, it managed to prosper despite the death of the gods. It will take about a week to get there on foot, granted we don't get rained on too much."

Eithne and Yocelin fell into conversation again, like twittering birds.

Darian strode next to Aram. "Those two are probably going to continue like that for the entire journey," he said quietly so that the girls could not hear him.

Aram was surprised to note the lack of annoyance in his voice. He thought that, despite his feigned grumbling, Darian did not mind the chattering at all.

"Most likely," Aram responded. "For now, I'm just happy that Yocelin has someone else to bother."

"Eithne seems relieved to have another female around." Darian looked back at the two women. "I suppose it's all right."

"You mean that she is socializing with a demon?" Aram countered.

"Yes."

Aram shrugged and looked ahead. Even though Darian had been raised with many prejudices, he was adjusting to the situation rather well. Aram could not help but to wonder what he would do if Darian ever learned that he was a werewolf. Those who had been turned could not help but to succumb to the predatory urges within. Most who had been bitten became more animal than human or elf and came to enjoy hunting and killing far too much. Aram constantly fought the wolf within, striving to maintain his true self. The power of it was seductively potent and difficult to resist. He was one of the rare few who had learned to control himself. It was why he sought solitude. During the years that he spent struggling to overcome his wolf side, he removed himself from society. Aram never wished the curse upon another innocent person. He was now confident around other people. Long ago, he had mastered the discipline of keeping the predator inside restrained—except for the nights of the full moon. He could keep from hurting people on those nights, but the wolf was so intensified at that time that he could not keep himself from changing. Aram always removed himself from others as a precaution during the full moon. It had been over forty years since he had been bitten, and Aram was proud to know that the only creature to have suffered from his curse was himself. Well, and the wildlife of the forest, but to his knowledge, Aram had never harmed a person, and he planned to keep it that way.

He glanced back at Yocelin. She was conversing in an animated fashion with Eithne. The smallest of smiles graced his lips as he thought of her positive outlook on life even after being rejected by her own family. For all his discipline, he had not been able to achieve that. She didn't know it, but their lives were more similar than anyone would think. Aram had been bitten probably around the same age that Yocelin's horns began to grow. His parents had also reacted with horror and disgust when they saw what their son had become. They cast him out into the forest with some supplies and told him to never return. There had been a small consolation in his mother's uncontrollable tears, but his father had been stern and straight-faced. It was a cold but logical reaction in his father's eyes, for his son had been replaced by a monster. Aram had been disowned. He turned his attention back to Darian walking beside him and wondered if he would have acted as his own father did in the same situation.

Luck appeared to be with them for the remainder of the week. The rain ceased completely, and the sun shone down with increased warmth. The biting cold dissipated and was replaced with the warm, happy breezes of summer. It was blissful for the companions and reminded them all of the days long past when this was what the late summer season felt like consistently. They were able to find their way to Eylme without consequence.

Things were far different from what they expected when they arrived at the city. Eylme was now a demon city. The way the walls were fortified and the guards standing outside the gates were blatant signs. Demons had very specific ways of guarding their cities. The four of them went out of sight before the guards saw them to further assess the unexpected situation. The group hid well in the forest outside of the city walls where they wouldn't be seen or heard.

"Finnis can't be in there," said Darian. "No elf simply walks into a demon city."

Everyone nodded in agreement. The contempt that elves felt for demons was equally reciprocated.

Darian gave Eithne an expectant look. "What about you?"

Eithne was confused. "What about me? I'm not going to walk in there!"

"I wouldn't want you to go in there," Darian clarified. He didn't like that she thought he was asking such a thing of her. "I'm asking whether you still have that feeling you demonstrated in the caves that led us to the stone."

"Oh . . ." Eithne trailed off, feeling embarrassed that she didn't catch his meaning before and at the mention of her apparent ability to sense the Stone of Elissiyus.

She noticed that Aram looked at Yocelin when Darian mentioned it. It was curious.

"I don't feel anything for the stone in the city, but I really don't know. I have no idea why I knew which way to go in the caves, or if I could still do it. Is this the only place Finnis could have run with the stone?"

"I agree that Finnis probably didn't come here, but since we are already here, maybe we should just check," Yocelin said helpfully.

She was also thinking it was strange that Eithne could also sense the stone. It was very interesting that they would have the same talent.

"Just how are we going to do that? Just let you go in by yourself? How do we know that you won't just run off with the stone if you find it?" Darian accused.

Both women scoffed at his questions, very offended.

Aram spoke before either of them could lay into Darian, "I will go into the city with her."

"How?" Darian asked in disbelief.

"I have developed certain skills and strategies for dealing with demons over the years. I will be fine."

Both Darian and Eithne were skeptical of an elf being able to simply walk into a demon city, but they trusted Aram knew what he was doing. He was not the type to make up wild stories or boast, so he must have skills that they did not. Eithne also had faith in Yocelin, even if Darian didn't. Both tribal elves nodded their consent to the plan. Then Aram and Yocelin went off, promising to be back before nightfall. Darian and Eithne would stay hidden in the forest until then. They were silent for a long time. They hadn't really been speaking to each other since their argument. Also, with Aram and Yocelin as company, neither had felt the need to reach out to the other.

"You're wound had been healing nicely," Darian indicated her right thigh.

Eithne looked down at where the demon's talons had cut into her during the raid. It felt like it was a year ago instead of a couple weeks. She remembered that Darian had stitched the wound for her and his kindness. She suddenly felt badly for how she had been treating him lately.

"Yes . . . it is," Eithne stammered. "Thank you for mending it so well."

Another long silence permeated between them.

"I'm sorry I've been so brash lately," Eithne apologized.

Darian looked at her with happy surprise and cocked an eyebrow at her. "Are you?"

"Not for what I did," she corrected stubbornly, "but for the way I did it. All this must be very hard for you, and the way I've been acting hasn't made it any easier."

Darian nodded his acceptance. "Thank you, Eithne. I appreciate it. It has been hard, but I'm glad that Aram is with us."

Eithne smiled with relief that they were talking again—though the feisty side of her was perturbed that she did not also apologize to her for his behavior. She pushed the urge to mention it down for the sake of keeping the peace. It wasn't worth arguing over anymore.

"So you and Aram are becoming good friends? I'm glad. I like both Aram and Yocelin a lot."

"I've noticed that on both counts," Darian grunted. His mood got a bit heavier.

Eithne let out an exasperated sigh. She didn't like his attitude toward Yocelin at all.

"I wish you would just accept her as part of the group. She's actually a lovely person and much more polite than many elves. Just because she's demon, you don't want to trust her intentions. You trusted Finnis, and look how he betrayed you!"

"Are you trying to spoil the moment, or do you just enjoy picking fights?" Darian countered.

Eithne took a breath and humbled herself. She gave a small laugh to relieve the tension. "I suppose I'm a defensive sort of person."

Darian relaxed at her admission. "For the record, I'm working on accepting Yocelin, and I think I'm doing well so far. I'm glad that you have someone to talk to. She simply will take longer to earn my trust. It seems that I have longer warming periods than you." He gave her a sidelong, almost-teasing look. Eithne grinned back.

Once Aram and Yocelin were out of sight from Darian and Eithne, Yocelin asked just how Aram planned to get into the city without drawing attention to himself. She was very curious.

He gave her a serious look. "I've worked very hard to maintain a high level of discipline regarding my curse," he explained abruptly.

Then Aram stood still and concentrated deeply for a few seconds. Yocelin watched in awe as his features became more wolflike—

sprouting a snout, pointed ears, canine fangs, and thick black hair that grew in around his handsome face and the backs of his hands. Even his eyes changed to something more lupine. The transformation only took a moment, but the change was drastic. He now stood before Yocelin looking the perfect grotesque balance of wolf and elf. He remained fully upright in his posture.

Aram looked down at Yocelin. "They will let me in like this without issue."

Yocelin nodded dumbly in agreement. She was going to have more trouble than him getting into the city now that he had changed. She thought that he must be a terribly powerful werewolf to be able to transform like that and maintain his composure. Yocelin didn't even know that sort of control was possible! She had heard of werewolves who were able to become a full wolf when the moon was not full but had never heard of any that could adopt only certain attributes of the wolf at will.

Aram ignored her astonished stare. He understood that he possessed an unusual talent, but he did not wish to dwell on it or talk about it at all. He suggested that they not lose any more time in searching the city for Finnis and the Stone of Elissiyus.

They entered Elyme with little resistance from the guards and spent a couple of hours inquiring after an elf carrying a strange stone. No one seemed to know anything, and Yocelin had no sense or feeling that the stone was nearby. The City of Elyme had certainly gone through many changes since either of them had last been there. It used to be a bustling trade city predominantly populated by humans. Sometime in the very recent past, demons must have taken over. The city still bustled and traded, but with a different population and wares. There were still prominent signs of human habitation, and even some humans in cages to either be sold into slavery or to become a pricey delicacy for some rougher demons. Both Aram and Yocelin had a strong distaste for those that dined on the flesh of other humanoids. There were not many who ventured to that particular diet but just enough for humans and elves to be justified in their fear of it. Aram and Yocelin wandered everywhere around the city with no trace of Finnis or the stone. When the afternoon sun began to wane, they decided it was time to return empty-handed to Darian and Eithne.

"Nothing?" Darian asked when Aram and Yocelin walked back to their hiding place in the forest.

Aram shook his head. He had reverted back to his full elf form so that there would be no reason for questions. He did not wish to reveal himself to Darian or Eithne. He was thankful to Yocelin for keeping his secret.

"No one had seen an elf or a strange stone. Also, Yocelin didn't feel the stone's presence at all," Aram elaborated.

"Wait, what?" Eithne was bewildered to hear that Yocelin had the same ability to sense the stone.

"Oh, right, I meant to say something about that earlier, but we sort of got off the subject," Yocelin grinned happily. "It seems that we share the same odd talent!"

"How strange!" proclaimed Eithne in excited amazement. "Do you think it has to do with us being female? Maybe there's some special locator enchantment on the stone that only women can sense?"

"That's doubtful. It's more likely that you two have something else in common that allows you to sense the stone. Why would Elissiyus place an enchantment on the stone that only females could sense?" Darian stated analytically, but there was an undertone of annoyance as he found Eithne's theory ridiculous.

Eithne rolled her eyes at his ridicule, but in the spirit of their recent making up, she decided not to say anything.

"It is odd that you two can feel the stone. It doesn't really seem to make sense, but it must be something that lies within both of you . . ." Aram's voice trailed off as he pondered for a moment. "Yocelin, you can't be entirely sure that you are a full demon given your background . . . Eithne, are you sure that you are a full-blooded elf?"

"What are you implying?" Darian was somewhat defensive of Eithne's heritage.

"Nothing. I'm only trying to reason this out as I don't understand it," Aram said soothingly. "Anyway, perhaps we should ask the two of you to concentrate to help us find a new direction?"

"We'd be glad to give it a try," Yocelin said cheerfully and smiled brightly at Eithne, who shrugged and nodded in a way that indicated she was willing to give it a try.

Neither of them really knew how to even try. When they were in the caves, it was just a feeling that sort of came over them. They hadn't done anything special to activate it. Aram suggested that they close their eyes and concentrate on the energy they had sensed before. So both women proceeded to close their eyes and sort of meditated for a several minutes. Darian and Aram felt a bit silly, relying on such an abstract thing, but what harm would it do to try? Finnis's trail had gone cold, and there was nothing to lose. Besides, if both women chose different directions, they would just have to fall back on tracking techniques and logic.

Eithne and Yocelin concentrated for what felt like a very long time. Eventually, they both slowly lifted their hand and pointed southwest as if in some sort of trance. When they opened their eyes to see that they had both chosen the same direction, there was a girlish explosion of excitement that neither Darian nor Aram had been prepared for. They giggled, bounced, and hugged then proceeded to speak so quickly to each other that neither of the men could possibly understand what was being said.

"Okay, this needs to stop," Darian said in his authoritative tone as he separated the two of them. "Don't get so excited over a little coincidence."

"Well, maybe it isn't a coincidence," Eithne retorted promptly. "It's not like we agreed on the direction beforehand to impress you. I really think that we both sensed the stone's energy!"

"I know I felt something," Yocelin chimed in. "Besides, you guys are the ones who asked us to try in the first place."

Yocelin and Eithne put their arms around each other and gave Darian a smart look. Darian sighed with resignation and looked to Aram for help.

Aram, who had been watching the scene in silent amusement, shrugged. "I don't see any harm in going southwest. It actually makes sense since the port town of Sali lies in that direction. There is a good chance that Finnis would go there."

Darian nodded curtly. "We'll camp here tonight and head southwest first thing in the morning."

Eithne smiled, thinking that Darian was trying his best to be the authority figure of their little group. It was endearing, but she also knew that he needed to have some control in order to maintain a sense of normalcy. She thought that Aram and Yocelin also recognized his need, for they obediently went along with Darian's orders.

CHAPTER TWELVE

*T*HE FOURSOME ARRIVED at Sali five days later. Thankfully, Sali had remained relatively unchanged, and all of them were able to enter the town without issue. Both Eithne and Yocelin had been buzzing with a good mood the entire trip from Elyme as they both claimed to continue feeling the stone more powerfully as they got closer to Sali. Now that they were in the town itself, both of them felt very strongly that they were on the right track. Their good spirits and energy influenced Darian and Aram, who were feeling more enthusiastic about the search. They had to be closing in on Finnis.

The companions inquired around town for some hours, and several people did remember seeing a tribal elf that fit Finnis's description, but they did not get a solid lead until evening. An innkeeper who had an establishment near the docks remembered an elf carrying something wrapped in cloth under his arm asking how much it would be for a room for the night. The elf had told the innkeeper that he was planning on boarding a ship early the next morning. Unfortunately, he had not mentioned where the ship would be headed. The innkeeper said that his rates were too expensive for the elf, so he went off in search of cheaper accommodation. This meant that the companions had tonight to find the traitor. Darian asked the innkeeper where Finnis may have gone for cheaper accommodation, and the innkeeper was kind enough to oblige.

"We should split up to look for Finnis," Yocelin suggested as they walked out of the inn. She wore a black hood in order to conceal her horns. It had turned cold again, so none passing by thought twice about it.

"I agree," Aram concurred absentmindedly.

Yocelin beamed with pleasure. Any agreeable statement from her friend was most welcome.

"All right, we will split into two groups," Darian started to take control of the situation. "Eithne, you're with me. Aram and Yocelin, you're together. Eithne and I will go this way . . ." He jerked his thumb in one direction. "Aram, you and Yocelin will go the opposite direction. We'll meet back here in an hour to report."

Aram nodded, and Yocelin saluted smartly. She meant it as a good-natured jest, but Darian had not yet accepted her enough to fully appreciate her jokes. He ignored Yocelin and turned to go with Eithne.

"She has no respect for authority," Darian grumbled quietly as they walked to the next inn.

"Oh, calm down," Eithne said with understanding. "She wasn't trying to offend you. You need to learn how to take a joke."

"Don't tell me what I need to do."

"Fine, but in my opinion, you take yourself too seriously. I think you would enjoy life more if you let go a bit," she advised with as much sweetness as she could muster. Eithne was not used to trying to charm others, but Yocelin had had an influence on her.

He shot her a warning look that told her that this conversation could go to a bad place quickly. Eithne took his hint and stopped talking. She had already made her point anyway.

Darian and Eithne checked with all the places of accommodation along their side of the docks. A few of the owners or patrons that way remembered seeing Finnis, but they all said that he did not stay. Darian was beginning to get a bad feeling. It was possible that Finnis decided to leave this evening instead of tomorrow morning. It made sense since he was obviously light enough on cash that he would choose not to pay for a night's accommodation and just hop on a ship tonight.

"What are you thinking?" Eithne asked, seeing his expression.

"I'm thinking that we should ask around the ships at the docks because something tells me that Aram and Yocelin are also having bad luck on their end."

They walked back to the agreed-upon meeting place and found that Aram and Yocelin were, indeed, just as empty-handed. Darian told everyone of his hunch that they should investigate the ships at the docks. The group split up again, each taking a side of the dock, and agreed to meet back at the same place in an hour.

Aram and Yocelin asked almost every sailor they passed about seeing a tribal elf carrying something wrapped in cloth. For a long while, they obtained no useful information; but finally, someone did have something interesting to say. However, it made their hearts sink to hear it.

"A tall tribal elf? Yes, I remember him. Seemed shifty. Anyway, he boarded on the *Persephone*. It left port about two hours ago. He's out at sea by now," said a sailor who was loading barrels unto another vessel.

"Do you know where the *Persephone* was headed?" Yocelin asked, anxious for the answer.

The sailor shook his head. "I don't keep track of the ships I don't sail on, but you could ask the quarter master. His office is right down there. The *Persephone* is a merchant vessel, so he should have record of where she's going."

They thanked the sailor and made their way to the quarter master's office, which was basically a neat wooden shack at the end of the dock. It took a small amount of bribery, but the quarter master was willing to tell them of the *Persephone*'s destination. Apparently, the ship ran a regular route from Sali to the port city of Doumo on the continent of Croissia. Croissia also happened to be an ocean away. The Stone of Elissiyus was turning out to be quite difficult to obtain. Aram and Yocelin started walking back to the agreed meeting spot a little early, wondering if Darian and Eithne had also learned of Finnis's departure.

"You know, I'm actually really enjoying this," Yocelin said as they walked. "It's nice to have friends."

Aram almost retorted that they were not friends, out of habit, but realized it would hurt her feelings if he said it, so he remained quiet.

"You must really enjoy having Darian around," Yocelin continued undaunted by his silence. "I really like having another girl around to talk to. I've adopted Eithne too . . ." Yocelin rambled on for a while.

Aram just let her talk. He had learned to tune her out. She was happy so long as she thought he was listening.

Then something caught his ear, "Eithne has a little crush on you, you know." Yocelin winked playfully at him. "Maybe you should explore that possibility."

"I don't think so," Aram said curtly. "She's not my type."

"What? The tall, gorgeous redhead with a feisty side isn't your type?"

"No. I prefer sass."

Yocelin stopped dead in her tracks. She couldn't believe her ears. Was that sarcasm from Aram just now? Did he just make a joke?

Aram stopped and turned. "What is it?" he asked impatiently.

"You made a joke!" she beamed and caught up with him. "A funny joke too! I didn't know you had it in you! I would have laughed if I weren't so surprised."

Aram found himself to be embarrassed by her outburst. "Calm down."

"I'm so proud of you!" Yocelin hugged him happily, which only embarrassed him further.

"Get off me, woman! Stop making such a big deal out of nothing," he fussed.

Yocelin stepped back with a girlish giggle that, despite its feigned innocence, seemed to express her sex appeal. "I'm just so pleased! I suppose I'm overreacting, but I don't care."

"Let's just get back to Darian and Eithne." Aram had no desire to continue talking about his joke, though he did not wish that he never made it. Deep down, he had to admit that Yocelin's overzealous approval of his humor felt good.

When they all met again at the meeting place, Aram and Yocelin told Darian and Eithne that Finnis had left on a ship bound for Duomo on Crossia a couple of hours ago. It was exactly the news that Darian had been expecting. His highest hope had been to catch

Finnis before his departure, but he must be aware that they were following him and was smart enough to move quickly.

"So we get on the next ship to Duomo, right?"

Darian cocked his eyebrow and regarded Eithne. She looked back up at him expectantly, waiting for an answer to her question. He thought that maybe she was getting too caught up in everything that was happening, but her suggestion did seem like the most logical course of action. They had already come this far for the stone. There was no going back now.

"Aram and I already checked with the quarter master, and the next ship leaves for Duomo tomorrow morning. It was probably the same one the Finnis initially intended to take," Yocelin offered helpfully.

Darian nodded. They shouldn't waste time. "Let's go see about passage on that ship. Then find a place to stay for the night."

All agreed on Darian's proposed course of action and set about finding the ship. It was a merchant vessel called the *Leviathan*. The captain did not usually have passengers but was happy enough to take those who offered fair payment. The *Leviathan* would leave very early the next morning and was expected to reach Duomo in a month.

Aram had been hesitant to agree to be on a ship during the full moon, for he had absolutely no wish to expose his secret to Darian or Eithne. Yocelin, however, had subtly suggested that he become ill for a day and night and ask not to be disturbed by anyone. It was doubtful that anyone would make the connection between Aram being ill and the full moon if he began feigning illness at the start of the day. Still, if they all continued to search together over several months' time, Darian and Eithne were certain to discover him. Aram did not worry so much about Eithne's reaction. Based on how she accepted Yocelin, she would probably have little trouble with the news that he was a werewolf. It was Darian that worried him the most. They were becoming friends, and he feared losing that friendship.

The foursome revisited one of the inns nearby to have a meal and find accommodation for the night. It was a small, unpopular-looking place that had clearly suffered for regular maintenance, but it would do. When inquiring after rooms, it suddenly became more complicated than expected when the matter of sleeping arrangements came up.

"Men and women shouldn't sleep in the same room unless they are wed," Darian insisted.

Despite the fact that he had been camping with Eithne and Yocelin lately, only feet away from them, somehow a room with a bed and a door was different. Eithne was feeling more and more that he was mostly putting up a fight for her sake. She could tell that he didn't want her sharing a room with Aram because he realized that she had a crush. She smiled to herself. Darian was chivalrous as ever, even if it did come off as ridiculous in this case, she still secretly appreciated the effort.

"Darian, we should just get the cheaper room with two beds instead of two separate rooms. Eithne and I will take one bed, and you boys will be in the other. No harm done," Yocelin said exasperated by his stubbornness.

"I just don't feel right about it," Darian grumbled.

"It's the best solution," Aram interjected. "Why should we waste money when we don't need to? We need to conserve all that we can."

Darian could not argue with their logic. He sighed and nodded his consent. He glanced at Eithne with mild concern as Aram went to arrange the room with the innkeeper.

Eithne gave his arm a reassuring squeeze. "I know it's hard for you to break with tradition so much, but we'll all be perfectly fine together."

Darian gave her a thankful smile and followed Aram and Yocelin upstairs to their room.

CHAPTER THIRTEEN

---

*T*HE NEXT WEEK went by seamlessly. The foursome cast off
on the *Leviathan* and was assigned to sleep in the hammocks
with the rest of the sailors. Yocelin was careful to always have
her hood over her head, as the captain and crew were not aware of
her heritage. So far, no one seemed to notice or care. Besides, the
sea winds were cold and strong, so it made sense that Yocelin would
keep her hood up in the weather. There was not much to do at sea,
and their days had fallen into a steady routine that helped the time
pass. They all slept late in the mornings, took a long breakfast, then
wandered around deck for a while. After lunch, they would usually
try to practice their swordplay or have a game of dice with the sailors—then some more wandering around the ship, dinner, and an
early bedtime. The days were generally boring with the exception of
swordplay and afternoon games. In fact, it was doubtful that any of
them would sleep at all at night without the activity.

One afternoon, Darian was looking for something to distract
him when he came upon Yocelin helping Eithne with her sword skills.
It looked like Yocelin was instructing her during sparring, which was
usually the most effective way to teach fighting techniques. It was
interesting to watch. Darian was usually the one teaching and rarely
got an outside look at a lesson. He noted that Yocelin seemed to be
a good teacher and Eithne, an apt pupil. One thing he would never
understand about women, however, was how they could do so many
different things at once. While both of them sparred, they chatted
about unrelated topics, during which Yocelin would seamlessly interject constructive criticisms on Eithne's technique. And occasionally,
they would both burst into laughter about something Darian didn't

understand. He watched them for a while, quite amused with their activity. He even had to admit that many of the moves Yocelin was teaching were very good. She was skilled with a blade, and Eithne took easily to the techniques. It occurred to Darian that two women practicing with swords was against the laws of his culture. It was amazing how much he had come to accept in such a short period of time. This strange journey was certainly having its effect on him.

"Do you have anything to add, Captain?" Yocelin's cheerful voice interrupted his thoughts.

She and Eithne had stopped their motion and were now smiling at him.

"No, it looks like you have it under control." He gave an awkward smile because he had been put on the spot but was happy to be included, nonetheless.

Yocelin beamed, and Eithne gave him an earnest expression of surprise and approval.

"I have something to add," Aram's interjection startled all of them as none had realized his approach. "You keep leading with your left," Aram indicated Yocelin's left arm. "It becomes somewhat obvious to an experienced fighter."

"Well then, why don't you show us how it's done?" Yocelin took his criticism well, but she was also curious to see what Aram was made of.

Aram nodded, drew his sword, and walked over to the two women. He bowed his head toward Yocelin to indicate who would be his opponent. Both readied their weapons, and Eithne stepped over to stand with Darian.

Aram and Yocelin began trading parries in a very concentrated, almost-studious fashion. Each was very intent on what the other was doing while maintaining politeness. Sparring is never meant to be violent but to be a learning experience for one or both parties involved. As they traded blows, it became clear that, while Yocelin was a strong and experienced fighter, Aram was better. Darian kept track of how many times Aram tapped Yocelin with the flat of his blade to indicate a hit. She blocked well, but he still managed to tap her five times during the match. After the fifth tap, Yocelin called a stop to things.

"All right, I'm dead," she stated jovially and held out her hand. Aram shook her hand somewhat awkwardly.

"So are you always this good?" Yocelin continued. She was hoping to draw Aram further out of his shell.

Aram shrugged. "I have a lot of time to practice. You really need to stop leading with your left, and you retreat too much."

"I'll be sure to work on that," she responded with heavy sarcasm. Then she looked to Darian, back at Aram, and cocked a mischievous eyebrow. "You know what I'm curious to see?"

"What?" Eithne was quick to encourage her.

"I wonder how Aram and Darian would match up in a fight," Yocelin placed her hands on her hips and gave both men a quizzical look.

"I'd be very curious about that as well," Eithne stated as she looked up at Darian with a smile.

He smirked back down at her. "You're being uppity again." His tone was not harsh at all. In fact, it seemed to indicate that he was feeling up to the challenge. Darian looked away from Eithne and regarded Aram. "What do you say?"

"I don't mind." Aram tried to sound indifferent, but he was truly curious to know how comparable they were in a fight.

Darian stepped over to him and drew his blade. Both men saluted then began slowly circling each other. They traded blows for a while, both testing the other. As they became more confident, the blows intensified, and they traded parries with rapid precision. There were several close calls where it looked like whether Darian or Aram would land a hit, only to have it blocked at the last second. It was clear that they were vastly different in the way they fought. Darian was cold and calculating, always anticipating his opponent's next move. He was stoic, never giving away his next move. If Darian was ice, Aram was fire. He operated purely on instinct, going after Darian with supernatural speed. Aram did not make any dramatic displays nor utter a sound, but his eyes burned with the thrill of the fight. He went at Darian in a controlled frenzy. Aram did not think about what he was doing; he just let his instincts guide him. It was clear that Aram's frenzy style was making it difficult for Darian to find a weak spot and attack. Aram had Darian on the defensive, and Darian did not like it. He decided to take a risk. As Aram stabbed at him, he knocked his sword to the side with his own and fluidly drove his shoulder into Aram's chest. The move would have allowed Darian the advantage over almost any other fighter, but Aram's fantastical speed allowed him to nimbly sidestep the forceful shoulder, and Aram got behind Darian instead of being pushed down.

Though Aram did not betray any signs of surprise, he had to admit that Darian almost had him there. If he weren't a werewolf, he would not have been fast enough to evade the maneuver. Aram did not have time to use his position to his advantage. Darian recovered quickly and spun around offensively to try and land a blow. There was a loud clash as both opponents lunged at each other to gain the advantage in the fight. For a moment, they gritted their teeth and pushed against each other, trying to over power the other. Aram suddenly circled his blade to the side, throwing Darian off balance, and he went after his stunned opponent by pushing him backward with a fierce frenzy of blows. Darian blocked and parried everything that Aram came at him with, but he could not find space to force Aram off of the offensive. He had to get more leverage. Darian tried to jump back, only to find that he had run out of places to go. Being confined on the deck of the ship had its disadvantages. Darian bumped up against the ship's railing and felt an instant of confusion. He was trapped and only had two choices: either concede the match or jump into the ocean. Darian stopped defending against Aram's blows and held up his hands in surrender. Aram tapped his chest with his blade. The match was over. The opponents saluted again and sheathed their weapons.

Some of the sailors had gathered to watch the two warriors fight. They all clapped in appreciation of the show. It was clear that Aram was embarrassed by the crowd. Darian did not seem to care, even though he had lost; he did not feel badly about losing to an opponent like Aram.

"Well, it's nice to know you're good at something," one of the sailors called out. "Your card playing lacks that kind of skill." The other sailors laughed in good humor.

Aram, still embarrassed, gave the sailor a nod. He didn't like being the center of attention.

Yocelin took notice of his discomfort and offered a distraction, "Speaking of cards, I haven't played a game all day! I think it's time we started one."

All present approved, and the sailors dispersed into the appropriate groups to play. Yocelin did not want to make Aram feel even more self-conscious by congratulating him on his win, but she gave him a look of pride. He had truly impressed her.

CHAPTER FOURTEEN

*T*HEY WERE ONLY three days away from the port of Duomo. Yocelin was up on the deck, gazing at the late-night stars peeking out brightly against the velvet sky. She didn't feel much like sleeping tonight. Perhaps she was just anxious about Aram. He had locked himself in a small room below deck with a bucket. He wasn't really ill; the bucket was part of the ruse. Tonight was the full moon, and Aram could not be seen. Eithne had been very concerned over his sudden seasickness, but he assured her that he was fine and simply wished to be left alone. Yocelin smiled to herself as she mused on her clever plan to conceal Aram's curse. She had even snuck into the galley and filled the bucket with the horrible porridge so that he would have something to dump overboard in the morning.

It was cold and clear tonight. Yocelin could see the stars plainly in the night sky. She found it very peaceful to gaze up at them while the waves rhythmically crashed against the sides of the ship.

Suddenly, she felt an intense pain in her chest—like her heart was about to explode! She clutched her chest and gasped for breath. Then she beheld a vision: her sight zoomed from the sky doom to a dock in Duomo, as if she were looking through another's eyes. Yocelin had the awful feeling that the person whom she was seeing through was very cruel and evil and that he wanted to find her. The vision zoomed back across the sea at a dizzying pace, up onto the deck of the *Leviathan*, and halted at her terrified face. Yocelin saw herself wide-eyed with fear, clutching at her chest desperately and gasping. Then she heard the horrible, throaty triumphant laughter of the man standing on the dock in Duomo ringing in her ears.

The pain came to an abrupt stop. Yocelin collapsed by the railing. It was a staggering relief to be released from the pain. She just sat for a few moments, catching her breath. As her heartbeat slowed and her breathing became more even, she began to realize that whoever the evil man was in the vision, he knew she would be at Duomo soon, and he would be waiting for her. The realization was terrifying.

Aram had noticed that Yocelin was acting fidgety for the past couple of days. She seemed less talkative than usual and kept to herself a little more. They were going to be arriving a Duomo this evening, and when it was mentioned, he noticed that Yocelin became even more anxious. Aram reasoned that she feared their arrival in Duomo for some reason. An old enemy perhaps?

"What's on your mind?" Eithne came strolling up to Aram with a smile.

He had noticed that she had a habit of approaching him when he was alone. Perhaps she really did have a crush on him and Yocelin was not merely teasing. Still, it did not matter to Aram. He liked Eithne but only as a friend.

"Yocelin seems very agitated about arriving today," Aram answered. His eyes were on Yocelin while she chatted with one of the sailors across the deck.

"She had a bad dream the other night," Eithne responded after following Aram's gaze. "She dreamed that there was something, or someone, very dangerous in Duomo who meant her harm."

"Yocelin told you that?"

Eithne nodded. "Yes, when I asked what was bothering her yesterday." She looked at him with a coy smile that Aram did not understand. Then she sighed. "I bet that if you asked her the same question, she would give you a similar answer."

Aram cocked his head at her. He understood what she meant but didn't know why women always had to play games.

"It's okay." Eithne patted his shoulder in mock patronization. "You're probably still a little muddled from being sick." Eithne walked away and left him to his own devices.

Aram looked back to Yocelin. She seemed to be enjoying her conversation with the sailor. He would approach her later.

"Why are you acting so anxious?" Aram's approach was brusque. He was not sure how to go about asking these sorts of questions. It really had been too long since he had had regular companionship.

Yocelin smiled at him. She was happy for the attention. "Something just happened that freaked me out a little."

"Eithne told me you had a bad dream."

She shook her head. "It actually wasn't a dream. I don't know why I told Eithne that. It was more of a vision."

Aram was taken aback. That was new. Visions are not common things anymore since Raashan now lacked magic. Such things were never really common, but now they were extremely rare. This caused Aram to also remember how both Yocelin and Eithne could somehow sense the power of the Stone of Elissiyus. Perhaps the two were related.

"What sort of vision was it?" Aram asked.

Yocelin told him the whole story about how and when it happened. It was obvious, as she spoke, that she truly believed that there was going to be someone waiting for her arrival in Duomo this evening.

"Did Eithne say that she had experienced anything similar lately?" Aram questioned after she had told her story.

Yocelin was confused. "Why?"

"Because you two seem to have the same ability to sense the power of the stone, and I wonder if your vision is related," he answered simply.

Yocelin shook her head. "No, she hasn't had any dreams or visions that I know about. I think she would have told me if she had."

"I agree." Aram thought for a moment regarding her as he pondered. "What do you want to do? We'll be at Duomo in just a couple hours."

"I know. I've been thinking about that, and I don't think I have much choice except to proceed with extreme caution. I really do believe that he's waiting to hurt or even kill me, Aram."

Yocelin looked up at him with her deep blue eyes. He could see that she was genuinely afraid. It triggered something in him. He felt a strong need to protect her.

"When we leave the ship, stay with me. I won't let anyone hurt you."

Yocelin was very grateful for his earnest words. Aram spoke them with a conviction that made her feel safe. She smiled at him with gratitude, and caught up in the moment, she hugged him.

Aram stiffened immediately. He didn't know what to do. Even though he was very uncomfortable with the contact, he felt it would be rude of him to push her away. After a few more seconds, Aram awkwardly cleared his throat.

"Erm . . . We should also tell Darian and Eithne about this so that we can all be prepared for an attack."

Yocelin released him. "Yes, that's a good idea. Thanks for making me feel better, Aram."

Aram looked away awkwardly. "It's nothing. Let's go find the others."

He tried to come off as nonchalant, but his discomfort was easy to see. He turned and began looking for Darian and Eithne. Yocelin went with him. She felt more relaxed and also taking some guilty pleasure in his awkward reaction to her hug.

They found Darian and Eithne with little trouble and explained the situation. All agreed in exiting the vessel and docks as quickly as possible. Of course, theoretically, if whoever this man was could locate Yocelin while she was at sea, then there was little doubt as to his ability to find her in the city. Still, it seemed that he was expecting her at the docks, so it was best to keep him looking. The captain of the *Leviathan* was already paid in full and carried very few belongings, so a quick exit would be simple to execute.

As soon as the *Leviathan* was anchored at the dock in Duomo, the foursome was walking off of it. Darian had already gotten directions to an inn that they could stay from the ship's captain. The group was going to go straight there and hopefully avoid any trouble. It was already late evening by the time they came in. The docks were practically deserted. The air smelled salty mixed with wood and smoke. It was cold enough so that they can see their breath in the fading daylight. The old docks creaked eerily as they made their way across the docks. Darian and Aram were careful to walk so that they two women were in between them. All were exercising caution, and they all had an ominous feeling that something was, indeed, going to happen. They were almost off the docks when a very large and formidable-looking human male stepped out in front of them, blocking their path. He was dressed in a warrior's clothing with heavy boots, a leather breastplate covering his broad chest, and a sword at his hip. His face was cruel and firm with dark eyes that seemed horribly dead inside.

Yocelin gasped for breath as she felt the intense burning pain in her chest again. She tried to control her reaction to it, but it was difficult since she found herself consumed with fear. This was the man from her vision. He had found her. She clutched Aram's arm to keep herself from crumbling to the ground. He instinctively moved closer to her in order to help support her, but his hand was on his sword. One did not need heightened senses to know that this human was very powerful. In fact, he may not even be fully human.

"Stand away from the she-demon," the large man ordered in a deep, throaty voice that dripped with cruelty and dominance.

No one moved.

"I have no business with the rest of you. Stand aside," his tone became even more forceful.

"Why do you want her?" Darian responded, sounding equally forceful.

"I am called Cavan, and I need to kill her. If you and your party do not leave, then I will be happy to kill the rest of you as well." Cavan drew his wicked-looking sword as he spoke. He meant what he said.

Darian and Aram both drew their weapons to show that they were not simply going to stand aside. As they did this, both men made sure that Eithne and Yocelin were behind them. Eithne had also drawn her blade but would not move forward to fight unless she had to. Cavan was an extremely intimidating opponent that she was happy tot let Darian and Aram handle. Yocelin had also recovered somewhat from the pain and managed to draw her sword, though she was not sure how well she could handle herself at the moment. Yocelin's attitude was that of Eithne's: best to let the boys handle this one.

Cavan emanated confidence and power as he lifted his hand and gestured with two fingers for Aram and Darian to come at him. They did not rush him as it seemed to be what Cavan wanted, and neither of them wanted to do anything to appease him. The pair stepped forward slowly and deliberately, fanning slightly as they approached in order to attack Cavan from two sides. Eithne and Yocelin looked on in awful anticipation as they watched the fight begin. Suddenly, Darian and Aram rushed Cavan at once! With amazing efficiency, Cavan dodged away from Aram's attack and blocked Darian. Then with a cocky grin, he maneuvered so that he put himself in between them so that he could take them on simultaneously. Neither Darian nor Aram could get an opening on the brute. He was quick, strong, and ruthless. Occasionally, Cavan would try to slash at them lethally with his sword, but Darian and Aram were able to narrowly avoid the strikes each time. Cavan's aim was incredibly accurate, and they both knew that if they were not able to dodge or dispatch even one blow, they would be out of the fight. Without warning, Cavan closed the distance on Darian and punched him hard in the side of the head, rendering him unconscious. Before Aram had time to react, Cavan kicked him squarely in the chest, causing him to go flying into a stack of barrels. Both of them were out of the fight, at least momentarily, and that was all Cavan needed.

He grinned menacingly at the two women and came at them. Eithne and Yocelin both readied their weapons apprehensively. If this brute could take out Darian and Aram so easily, then they didn't stand a chance. Still, they had to at least try and defend themselves.

"Out of my way, elf!" Cavan ordered as he clashed swords with Eithne.

She tried to hold against him, but he was pushing her down with his blade and was much stronger. Eithne stepped backward to try to get out of her predicament, and Yocelin took the opportunity to attack him from the side. He blocked her with ease and ruthlessly slammed his heavy boot down unto the arch of her foot. Yocelin let out a yelp of pain as she felt the bones in her foot crack. Cavan grabbed her wrist and twisted it sharply so that she dropped her sword. The weapon clattered onto the dock. Cavan's face contorted with intense evil pleasure as he savored the seconds before running her through. Yocelin was in incredible pain and terrified. She was about to die! All of a sudden, Eithne threw herself at Yocelin, ripping her away from her would-be murderer. Both women fell hard onto the dock with Eithne on top of Yocelin. Eithne scrambled to get back on her feet and tried to get Yocelin up as well, but her foot was broken and she couldn't stand. Cavan was coming at them with fury in his eyes. Eithne stood protectively over her friend and readied her sword shaking. Every fiber in her body urged her to run, but she could not allow him to kill Yocelin. Behind her, Yocelin managed to stand wobbly on her one good foot and drew a small dagger out of her boot. Her sword was out of her reach, so the dagger would have to do.

Suddenly, Aram was between Cavan and the women with his sword at the ready.

"I've had enough of you!" Cavan shouted.

He knocked Aram's sword aside with his own, causing Aram's weapon to fall from his grip. His other hand shot out with lightning speed, grabbing Aram by the throat. Eithne and Yocelin looked on in horror as Cavan lifted Aram off of the dock with one arm while choking him. Aram gasped and clawed at the large hand crushing his neck, but he could not get free. He had never battled anyone so physically superior to him before. Cavan certainly was not human. All the pain and fear were rising up into Eithne and Yocelin's throats. They both felt the same utter terror as they watched helplessly as Cavan took sick pleasure in choking the life out of Aram. Eithne looked to Darian for help. He was staggering to his feet and trying to come to their aid, but he would be too late. Both women felt such a strong surge of emotion as they watched the scene play out. Both of them seemed to share another experience as they began to black out . . . Something happened.

The next thing Eithne and Yocelin knew, they were fleeing the docks with Darian and Aram with a speed only true fear can inspire. Darian held fast to Eithne's hand as they ran deeper and deeper into the large city. Aram carried Yocelin in his arms but was able to keep pace with Darian and Eithne very well. They twisted and turned their way into the center of Duomo, propelled by terror, until they felt certain Cavan was no longer following them. Then they found an inconspicuous inn off of the main streets and got a room for the night. The patrons of the inn all stared as the foursome entered and asked for lodging, so they were quick to pay and go to their room.

Aram lay Yocelin down on the bed so that Eithne could begin tending to her foot, which she did immediately. Long moments passed before anyone spoke.

"All right, what exactly was that back at the docks, and did you know that you were capable of it?" Darian questioned firmly to Eithne and Yocelin.

Both women looked at him perplexed. They did not know what had happened at all, actually.

"What do you mean?" Eithne asked.

Yocelin was paying attention but trying not to speak for once due to the pain in her foot and wrist. She was afraid that any sound she tried to make would just come out in a pathetic whimper.

"Do either of you realize what happened back there?" Aram said, flabbergasted.

Eithne shook her head. "No, I seem to be missing a chunk of time. I remember Cavan choking Aram and seeing Darian too far away and feeling very hopeless . . . The next thing I can remember is us all fleeing through the streets of the city. I don't know what happened to get us to that point."

Eithne did not look up as she spoke but kept her attention focused on Yocelin's foot. There seemed to be multiple fractures in the bones. It must be very painful, but there wasn't much that Eithne could do except to wrap the foot and tell Yocelin to keep her weight off of it while it healed, which would be a long time.

"It was the two of you that warded Cavan off long enough for us to escape," Darian stated.

Eithne and Yocelin quickly looked up at him with shock and confusion. How could they have done that?

Darian was amazed that they did not recall the amazing feat, but he could see that they were sincere in their confusion.

"Things were looking very dire, then, out of nowhere, you two created blasts of some kind of magical beams and knocked him half-way across the docks! Aram and I seized the opportunity to run, grabbed the two of you, and didn't look back. Did either of you have any idea that create magical beams? It was truly amazing. I've never seen anything like it."

"Nor have I," Aram added.

"What? No, of course not. I didn't know I could do that! I've never used magic at all before. I wouldn't even know where to begin. Are you sure the beams came from us?"

Eithne suddenly felt panicked. It was impossible that she could do something like that. That Darian and Aram said that she and Yocelin had blasted Cavan with magical beams sounded completely ludicrous and made her very uncomfortable.

"I've never used any sort of magic either. Like Eithne said, I wouldn't even know where to begin," Yocelin argued in a pained voice.

Darian and Aram scrutinized the women with hard stares as they thought about what had happened. How could neither of them remember doing something so incredible?

"Maybe the strange ability you both possess to sense the Stone of Elissiyus is somehow connected?" Darian pondered out loud as he rubbed his temple. He could feel a welt coming through from where Cavan punched him. His head still throbbed terribly.

Aram nodded in concurrence. He also thought there must be a connection between the two strange abilities.

Eithne shook her head as she tended Yocelin's foot. She had torn strips from the bedsheet that she was using to wrap the injury. Yocelin was tolerating the pain well and remaining still.

"It doesn't make any sense to me. Something like that, magic of that kind, isn't really seen anymore, and when it is, it's from wizards or shamans of great power, not people who have absolutely no experience with magic."

"I don't think I could be capable of that kind of power either," Yocelin said as she winced from Eithne's handling.

"Denying it doesn't make it untrue. I saw very clearly that the magical force that stunned Cavan came from the two of you," Darian affirmed resolutely. "It was as if a blackish beam of light emerged from Yocelin and a yellowish white light from Eithne. Then the two beams converged and blasted Cavan clear across the docks. I agree that it seems completely crazy, but I saw what I saw. Plus, the fact that the two of you can sense magic suggests that you probably do have some sort of hidden abilities. Just because you don't know it's there doesn't mean it doesn't exist."

Eithne didn't like talking about this. She was so confused and upset by the whole situation. She exchanged a look with Yocelin that told her that she felt the same, if not even less inclined to speak about it given the pain she was currently experiencing. They could both feel Darian and Aram staring at them waiting for a response.

"I can't talk about this right now, and I don't think that Yocelin wants to either," Eithne said in a quiet voice. Yocelin nodded her support of the statement. "Can we just leave it for now and talk about it after we've had the opportunity to fix her foot and calm down?"

Her plea made Darian and Aram feel a bit sheepish as they realized that they had been putting a lot of pressure on their friends when they were just as confounded and stressed over the situation as they were. An almost-tangible silence fell about the room. Eithne busied herself with Yocelin's foot and wrist and dug about in her pack for possible herbal remedies to soothe the pain. No one made eye contact or spoke.

The still silence was becoming stifling when it was broken by a man's voice barking loudly downstairs. All four of them immediately looked at each other as their hearts simultaneously jumped into their throats. It was Cavan! He had found them already and was yelling at the innkeeper, demanding to know what room they were in. They all moved without words and fast fluidity. There was no time to ponder what to do, and they didn't need to think about it. The course of action was clear: run!

Chapter Fifteen

RAM GRABBED HIS weapon and scooped Yocelin into his arms. Darian had already opened the window to exit the inn. Aram nimbly jumped out the window and landed cleanly on the cobblestone street below. Eithne was right behind him, her pack and sword in hand. Darian was last to leave immediately after Eithne. It was only a short jump down to the street, and as soon as their feet hit the cobblestones, they were running. None of them knew where they were running except away from Cavan. Where could they possibly be safe? He was able to locate them so quickly! All of them were certain that he was right behind them, and he was angry. There was nothing else to do but to keep running until they could find a place to hide or until they simply couldn't run anymore.

"Over here! Come this way!" a teenaged human boy yelled out to them as they ran down a residential street.

It might not have been the smartest course of action, but Aram was ready to take anything over Cavan right now. He veered toward the boy's voice, and the others followed without missing a beat. The boy ushered them into a cellar door and slammed it shut behind them. They practically skidded to a halt as they were plunged into the inky darkness of the cellar.

Without warning, Yocelin began screaming in terrible pain!

"What the hell is going on here? What have you done?" Aram shouted lividly. He sounded more animal than human.

"She will be quite all right," came a soothing voice male voice.

A soft white light illuminated the cellar to expose an old, yet strong-looking human with a long white beard wearing deep purple wizard's robes. He glided over to where Aram stood holding the shrieking Yocelin. The old man took out a small glass vial from his sleeve and proceeded to uncork the vile and carefully tap a few drops of the clear liquid into Yocelin's mouth. Aram watched fuming, but he allowed it nonetheless. Instinctively, he felt it was the right thing to do. Seconds later, Yocelin quieted and suddenly fell asleep.

"That's much better," the wizard stated as he tucked the vile back into the sleeve of his robe. "Now then, I've been expecting you four."

"What is going on here?" Darian demanded with his sword raised defensively.

The old wizard held up his hands to show that he meant them no harm. "I am happy to explain, but perhaps upstairs, where it is more comfortable?" he sounded as though he were speaking to invited guests.

"No. I think that I would like to hear it right now," Darian returned defensively.

"Very well. First of all, let me say that you will be safe here from Cavan. He cannot enter my home. Consequently, that is also the reason that you're friend was in such great pain upon entering my cellar, for a small piece of the same evil lives in her as in Cavan," the wizard answered politely, but he seemed annoyed that his invitation to convene upstairs was rejected.

"Excuse me?" Aram growled. He found that he didn't enjoy hearing that Yocelin could have something in common with that monster outside.

"Calm yourself," the wizard commanded firmly. "I will explain myself fully, but understand that you must allow me to finish speaking before asking questions. Is that understood?" He locked eyes with Aram and gave him a hard look. "I do not fear your kind as most do."

Aram's eyebrows shot up, but he did not speak. For some reason, the weight of he wizard's authority lay heavy upon him, and he knew that he must obey. Aram nodded affirmatively.

"Good. Now, as I was just saying, I foresaw that you four would come here. You are all quite important, you see. You're all going to save the world, and I'm going to help you." The wizard's pale-blue eyes twinkled mischievously, but his tone was casual. He appeared to be a complicated, and possibly crazy, old man.

Aram, Darian, and Eithne stood flabbergasted. The old man must be mad! What was he talking about? They all stood agape, unable to respond. None of them knew what to say after hearing such a claim.

The wizard took their befuddlement as an opportunity to further explain.

"I see I have left you all speechless, and probably in denial, which is quite understandable. You see, the four of you did not happen to come here by chance, nor did you meet each other by chance either. It was foretold that you would all end up here together. None of you are normal elves or demons. There is a touch of something divine in each of you that will enable you to fulfill your destinies. I happen to be familiar with this prophecy. I am set on helping you all in your quest." The wizard then stood quietly and politely gazed at his guests.

This supposed explanation only baffled them further. Even if Yocelin were awake, the shock and absurdity of the wizard's claim would have been enough to silence even her. The room was still and silent for long moments. No one knew what to do or say. The wizard simply kept his polite stare on them, waiting for a reply.

Eithne hated awkward silences, and she did not wish this one to continue, especially since she needed to know whether or not their apparent savior was insane.

"Okay, could we possibly start with something more basic? Who are you?"

The old wizard smiled broadly, exposing even, white teeth. "Ah, yes, pleasantries are much easier to digest. You may call me Tim."

"Tim?" Darian questioned. It seemed a very odd name for a wizard.

"My full name is long and difficult to pronounce correctly," Tim said with a dismissive wave of his hand. "Now then, what are all of your names?"

"You don't already know?" Aram asked a little sarcastically.

"Well, I may be good, but no one is that good. So what may I call each of you?" Tim replied respectively. He ignored Aram's sarcasm.

"I'm Eithne," Eithne offered promptly. She felt much more comfortable when dealing in the business of names—though her candor earned a suspicious look from Darian.

"I am called Darian," Darian begrudgingly offered after a pause.

"Aram," Aram growled flatly. "And you may call her Yocelin." He indicated the sleeping she-demon in his arms.

"Excellent. I am happy to be properly acquainted with all of you. Oh, and this is Tristin, my apprentice." Tim gestured to the teenaged boy who had directed them into the cellar.

Tristin nodded his head but said nothing.

"Shall we all go upstairs and talk about this new situation? I will be happy to mend your friend's foot as well." Tim turned without waiting for a response and began walking up the stairs.

"Why should we trust you?" Darian barked. None of them had moved.

Tim half-turned to look at them over his shoulder. "What choice do you have?" Then he continued upward.

The three of them looked at each other. What choice did they have? If they went back outside, Cavan would surely be waiting to kill them. It was an unspoken decision to put some trust in the old wizard for now. They waited for Tristin to follow his master up the stairs before going up.

The cellar stairs led into a large kitchen. From there, they were directed by Tristin into a sitting parlor where Tim sat in a large comfortable-looking leather armchair with a glass of red wine in his hand. He gestured for all of them to sit on the large leather sofa and other armchairs adjacent to him.

"Lay her down on the settee, and I will mend her foot now. She should be mended and awake for this conversation," Tim commanded, and Aram obliged cautiously.

Tim then set his wine glass down on the mahogany table next to his armchair and went over to Yocelin. He gently undid the wrapping that Eithne had put on, placed both of his long-fingered hands unto her foot, and closed his eyes. No one spoke while Tim concentrated. A faint glow began forming under his hands, peeking out through his fingers, and Yocelin stirred. Tim lifted his hands away and went back over to his armchair, looking a little tired.

Yocelin opened her eyes and sat up quickly. "Where are we? What's going on?"

The wizard, Tim, answered before any of the others had the opportunity. "You are in my sitting parlor, Yocelin, and you are safe. My name is Tim, and we are all going to have a talk about your destinies."

Yocelin blinked at this person who called himself Tim then looked at her friends, who were all sitting on a leather sofa nearby.

"Well, that all sounds very heavy," she stated plainly.

Eithne could not help but to giggle, as her friend's frankness had struck her as funny and laughing helped to relieve some of the tension in the room. Tim joined her with a chuckle. Even Darian and Aram seemed amused.

"Hey! My foot isn't broken anymore!" Yocelin exclaimed as she rotated her ankle. "How did that happen?"

"He fixed you," Aram said and motioned to Tim. "He is a wizard of great power, it seems." His tone was still suspicious even though he was beginning to trust Tim's intentions.

"Thank you so much!" Yocelin showed her gratitude with earnest joy. "Why are you helping us?"

"That is what we are going to talk about, but first, we must get you caught up on what I have already told your friends."

Tim then briefly and bluntly told Yocelin what had been discussed in the cellar, including the proper introductions. Yocelin was left just as the rest of them had been: in stunned silence. She wanted to ask questions right away but had not absorbed the information enough to know where to begin, so she was simply shocked.

Darian, upon hearing the conversation a second time, had decided on a rational course of questioning.

"So what exactly is this prophecy that you speak of? What does it have to do with us?"

The old wizard was happy to oblige an answer.

"It is not well known, nor is it very old, but it is something that I personally foresaw at the time of the death of the gods. You see, two of the gods are not quite dead."

He paused to sip on his red wine. All four of his guests were staring at him, eager to hear more. There could be hope for Raashan yet, if even just one of the old gods survived. Perhaps order could be restored!

"You see," Tim continued. "Muntros, the dark god of fear and destruction, realized that the Heavenly Wars were going to end in the death of all the gods. Being the god of destruction has its perks, of course. So he formed a plan to break himself into hundreds of pieces and cast them out to attach to various hosts, mostly humanoid. Eventually, one of these hosts would realize that they carried a piece of something divine and set out to gather the other pieces from the other hosts. Once all of Muntros was back into one body, he would be reborn of the host and rule over the world unchallenged. Fortunately, his plan was discovered by Anut, light god of the sun and righteousness, who could not allow Muntros to rule over the world alone, for he would only cast Raashan into further turmoil. So Anut also broke himself into many hundreds of pieces and cast them off into many hosts to be one day gathered altogether and reborn, thus maintaining the balance of good and evil.

"What I have foreseen is that two people who are host to a piece of each god will search together for the rest of the god pieces and collect them at the same pace. Once all the pieces of each god have been collected, the hosts will perform a ceremony for both Anut and Muntros to be reborn at the same time so that neither god will have the opportunity to gain an advantage over the rule of our world, therefore restoring the balance between good and evil." Tim paused for another sip of wine as well as to allow the information settle with his guests. "I believe that those two are among your party," he concluded.

The room was silent and still. Tim patiently waited while the companions slowly came to comprehension of all they had just heard.

"You believe those two hosts to be Eithne and Yocelin," Darian did not ask this but stated it as fact.

Tim smiled and slowly nodded his head. "Very astute of you, Darian. How did you know?"

Aram answered for him. "We have already seen evidence that they may possess something divine. We simply had no explanation for it until now."

"Is that why Cavan wanted to kill me? So that he could claim another piece of Muntros?" Yocelin spoke in a quiet, resounding tone. It all seemed so crazy, yet it made sense of so many things.

"Yes, that is why he wanted to kill you. You carry a piece of Muntros within you, and Eithne, a piece of Anut," Tim replied.

"So you want us to gather the pieces and perform the ceremony for the gods to be reborn so that we can save the world?" Eithne asked, still astonished, but she was beginning to piece it all together. She still found the whole thing very bizarre.

"Precisely," Tim answered and sipped more of his wine.

"Seems an awful lot to ask of two young women who are strangers to you," Darian said defensively.

"I quite agree. However, when faced with the choice between ultimate salvation and utter apocalypse, one tends to forego tact and politeness for absolute clarity. Besides, I am not only asking for their help. The two of you are required as well." The wizard nodded at Darian and Aram and took another sip of wine.

"Please clarify further," Aram requested bluntly.

"The two of you feel strangely protective of these women, do you not?" Tim asked.

Darian glanced at Eithne; and Aram, at Yocelin. It was true. Their feelings of protection over each of them were stronger than the usual instinct a man feels to keep a woman safe. Yocelin smiled at Aram when he looked at her. She felt very happy to know her friend cared so much for her safety. Eithne found herself to be embarrassed by Darian's gaze. She looked away and blushed slightly pink. Darian realized her discomfort and looked back to Tim.

"What of it?" Darian sounded somewhat argumentative.

"It is because your friends will require protection and help along the way. Each of you was drawn to them because you are meant to be their protectors on this journey. You both possess exceptional fighting abilities and are both highly intelligent. I also assume that the two of you became fast friends. The kinship shared between you is rare and strong," Tim explained patiently.

Darian and Aram exchanged a look as they both recalled how they were so inclined to trust each other upon their first meeting. Each knew that if the stranger they had met that day had been anyone else, their reaction would have been quite different. They each felt instinctively that they could trust the other with their very life.

The old wizard regarded his guests as they had a quiet moment of contemplation. It was an awful lot of information for all of them to process at once, not to mention that they had heard it all immediately after running for their lives from Cavan. It had been a very long night, and the four of them were sorely in need of a good night's sleep.

"I see that I have given all of you much to ponder. I will not vex you any further tonight. It is late, and we all require rest." Tim stood from his armchair and downed the last bit of wine from his glass. "You are all my guests and may find your rooms upstairs. We can speak of all this more in the morning."

That said, the wizard left the room to retire without a second glance back at his guests, but they were not left to idle.

"I will be happy to show you to your rooms," the young Tristin stepped forward and gave a small bow.

They were all too tired to argue the point. Tim's house seemed quiet and much safer than any inn, and the beds, just as comfortable. The foursome followed the apprentice up the deep red-carpeted stairs. Darian and Aram were to sleep in one room with Eithne and Yocelin directly across the hallway in another.

CHAPTER SIXTEEN

OSALIN BRUSHED HER reddish blond hair at the small vanity in her bedroom. She was wearing one of her best dresses, a deep amethyst gown with silver embroidery around the hem and neckline. She smoothed her hair to one side over her left shoulder and braided it. She stood and smoothed out the woolen gown while inspecting herself in the mirror. Rosalin felt that she looked very nice but wondered if she ought to bring a cloak. It was unusually, bitterly cold out today, and the wool dress may not be enough to keep her warm. It seemed a shame to cover the embroidery. She was going to meet Theryl for a walk in the village square.

Theryl had been courting Rosalin for the past month, and she liked him very much—maybe even loved him. He was kind to her and her family, even though some others in the village had started snubbing her family once it was revealed that Eithne had run away. Theryl was the eldest son of one of the village council members, and he was very bright. Rosalin genuinely hoped that he liked her enough to ask her hand in marriage in the near future. He had given her and her parents some joy over the past month, which helped to bring them out of their depression over Eithne. They had received another letter from Darian, not long ago stating, once again, that Eithne was well and that he would continue to look after her. Darian did not send letters to Rosalin personally, and she did not find herself as disappointed at this as she thought she would be. While Darian would be a wonderful husband to someone, Rosalin had realized that her infatuation for him had diminished quickly once he was gone. She assumed that he felt the same way since he did not send her letters of courtship. This was all for the best, as far as Rosalin was concerned.

A couple of weeks back, Proithen had come to visit the family with further news of Eithne. Her parents were at once hopeful that, since Proithen had been with Darian's party, they had all returned. That hope was quickly dashed as he explained what had happened back in the caves on the Southern Continent. The news that he brought was disquieting to say the least. Stories of Eithne killing demons on the road and fighting a giant cave worm were both amazing and upsetting. Proithen further surprised the family when he expressed admiration for how capable Eithne was in battle. It had made Rosalin feel pride swell up inside for her little sister. While it was forbidden for women to fight in their culture, and she should be appalled, Rosalin somehow knew that it was good for Eithne and that made her happy. However, when Proithen told them that Darian and Eithne had opted to chase after the Stone of Elissiyus with a she-demon and outcast city elf, it caused great emotional strife. It was even more distressing that Eithne seemed to have befriended the she-demon! Her mother had broken out into tears again upon hearing that news, and her father's face went rigid. The city elf was not so bad to think of, but how could an evil demon be allowed to travel with them? Proithen had said that the demon looked like an elf and was odd in that she was extraordinarily friendly, but a demon was a demon all the same. It was of great concern that Darian would agree to travel with such filth, but nothing could be done about it. All they could do was put their trust in Darian's judgment and hope for the best. They all knew that he was an honorable man.

There was a knock at Rosalin's door.

"Sweetheart, Theryl has come to call on you!" her mother called from the other side of the door.

Rosalin forgot her thoughts and excitedly went to greet her suitor.

CHAPTER SEVENTEEN

*E*ITHNE AWOKE SUDDENLY the next morning. There was no noise to disturb her, only the very startling thought of what she had learned last night. She sat upright and looked around the small, faded-yellow room. Yocelin was snoozing peacefully in the bed next to her own. There was a washing stand with a porcelain bowl, pitcher, and towel with an oval mirror hanging above it. Only a few feet away, against the wall, there was a large cedar wardrobe. The two twin beds that Eithne and Yocelin had slept in had a nightstand in between them on the wall opposite the wardrobe. The curtains hanging over the small window to the right of the wardrobe were drawn, but Eithne could see sunlight piercing through around the edges. It seemed to be a bright and sunny morning. The room felt warm and safe. It was painted a harvest yellow color, which was now faded with time, with dark wood furniture and warmly colored rugs covering the floor. It struck Eithne as odd that she should feel so warm during the late autumn months in a room with no fireplace, but she was grateful all the same.

Despite the somewhat horrifying thought that had awakened her so abruptly, Eithne felt very well rested. She had slept soundly. Still, what had happened last night? Had she truly heard everything correctly? She felt heavy, just thinking about it. How could she carry a piece of a god within herself? She supposed that it at least made sense of the strange magical blast she and Yocelin had created to repel Cavan. The thought of it all made her uncomfortable in her own skin. Was this why she was always so different? An outcast among her own people? That seemed to make sense. Yocelin was an outcast, as apparently Aram was too. Darian was the only one of their group who seemed to fit into society properly, though Eithne had always suspected him of being stranger than he let on. She smiled to herself, thinking of how he had kept her secret back in the village. If he were not a bit different himself, he would have never understood and kept quiet.

Eithne let out a sigh as she swung her legs over the side of the bed and went over to the washbasin. She found the pitcher full with water, so she poured it into the bowl and splashed her face. Yocelin stirred when she heard Eithne moving about the room. She sat up and stretched, making a little squeaking noise as she did. Eithne turned to look at her as she blotted her face dry with the towel.

"Good morning," Yocelin said with a mixture of cheeriness and sleepiness.

"Morning," Eithne replied.

The two friends went about the room in a morning-time routine without words for the next few minutes. After Eithne was finished at the washbasin, Yocelin used it and was pleasantly surprised to find that the water Eithne had used had vanished with a pitcher of fresh water in its place. The towel also felt as though it had not been used. While Yocelin washed her face, Eithne opened the wardrobe and pulled one of the dresses over her head. The wardrobe had a small number of very plain dresses inside and two apprentice robes that a female apprentice might wear. Eithne would have felt strange wearing wizard's garb, so the plain gray shift dress would have to do. Her own clothes were very worn and dirty. It felt good to have something clean to wear. She looked at herself in the mirror and clucked her tongue in mild disappointment. The dress didn't exactly accentuate her positive characteristics. She knew it wasn't very important to look pretty, but she didn't like the idea of looking frumpy in front of Aram. She took a belt and cinched it around her waist, then began braiding her long red hair over one shoulder.

"That dress looks nicer on you than you think," Yocelin offered sweetly as she put on a very similar dusty-blue dress from the wardrobe. "You brighten it considerably."

Eithne smiled. "You're too kind, but thank you." She looked back into the mirror. "It's odd to wear a dress again. It's been so long that I forgot how comfortable they were."

"Yes, it's too bad that dresses aren't more conducive to traveling," Yocelin agreed absentmindedly.

The two women finished getting dressed then left their room to go downstairs. It was funny how neither of them felt awkward about wearing the dresses or walking about the wizard's mansion. Perhaps the shock of what was told to them last night simply outweighed any feelings of discomfort. They found the kitchen and saw that Darian and Aram were already they chatting with Tristin. The wizard, Tim, did not appear to be around.

"Good morning, boys!" Yocelin announced happily.

They all said, "Good morning," in return, though not nearly as energetically. Yocelin noted how the young apprentice looked at her and Eithne when they walked into the kitchen. The poor boy probably didn't get to see many pretty girls, and she and Eithne were prettier than the usual sort. Yocelin smiled deviously. She may not be able to resist the urge to tease the young apprentice. After all, she didn't know how long they would be staying here, and things might get boring.

"How is your foot?" Darian interrupted her thoughts.

Yocelin beamed at his concern. "Good as new! It's as if nothing ever happened to it."

"Glad to hear it." Darian returned and took a drink from a brown clay mug.

Upon seeing Darian drink, Tristin was reminded of his duties.

"May I get you, ladies, something for breakfast? We have some hot cider to drink." As he spoke, he busied himself with pouring two mugs of cider and bringing them over to Eithne and Yocelin.

"I'm happy to eat whatever is already made," Eithne offered regarding breakfast.

"We have porridge made," Tristin answered.

"That's great, thank you."

Yocelin nodded to show that she would have the same. Tristin went to the stove where the porridge pot sat to keep warm and scooped out two portions.

"Tristin was just telling us more about his master," Aram said. "Apparently, he used to keep many young apprentices at the house, but since the death of the gods, things have been much more scarce. Tristin is currently the only apprentice."

"So the rooms we're staying in used to be for Tim's apprentices?" Eithne asked. She was hoping the conversation would prove fruitful of new information about Tim.

"Yes, most of the rooms upstairs are now empty because they were apprentice quarters," Tristin answered dutifully.

"How long have you been here?" Yocelin asked as he put the bowls of porridge on the table in front of them.

"I have been here since I was twelve years old. I am now fifteen."

"Were there other apprentices when you started three years ago?" Eithne asked.

Tristin shook his head. "I am the first in at least ten years. Master Tim says that he is amazed that he even found one boy in the city who showed some magical talent." At this, Tristin beamed with pride but still humbly continued his tasks.

"You must have quite a talent," Darian stated. "How old is your master?"

Tristin shrugged and shook his head.

"You don't know?" Yocelin asked.

"No one is really sure. My grandparents remember Master Tim being old when they were young children. As far as anyone knows, he has always been here," Tristin answered with another shrug.

"So he's not human," Eithner concluded. Such a long life span was not at all uncommon among elves or demons. She herself was over one hundred years of age and still considered to be very young.

"He's human. At least, that's what he was born," Aram stated matter-of-factly. "Seeing how he has such great power, perhaps he used magic as a means to maintain unnatural long life."

"How do you know he's human?" Darian inquired, intrigued by Aram's certainty on the matter.

Tristin glanced nervously between the two friends, as did Yocelin. Eithne took no notice of their reaction as she was innocently looking to Aram for his answer.

Aram cleared his throat. "I've never seen an elf who looks as he does, and he's certainly not a demon. That effectively rules out the two races of extreme life longevity on Raashan. Besides, he looks and acts human." Aram then tried to appear nonchalant by sipping his cider. He hoped this was a rational-enough explanation. The truth of the matter was that he could simply smell that Tim was human.

Darian shrugged. It was a satisfactory response, but he still had his doubts about Tim being human even if Aram was sure that he was.

"So, Tristin, what sort of things does Tim teach you?" Yocelin asked. She was bored with the musings on Tim's origins.

"I am not at liberty to discuss my lessons," he replied shyly.

"I will thank you all to stop pestering my apprentice." Tim stopped into the kitchen and gracefully sat at the table with Yocelin and Eithne. "If you wish for more information, I will be happy to oblige you."

Tristin got a renewed rush of energy when his master came in and quickly went to work, preparing a bowl of porridge and mug of cider for him. Tim calmly took a seat at the table and folded his hands in front of him. He looked to each of his guests expectantly. There was a long pause as Tristin brought the wizard his breakfast, and Tim waited for his guests to speak. None of them spoke, for they were all questioning Tristin because none were entirely trusting of Tim yet. Fortunately, the old wizard was wise to such emotions.

"I understand that all of you would have difficulty trusting some strange old wizard who seems to know too much and ask huge favors of you." Tim paused to take a bite of his porridge and made a noise to indicate that he thought it tasty. "So ask me anything you like. I will not keep secrets from you and will answer your questions with the utmost honesty. Feel free to start anytime. I have nothing to hide." He continued enjoying his breakfast while he waited for their questioning to begin.

Yocelin looked at all her companions and shrugged. What the hell, they didn't have any reason to think Tim a liar. "How old are you, and are you human?"

"Ah, a good start," Tim praised with satisfaction. "Well, I was born human, and technically, I still am. However, through my magic, I have, in a way, accidentally been granted extreme longevity. I am now 972 years old by my reckoning and feel quite healthy. I don't know how long I will continue to live."

"What do you mean by 'accidentally granted longevity'?" Darian asked.

"Well, it sort of comes as a side effect of great magical power. Once a wizard reaches a certain point in his capabilities, the magic itself becomes a part of him, almost like it gets into your blood. We all know, of course, that magic has no real age, and it's almost like an immortal force. So once your power grows to the point that magic is infused in you, living far beyond your normal life span is a side effect," Tim explained casually as he continued to enjoy his breakfast.

"How many wizards achieve that kind of power?" Eithne asked, agape with awe. The conversation had caused her to forget her breakfast entirely.

"Very few, indeed. I believe the most famous wizard to achieve it was Elissiyus, and there are many who believe his story to be fiction! He died long ago, but he was real, to be sure. I was his apprentice, actually, and I'm rather proud of that." Tim gave a boyish grin that would have looked out of place on the face of another old man. "He was a very kind man but still a firm master. He must have died about nine hundred years ago . . . He was hiding his magic rock, or something, and never came back. But I digress. So sorry, us old folk will prattle on." He ate another spoonful of porridge and smiled pleasantly.

All four of them stared at him. Not only was Tim the student of the most famous wizard that ever lived, but the magic rock he mentioned must be the Stone of Elissiyus! If they were able to track the stone down and retrieve it, then Tim would surely have some idea of how to invoke its power! Of course, their pursuit of the stone seemed somewhat insignificant now. The four companions all glanced at each other. They had the feeling that they were all thinking the same thing.

"Okay, putting that long line of questioning aside, how did you come to know of the prophecy you told us about last night, and what makes you so sure that we the proper people to fulfill it?" Eithne needed to keep things on track. She wanted to hear more about Elissiyus, but that was less important right this moment.

"Ah, well, prophecies are tricky creatures. Once they are written down with quill and ink, people are more accepting of them, but they never come into being that way. I first became aware of it through a dream."

"A dream? What kind of dream?" Yocelin found herself intrigued.

"In this dream, I saw a great many scenes flash by: I saw Muntros breaking himself apart and Anut doing the same, then a piece from each of them floating down and each resting with a young beautiful woman." Tim nodded his head at Eithne and Yocelin sitting across from him. "I saw each of you quite clearly." He allowed a couple seconds pause for effect. "Naturally, I chose to further investigate such a clairvoyant dream using my magical skills. Through these methods, I came to better understand that the dream was quite literal and the gods were indeed Muntros and Anut. Several nights later, I beheld a second vision of the gods being reborn. Once again, I investigated and came to the conclusion, which I have already shared with all of you. I'm certain that I am correct. I have used many different spells and devices, and my conclusions do not vary." Tim took the last couple mouthfuls of his porridge and leaned back in his chair cider mug in hand.

"How long ago did you foresee this?" Eithne prompted.

"Only about twenty years ago, not very long ago, by my standards."

"How long did it take you to finish all your investigations?" Darian asked.

"A couple of years after having the dreams. I worked on nothing else during that time." Tim took a drink from his mug. "After I was sure of my results, I set about trying to locate you lot. I was very pleased when I learned that the four of you would all find each other easily and then come right to me. Of course, what is meant to be will always find a way to run smoothly, at least in the beginning. Oh, and I was sure to write the prophecy down properly for the sake of validity." The old wizard smiled at the last part as it seemed to be a personal point of humor.

"What's in it for you?" Aram's question was blunt and ruined the pleasantly polite air hanging about the kitchen.

"Do you mean to ask why I care what happens to the world?" Tim countered.

Aram nodded. He had a suspicion that Tim's motives were not wholly noble.

"I expected you would realize the answer to your own question, Aram. I live in this world, as do all of you. I do not wish to see my home in ruin. Also, it seems that I have been chosen to help all of you since I was shown the prophecy. Raashan has been slowly dying ever since the death of the gods. Unless something is done to stop it, the entire world and all that inhabit it will perish."

"See, now that's something I don't understand," Yocelin interjected and earned an expression of raised eyebrows from Tim. "How can it be that you are receiving prophetic dreams even though the gods are all dead and gone? From what you've said, the only two who could potentially be reborn can't do anything until they are brought back to life."

Aram gave Yocelin a pleased look and nod. He thought her question to be a great one. However, Tim's slight chuckle brought him back down a bit.

"That is a common misconception about visions and prophecies," Tim explained. "You clearly know that there is still some magic in this world. It is not as strong as it once was, not as prevalent, but it's there. The gods would occasionally create a prophecy or two, this is true, but most prophecies have come about through the mysterious workings of the magic of Raashan itself. The gods themselves would come to learn most prophecies as we mortals do. Try to think of the old gods as a sort of maintenance staff that kept things running smoothly." The wizard took a satisfied sip of his cider.

Yocelin shrugged at Aram, as if to say that she tried.

"Now then," Tim stated, "have you all decided whether or not you will save the world by choice?"

"Choice?" Darian asked confused by Tim's wording.

"Yes, well, these things have a way of happening whether you want them to or not. You're already involved, so now you only have to choose the easy way or the hard way. Which will you choose?" the wizard explained.

"How exactly are we supposed to gather the pieces of the gods anyway?" Eithne asked.

All this talk about "already being involved in some sort of quest to save the whole world" made her very uncomfortable. She really didn't know how to process it, so she figured that the best way to deal with it was to be sure of all the details before agreeing to anything.

"An excellent query, Eithne. Well, there is a traditional way of gathering those pieces—"

"Which is killing the other person and somehow absorbing the energy as Cavan was trying to do with me?" Yocelin finished for the wizard.

"Precisely," Tim confirmed.

"What's option number 2?" Eithne did not like the idea of killing hundreds of people, even if it did mean saving the whole world.

"Magic, of course!" Tim was happy to answer. "While waiting for all of you to come to me, I devised a second option for gathering the pieces. If you will follow me," Tim stood and gestured for them all to follow as he walked out of the kitchen, through the sitting parlor and through a pair of tall, ornately carved wooden double doors that led into his study.

Tim's study was small and round but grand with a very high-domed glass ceiling and ancient books lining all the curved walls. There were many strange-looking artifacts and devices on the large mahogany desk at the center of the study and on the shelves, squeezed tightly in between the books. There was also a very thick but pleasant smell in the room of various crushed herbs and other potions ingredients. The old wizard walked up to his desk, where a small wooden box sat among other trinkets, and opened the box. He took out two bracelets. The bracelets were of a dark silvery metal that none of them had ever seen before, and embedded in each of them was a precious stone: one, a dark-blue sapphire, and the other, a vermillion ruby. They were very simple pieces but quite lovely in their simplicity. Tim handed the sapphire bracelet to Yocelin and the ruby to Eithne.

"You may use these to drain the power of the god from individual people and transfer it into yourselves without killing the other host. However, I will have to train you in how to properly use the bracelets."

"Will this hurt the other person?" Eithne asked as she examined the bracelet in her hands by turning it over and smoothing her thumb over the ruby.

"The other host will feel temporarily weakened, but it does not hurt them," Tim replied sympathetically.

"How will we even know which people have pieces of the gods inside them?" Yocelin asked curiously.

"That is much more difficult to learn. I will also have to help you mentally discipline yourselves enough to recognize them. I will train the two of you as well." Tim nodded toward Darian and Aram. "You should also be able to recognize hosts of god pieces at least to a degree."

"How long will all this training take?" Aram asked.

"Why? Do you have somewhere else to be?" Tim's tone was somewhat sarcastic. The wizard knew very well why Aram concerned about timing. "You know, they're going to find out eventually."

"Find out about what?" Darian didn't like how Tim was addressing his friend. It made him uneasy.

"You'll know soon enough," Tim answered dismissively with a wave of his hand. "As for your original question, Aram, the training will take as long as it takes. There's no real schedule to it. It simply depends on how quickly all of you catch on to the techniques."

Aram crossed his arms defensively and gave Tim a dark look. He didn't like the idea of telling anyone his secret, and it was extremely irksome to him that the wizard already knew all about it.

"What will this training consist of?" Darian wanted to get back to the matter at hand and away from the uneasiness of Aram's predicament. He was concerned about Tim's methods.

"It is not physically demanding training. It consists of a certain disciplining of the mind and a very little bit of memorization of an incantation to bring out the power of the bracelets," Tim responded.

"It doesn't sound like it will take very long. You make it seem pretty simple," Yocelin said with a cheery smile. "When shall we get started?"

Tim smiled warmly at Yocelin. "I have never met a demon so cheerfully pleasant and eager," he complimented, and it earned a brilliant smile from Yocelin. "We will begin your training immediately since some of you are so anxious." The wizard gave a look at Aram and moved to leave his study.

When the rest did not immediately follow, he stopped and cleared his throat at the entry to let them know that they should all leave his study. The foursome promptly recognized and walked back out into the sitting parlor. Once there, Tim called for Tristin to bring "the books," and the apprentice hurried off to fetch them. Thankfully, Tristin was not long in retrieving the books and came back after only a moment or so, carrying four separate volumes. He set them on the table for Tim to distribute and then went back into the kitchen after his master nodded at him.

Tim did not pick any of the books up but simply stood near the table they sat on.

"There are all books on how to properly meditate and discipline your mind. You will have to learn these basic techniques before I start teaching you how to more specifically hone in on certain energies. You shall each choose one volume and begin reading it as well as putting into practice its lessons. Tomorrow morning, you will all begin doing morning meditations with me every day." He waited a brief moment for questions on his instructions. When none of them spoke up, Tim turned and walked back into his study and shut the door behind him.

The four of them stood in silence. When exactly did they all agree to save the world? None of them had actually voiced any approval of taking on the gargantuan task, though Tim had said that they would be forced into their fates whether they liked it or not, so perhaps it was best to play along for a while. At the moment, they were only being asked to meditate, which was easy enough. Also, they were safe from Cavan so long as they remained in the mansion. It appeared that the best course of action was to stay safe and learn how to meditate.

"This training just went from quick and simple to really boring," Yocelin stated grumpily as she eyed the small pile of books on the table. "Just how mentally disciplined are we supposed to be?"

"Look at it this way: the sooner you start, the sooner it's over," Aram said as he bent down and indiscriminately grabbed one of the books.

Personally, Aram felt that he was already very well mentally disciplined. Dealing with controlling the bestial urges inside him continuously took an extreme amount of mental control and meditative talent. He was planning on leafing through the book briefly for the sake of following instructions but didn't feel that he needed to do anything beyond that in preparation for the next level of training.

Yocelin made a little huffing noise and eyed Aram as he went upstairs. She quickly snatched the thinnest of the three remaining books and stomped off to the mansion's library. She looked like a kid being punished by her parents, but in a rather cute way.

Eithne smirked at her very put-out friend then read the titles of the two remaining volumes.

"Do you care which one I take?" she looked back to Darian.

He shook his head. "I don't care. I can't pretend not to be a little disappointed at the start of all this."

Having always had a love of reading, Eithne really didn't mind at all. In fact, she was excited to be able to sit with a book in a comfortable chair to read for a while. Perhaps she would take some of the cider with her while she studied. Seeing Darian's lack of enthusiasm, however, she gave him a mischievous smile.

"Tim never said that we had to read the books thoroughly." She chose one book and handed the other to him with a wink.

Darian cocked an eyebrow at her and watched Eithne walk upstairs to her bedroom. He should have expected her rebellious nature to come through. He then peered at the book in his hand and gauged how long it would take him to read it cover to cover. Perhaps a little quiet rebellion was not so terrible in this case.

CHAPTER EIGHTEEN

*T*HE NEXT FEW days at the wizard's mansion were spent reading their respective books, daily morning mediations, and taking exercise in the form of sword practice in the courtyard. It became tiresome very quickly, especially since the four of them had recently spent a month on ship in a somewhat similar routine. They were all ready to be out of the rut.

On the eighth day, after their morning meditation, Eithne and Yocelin had an announcement.

"Eithne and I feel we are ready to move to the next level," Yocelin stated plainly but still with a smile. Eithne stood beside her and nodded in agreement.

Tim raised his eyebrows at the two of them. "You two have a fair amount of pluck about you, don't you?"

"Yes," Darian and Aram tersely affirmed in unison, which earned a grin from the old wizard as well as annoyed expressions from the girls.

Eithne and Yocelin decided not to respond to the boys' too-quick reply to Tim's remark and looked back to the wizard for his answer.

"Well then, we shall see if you are as ready as you think you are. Today I will try to teach the four of you to recognize others who carry god pieces. I think you'll find that possessing proper mental discipline is key."

Tim walked from the sparse, simple meditation room and into his study. The rest of them assumed that they were to follow. They had all grown accustomed to Tim expecting them to follow when he left the room, even if he had not indicated it. Over the eight days of living at the mansion, Yocelin had actually grown somewhat spiteful in her attitude toward the old wizard. There as no real reason for it, except that she had a little problem with authority, and she didn't like that Tim was always telling them what to do. After all, they were all doing him—and the rest of Raashan—a big favor by agreeing to undertake this quest. One would think he wouldn't be so arrogant about it.

Once they were all gathered in the study, Tim began the lesson. "Why don't we begin by you all telling me what you think you are looking for in other hosts of god pieces?"

There was a long pause while the four of them thought about how to answer the question. Traits of other hosts were not something they had previously discussed or even really thought about.

"I would assume that they are all humanoid," Darian stated. It was the one thing he felt fairly sure of.

Tim nodded his concurrence and waited patiently for the other three to give their answers.

"They would all have magical energy that we would be able to sense," Aram said and also earned a pleased nod from Tim for his answer.

"Would that energy be subconsciously sensed by other hosts, drawing them to unknowingly live in the same areas, therefore having higher population densities of hosts in certain places?" Eithne presented her answer as a question because she was uncertain of her theory, but she couldn't think of anything else to say.

She was extremely pleased when Tim was impressed with her answer and gave her an affirmative nod. The approval made her grin foolishly, but she didn't care. Eithne was just happy to have given a correct and impressive answer. Academic achievement was something she always strove toward.

"Would they all be fairly young?" Yocelin's mind was completely blank.

She had actually thought the same thing as Darian, but he answered before she had the opportunity. She was all out of ideas. It only made her dislike Tim more when she did not get the nod of approval that her friends had gotten. The wizard shook his head at her and looked down briefly. Yocelin crossed her arms tightly and fixed her face in a grumpy expression. Stupid Tim.

"Now then, those were all very well said," Tim congratulated. "Those three indicators are the only evidence you will have at your disposal. The energy is the important thing. That kind of power will leave a sort of signature, something you can sense if you concentrate. Now, the energies of Anut and Muntros are very different, so each pair of you will have to learn how to hone in on them in different ways. Does that make sense?" He paused for questions.

"So we are to be taught in separate pairs?" Aram asked.

"I think it would be easier, yes," Tim answered. "Which pair of you would like to go first?"

"We will," Aram replied promptly. He wanted to get it over with.

Yocelin quickly turned her grumpy stare on Aram in protest. "What if I don't want to go first?" she was very annoyed and sarcastic.

Aram gave her an exasperated look. "You will get over it."

Yocelin was sorely tempted to get uppity. She didn't like his tone at all. Besides, she always felt that she couldn't really take her frustrations out on Tim because he was such a great and powerful wizard. She had no wish to be turned into something unseemly.

"We'll be out in the parlor," Eithne interjected as she hustled Darian out of the study. It was obvious Darian did not appreciate her needless hustling, though he still left wordlessly.

"This will probably take a couple of hours," Tim called after them so that they would know how long to wait.

He then gave a meaningful look to Yocelin that meant that she best curb her irritation. He was well aware that she did not much care for him. She was terrible at hiding her feelings for others. The irony was that it only made Tim appreciate her personality more.

"Stop pushing me!" Darian said very firmly to Eithne once they were out of the study. "You have no right to treat me like a child."

He was very annoyed with her and felt that she needed to understand that such behavior would not be tolerated. Darian was not used to being pushed around.

"Sorry," Eithne flippantly apologized, "I was just in a hurry to get out of there. Yocelin really doesn't care for Tim."

"That is obvious to everyone, and I don't believe that you are truly sorry."

Darian crossed his arms across his chest and locked eyes with her. He didn't know why he was pressing the issue. It was only going to lead to a fight, but he felt that she needed to treat him with a little more respect and courtesy at certain times.

Eithne bristled at his tone. So what if she wasn't really sorry? It didn't really matter, anyway. Darian could be so sensitive sometimes. She began to feel herself getting angry. She didn't know why Darian brought out this side of her so easily. It was as if he knew exactly what to say to make her want to argue.

"Well, maybe I'm not sorry because I don't feel that I have anything to apologize for. Maybe you're just being too sensitive!" Eithne fired back at him, her grass-green eyes blazing.

Darian had to stop himself from retorting in a way that he would only regret. This was not the proper way to handle the issue. He looked at her with the fire in her eyes, flushed cheeks, and defensive stance. She was actually quite lovely in a fierce way when she was angry, but that was no reason to make her that way.

"All right, I'm handling this poorly. Calm down, and stop being so feisty." He calmly crossed over to her and rested his hands on her delicate shoulders. "I'm only saying that sometimes, you get carried away in the moment and do or say things toward me that I don't appreciate. We have to get along better than this if we are to be on a long quest together. So don't get riled up when I tell you I don't like something. I'm only communicating my feelings to you. You should feel free to do the same with me."

Darian gently rubbed his thumbs over her shoulders as he spoke to better soothe her, and it seemed to work. He felt her muscles relax, and her expression changed from angry to sympathetic. As he watched the physical transition of her emotions, he caught himself thinking how lovely she is again. There was certainly something about her that was very attractive beyond her physical appearance. Darian also became very aware of how close he was to her and felt his heart make a resounding thump. Eithne smelled like fresh spring rain. He hadn't really thought about how often he had been close to her like this in the last two months until this moment.

Eithne let out her breath to relax herself and release her temper.

"All right, maybe I'm overreacting, and I will try to be more respectful of your feelings. We do have a long way to go together." She looked up at him and smiled. "Besides, if you marry my sister when we get back, I'm never getting rid of you."

Darian blinked as if coming out of a daze. Rosalin hadn't even crossed his mind for a very long while. All of a sudden, he felt guilty for his musings on Eithne's beauty. It wasn't right to look at his future sister-in-law that way. He released her shoulders and let his hands drop to his sides.

"Yes, well, I'm glad we understand each other better now," he stammered.

Eithne knitted her brow in a confused expression. Why the sudden change in Darian's demeanor?

"Are you all right?"

"Yes, fine, just had an odd thought." Darian walked past her toward the courtyard of the house. "I'll just be out in the courtyard practicing, so let me know when Tim is ready for us."

"All right, I will." Eithne was still confused by his behavior.

She was very curious to know what his "odd thought" was, but she would not press the issue. After all, Darian had just asked her to be more respectful of him.

Hours later, Yocelin and Aram emerged from Tim's study. Yocelin was wearing a miffed expression on her face, but that was probably only on account of her being in a room with the old wizard for so long. Aram seemed stoic and ready to be alone for a while.

Eithne was reading in the sitting parlor when they came out. She had chosen not to bother Darian while she waited. "How was it?" she asked as they came out.

"Fine," Aram answered bluntly and walked away without further ado.

"It wasn't bad, I guess. I just wish Tim didn't have to be so pompous all the time," Yocelin said with mild irritation.

"So it wasn't too difficult to learn the technique?" Eithne prompted.

Yocelin shook her head. "It's a simple concept. The concentration is the hard part."

"I'm so glad you approve," Tim stated with some sarcasm from the doorway.

Yocelin rolled her eyes at the wizard's comment and went into the kitchen.

"Are you ready for Darian and me now?" Eithne asked politely.

Tim rubbed in face with his hand. It had been a very long lesson. Aram was extremely easy to teach and picked up the skills almost immediately, but Yocelin was much more difficult. Of course, she had not been trained in the way Aram had been training himself for years in the way of mental discipline; however, she was also simply resistant to learning the techniques because of her dislike for him. It was very tiresome.

"I think we can begin in an hour or two just as well. I need time to clear my head."

Eithne nodded that she understood and let Tim retreat back into his study. She then followed Yocelin into the kitchen. It was lunchtime, anyway. She found Yocelin snacking on some dried meat at the table.

"So your personal feelings for Tim aside, what is your take on all this craziness?" Eithne asked. It felt good to speak with someone after hours of silence.

"It's pretty crazy. I'm still having difficulty with the whole fate-of-Raashan-resting-in-our-hands thing," Yocelin replied as she chewed her snack.

Eithne got herself a plate of bread and cheese and sat at the table with her friend. "I know exactly what you mean. A part of me just doesn't believe it's true, like this is all a dream we'll wake up from at any minute."

Yocelin swallowed the bit of meat she was chewing and gave a womanly chuckle. "I've already pinched myself and found that I was very disappointed."

Eithne laughed at the joke. It felt better to talk about their unique situation.

"It's just so big, you know? I don't know if I could handle the entire concept in one thought. I bet one of the reasons that Tim is keeping us here and teaching us mental discipline is to give us time to deal with our newfound duty."

"You might be giving Tim too much credit," Yocelin grumbled and bit off another piece of meat.

Eithne shook her head. "I know he can be bossy and a little arrogant, but he's almost a thousand years old and is a wizard of immense power. I think that you don't give him enough credit."

"I don't like that you're defending him," Yocelin's tone was pouty. "I didn't think you liked him either."

"I don't much care for his personality, but I do respect him. I think you will find that is the difference." Eithne gave her friend a silly smile to keep things light and munched on her food.

Yocelin stuck her tongue out in response, and Eithne reciprocated. They laughed and forgot the seriousness of their conversation.

"I see that I have walked into the mature room," Darian stated as he entered the kitchen.

The girls turned and smiled a friendly greeting his way.

"Tim will see us in an hour or two," Eithne told him before she forgot.

Darian nodded. He then got something for himself to eat and left the kitchen with his plate and no further words.

"He's quiet today," Yocelin commented after Darian had left the room.

"Yeah, we had a tiny tift, which was quickly resolved. Then he suddenly had an 'odd thought' and left to be alone," Eithne explained while she continued to eat.

Yocelin found that she was excited to know more. After all, she was a busybody and not at all ashamed of it.

"What sort of 'odd thought'?" She leaned over the table eagerly.

Eithne shrugged. "He didn't tell me. I didn't want to push since he had just asked me to be more respectful of his feelings."

"Don't you want to know?"

"Well, of course, I do. But apparently, he doesn't want to share it with me," Eithne replied.

Yocelin let out a sigh. This topic was not as exciting as she had hoped. They would have to find something else to talk about.

Two hours later, Eithne and Darian met with Tim to begin their training as scheduled. They were also in the study for quite some time. Afterward, during dinner, Tim informed his four guests that they were also to devote a certain amount of time per day to mastering the new honing techniques they had learned today. There was some eye-rolling from Yocelin, but all four of them agreed. It felt as though they were all children in school again, though it was much easier to devote their thoughts to meditation and honing techniques instead of focusing on how they were all supposed to use them to save the entire world. Right now, it was much less complicated to take one step at a time.

CHAPTER NINETEEN

*A*RAM AWOKE AND rolled onto his back to stare at the ceiling. They had all been staying at the wizard's mansion for almost a month. Tonight was the full moon. Aram needed no calendar to tell him that. He could feel the full moon coming for days before it happened. His body was humming with the bestial change to come. Aram was disciplined enough to control the beast within himself from harming others, but he could not stop his body from changing on this night. The power of the moon was too strong.

Aram turned his head to look at Darian sleeping in the other bed a few feet away. This was the night he had been dreading. Now, he had no choice but to tell Darian and Eithne what he truly was. Would Darian cease to be his friend? He hoped not, but Aram could not know what his reaction would be. Perhaps he should have already come out with the truth of his situation, but it wasn't as if there were ever a proper moment to broach such topics. He looked back up at the ceiling for a few more minutes before sitting up and getting out of bed. Aram would tell his friends after morning meditations.

Breakfast and morning meditations all went as usual. The boys were the first to arrive in the kitchen for breakfast, while Eithne and Yocelin came in shortly after. They girls always discreetly teased Tristin until Tim came in and scolded them for their bad behavior. Then after finishing their meal, they all went to the meditation room to meditate for an hour.

Aram found that his meditations were not as relaxing as usual. He had trouble clearing his head of the conversation that would take place afterward. He kept trying to come up with the best way to begin the conversation. How does one even approach such a topic?

Aram had never actually had to sit down and tell someone what he was before now. It was a new and frightening experience.

When meditations were over, they all walked out of the room to go their separate ways for a while until lunch. Now was the time. It would not do to wait any longer.

"I would like to speak with everyone," Aram announced awkwardly.

Everyone stopped and looked at him. It was very strange that Aram would suddenly announce anything. Still, it wasn't as if it were a bad time. Only Tim seemed to be expecting something from Aram this morning.

"What is it, Aram?" Eithne was concerned.

Even though her crush on him had lessened considerably once she realized he did not return her feelings, she still cared for him as her friend a great deal.

"Perhaps we should all sit in the parlor first?" Tim suggested.

He knew what Aram was going to say and felt that Darian and Eithne may need to be seated. Aram nodded that he thought it was a good idea.

After all of them were properly situated in the sitting parlor, Aram decided to just say what he needed to be said: "I am a werewolf."

He immediately looked to Darian for his initial reaction, which simply looked to be shock, much to Aram's relief.

"I have been a werewolf since my adolescence. It is why I was cast out of my home city of Amara. I am not dangerous to any of you, even during the full moon. I have learned to control the animal urges and do not harm others."

"I can't believe you told them! Good for you!" Yocelin's blind encouragement of his actions was positive, but Aram was not concerned with her thoughts on the issue. He sat and waited to hear what Darian and Eithne would say. Tim remained a silent observer.

"So you were never sick when we were on the *Leviathan*, and that's why you lied about taking a new direction just before the caves?" Darian stated thoughtfully.

In hindsight, he felt a bit foolish for not noticing sooner, but it wasn't as if he were looking for signs that Aram was a werewolf either.

"Yes, that is the truth of both of those situations. I hope you can understand why I had to behave that way," Aram answered. He was very nervous. He kept clenching his hands out of anxiousness. At least, Darian was talking to him. That was a good sign.

"Why are you telling us now?" Eithne asked.

She really didn't know what to think. She had just started getting used to the idea of being a part of saving the world. Now, one of her best friends was a werewolf. Honestly, with what she already knew about Aram, and everything else she had to sort through emotionally, Eithne was ready to simply accept him as a werewolf and move on.

"Because we will all be traveling together for some time. It is not right to keep my secret from the two of you under such circumstances. You have a right to know," Aram replied, still tensely clenching and unclenching his hands.

"Well, you wouldn't be able to keep it a secret," Darian stated plainly, though Eithne perceived his tone as being a little harsh. "Would you have told us if you thought you could keep it hidden?"

Aram held strong. He knew that Darian was not accusing him of anything yet, but he feared it could go in that direction.

"I would like to say that I would have told you regardless, but I do not know for sure. I am sure that you are aware of the reputation that werewolves have. I cannot lie to you, I could not control my own wolf side at first either, but I did remove myself from society and learned how to control it. I am very confident in my ability to do so now."

There was a quiet moment while Darian and Eithne processed the information. Aram wanted to know exactly what was going on in their heads. He hadn't realized until now just how important their opinions of him were. It had been so long since he had had any real companionship, and he didn't want it to go away. Yocelin saw how upset Aram was and squeezed his hand supportively. He nodded at her thankfully and stopped his nervous clenching.

"Okay, Aram, I believe you, and I trust you," Eithne stated with satisfying conviction.

She looked Aram in the eyes as she spoke to show him that she meant what she said. She reasoned that Aram had had plenty of opportunities to hurt them and never had. Besides, he was their friend, and real friends trust each other.

Aram was grateful and relieved at Eithne's acceptance, but he was still feeling nervous about how Darian would react. Still, Aram gave Eithne an appreciative nod and relaxed somewhat.

After torturous, long seconds of contemplation, Darian spoke, "I believe you as well, and you have been nothing but a friend to me since we met. However, I am still not totally comfortable with this new information. I want to talk to you more about it, as a friend."

Aram relaxed completely and nodded his accord to Darian. This was the best possible reaction he could have hoped for. He understood why Darian would want to talk about it. Darian would probably have more confidence in him after he was better able to comprehend it all and have his questions answered.

"I appreciate both of your understanding." Aram thanked his friends with full sincerity. "I will answer any questions you may have about my particular condition."

Darian stood and looked at Aram straight on. "I'd like to talk now if you have the time."

Aram nodded, and the two of them went to the library to discuss things privately.

"You took that well," Tim mentioned to Eithne after the boys had left the room.

Eithne shrugged. "He's still Aram, no matter what. He's been a werewolf all this time and been perfectly fine. Besides, with all the shocking news and changes I've had to digest lately, things don't seem as astounding or upsetting as they used to . . . Wait a minute! How come you two already knew?" She looked at Yocelin and Tim expectantly.

"I knew what he would be before you all arrived," Tim said dismissively and stood to leave. The wizard made his way upstairs and called for his apprentice.

"Demons have a better sense of smell than elves. I can smell that he is a werewolf, so I have known since I first met him," Yocelin offered happily. She was happy to talk with Eithne without the wizard present.

"Does Aram have a better sense of smell too?" Eithne was intrigued at how heightened Yocelin's sense of smell was.

"Yes, all his senses are heightened. He has better reflexes, more strength, and can run faster than any elf or human," Yocelin answered proudly.

Of course, demons were also superior to elves and humans in these same ways. It was one of the reasons elves and humans had such a strong dislike for demons. They know that they are physically superior, and it is frightening. Also, demons that looked like Yocelin were extraordinarily rare. Most demons were considered to be utterly repulsive to other humanoids.

"So is Aram considered to be a strong werewolf since he can control himself like he does?" Eithne continued her questions.

Yocelin widened her eyes and gave one big nod. "Oh, yes, Aram is a very powerful werewolf. I didn't even know it was possible for them to have the self-control and abilities that he does. Did you know it was possible for them to go only halfway with the transformation? Or that they can transform even when there isn't a full moon? Aram can do that! If he wanted to, he could just sprout the ears and tail and leave it at that!"

"Wow. I had no idea that was possible. I'm glad he's on our side."

Eithne had read about werewolves a little bit in her personal studies but had never come across anything that said that werewolves could have that sort of control. In fact, everything she had ever read about them had been extremely negative. Most werewolves completely surrendered to the beast within and lived only for the thrill of hunting down innocent victims. The urge to bite and spread the disease was said to be completely irresistible. But apparently, if someone was strong enough, they could overcome it, as Aram had—though Eithne realized that he must live with a constant struggle against the wolf within him. She also had a more horrifying realization that if Aram was that powerful and Cavan was able to defeat him so easily, defeating Cavan would be nigh impossible. She shook her head of that thought. There was too much in her head already, and she could not stress about Cavan right now.

Eithne and Yocelin continued to talk for an hour or so. Sometime later, Darian and Aram emerged from the library, and the four of them talked more about things together. Aram's announcement had settled well among the foursome, and for that, Aram was very grateful. It had been a very long time since he had been in the position of having friends. It felt brand-new and strange, but it made him happy.

CHAPTER TWENTY

✦

*T*WO WEEKS AFTER Aram had told his friends that he was a werewolf, Tim had an announcement of his own. The past weeks had gone by in the same routine as before, but there had been something different about the feeling of it. All four companions felt as though they were doing everything right. The techniques had become easy, and they each felt comfortable using them. Even Yocelin, upon finally receiving some compliments from Tim, had become less spiteful about the whole situation. The wizard had asked all of them to meet him in the sitting parlor after morning meditations because he had something important to tell them. So they all dutifully filed into the sitting parlor after meditations and waited for Tim to speak. Tim decided not to sit in his favorite leather armchair, to everyone's surprise, but chose to address them while standing.

"It had become clear to me that the four of you have learned the techniques well enough to begin your journey. Tomorrow, you will all set out for the elven city of Lupia. I have already told my friend, King Reimus, to expect you. He is a trusted friend of mine and is aware of your quest. He will help you as much as he can." The wizard smiled proudly at them as he spoke.

"So we graduated?" Yocelin asked with a satiric smile.

Tim nodded at her use of the term *graduated*. He liked it. "You could say that you did, yes."

"Why are you sending us to Lupia?" Darian asked quickly before Yocelin could get them further off the subject. He needed to fully understand where they were going and why before leaving.

"Lupia is one of the most densely populated cities in the world. There is bound to be at least one other person there who carries a god

172

piece. It simply seems like a good place for all of you to start. Besides, it's an elven city, so you all shouldn't have any trouble blending in," Tim explained patiently.

"What about me? I don't exactly blend like the rest of us," Yocelin piped up and gestured pointedly at her horns.

"I have already devised a solution for that," Tim answered with an arrogant smile. "I will show you when we are done here."

Yocelin was pleased enough with his answer, though she still wrinkled her nose at his arrogance. She was very excited to be leaving the wizard's mansion. She was beginning to feel as though the walls were closing in on her.

"Where will we go from Lupia?" Eithne asked. It was going to be a very long quest, and she hoped for further directions than just one city.

Tim smiled kindly at her but did not provide the answer she hoped to hear. "I trust that all of you will be able to decide that yourselves. Just go where your instincts take you. You will travel quite extensively during this quest. I would suggest going in the direction where you sense the most magic."

Eithne's cheeks grew a little pink. She suddenly felt that her question had been stupid. Darian noticed her embarrassment but held back from reacting. His hand only twitched slightly as he fought the impulse to rest it on her shoulder.

"Are there no other questions?" The wizard looked at each of them expectantly. It appeared no one had anything to add. In fact, Yocelin was almost bouncing to get up and leave. "Good. Darian, Aram, after lunch, I will need to speak with the two of you in my study."

Both Darian and Aram nodded that they understood. Then Tim indicated that it was time to leave, except for Yocelin, whom he took to show her his solution for disguising her horns. The other three went to start packing their belongings.

After lunch, Tim sought out Darian and Aram to have the discussion he had told them about earlier. He found them getting their things in order in their room. Aram was packing supplies into this pack, while Darian cleaned his weapons. When Tim entered through the open door, both men stopped what they were doing and gave the wizard their full attention.

"Would you both be so kind as to join me in my study?" Tim politely commanded, and they obliged.

Once inside the wizard's study, Tim closed the heavy wooden doors and invited them to sit, which they did. Tim then took a seat behind his large mahogany desk, facing them, and folded his hands neatly in front of him.

"What I am going to say to you does not leave this room," Tim began. "Neither Eithne nor Yocelin are to know of what we discussed, no matter how much they may pester you to tell them. Is that clear?"

Both Darian and Aram were confused by the way this conversation was beginning, but they had also learned to trust the great wizard and his methods. They both nodded in agreement to the terms and waited for him to continue.

"Good. Well, I will get straight to the point of this meeting." Tim paused to clear his throat before continuing. It was an awkward subject to approach at any age. "Both Eithne and Yocelin are very appealing, physically and mentally. Many men would find them to be tempting prospects."

Darian and Aram became even more confused and now feeling slightly uncomfortable. What did any of this have to do with anything? Did Tim mean to caution them about protecting them from possibly violent men besides Cavan? Of course, they would already do that.

Tim could see their confusion and decided to stop tiptoeing around his point.

"Neither of you are to be romantic with either of them in any way. It will be tempting. You are all young, attractive, on a long quest together, and you already feel a strong bond to them because you are their chosen protectors. Just don't fall in love with them." Tim leaned over and gazed formidably at them from across his desk to further impress his point.

The boys were very taken aback by Tim's statement. It was certainly the last thing they were expecting to hear. Both friends looked at each other and then back to the old wizard, who continued to glare. They had no idea how to respond.

"I'm afraid that I don't know how you want us to respond," Darian countered awkwardly after he couldn't take the old wizard staring at him anymore.

"The two of you swearing a blood oath that you will not get romantically involved with either of the girls in any way will do just fine," Tim answered plainly. He clearly felt very strongly about this.

"Don't you think that a blood oath is a bit extreme?" Aram asked. "I mean, they are beautiful, but we are more than capable of controlling any urges we might come to feel toward them."

Tim did not answer verbally but gave Aram a skeptical hard look. It made Aram feel as though he were being treated like a child, which he did not like at all.

"Look, I hereby swear to keep my hands off of Eithne and Yocelin. Are you satisfied?" Darian swore in an exasperated tone.

This whole conversation was beginning to make him question Tim's sanity. After living for almost a thousand years, one could understand how someone would become a little off mentally.

"Not with that attitude, I'm not," came Tim's blunt reply.

He didn't appreciate Darian's tone at all. It seemed they were not taking this seriously. He knew just how crazy it sounded that he was telling them not to fall for the girls, and he didn't care if Darian and Aram did think that he was a crazy old man, so long as they did as they were told. It was more important than they realized.

Darian sighed. He felt that this whole discussion was ridiculous. He just wanted out of the study so that he could forget it. He didn't even care why they weren't supposed to fall in love with Eithne or Yocelin. He just needed to say something convincing enough to satisfy the old coot.

"Well, I have absolutely no intention of pursuing either of them. I happen to be practically engaged to Eithne's sister, Rosalin. I will not be pursuing any new romantic interests."

Darian crossed his arms and leaned back in his chair. He was certainly exaggerating about his relationship with Rosalin. In fact, he was certain that he would not be courting her for marriage now, but Tim didn't need to know that. Darian knew enough about the old wizard to know that he couldn't read minds, so if misleading him about marrying Rosalin was what it took to get out of the study right now, then that is what he would do.

Tim looked back at Darian, unblinking, for a moment, as if he were going to make him admit to something. Darian stared back with his steely blue gaze. Then it seemed that he accepted Darian's statement.

"All right, I will believe you in this. I am satisfied."

That was a relief. Darian and Aram stood and started to leave.

"Wait a minute. I said that I was satisfied with the reason Darian gave. I have not yet heard what I need to hear from Aram," Tim stated sharply.

Aram turned back. He was tired of this talk.

"Very well, I do swear to not get romantically involved with Eithne or Yocelin. I will act as a protector and friend, nothing more."

Aram looked Tim squarely in the eyes as he made his statement. He didn't want Tim to think that he was only saying it to leave the room, which he was, in part. He also did mean what he said. Aram had no intention of getting involved with either woman.

Tim gave Aram the same long look he had given Darian before conceding to accept his intentions as true. "Very well, I am also satisfied that you will not touch them either."

Darian and Aram were very relieved and tried again to make their exit.

"Just one more thing," Tim said from behind his desk just as Aram was about to pull open the door. The men turned around again but did not move away from the door. "I want to discuss the Cavan situation with you."

Darian and Aram continued to stand by the door. Neither felt like sitting down again. Tim was displeased by their quiet refusal to sit back down but decided not to press the issue.

"Cavan is very dangerous, as you already know, and he will continue to seek your group out in order to kill Yocelin. He has already come to realize what he needs to do to collect all the pieces of Muntros. The reason he is so powerful is because he has used old incantations to bring out the strength of the god within him. The more pieces he gathers, the more powerful he will become. Therefore, Yocelin should kill him sooner rather than later. She must be the one to slay him, or else she will not be able to absorb all the pieces of Muntros that Cavan has already collected. I also do not recommend using the bracelet to absorb his power. He is too dangerous, and if left alive, he would only continue to come after you."

"Do you think that Cavan is still in the city?" Aram asked.

"No, I have been monitoring his activities here, and he left some time ago once he realized he could not get past my barriers. He will still seek out Yocelin, however," Tim replied.

"Any idea where he is now?" Aram pressed, anxious for as much information as possible.

"North of Lupia somewhere, but I cannot pinpoint his precise location. Anyway, Yocelin is able to sense when he is close by," Tim responded helpfully.

"If Cavan gets more powerful with each piece he collects, will the same thing happen to the girls?" Darian asked. It seemed a logical deduction.

"Not exactly. Cavan has used old incantations to magnify the effect that absorbing god pieces gives. The girls will very slowly and discretely become more powerful, but they probably won't even notice a discernible difference in their abilities until over half of the pieces are collected within each of them," Tim explained.

"But they were able to manifest that blast before," Darian countered.

Tim acknowledged Darian's argument with a slow nod. "It is truly incredible what a strongly felt emotion can do in times of crisis. That was simply an amazingly lucky anomaly," the wizard further explained patiently. "Is everything clear to you both?"

Both Darian and Aram nodded in unison.

"Excellent. I am counting on you two, and don't forget to keep your feelings in check. You may go now."

Tim dismissed them with a wave of his delicate hand. They left in a hurry, thankful the conversation was over. It was obvious that they couldn't wait to leave. Tim leaned back in his chair and sighed. He knew that his forewarning against falling in love must have seemed ludicrous, but he knew what could happen if they did. The wizard had watched how they all interacted and looked at each other. The danger of them falling for each other was very real. He had debated greatly over even having that conversation with Darian and Aram, but in the end, he decided it would be best to try preventative measures. They would only end up devastated if they fell in love with Eithne and Yocelin.

CHAPTER TWENTY-ONE

*T*HE FOUR COMPANIONS set out for Lupia the next morning. It was an extremely hot and bright day. It was now the middle of winter, and it felt like the height of summer. Of course, tomorrow would probably bring a freezing blizzard, so they counted themselves lucky to have clear roads to travel on for now. All four were happy to be on their way. It had become stuffy in the wizard's mansion. Tristin was sad to see them all leave. The young apprentice had enjoyed having other male companionship as well as the teasing from such beautiful women. All said warm good-byes, then the foursome mounted up on the horses provided by Tim and left.

It was a three-day ride to Lupia from Duomo. The road there was well-traveled and relatively safe. They passed other travelers on a regular basis, but there was little to no interaction. Yocelin was forced to keep her hood up in the sweltering heat in order to hide her horns. Her friends felt very sympathetic for her when they saw the beads of sweat dripping down her face. In the afternoon of the second day of travel, the weather turned suddenly from blistering heat to bitterly cold again with a biting wind. At first, it was a welcome relief from the heat, but after an hour or so in the cold, they all wished to be warm again. The unprecedented changes in weather made the companions talk of their quest and how Raashan really was in need of saving. They were all old enough to remember what the world was like before the death of the gods and longed just to have normal seasons again. The people of Raashan had grown accustomed to the chaos, but that was not how it was supposed to be.

At dawn on the third and final day of travel, the foursome was packing up their camp after a light breakfast and getting ready to leave. The freezing wind had died down, but the damp cold still seeped into their skin, so all of them moved about as much as possible to stay warm. They estimated that they would be in Lupia by early evening if they did not experience any holdups along the way.

Yocelin took out a corked glass vile that was filled with a greenish potion from her pack and approached Eithne with unusual secrecy.

"Eithne, would you mind coming with me for a few minutes?" she asked quietly.

"Is something wrong?" Eithne found Yocelin's quiet demeanor to be strange.

"No, nothing really, I'm just nervous about using this potion that Tim gave me to get rid of my horns. I'm not certain what will happen when I take it and don't want to do it by myself," she answered sheepishly.

"Oh, of course, I will come with you." Eithne was immediately at ease.

Obviously, her friend was just nervous, and she didn't blame her. Eithne wouldn't like taking strange potions either. The two women left what they were doing and walked into the forest just out of sight of their protectors.

"Where do you think they're going?" Darian said to Aram as he noticed the women leave.

"To relieve themselves, maybe?" Aram guessed.

"Together?"

Aram shrugged and secured his horse's girth.

Darian shook his head. "Women are strange creatures."

Once out of sight, Eithne and Yocelin stopped for Yocelin to drink the potion. She nervously uncorked the vile and took a deep breath. Before drinking, she tentatively sniffed the greenish liquid and immediately recoiled in disgust.

"It smells like fertilizer!" she exclaimed and made a bad face. "I hate Tim."

"It can't be that bad if you're supposed to drink it," Eithne said and took the vile to smell it herself. "Never mind, that is awful! Um, just hold your nose when you drink it and chug it really fast."

Yocelin stuck out her tongue in a form of mild protest but took back the vile and did as Eithne instructed. She held her nose and threw the potion down her throat, trying to swallow it before she could taste it. She coughed as her gag reflex reacted to the horrible taste, but she kept it down. They stood there for a few seconds, waiting for something to happen. Then Yocelin let out a painful groan, grabbed her head, and dropped to her knees. Her eyes squeezed tightly closed, and her teeth clenched.

"Are you all right?" Eithne was alarmed.

She dropped down next to her friend and put her hand on Yocelin's shoulder. She was very concerned but reminded herself that it was just the potion working and that her friend would be fine. Eithne tried her best not to overreact.

Yocelin's black curling horns began to slowly corkscrew back into her head! It was obviously very painful as Yocelin continued to groan and make other expressions of extreme pain. Eithne gave Yocelin her hand to squeeze and was almost sorry that she did as her friend squeezed it so hard that Eithne almost let out a yelp of pain herself.

Thankfully, the pain only last for a moment, though it felt like longer. When it subsided, Yocelin released Eithne's hand and let out a deep sigh.

"How do you feel?" Eithne asked as she helped her friend to her feet again.

"I have a splitting headache, but that's a lot better than it was a minute ago." She rubbed her head where her horns used to be. "Wow, that potion really did work! How do I look?"

Eithne stepped back to better look at Yocelin. "Still very pretty, but now I feel like something is missing. How long will the potion last?"

Yocelin shrugged as they took the short walk back to camp. "Tim said about ten days, give or take."

When they emerged from the forest, the boys gawked at the sight of Yocelin without her horns. It was just so different, even though it was a very small change. Somehow, she didn't look like herself anymore.

Yocelin pouted at their reaction while she rubbed her temples to help ease her headache. "I look ridiculous, don't I?"

"No!" Darian was very quick to react.

He had been around women enough to know that when they said that they didn't look nice, a man should immediately dispute it, no matter what they looked like—though he really didn't think she looked ridiculous at all. Really, he was just so surprised at how elflike she looked without her horns. It was very easy to see how her adopted parents would be able to believe she was an elf until her horns grew in.

"You just look so different without your horns, but you look very pretty."

Eithne smiled at Darian. She was happy to see them being friends.

"You just look like a short elf woman now," Aram said bluntly.

He meant the statement to be more comforting than it sounded. He saw Darian and Eithne both give him a disapproving look that told him he needed to amend his statement.

"Erm, but a beautiful short elf woman. Very pretty," Aram amended awkwardly.

He decided to take a cue from Darian and just tell her she was pretty. Aram really wasn't sure why it worked so well, but he had noticed that whenever the girls were getting uppity with Darian, he would tell them how nice they looked, and they seemed to calm down.

Yocelin smiled weakly but winced from her headache. "Well, thank you. It's nice to know that I haven't lost my charm."

Eithne gave her some herbal remedy to chew on the help ease her headache, and it seemed to help her feel better.

The companions made it to Lupia just ahead of schedule. The freezing weather had caused them to move faster than usual. Tim had instructed them to go straight to the palace at the city center. They were to tell the guards that they were guests of King Reimus sent by the wizard Tim, so that is exactly what they did.

Lupia was a truly lovely city. It had been built in the center of a great forest, and the elven ancestors who built it had allowed most of the original trees of that forest to remain. The beautiful foliage was contrasted against gleaming silver architecture that arched upward in graceful lines as if all the buildings were reaching to touch the sky. It was like walking through a dream. There were white-washed cobblestone streets for the main roads, but any side streets were more like animal paths through the forest that led to clusters of homes and shops glinting silver from in between the ancient trees. It wasn't uncommon for the elves of Lupia to see a herd of deer grazing by their front door in the morning, or many other forest creatures scampering by as they went about their daily routines. The natural world and city culture existed in a state of perfect harmony here. It was truly a unique and gorgeous place. There were also many park squares, where patches of the original forest had simply been left to grow and thrive inside the city. It was in stark contrast to the elven cities in which Aram and Yocelin had been raised. Most elven cities were very beautiful, but they did not harmonize with nature as Lupian elves did.

Aram's home city of Amara had many squares and parks, but they were all planned and organized. Things were not allowed to grow wildly as they were here. Elves were known as great lovers of sunlight, so the silver and crystal architecture was something that was common in elven cities so that the sunlight would be always reflected, making the cities themselves glow like beacons. On nights when the moon was full, Aram remembered how beautiful Amara was. The reflection of the moonlight lit the entire city without needing to light lanterns. The people used to go out in the streets and celebrate the beauty with nighttime festivals and dancing. Aram shuddered as he recalled that it was on such a night that he wandered outside of the safety of the city walls to admire the full moon without the reflection of the buildings to cloud the details of its surface. He should not have wandered alone; for that was the night he was attacked.

He had simply been standing still, within sight of the city gates, mesmerized by lunar beauty, when the black, hairy beast jumped upon him and sunk its fangs into his left shoulder greedily. Aram remembered being so horrified and stunned at first that he did not even cry out. He had always been a quiet child. The golden yellow eyes of the werewolf were veined with red and had slit black pupils. Aram could not even begin to describe his terror as he locked eyes with that monster. It had let its fangs sink into his flesh slowly, savoring his taste. When it bit down harder and cracked the bone in Aram's shoulder, the shock of pain brought him out of his narcosis. He screamed as loudly as he could for help. The guards at the gate came running to his aid, and the werewolf released him, vanishing into the night. When the guards got to him, the werewolf was gone and Aram was in such a state of shock that he couldn't clearly describe the monster that had attacked him—except for the eyes; he would never forget those horrible yellow eyes. The guards surmised that it must have been a bear attack and brought Aram back to his parents. He himself became convinced that it had been a bear. His wound was properly treated and seemed to heal faster than it should. Werewolves are fast healers. It wasn't until the next full moon that Aram and his family knew what had really bitten him. Thankfully, his father's fast reflexes had stopped him from maiming his little sister, and his father had managed to barricade his son in the cellar for the night. The next morning, his parents took him outside the city walls and disowned him. Aram did his best to push away that painful memory. It was a long time ago and could not be changed. Still, he couldn't help but feel that he had been treated unfairly. He could not help being bitten and was only an adolescent boy at the time. Aram had learned long ago that life was never fair.

As the companions walked along the white-washed cobblestone streets of Lupia, the four of them could see that even in this wondrous city, the signs of cataclysm were apparent. One of the gleaming silver monuments they passed had been partially crumbled and blackened by fire. Many other buildings and trees showed their own deep scars. One of the patches of original forest that had been left to thrive was simply dead and brown. Nothing could live or grow there now. Still, Lupia was considered to be one of the lucky cities of Raashan. Even though it bore some damage, it still remained an active and prosperous place. In a way, the death of the gods was beneficial to the city as many elven refugees flocked to Lupia to start a new life and boosted its economy. The city had also managed to remain peaceful during these difficult times. Of course, there were always confrontations with outlaws who lived in the surrounding forest, but Lupia was officially considered to be neutral and formed no alliances with other cities or nations. It kept life here simple and peaceful for its inhabitants.

The great palace was not at all difficult to find. It was like a glorious pillar of light that shot up from the center of the city. The palace was encircled by a moat, which was now frozen solid, that was deep and wide enough to discourage those who thought to sneak into the palace. There were four white cobblestone bridges that lead to the north, south, east, and west entrances. Only the western bridge was used regularly; the other three remained with their polished silver gates heavily locked.

As the companions approached the west bridge, they saw that the gates were ajar with five guards standing in front of them. No one else seemed to be trying to gain entry to the palace at this time. As they all walked up to the gate, Darian found himself at the front of the group. The other three hung back slightly. Darian noticed their subtle actions and smiled to himself. He supposed that he would be the one to do the talking, and it made him feel like the captain of the guard again. It felt good to take charge, made him feel more comfortable.

Darian approached the guard confidently and told him that they were all guests of King Reimus, sent from the wizard Tim. The guard nodded and told them to wait there while he confirmed with his superior inside. The guard did not take long, and he reappeared with a more official-looking elf. He was tall and wearing the clothing of a royal court adviser. His face appeared to be middle aged, but his hair was stark white, and his eyes looked as though they had seen more years than only half a lifetime.

"Welcome, friends," the elf said and opened his arms in a formal gesture of welcome. "I am Trias, one of King Reimus's advisers. It is a pleasure to meet you. I will be happy to escort you to the king and then to your rooms so that you may clean up and change before dinner with the king."

"Thank you, Trias. We are much obliged. I am Captain Darian, and these are my companions: Aram, Eithne, and Yocelin. We are fortunate and pleased to accept your hospitality," Darian responded, sounding very official.

In fact, his sudden courtly manner caused Eithne and Yocelin to exchange glances and control a nervous snicker. Darian noticed their reaction but paid it no mind. That is how one is expected to present themselves in such company.

Trias led them across the bridge and into the gleaming palace. They went up a great spiraling staircase to the top of the highest tower. It felt like a very long and dizzying climb to the foursome who had been traveling for days. Finally, they arrived at the throne room of King Reimus.

It was a glorious room! The tall arched ceiling peaked at a single circular skylight that beamed a ray of sunlight directly unto the ornate silver throne below it. On the throne sat King Reimus, wearing pale-yellow and gray robes in the style of the city elves and a simple platinum circlet crown resting on his brow. The throne room was sparse, except for the throne and four decorative tapestries on the walls depicting the four seasons. King Reimus smiled broadly at the companions and opened his arms in the same gesture of welcome that Trias had shown them. His face crinkled in smile lines as he grinned at his guests, and his bright-blue eyes shone with a youthful spirit, even though he looked to be at least 550 years old, which is considered to be late middle age for elves.

"Welcome to you all, my friends. I am King Reimus. I am very pleased to meet all of you. I do hope that your journey to Lupia was pleasant," the king stated in a warm echoing voice.

Darian bowed low from his waist respectfully.

"We are honored to make your acquaintance and receive your hospitality, Great King. I am Darian, captain of the guard of the Aranni tribe. These are my companions: Eithne, also of the Aranni, Aram of Amara, and Yocelin."

He indicated each of them accordingly, and as they were introduced, each of them bowed to the king, mimicking Darian. They all figured that Darian must know what he was doing and saying in this setting. None of them were as familiar with formalities.

King Reimus greeted each of them in kind. They exchanged a few more courteous pleasantries, and the king invited them to dine with him this evening. Naturally, the invitation was accepted gladly. Even Aram knew that one did not decline such invitations from kings. Besides, the meal was sure to be excellent. Only Yocelin—who was, of course, a carnivore—was concerned about what would be served, but she did not show any indication of her concerns.

After the formal meeting, the four companions were escorted by Trias to their separate rooms. They were all located in the same hallway of the palace, but each had their own private room. That in itself felt like a great luxury, for none of them had slept alone in months. The rooms were almost identical, each only with small differences in decor. Once settled, they were then given the opportunity to bathe and dress for dinner.

All four of them were taken aback with the royal treatment they received while getting ready for dinner. It seemed too lavish. Aram found the constant attention uncomfortable and didn't wish the servants to be so attentive. He felt as though his privacy was being imposed upon. After all, he had just gotten accustomed to Darian, Yocelin, and Eithne being around all the time. All these extra people coming along so suddenly was disquieting. When they tried to bathe and dress him in clothes for dinner, Aram had had enough. He asked the servants to just leave the clothing on the bed. He was certainly capable of cleaning and dressing himself properly on his own.

Yocelin, on the other hand, loved all the extra attention. She chatted unendingly with the servant girls while helped her to bathe and dress in her dinner clothing. She was so excited to be receiving such treatment. Even if it was just for a few days, Yocelin intended to take advantage of every moment of it. Besides, after leaving Lupia, it would be back to a hard life on the trail and questing for god pieces. There was absolutely no reason for her not to indulge in this experience to the fullest. Yocelin also lavished in the beautiful gowns she was able to choose from for her dinner attire. Even though the maids only offered three options, she felt spoiled for choice. After trying on all three and admiring herself in each one, Yocelin decided on a dark-blue silk gown that had billowing sleeves and was fitted to the waist. Silver embroidery embellished the gown further, and the matching velvet slippers she was given to wear completed the ensemble nicely.

Darian found that he was a little uncomfortable with the extra attention but tolerated it nonetheless; though, like Aram, he could not fathom allowing someone else to bathe or dress him. It seemed ridiculous and unnecessary. Darian politely told the servants that he would bathe and dress himself when the time came, and they left him to it. The fashions of city elves were very different from what was generally worn by tribal elves. He had visited elven cities before but had never taken note of their clothing. He had been given a long gray tunic to wear with a matching pair of leggings. The shoes he was given were a sort of moccasin slipper that he did not care for. Darian donned his black leather boots instead after shining them up a bit. If anyone mentioned something about his shoes, he determined that he would simply say that the moccasins did not fit his feet.

Like Yocelin, Eithne enjoyed the attention of having maids attending her, but not so much as her friend. She still felt a bit strange with the maids trying to do everything for her. Even though Eithne came from a well-to-do family in her own culture, Aranni tribal elves simply did not stand on as much ceremony as city elves did. She continuously found herself getting in the maids' way as she would automatically try to tie her own laces or just do anything for herself. In the end, Eithne decided to try and stand still unless otherwise directed by the maids, and that seemed to work best. She did catch the maids giving each other secret smiles as they had nonverbal jokes about tribal elves, but it did not bother Eithne. Their two cultures were just different. Of course, she did smile proudly to herself when the conservative maids reacted to the massive phoenix tattooed down the left side of Eithne's lithe body. Tattooing was not something city elves did, and they gawked at the body art. Even though their reactions may not be construed as positive, she was happy that someone else finally got to see the spirit guide that she was so proud of. Eithne was fitted into a pale-yellow gown, which was very similar in style to Yocelin's dress. She felt very pretty as she looked at herself in the mirror. Eithne had never worn a dress this expensive before. Her sister would have been the jealous one for once.

A servant came to each of their rooms to show them the way to the dining hall. As they were all staying in the same hallway, the four companions ended up walking together.

Yocelin could not contain her excitement when she saw her friends.

"Everyone looks so nice!" she exclaimed happily. "I just love all this pampering! No wonder people talk about the high life of the city elves. I don't think I would mind living like this all the time."

The servant who fetched them was clearly stunned by her outburst and blinked at the companions for a few seconds. He did not know if he should continue leading them down the hall or to let them stop and talk for a moment. He composed himself and decided to wait it out until he was given the signal to lead onward. The others had all grown accustomed to such outbursts from Yocelin and did not think anything of it.

"You look really beautiful in that dress, Yocelin. I'm glad that you are enjoying wearing it," Eithne complimented sweetly. She always enjoyed Yocelin's cheerful way of expressing herself. It made Eithne smile.

"You guys look so handsome too!" Yocelin embarrassed Darian and Aram as she said this.

Aram was not used to compliments, and Darian felt that it was inappropriate somehow. Neither of them had much of a reaction for her, much to Yocelin's disappointment.

"I don't think we should continue to linger in the hallway. I'm very hungry," Aram said brusquely. He wanted to halt any further chatter from the girls and get to dinner.

Yocelin pouted at him, for she knew exactly what he was doing. She decided to tease him for trying to dampen her spirits.

"Well, I'm hungry too, but I'm not going anywhere until I am properly escorted." She then tried her best to look like a proper lady waiting for her escort.

Aram was exasperated by her games. "You're kidding."

Yocelin shook her head and daintily held out her hand to show that she was not.

Aram stalked over to her and curtly offered his arm. He just wanted to eat, and if this is what it took to get to the dining hall, so be it. Yocelin preened happily as she accepted his arm. She had the glow of triumph. Aram could not help but to notice her effulgence. She looked lovely in her dress, and that she was in such good spirits only made her more beautiful. Of course, he would not say so to her. It would only encourage another embarrassing outburst. Though as he felt the unfamiliar pride that comes to a man while escorting a beautiful woman, Aram remembered Tim's warning about falling for Yocelin. It suddenly didn't seem like such a ludicrous caution.

As Yocelin pouted for Aram's arm, Eithne realized that it seemed like a lovely thing to experience. She had never been formally escorted by anyone but her father, and what better an opportunity than now to change that. Her approach was different than Yocelin's, however. Eithne smiled brightly at Darian, who was waiting patiently to go to dinner, walked up beside him, and cleared her throat. Darian cocked his head slightly as he looked down at her. He tried to wear an expression of annoyance, but Eithne could see his steel blue eyes showing with an amused warmth. She looked at his arm, then back to his face, making it completely obvious what she wanted. He cocked his eyebrow smartly at her as he offered his arm. Eithne took it with mock formality and looked on ahead as if to say, "Lead on." Darian shook his head and allowed himself to smile. What could he say? It was cute.

The servant couldn't have been more confused as he watched the scene play out. As far as he understood, neither pair was a couple, but they did seem to be acting that way. He shook his head to clear it and decided not to think about it anymore. Darian nodded at him to lead them onward to the dining hall, and so he did. He had a feeling that the king's new guests were going to cause some interesting gossip at court.

They arrived at the dining hall to find that they were the last ones there. It was not a large gathering by royal standards, but to the companions, it seemed like an awful lot of people for one dinner. Besides King Reimus and his queen, there were eight other guests at the long table, who were obviously all members of the royal court. One of whom was Trias, the advisor who had escorted them into the palace earlier today. The rest were finely dressed city elves, and they all smiled politely as the four companions entered. The dining hall was a long, narrow room with windows lining three sides of it. The remaining wall was, of course, where the grand, intricately carved rosewood double doors were. To complement the doors, a very long and similarly carved rosewood table had been placed in the center of the room with matching high-backed chairs lining each side of the table. It could actually seat up to twenty-four guests, but since there were less than twenty-four dining this evening, all the guests were grouped at the far end of the rectangular table. In between the windows of the longest opposing walls were hidden doors for the servants to hurry in and out of with food and drink. The tapestries that hung in between the windows to conceal these doors were richly embroidered with dark robust colors and depicted various scenes that one might find in the forest. Like all of the palace, the walls were a gleaming silvery white that reflected the fading evening sunlight filtering through the many windows beautifully. The contrast of light and dark in the hall was very pleasing.

The table was already laden with food. There was so much to eat! Three different meat courses (which Yocelin was very glad to see), several bowls of various vegetables, and baskets of freshly baked breads all sat on the table untouched. Those already gathered had politely waited for the new guests to arrive before eating. The delicious smells filled the nostrils of the companions, and they all realized how hungry they really were. Eithne's stomach made a little growling noise that she hoped no one noticed.

"Welcome, all of you!" King Reimus greeted sincerely.

The companions all smiled back, except for Aram, who wasn't used to smiling, and bowed to the king.

"Please be seated." King Reimus gestured to either side of himself and his queen, who was seated next to him at the head of the table. At each side of the royal couple, there were two empty chairs.

They all made less formal bows in thanks and went to take their seats. Darian escorted Eithne to the chair closest to the king and pulled out the chair for her. She gracefully sat, and he pushed the chair up to the table for her before taking his seat next to her.

Aram took note of what Darian did to seat Eithne and tried his best to mimic it. However, when he pulled out the chair for Yocelin, it dragged harshly on the marble floor, making an awful noise. Then he pushed the chair back in too abruptly and too far, causing Yocelin to put her hand to the edge of the table so that she wouldn't bump into it. She looked more amused than offended as she put her other hand to lips to conceal a smile. Aram hurried to take his seat next to her in the remaining chair. His expression had turned brooding. He was thankful that everyone gathered was polite enough to ignore his awkwardness, but he was certain that they all noticed. Being in such a formal setting did not suite Aram, and he didn't know how to act. It was almost like going through puberty again.

As they all began to dine, the questions began. The members of the royal court who were present, and the king and queen themselves, were very curious about their guests. Darian handled it well and politely answered their questions as he felt appropriate. Aram barely spoke at all. He felt that as soon as he took a bite of food, someone was asking him a question. Then before he could swallow and speak, at least one other question was posed to him. It was all terribly hectic. Eithne was a bit embarrassed by all the attention and, like Aram, felt the questioning to be hectic, though she handled it much better than Aram did. She had sat at fine dinners before with her family but was more accustomed to her sister being in the spotlight. She wasn't used to people wanting to speak to her so much. Even though Yocelin had never dined at a formal dinner table before, nor interacted with people from any royal court, she handled the situation like a professional. She was charming and light and kept pace very well with all the questions. It seemed that everyone at the table was enchanted by her, and she loved it. Of course, none of the foursome spoke of what their quest was. At the beginning of the conversation, Darian had said that they were questing for the Stone of Elissiyus and happened to be passing through Lupia. The other three all stuck to this story. It wasn't a good idea to make their real objective known. Besides, up until recently, they were searching for the stone. So it was an easy thing to say.

Toward the end of the meal, King Reimus had an announcement. He cleared his throat and waited for everyone to stop talking before he spoke, which was a matter of seconds.

"In honor of our guests, I have arranged to have a ball. It will happen three days from tonight in the grand ballroom of the palace. I want our guests to have a most pleasant and luxurious experience here before they must go back to their quest." He then turned his attention to his four guests. "I hope that you will all accept this invitation and enjoy the full hospitality Lupia has to offer."

Yocelin almost jumped out of her chair with glee and almost shouted an undeniable "*Yes!*" But luckily, Darian spoke before she could manage the outburst.

"We are all delighted and honored to accept your gracious invitation. Thank you."

King Reimus smiled graciously and nodded his approval.

After a long evening of dining with the royal court, the four companions were escorted by the same servant back to their rooms. As they walked, Darian once again had Eithne on his arm, and Yocelin was on Aram's.

"You do realize the king's real purpose for holding a ball in our honor?" Darian bent low and whispered to Eithne.

"What?" she whispered back.

"King Reimus knows of our true reason for coming here. Tim must have told him about our quest. He is holding the ball so that we will have a better opportunity to seek out those in Lupia who carry god pieces and gather them," he explained.

"Oh, how very clever! We will have to make the most of the opportunity. I will try really hard to concentrate at the ball," Eithne responded.

Darian nodded and smiled at her. That was exactly what he wanted to hear from her. He had been slightly concerned that she would get caught up in the girlish delight of attending a ball and forget her duty.

"Now, we just have to make sure that Aram and Yocelin are aware of what they need to do at the ball," Darian whispered more to himself. They could not speak openly in front of the servant.

Eithne smiled at him. "I think they already know. You forget that they both have super hearing."

She glanced over to her friends. Yocelin gave a sly nod and a wink to let them know that she and Aram had heard everything.

"See? We are all up to speed on the situation now." Eithne looked up at Darian, feeling very pleased with herself.

"Having friends with exceptional hearing is both a benefit and an inconvenience," he joked quietly.

Eithne and Yocelin both giggled at Darian's joke. Aram looked at his friend and shook his head at the girls' reaction.

The servant leading them once again found the companions to be very strange, indeed. He knew they were all communicating with each other, but somehow, it mostly seemed unspoken. These new guests were acting suspiciously as far as he was concerned, and it worried him that the king would have such guests and treat them so lavishly. Perhaps these people had some evil power over the king. They did not appear evil outright, but they were definitely keeping secrets. All elves were naturally distrustful of the unfamiliar, and the foursome was as unfamiliar as it could get. The servant decided that he would take care to keep a close watch on them, for he was very loyal to the royal family. He wanted to be ready to alert King Reimus to any danger passed by these strange people immediately.

The servant led each of them back to their rooms. They all said good night to one another in informal ways. He did not understand this either. These people were obviously not of noble blood. So why were they so friendly with King Reimus? Why was the king going out of his way for a small gang of no-name peasants? It did not make sense. The servant smiled to himself as he went back to his other duties. He would be greatly rewarded if and when he helped save King Reimus, perhaps all of Lupia, from these untrustworthy strangers.

CHAPTER TWENTY-TWO

T HE DAY OF the ball had arrived! Eithne could hardly believe it! She had just awakened and was still in bed but was immediately fully awake due to her excitement. A real ball! She knew that she had to remember her quest and what she was really supposed to be doing at the ball, but that didn't mean that she couldn't take in a few dances and eat some amazing food. After all, she needed to give the appearance of just having a good time. She smiled devilishly to herself as she thought of all the fun tonight would bring. How glorious it would be!

Eithne reached over from her feather bed and pulled on the thick satin cord that hung nearby. As she leaned back into the soft pillows, she mused on how quickly she had adjusted to living at the palace. Mere minutes from now, servant girls would flood into her room with breakfast served on silver trays. Then once Eithne was done eating breakfast, they would help her to bathe and choose a dress to wear today. The maids would probably even hand-feed her if she requested it. She laughed out loud as the mental image of her, a grown woman, being hand-fed breakfast in bed formed in her mind. How very ridiculous that would be! Still, Eithne wondered if that sort of thing was at all common for the inhabitants of the palace. Perhaps she would ask the maids when they came in. She had been chatting with them a lot over breakfast in the mornings and had learned many things about what life was like at the palace. It was all very fascinating. Eithne had never had experience with city elves before, and now she had the joy of a full-blown education on the subject. She felt very lucky to be staying at the palace. Eithne was even a little worried that she had perhaps thanked King Reimus too much for his hospitality. She realized that she had thanked him every time she saw him over the past three days. Perhaps he was beginning to find her gratitude tiresome.

The maids came in with breakfast right on cue. They placed the serving tray over Eithne's lap and put down a silver plate of food on top of it. She sighed happily as she saw another delightful meal in front of her. This morning, she was served freshly baked bread with butter and honey, sliced ham, a mixture of nuts, and dried fruit with hot tea and milk. It was as if the people of Lupia never suffered from bad harvests and food shortages. She thanked the maids and began to eat. Eithne chatted politely with the maids as she ate. She knew that they were not used to being spoken to when serving breakfast to guests, but she felt too awkward having them in the room but not speaking to them. Eithne assumed that the maids who served Yocelin got even more of an earful.

After breakfast, Eithne luxuriated in a warm bath scented with oils. Then she was fitted into a dark-green dress that was bejeweled along the hem and had a scooped neckline. It was made of soft velvet and felt so good against her skin. She needed a warmer material to wear as it had grown quite chilly. Winter was surely here now. Of course, that could all change by the afternoon. Since Raashan no longer upheld regular weather patterns, it could become blazing hot in a few hours, or perhaps there could be a horrible snow storm. Eithne suddenly became worried that the ball would be canceled because of bad weather but quickly took a deep breath and told herself to stop thinking negatively. She wouldn't let anything spoil her happy anticipation.

"Madam?" one of the maids interrupted her thoughts.

Eithne smiled at the maid. "Yes?"

"Madam, did you hear the question? When would you like to select your gown for the ball tonight?" the girl repeated patiently.

Eithne felt a rush of joy at the mention of ball gowns. "When does a lady usually choose her gowns for such occasions?"

Eithne wanted to look at the gowns now but sensed that was somehow incorrect. However, she was not afraid to ask the question even if it did make the maids giggle. She would rather ask and be giggled at privately than be humiliated publicly.

"It depends of the lady, Madam. Perhaps you would like to start looking at the gowns and getting ready after lunch?" the maid mercifully offered.

"That sounds perfect." Eithne smiled contentedly as the maids finished tending to her. She felt that she would be happily buzzing off her good mood all day long.

"Isn't it just like floating?" Yocelin proclaimed as she and Eithne were presented with ball gowns.

The friends had decided to get ready for the ball together so that they could share in each other's excitement. Eithne laughed and agreed with her friend. They each stood on a small dressing pedestal in Yocelin's room while six maids buzzed around them, showing them different gowns. Both Eithne and Yocelin had already been fitted into the proper undergarments and were standing in just those undergarments now. Neither of them had worn a real corset before today. Corsets had to be the most restrictive and uncomfortable things either of them had ever had on their bodies, but it only took one look in the mirror, seeing their already tiny waists shrunk even smaller, and both were happy to sacrifice pain for beauty.

The array of gowns that were offered to them to wear was somewhat overwhelming! There were so many, and they were all so beautiful. The two friends giggled gleefully as they tried each gown on and chattered endlessly about how lovely everything was to wear. The maids may have been annoyed at having to spend so much time helping two people choose a ball gown, had it been anyone else. However, Eithne and Yocelin's good humor proved to be infectious, and they encouraged the maids' opinions, and interaction made the experience much more fun than a palace maid was accustomed.

"This is it! I never want to take it off!" Yocelin declared with a big smile.

She stood on the dressing pedestal in a voluminous pale-pink silk gown with a fitted bodice that came down in a sharp *V* at her waist. The skirt was full with several layers of pink silk and a hoop skirt beneath it. The bodice was embellished with small crystal beading that was sewn on in such patterns that it accentuated Yocelin's petite, curvy figure perfectly. It was off her shoulders but still had long sleeves that formed another *V* shape over the top of her hands. The pale-pink color contrasted beautifully with her cinnamon skin and violet hair.

"You really are stunning in that one," Eithne exclaimed.

Everything about it was just right on Yocelin. It suddenly occurred to Eithne that this might be the first time that she had finally allowed herself to enjoy being a girl. Back in her village, she was so wrapped up in being different and sneaking away to practice with a sword that she had never let herself have the pleasure of being a silly girl obsessed with pretty things. She beamed at Yocelin with happy gratitude. Eithne was so pleased to be sharing this moment with such a good friend.

"Enough about me. Look at what you're wearing now! It's gorgeous on you!" Yocelin exclaimed happily.

Eithne turned back to the mirror while one of the maids finished lacing the bodice of her gown. She beheld herself in a sapphire-blue gown with beaded cap sleeves. Like Yocelin's, it had a fitted bodice, but instead of a *V* it made a more swooping *U* shape at her waist. The skirt was not as full either. There were some layers to the skirt, but it did not puff out as much, which suited Eithne's willowy frame very well. The dress did not have a lot of embellishment, but there was some pale-purple crystal beading along the scoop neckline, and the back had some lovely bustled ruffles that were very flattering to her backside. Eithne was not used to wearing dark colors because she was so pale, but she found that the deep sapphire color complimented her creamy skin nicely and even brought out a slight glowing pink in her cheeks. She smoothed her hands down the bodice while examining herself in the mirror. Yes, this was her gown tonight.

"I can't believe how pretty I feel," Eithne breathed with a hint of awe.

"We are no done yet, madam," one of the maids said with a smile as she brought over a small chest full of accessories and jewelry.

Eithne and Yocelin gasped at the sight of the chest of shiny treasures. To be further adorned seemed impossible, but they accepted it gladly.

Darian tugged uncomfortably at the collar of his shirt. He was used to wearing his military uniform for special occasions but found the suit he was given for the ball to be even more confining and stiff. He wished he had his formal uniform now to wear, instead. He stared at his reflection in the mirror. The suit he had chosen to wear was black with very little embellishment and very clean lines. The only detailing was some cream-colored embroidery along the hems of his sleeves and collar. Darian preferred not to stand out too much. He had to admit to himself that he looked good in it. The collar was still too tight, though.

There was a knock at the door. Darian called for the person knocking to enter, and Aram walked in, wearing a very similar black suit—the main difference being that the embroidery on Aram's suit was also black, giving it a monochromatic look that suited him well.

"I have never been so uncomfortable. How long do I have to wear this?" Aram's sounded irritable.

Darian's mouth twitched as he tried to keep from showing his amusement. "You have to wear it until the ball is over."

Aram didn't like the sound of that. He had never been to a ball before, but he knew that they could last all night. He would just need to make certain that he made Yocelin leave before too long. He inserted a finger into the high collar of his jacket and gave it a tug. The entire ensemble just chaffed and annoyed him. Aram assumed that his discomfort must show plainly.

Darian smirked as he turned and checked his appearance in the mirror one last time. He supposed that he looked all right. He was less nervous than Aram but still felt anxious with the situation. He couldn't remember the last time he had danced, and he was certain that he would be made to dance tonight. Then the sudden thought occurred to him that Aram had probably never danced. He may be rusty, but Aram was likely clueless. Darian made a resigned sigh to himself as he turned back to his friend, who was still plucking at his suit uncomfortably.

"Do you know how to dance at all?" Darian asked.

Aram blinked at him for a second then dropped his eyes and shook his head. "I was hoping to avoid it," he mumbled.

"I doubt that you can with Yocelin on your arm. She's the type to insist."

They held an awkward look for a moment before Darian cleared his throat and looked away. "I suppose I will have to teach you."

Aram nodded. Darian was right. Yocelin would make him dance. He had to at least learn some basic steps.

Darian and Aram had been practicing dance steps for what seemed like an eternity when there was a knock at the door. The two men stopped immediately and stood stiffly as they called for the servant to enter. Neither would ever speak of the dancing.

The servant entered and told them that their ladies were ready to be escorted. Darian felt the urge to correct the servant as neither pair was a couple but decided that it really didn't matter what they thought about it. The men nodded and proceeded out into the hall to find Eithne and Yocelin.

Both protectors found that they were stunned by the ladies they were meant to escort to the ball this evening. Neither had ever seen nor imagined Eithne or Yocelin as such proper and beautiful women. Darian and Aram had grown used to seeing them in traveling clothes or the plain dresses they had worn while staying at the wizard's mansion. The lovely gowns they currently wore seemed to flatter and exaggerate every positive physical feature—which the protectors realize, each woman had a great many such features.

As Darian's gaze glided over Eithne's willowy, lithe frame in the sapphire gown, he found that he felt a bit breathless. The deep blue of the material caused her pale, rosy skin to glow. Her red hair had been pinned half up with jeweled hairpins and the rest of her fiery locks rested over one shoulder. Suddenly, he took note of how very pink her cheeks had grown and realized that he must be staring.

Darian smartly snapped out of his reverie and approached Eithne to offer his arm, feeling awkward about his behavior.

She gave him a sweet little smile. "You look very nice this evening," she offered quietly so that no one else would hear.

"I hope I didn't embarrass you too much just now," Darian responded. Her comment helped him to relax after his faux pas. "It's just that I didn't know that you cleaned up so well. I hope that you can forgive me."

Eithne's cheeks grew pink again. "You don't have to worry about being forgiven. You generally don't need to worry about that at all," she mumbled the last sentence under her breath, and Darian smiled as he heard it. He was glad that she felt that way. Sometimes he wondered about that with Eithne.

After some time of musing as they walked, Darian remembered the true purpose of the ball. "Are you wearing the bracelet that Tim gave you?" he whispered.

Eithne nodded. "I am. Don't worry, I remember what tonight is about."

She did remember, but she had to admit that, in that moment, she had forgotten. Even though Eithne did not stare, Darian was having an odd effect on her as well. He had always been handsome, but it seemed as though this was the first time that she really noticed. Eithne had the small epiphany that knowing something to be true and realizing it for yourself were two very different things. It made her feel a bit guilty to find Darian so attractive. She would try her best to concentrate on finding god pieces tonight.

Aram would have liked very much not to have been stunned by how beautiful Yocelin looked in her dress. However, the damned she-demon had succeeded in shocking him again. He had never thought that such a seemingly innocent color of pale pink would suit her, but it did. Yocelin looked very girly with her pink dress and purple hair adorned with sparkling hairpins, but her innate sexiness always shone through. She was giving him a knowing smile as he stared at her. That smile usually would have annoyed him, but at this moment, he was too annoyed at himself. Aram cleared his throat, walked up to her, and curtly offered his arm.

"What do you think of my gown?" Yocelin batted her eyelashes at him and smiled.

Aram's reply was gruff: "It's fine."

He knew that this initial reaction had shown more than his comment, but he did not wish to give her anymore to tease him about later. He decided to lay some ground rules before she got too carried away with the embarrassment of him tonight.

As always, Aram was blunt: "You have to remember to work on identifying the proper people tonight. You can't be having fun all night."

Yocelin's fantasy was somewhat deflated by Aram's statement, and she made a pouty face. She knew what the real purpose of the ball was, of course, but did he have to go and try to take all the fun out of the experience for her? Well, Yocelin was far too much of an optimist to allow that. She was going to do her job, but it would not stop her from enjoying the evening.

As they followed the servant to the ballroom, she patted Aram's arm reassuringly. "Don't worry, handsome. I've got my bracelet on and everything."

Aram tilted his head toward her when she referred to him as *handsome* but said nothing. He simply nodded to recognize her statement. He was glad she hadn't forgotten the purpose of the ball.

Yocelin devilishly waited to see him relax before pouncing on him verbally, "Of course, we must keep up proper appearances. So you will dance at least two full dances with me tonight."

Aram felt stiff and uncomfortable again. He shot her a dark look, for he knew that she enjoyed watching him squirm. She was giving him her knowing little smile and her deep blue eyes were twinkling with amusement. Aram would not give her the satisfaction of a response. He simply faced forward and did not look at her, though he knew that there would be no avoiding the two dances she required.

Once again, the servant felt more than a little suspicious of the four guests. They actually didn't require to be led to the ballroom anymore. They had been at the palace long enough to find their way to the major rooms, but the servant wanted every opportunity to monitor them. Both couples were whispering to each other as they walked. They always seemed to be whispering. He had shared with another servant at the palace that he thought the strange guests to be constantly plotting against the king. His friend had dismissed his suspicion, but he would not let it go. He was determined to expose these four strangers and whatever their devious plot may be.

The ball was the most extravagantly marvelous thing any of them had ever experienced! Bright colors, beautiful people, delicious food, harmonious music drifted through the air, and all seemed to be pleasantness and laughter. The good mood was infectious. One could not help but to smile when they entered the grand ballroom. The ballroom itself was huge. The entire room seemed to be gleaming white marble except for the domed ceiling, which was frescoed with heavenly scenes of the old gods watching and laughing at those below. There were also dozens of platinum and crystal chandeliers dangling from that ceiling.

Eithne gasped with delight as she and Darian were announced and walked inside. She found herself immediately entranced with the entire scene. She wanted to see and do everything the ball had to offer!

"Stay focused," Darian whispered kindly. He could tell how swept away Eithne was with the ball.

She gave him a sheepish nod. He was right, as always. She had a job to do tonight, but the ball was seducing her with all its merriment.

"Will you at least dance one dance with me?" Eithne pleaded sweetly.

She needed at least one dance this evening. It would be a tragedy to miss dancing at a ball like this.

"Of course, I will," Darian responded warmly.

Even he felt himself being caught up in the spirit of the ball. He mused that he may even enjoy dancing this evening, so long as he didn't have to dance too much. For now, his military mind was taking over as he worked out a strategy for the evening. Given the monstrous size of the ballroom, and the hundreds of people filling it, the best course of action would probably be to start at one side of the room, circulate all around to each area and end up where they started. It would take a long time to circulate just once. Probably an hour at least, and to be thorough, Darian would want to go around at least twice. He looked to Aram, who was standing nearby with Yocelin and already developing a headache from Yocelin's excited chatter. Darian walked over closer to Aram to share his plan. Their conversation was brief. Aram agreed that Darian's strategy was a good one, and they decided to start on opposite sides of the great room. Each pair would work in a serpentine pattern up, down, and across the ballroom in order to cover the most ground. Each pair separated and began the slow progress through the ball.

"Do you need a moment to clear your head before we start sweeping?" Darian asked Eithne quietly as they arrived at his starting point.

Eithne nodded. She already felt very distractd and needed to compose herself to properly reach out with her mind. While they stood by the wall, pretending to observe the people around them, Eithne closed her eyes and took a deep cleansing breath. She allowed herself to clear her mind of all things, letting each noise and smell slip away from her attention. Once all the distractions had been pushed away, Eithne conjured up an image of Anut glowing brightly with the warmth of the sun. Then she imagined him falling apart into hundreds of balls of light and drifting away into the atmosphere. Eithne concentrated on where those balls of light fell and which were closest to her now. She focused on the vibe of them and the type of energy they gave off.

Eithne opened her eyes and nodded at Darian. She was focused and ready now. The pair began to move about the ballroom.

They were a little more than half done with their first circulation, and it had taken slightly longer than Darian had originally estimated as they socialized, snacked, and otherwise behaved like normal party guests. It was pleasant enough, and Eithne certainly seemed to be enjoying herself. People also appeared to be enjoying her company, Darian noticed. Despite that she could be shy at times, she was absolutely charming tonight. Of course, none of the other guests had seen her stubborn, feisty side as Darian had. That side of her was not so charming.

Eithne stopped walking and gave Darian's arm a little tug. He looked down at her. She was staring at an elven man in a blue coat and cream-colored pants. The elf looked to only be a few years older than Darian. He was with an elf woman, probably his wife, by the way they were relating to each other.

"So how am I supposed to get him alone in this crowded place?" Eithne whispered, feeling worried as she suddenly realized how difficult her task was in the setting of a crowded ball.

"I have a thought . . ." Darian's voice trailed off, and he began moving closer to the couple with Eithne on his arm.

"What are you doing?" Eithne whispered back harshly. She was upset that he wasn't sharing his thoughts before implementing them.

"Be quiet. Be sociable, and follow my lead," Darian ordered as they came up to the couple. Eithne swallowed hard as she was forcibly dragged toward the couple. She had a bad feeling that Darian was going to leave her alone.

Darian bowed and introduced himself and Eithne to the couple as well as the other people speaking with them. All were cordial and invited the newcomers to join their conversation. They all talked pleasantly. Eithne noticed very early on that Darian was trying his best to charm the elf man and his wife, and she realized where he was going with his ploy. She also made a special effort to charm the couple. After much effort, Darian and Eithne had managed to enamor themselves to the couple. They laughed at all their jokes and pretended to have more in common than was true. Eithne realized that Darian was not only a great military leader but also quite skilled at social maneuvering. It made her think that he would make a great politician.

"Could I be so bold as to ask your lovely wife for a dance?" Darian requested of her husband. The question brought Eithne back from her musings.

"I don't believe that she would have any objections," the elf replied and smiled at his wife, who accepted Darian's arm to go to the dance floor.

"Lady Eithne, would you do me the honor?" the elf held out his hand to her.

Eithne nodded and curtsied as she took his hand to follow the other two to the dance floor. She smiled to herself as she thought how intelligent Darian's plan was. It had worked like a charm. Now, she simply had to fake a minor injury so that she could sit aside with the elf and use her bracelet to take the piece of Anut. She could feel her body humming with energy and recognition of the same energy in another person. They began to dance, and Eithne was grateful that it was a fast-paced dance. It would be easier to feign twisting her ankle with an upbeat tune. A short bit into the song, her partner tried turning with her, and Eithne found her opportunity. As she spun, she purposefully tripped a little and let out a very pathetically girlish squeak of pretend pain.

"Are you all right, Lady Eithne?" the elf was very much a gentleman.

"I'm simply too clumsy. I'm afraid I may have twisted my ankle," Eithne responded meekly. "Would it be awful of me to ask you to help me leave the dance floor?" She gave him a weak smile and held out her hand to him for help.

Being a proper gentleman, the elf obliged. Eithne couldn't help but to feel like some kind of predator as she manipulated him to do what she wanted so that she could pounce. It made her feel slightly uncomfortable that she enjoyed the sensation of playing a predator as much as she did. The elf took her over to a couple of chairs and sat with her there. Eithne pretended to fuss over her ankle and made small talk about her clumsiness while she tried to concentrate into the power of the bracelet in order to draw out the piece of Anut from him. It felt like very long moments passed before she tapped into the divine energy, but she managed it. Eithne shifted closer to him discretely and closed her eyes as she faced down toward her feet. It felt as though she were physically pulling something out of him very carefully. She felt herself gaining power. Her body was filled with wonderful warmth for a few seconds. It was a very heady experience, one that was perhaps over too quickly. Eithne opened her eyes and saw that the elf gentleman was holding his head and looking pale.

"Are you all right?" Eithne asked, even though she knew exactly what was wrong with him.

She did feel badly about making him feel unwell, but it would pass. Besides, it was so much better than having to kill him.

"I seem to be very tired suddenly. Perhaps I am not well," he replied.

Eithne acted very concerned for him and asked if there was anything that she could do. Of course, there was not, but he appreciated her concern. Soon after, his wife and Darian approached as the dance had ended.

"Are you both all right?" Darian asked when they got close enough to see their discomfort.

Inside, he was pleased to see the elf feeling ill, for it meant that Eithne had been successful. Of course, he did not let on about his true feelings.

"It seems that I am struck with a sudden tiredness. Perhaps I am coming down with something," the gentleman replied.

"Darling, if you do not feel well, we should leave at once," his wife said in a reassuring tone. She was much more concerned with her husband's welfare than social engagements at the ball. "I will call to have our carriage brought around."

She politely thanked Darian for the dance and asked if he and Eithne would be kind enough to stay with her husband while she called on the carriage. They were happy to oblige, and she went off.

Once the elf and his wife were safely on their way home, Darian and Eithne resumed combing the ball for more people who possessed pieces of Anut. They were both elated that the first person had gone so smoothly. They did feel a little badly that the elf had to spend the rest of the evening not feeling very well, but that guilt was alleviated as soon as they thought of the other option for gaining god pieces.

Before the evening was complete, Eithne would be lucky enough to gain a second piece of Anut from a young lady, with whom she was able to steal a private conversation. When the young lady began to feel weak and dizzy, Eithne cleverly suggested that her corset may be too tight and took her outside for some fresh air. All in all, Eithne had a very successful evening and managed not to draw any undue attention to herself. She even got Darian to dance with her twice, which made her very happy, indeed. She found that absorbing the god pieces put her in a sort of euphoric state. It made her feel light on her feet with lots of energy. It was a lovely feeling, and she couldn't stop smiling for a long while.

Yocelin and Aram were not feeling so successful. They had already circulated the ball room one full time and were coming close to completing the second round without locating anyone who possessed a piece of Muntros. Yocelin had already insisted that Aram dance with her once, and he was painfully aware that she would make him dance at least one more time tonight. He was also aware, and annoyed, that she did not seem quite as concerned about their lack of progress as he thought she ought to be. In fact, Yocelin seemed rather pleased with everything going on around her, and Aram wondered if she were concentrating at all. He looked down at the flirtatious she-demon on his arm. Without her horns, she really did look just like an elf with an unusual hair color. Yocelin was chatting up some gentlemen, one of whom seemed simply ancient. Aram was surprised that he could even stand for so long. Aram was not participating in the conversation. He simply stood quietly and let Yocelin do the talking. She was pretending that he was included by acting more familiar with him than she really should be. Whenever one of the gentlemen would address Aram, Yocelin would answer the question for him and continue prattling on and on about whatever the topic was. Truthfully, Aram had no idea what the conversation was even about. He only knew that he had been standing there for some time and wondered when they could get on with going around the ballroom in search of potential god pieces. These social stops seemed to be a ridiculous waste of time.

Aram cleared his throat and gave Yocelin a look to let her know it was time to move on. She ignored him and continued to talk with the gentlemen. It was very annoying. He was about to tell the gentlemen to please excuse them and drag Yocelin away when the ancient one faltered.

"Do you need some help?" Yocelin blurted, apparently very concerned with his health.

"Perhaps so," the old elf feebly replied. "I believe that I have been standing too long." His old eyes scanned the ballroom for empty chairs nearby that he could sit down on.

"Maybe you need some fresh air. Aram and I will be happy to walk out to the courtyard with you. It's too stuffy in here anyway," Yocelin was quick to offer aid and did so with her classic sweet smile.

Aram almost snarled at her. They had already wasted enough time! They didn't need to be taking the time with some old elf who should have probably been dead years ago. Still, he didn't want to make a scene and draw attention to them. Besides, she had already offered to help the ancient one, and he seemed to be very grateful.

The old elf took Aram's arm, and he and Yocelin began walking him out to the courtyard. As they walked, Yocelin daintily cleared her throat and made eye contact with her protector. At first, he gave her an irritated look, but his expression soon changed when he saw her gesture with her eyes toward the old elf. She had spent all that time with him and offered to take him outside as a ploy to get him alone as she sensed a piece of Muntros within him! Aram gave a curt nod to show that he understood and guided the elf to a secluded bench in the courtyard to sit. It was a cold winter evening. It was clear, however, and the stars shown brightly in the night sky. The sharp bite of the cold was actually refreshing when walking out of the hot, cramped ballroom.

"Some cold air feels good in this old chest," the ancient elf said after taking a deep breath. "I don't want to stay out too long, though, just enough to refresh myself."

Aram and Yocelin helped him to sit down on a bench surrounded by trees just off the garden path. They probably didn't need to be so cautious as no one else seemed to be outside tonight. It was too cold for most people to tolerate.

"We won't stay out too long," Yocelin promised as she patted his wrinkled hand. "Just let us know when you're ready to go back inside."

The old elf nodded and smiled at her. He closed his eyes and relaxed by taking some deep breaths.

Yocelin saw her opportunity, and with her hand still resting on his, she began to concentrate on drawing out the piece of Muntros. There was a rush of ice cold through her veins, and she felt as though a force of wind had hit her. She felt it acutely as she drained the old elf of his god piece. The sense of power was intoxicating as she took away the energy. It was almost as if she were stealing away his very life's essence! Yocelin almost savored it, and she didn't like that she enjoyed the sensation so much. Despite being a demon, Yocelin still thought of herself as a sweet person and did not enjoy causing others hardship. She snapped out from her trance and felt the chill leave her body, though being outside in the cold did not help her to feel warm again. The old elf seemed to be asleep, which made sense to her given his age. The strain of taking his god piece probably caused him to black out.

"We have a problem," Aram stated seriously.

Yocelin looked up at him and blinked in confusion. The old elf being unconscious was not that big of a problem.

"He's dead," Aram's statement was blunt.

"No, he's not!" Yocelin was immediately in denial.

"Yes, he is, Yocelin. That piece of Muntros was probably the only thing keeping him alive, and you just took it away," Aram replied calmly yet frankly.

He felt that she needed to accept that she had killed the old elf and move on.

Yocelin placed her hand on the old elf's chest to feel for a heartbeat. There was none. She then put her finger under his nostrils; he was not breathing. Aram was right. He was dead. How could she have done such a thing? Her eyes grew wide with shock and turmoil as she stared at Aram.

"What are we going to do? We can't just leave him here!" Yocelin said, still feeling shock and appalled at herself for killing a nice old elf.

Aram sighed. He was no good at comforting people, which she obviously needed right now, but he was a decent problem solver. So that is what he was going to concentrate on for now. Besides, solving the problem was probably the best way to comfort Yocelin.

"Okay, you're right. We can't just leave him here. He was so old that it plausible that he had a heart attack. We could just be innocent bystanders here," Aram reasoned out loud, and it all sounded logical to him as he said it. He thought a moment more while Yocelin gazed at him, desperately hoping that he would make everything all right. "I know what we are going to do about this."

"What?" Yocelin blurted desperately.

Aram gently helped her up from the bench and began to walk with her back toward the entrance to the ballroom. "We will find a guard, tell him that the old elf wasn't feeling well, so we brought him outside for some fresh air. While sitting outside, he seemed to fall asleep and died. We can speculate that it was a heart attack."

Yocelin blinked up at him as she processed his plan. It was brilliant! Not only was it mostly true, but it also made them seem more credible since they would report the old elf's death themselves.

"You're such a great protector," she said, her voice full of warmth, and hugged onto his arm. "I can see why we were meant for each other."

Aram stopped in his tracks and stiffened. What did she mean by that statement? He wasn't sure, all of a sudden, if he liked the level of familiarity that Yocelin had with him. He turned his head sharply and gave her a look of confusion.

Yocelin immediately recognized his stress response to her statement and was sorry she said it. Her words had come out all wrong.

"I meant professionally, you dope," she teased. "Now let's take care of this dead body situation."

Aram knitted his brow at her and shook his head. How could anyone change their mood so quickly? She just went from vey upset, to relieved, to affectionate, and now flippant—all within just a couple of minutes! He didn't know how to react to her most of the time, but he supposed that he wasn't the only one. Yocelin was very strange. Anyway, there were much more important matters at hand other than her fluctuating emotions. He continued walking back to the entrance of the ballroom.

There was a guard standing and looking very bored and cold once they got to the entrance. Aram told the guard the story about the possible heart attack as discreetly as possible. He was sure to mention that he didn't know what else to do and acted as shocked as possible. Yocelin, of course, played her part beautifully as well. The guard bought the act easily and said that he would tell the proper authorities after they showed him the body. The old elf looked so peaceful on the bench that the guard had no reason to suspect foul play. It was a shame, though, as the guard recognized the old elf as King Reimus's great-uncle Aeil. The death of a member of the royal family would not be taken lightly. However, Aeil was so old that it wouldn't be a surprise to anyone. The guard told Aram and Yocelin to go back to the ball and thanked them for notifying him. He did not tell them who the old elf was and thought it best that they did not have any further involvement. The pair obliged gratefully and returned to the ball.

As Yocelin and Aram exited the gardens and went back inside, they were so consumed by relief that they did not notice the servant hiding among the trees. He now felt that he finally had the proof he needed to expose these strangers. The servant crept from the trees over to where the guard stood, trying to figure out how to best handle the situation. He practically shivered with anticipation as he thought about how his clever spying had probably saved King Reimus's life. The king was most certainly their main target, and it could have been a coincidence that they had just killed a member of the royal family. Also, the pair of tribal elves seemed to have brought on sudden illness to one of the other guests at the ball earlier this evening. Whatever their plan was, the loyal servant was certain that it was not a positive one for the king or the City of Lupia.

"Lord Aeil did not die of a failed heart. They did something to him," the servant announced quietly to the guard as he approached.

The young guard was taken by surprise, not only by the sudden presence of another person, but also by his claim. "What do you mean?"

The guard did recognize the servant. He was called Rane and had been working at the palace practically from birth since both of his parents were servants at the castle as well. Rane was well trusted by the royal family and was known for being well intentioned in his actions.

"I've been paying some extra attention to the king's strange guests because I suspected them of plotting against the king. I swear to you that the purple-haired woman did something to Lord Aeil, and he died because of it," Rane stated.

"It doesn't look as though any violence was done to Lord Aeil," the guard answered skeptically as he surveyed the lord's peaceful body. There wasn't a mark on him.

"She did not hurt him violently," Rane responded almost in a whisper as he took an eager step closer. "It was some sort of witch-craft! She touched him and concentrated hard. Then the jewel on her bracelet glowed with a strange light, and she seemed to receive some sort of energy as Lord Aeil took his last breath."

"A witch?" the guard was flabbergasted and frightened by the notion. Such people were not often heard of these days, which made it all the more upsetting when one was identified.

"I also suspect the other two guests. I saw one man, who a moment before, was the picture of health, fall immediately ill when in the presence of the red-haired tribal elf. She even seemed to have the same strategy as Lord Aeil's murderer. She sat close enough to touch him, concentrated, and appeared to gain some sort of energy as the man fell ill. Perhaps she would have killed him if she weren't in a crowded place. I tell you, neither of them should be trusted. I fear that they mean to harm the king. They have already disposed of one member of the royal family. They must be stopped before they cause any further damage," Rane's voice was powerful and confident as he made his accusations. He felt almost as though he were a divine messenger.

The guard looked back at him, feeling rather moved by his speech. There was still a nagging doubt in the back of the guard's mind. Why would they have reported Lord Aeil's death if it really was murder? Then again, that was also one of the best ways to take suspicion away from themselves. The guard made eye contact with Rane and saw the absolute conviction in his eyes. Rane had never been one for wild stories, nor had he ever vied for attention as some do. The guard found that he believed the servant completely.

The guard nodded resolutely after a moment of thought. "Let's go talk to my captain."

Rane smiled in smug triumph and went with the guard. Those vicious murderers would not reach King Reimus.

CHAPTER TWENTY-THREE

*L*ONG AFTER THE ball had ended, all had gone to their beds and slept soundly. The night was sharply cold and peaceful—almost too calm, as if there were some disturbance to come.

Darian bolted upright from a deep sleep as Aram rushed into his room and woke him. Darian did not know what was going on, but he gripped the hilt of his sword that leaned against the wall next to his bed.

"We must leave immediately," Aram whispered urgently. "Get on your boots and your sword. Retrieve Eithne from her room, and meet me in the stables in fifteen minutes. There is no time to explain."

Darian saw in Aram's eyes that the situation was truly as urgent as he projected. Darian simply gave a curt nod of understanding to Aram and swiftly got dressed quickly and buckled on his weapons. There was no time to gather all his belongings. He could only take what was still in his travel pack as he left.

Aram left as quickly as he had come in once Darian nodded at him. Aram headed straight for Yocelin's room. He was thankful for his incredible hearing, for he never would have heard the guards talking if he did not possess the extraordinary sense. He was also thankful that he was not able to sleep after the ball. Aram had felt tired, but something in the back of his mind kept him awake. The events of the evening bothered him. He had gone out of the balcony to get some fresh air and clear his head. Below his balcony, speaking in low whispers, were a group of guards. A normal elf would not have been able to discern what they were saying, but Aram heard them as if he were standing there among them. What he heard caused him to fly into action. The guards said that the murder of Lord Aeil had been witnessed by a trusted servant and that there was other foul play suspected at the ball. The four strange guests of King Reimus were to be arrested at once for murder and suspicion of witchcraft. They planned to take them all from their beds as they slept so that they would be caught completely by surprise and have no opportunity to work their magic on them. Aram knew that the guards planned to set their plan into action within the hour, so it was imperative to get out of Lupia before they even started looking for them in their rooms.

Aram arrived at Yocelin's room and slipped in soundlessly. Yocelin slept and did not stir. He grabbed her boots, put them beside the bed, as well as her sword and winter cloak. He then leaned over and gently shook her shoulder. She opened her deep-blue eyes and gave him a groggy look, which quickly changed to alert when she comprehended his expression.

"What's going on?" she asked as she sat up.

"I'll explain later, for now we must get out of here as soon as possible," as he spoke, he guided her to put on her boots and cloak then handed her sword and pack to her.

Yocelin went along with his movements easily. Her mind flooded with questions, but now was not the time, and she trusted him. He would tell her what she needed to know once they were out of whatever great trouble this was.

Aram was already halfway out the door, making sure the coast was clear to leave. He then looked back at Yocelin and gestured that she should stay close to him, which she hurriedly did as they slipped out into the hallway. Everything was dark and still, and they swiftly and silently fled down the hall to the stairwell. Aram was acting cautiously but also with great speed. Whatever the trouble was, it was apparent that they needed to get out of the palace unseen. The thought of leaving the palace made Yocelin frown. Her overly pampered dream would end sooner than she expected. It was a sad thought. She suddenly realized that they were on their way to the exit and did not have their friends with them!

"Wait!" Yocelin called out in an anxious whisper. "What about Eithne and Darian?" She stood rooted to her spot. Yocelin cared too much about her friend to leave them behind.

Aram had such forward momentum going that he had to return a few steps to Yocelin. "They are meeting us at the stables. Now come along." He took her by the wrist and continued guiding her through the palace. He did want any further interruptions while they were making such good progress.

Yocelin nodded and continued with him. She trusted him as well as Darian and Eithne to get themselves to the meeting place. They made it to the ground floor without incident. They only had to dodge a few guards by ducking into nearby corridors. Luckily, most of the guards were assembling to go upstairs to surprise them at this time and did not suspect that they would be wandering about the palace. The hardest part of the journey came when they had to cross the palace grounds and get to the stables. They would be in the open and at their most vulnerable while crossing the grounds. Aram hugged the exterior wall of the palace with his arm out across Yocelin's midriff to be sure she did the same, though there was no need for the extra coaching. Aram scanned the stretch of ground from where they stood to the stables. There were no guards on the ground, but there were sentries on the walls above. Aram only hoped that their eyes would be focusing elsewhere when they crossed. An icy breeze blew past them, and Aram knew that it was now or never. He gripped Yocelin's hand tightly and took off at the fastest sprint Yocelin had ever felt! She stumbled as he jerked her away from the wall but got her feet under her efficiently enough to keep from being dragged. The rush of air on her face was such that her cheeks burned with cold and her eyes watered. It almost made her want to close her eyes, but they were nearly there. The brief obsession of making it to the stables without being seen distracted her from the biting chill, even though Yocelin only wore her winter cloak over her nightgown. Her adrenaline was pumping too hard for her to notice.

Darian was less subtle than Aram when he entered Eithne's room. He moved silently but immediately shook her awake. When her eyes burst open to find Darian's face right in front of her, Eithne's reaction was to open her mouth and ask what was going on. However, Darian was quick to put a finger to her lips to silence her.

"Get on your cloak and boots, and grab your pack. We have to leave now. Be silent," he ordered her in a calm voice.

His tone was meant to keep her from feeling alarmed, but Eithne's heart pumped faster as she sensed danger. She did not allow it to control her, though. Darian could see the urgent emotion on her face, so he was grateful when she simply nodded and began following his instructions. He admired that she could be so upset yet function properly at the same time. Eithne was the type to simply do what needed doing, even when it frightened her. Eithne was ready to leave inside of a minute. Darian was already checking to be sure that the hallway was empty of anyone else.

"Let's go," Darian whispered, and he left the room. Eithne followed, almost on top of him.

They followed the same path that Aram and Yocelin had taken moments before. They too made it through the palace without incident. As they ran across the open patch of ground to get to the stables, it looked as though they would get away without being seen. Just before running inside the open double doors of the stables, however, Eithne felt a terrible chill course through her body when she thought she heard a guard from above shout.

Darian heard that guard shout as well. They had been spotted entering the stables, and someone would be here shortly to investigate. He quickly surveyed the dark stable for a good place to hide. Without warning, he shoved Eithne into the best spot he could see on such short notice. Darian pushed her down into a small space between the stack of hay bales and the wall. Luckily, there was a pile of loose hay to fall onto as Darian simply went down on top of her and hurriedly threw some of the loose hay over both of them. He did not have the time to find separate hiding places for each of them.

Eithne lay stiff and quiet beneath him, but her heart beat so fast that she feared it would burst from her chest! She was not expecting this situation to arise! It was almost completely black around them except for a shaft of light that fell across Darian's eyes. He was not looking at her but had his head up and alert, looking toward the entrance. Eithne began to breathe harder. Having a man on top of her felt like a very compromising position. It wasn't right that Darian was making her feel this way. Her body was responding with feelings that she had not felt before, and her feminine instincts were telling her to get away from him. The internal conflict caused her to shift uncomfortably and let out a meek whispering plea to Darian. His eyes darted and met hers intensely. He wanted her to be still and quiet. It was obvious that he was not thinking of this position in the same way as she.

Just then, they heard a small group of guards enter the stables. Eithne held her breath to keep from making noise. Given all the emotions she was feeling, she didn't know how else to stay quiet.

"You're sure you saw two people run in here?" one of the guards asked gruffly.

"Yes, sir, two figures," another replied.

"Well, let's have a look then," the gruff one ordered.

The group then began searching about the stables. They opened stall doors and poked around halfheartedly. They did not search long, but it felt like she longest moments of Eithne's life. When they poked at the hay bales that she and Darian were concealed behind, Eithne squeezed her eyes shut and silently prayed that they would go away. Thankfully, they did, and the guards reassembled.

"No one found, sir, and all the horses are present and accounted for," one of them reported.

"Probably just some delinquents running around after the ball. No doubt they've moved on by now," said the leader. "Come on. We have more important things to do tonight than chasing after reckless drunks."

The guards all left. Eithne could hear their heavy footsteps getting farther and farther way as they marched across the yard back to the palace. She allowed herself to slowly exhale when she felt certain they could no longer hear her. She felt herself relax from the tension and then promptly became tense again when she realized that Darian still lay on top of her. He seemed to be waiting to make sure that it was safe to move.

"Darian, please," Eithne pleaded quietly as she looked up at him.

He locked eyes with her again, and his eyebrows shot up. He swiftly moved off of her when he realized why she was so anxious and uncomfortable. Darian mumbled an apology as he helped her up from the hay. He was suddenly finding it to be very difficult to forget what she felt like beneath him.

"Are we supposed to meet Yocelin and Aram here?" Eithne asked as she pulled her cloak tighter around herself.

Darian nodded. He scanned the stables for their friends. He assumed that they would have gotten here first, and he knew that the guards had not found anyone during their search. Not seeing them made Darian concerned that they had been elsewhere delayed or even caught.

"You can stop worrying, Captain. We're all here," Yocelin chimed as she and Aram stepped out from the tack room.

Eithne embraced her friend gratefully. Darian and Aram simply nodded at each other.

"So what now?" Eithne asked. She and Yocelin were still completely uninformed on the present situation.

"We are leaving Lupia tonight," Aram announced. "We need to find the fastest and best way out of the palace. With the four bridges and the guards, it won't be easy." Aram looked to Darian for strategic aid. As the best military mind among them, he ought to have some helpful input.

Darian was already in the process of considering the different avenues to escape. He looked at the horses in the stalls around them. It would be nice to have a couple of them, but it would also make it much harder to escape without being seen. They may have to forego that particular luxury. It wasn't worth the risk. He continued to think for a few more minutes. He devised a simple plan that he hoped would yield minimum risk. The others patiently let Darian think. Eithne and Yocelin huddled together as they had never broken their initial embrace. It was too cold not to take advantage of the body heat.

"We will leave from the east side of the palace, as it is the least guarded. The moat will hopefully be frozen enough for us to simply walk on it, and I think it will be, given these freezing temperatures. There is no need for us to trouble ourselves with the iron gates or possibly being spotted on the bridge. Are you all okay with climbing the rocks in and out of the moat?" Darian looked to his friends to seek approval of his plan. He was thankful when they all nodded their accord.

Aram went to check to see if it was safe to leave the stables. Since they would be exiting by the east side of the palace, they would not have to cross the stretch of exposed ground again. That was a very positive point in the plan. Now they could just hug the outside wall of the stables and palace until they made it to the east bridge where they would climb down to the moat and cross. Hopefully, they would be able to do all this without further incident. It seemed safe, so it was time to leave. Aram still felt a strong sense of urgency. The guards would be assembling, or already be assembled, to go capture them from their rooms. There was little time until they were discovered missing.

Darian was in the lead; the girls were in the middle, and Aram came up the rear. They all moved quietly and swiftly along the wall to the east bridge. Darian climbed down first to test the ice and make sure it was solid enough to support their weight. He breathed a deep sign of relief when it held firmly beneath him. He then helped Eithne and Yocelin down and got them moving across the icy surface. He made sure they stayed under the bridge so that there would be less chance of being spotted. Aram was the last to come down and cross the moat. They all made it to the other side without incident, excepting their feet slipping here and there. As they were climbing the rocks out of the moat, it began to snow. The puffy white flakes drifted down lightly at first but soon became thick and heavy. This was good and bad. On one hand, the snowfall made it harder for the guards to see them. On the other hand, it made climbing out of the moat even more difficult. The rocks were already covered with a thin layer of ice. They were extremely cold and slick. None of the companions wore gloves, and their hands were going painfully numb as they tried to grip the rocks. It was taking a dreadfully long time to climb out, too long.

Uproar was heard in the palace, and an alarm sounded. They had been discovered missing, and they weren't off the palace grounds yet! Aram would not delay any longer. There was a way that climbing the rocks would become much easier for him. He held fast to his position as he concentrated on the change. He felt the hair sprout from his body, felt the beast within become more apparent. He was careful not to change entirely, for he still may need to speak clearly to his friends. What Aram really wanted were the claws. He had instant traction once he had changed halfway and was able to almost bounce up the rocks to safety. Now, he could help the others.

Yocelin, who had seen his change once before, was the only one who did not falter at the sight of him. Eithne's eyes became as huge as saucers, and she felt her heart seized with innate fear at seeing Aram as a monster. She knew what he was, but she could not help her reaction. It was all she could do not to cry out when he came to her and dragged her up the rocks. Eithne shut her eyes tightly and just kept telling herself that she could trust him. Aram got Eithne to the top as fast as he could and went back for Yocelin. He did not blame Eithne for her reaction. In fact, she took seeing him like this rather well, considering the circumstances. After helping Yocelin, Aram got Darian, who seemed hesitant but accepted his aid nonetheless. Darian was also taken aback by his seeing his friend in such a state. His form was still humanoid, but his features were no longer delicately handsome. Aram seemed half wolf, half elf, and it was a very unnatural countenance.

Once all were safely out of the moat, Aram reverted to his full elf form, and the four of them broke into a run. They could walk once they were out of the city and under the cover of the forest. As they ran, the alarm at the palace became more distant and gave them all a great sense of comfort that they would not be captured. The heavy snowfall helped in covering their tracks so that it would not know which way they ran.

Eithne did her best to keep pace with her friends but was finding herself faltering as she went. She was very hot as if she were burning up from the inside, and her vision blurred. The effect on her physical performance was awful, and she hated feeling so weak. Eithne didn't realize that she was falling, nor was she conscious of Darian lifting and carrying her the rest of the way out of the city. She was too feverish.

Darian was very concerned for Eithne, but he could not stop running until they were certain that they could be safe. Her cheeks were flushed with fever. She felt so light in his arms. He gripped her tighter to him. They would need to find or make some kind of shelter and soon. Darian very much wanted to tend to her as soon as possible.

They ran deeper and deeper into the forest, taking a sort of zigzag pattern as they went so they would be harder to track. None of them knew exactly where they were going, and it didn't really matter so long as they were headed away from Lupia. The forest was rumored to be full of outlaws, but none of the companions believed that they needed to be concerned about that on a night such as this. Anyone who didn't need to be out tonight would be safely huddled by a fire.

They must have been running for almost an hour when they finally slowed to a walk. They were now completely safe from being caught, and no one would be able to track them at this point. Their tracks were covered by the snow, and they were deep the forest, off of the main trail. It was time to find some shelter and get some rest.

"Okay, so I would love an explanation for all of that fleeing now," Yocelin said promptly and breathlessly after they started walking.

"Someone saw you accidentally kill the old elf during the ball," Aram explained. "Unfortunately, he was a member of the royal family, and they thought that you were a witch with an agenda against the royal family. It was assumed that we were all witches, so they planned to barge into our rooms and arrest us while we slept. That is why we needed to run."

"You killed an old man?" Darian was hearing all this for the first time and was understandably surprised. In fact, his tone sounded rather more accusatory than he meant it.

"I didn't mean to!" Yocelin blurted defensively. "I was concentrating on taking the piece of Muntros, and he was just really, really old! Once I took that bit of energy from him, he just died. I feel just horrible about it. Even more so now that I know he was a member of the royal family."

Darian realized that he must have sounded as though he were accusing her of killing the old elf on purpose. He nodded to her to show that he understood and accepted her reasoning. He did not mean any offense. Then he turned his attention to Aram.

"How did you know that they planned to arrest us tonight?"

"I was awake, standing on my balcony, and I overheard some of the guards talking about it. I came and got you immediately after that," Aram responded as he walked. He was very aware of the need to find a place to settle in for the night.

"Lucky you were awake." Yocelin came up next to Aram and invaded his personal space more than he would have liked. "I'm very glad not to be in the dungeon right now." She smiled up at him thankfully.

"I am glad of that happenstance as well," Darian echoed Yocelin.

He looked to Eithne in his arms. She was unconscious and breathing much harder than she ought to be. He needed to get her out of the snow and warm. He couldn't understand why she had suddenly fallen ill. Perhaps she had not been feeling well for a while and had chosen not to mention it to anyone. Either way, it was obvious that she was quite sick now.

They all walked in silence for a while. All were focused on finding a place to stay for the night. Yocelin remained very close to Aram as they walked, which annoyed him mildly. He would subtly move away from her, and she would simply close the distance again. He supposed that she was only trying to share body heat because she was cold, but the physical closeness made him somewhat uncomfortable—especially given Tim's warning to he and Darian. Ever since then, Aram could not help but to notice Yocelin's more positive qualities, both physically and of her character. He found that he now noticed a great many positive qualities on both counts. He had also discovered that his annoyance toward her stemmed more from his own feelings rather than her actions.

"Look there!" Yocelin suddenly exclaimed and bounced a little as she gestured toward what looked like a small structure. It was covered with snow, and it was hard to tell how useful it would be, but it inspired them all to hope and pick up their pace as they moved closer.

They approached the little shack with caution as there may be outlaws occupying the place, but there was no telltale curl of smoke emanating from the structure. Also, neither Aram not Yocelin sensed the presence of anyone else. It was deserted. They entered gratefully into the small, one-room structure. There was not much space, just barely enough for the four of them to lie down and sleep around a fire. Aram set to work on the fire while Darian began tending to Eithne. As they had left in a rush, they did not have all their belongings and were short on bedrolls, though Eithne's pack did contain a blanket. Darian laid out one of the two bedrolls they did have and laid Eithne on it with the blanket over her. Her skin was hot to the touch and flushed with fever. She needed water and perhaps some sort of herbal remedy, but Eithne was the one in their group who knew of such things. Neither Darian nor the others had any idea if the small supply of herbal medicines in Eithne's pack would be of any use at all.

Darian gave her water and kept her warm for the rest of the night. Yocelin, who was also very anxious over Eithne's welfare, tried to help as well, but it was a one-person job, and she could see that Darian was intent on tending to her. Yocelin resigned herself to fetching things when asked. Besides, Eithne seemed to be doing well enough under Darian's care.

Aram tried to encourage Yocelin to get some rest by offering her the remaining bedroll, and she did try to sleep, but to no avail. The mad dash of an escape had made her too tense, and her mind was too active to sleep now. Anyway, they probably wouldn't be moving Eithne for a day, and Yocelin did not foresee any strenuous activities happening tomorrow.

"Let's play a card game," Yocelin suggested hopefully to Aram while they shivered by the fire.

The fire offered much-needed warmth, but it was small, and it was very cold outside. The poor little flame couldn't properly combat the winter chill—not to mention that Yocelin was not of the benefit of being fully dressed beneath her cloak. Thinking back, she wished that she had grabbed some extra clothing to put on later when they fled the palace.

"I don't think we have the cards," Aram responded evenly. He was staring into the fire. His mind was elsewhere.

Yocelin wanted to be sure of his statement, so she went through their now-meager possessions to be sure. When she found that Aram was correct, she let out a heavy sigh and sat back down next to him. She decided to try staring into the fire for a while herself. She let her eyes relax as she gazed at the flames and let her mind drift away.

Aram shifted uncomfortably when Yocelin sat too close to him. Her shoulder grazed his, and if either one of them moved at all, they would definitely touch. He scooted away from her a little, and she didn't seem to notice.

As Yocelin stared at the fire, her thoughts drifted to that night on the *Leviathan* when she had her first vision of Cavan. She shivered again as his soulless laughter filled her mind. He was chasing her still. Cavan would not stop coming for her until either she or he was dead. Knowing such a powerfully evil man existed in this world was bad enough; that he was coming after her personally was terrifying beyond explanation. Yocelin squeezed her eyes shut and shook her head. She didn't want to think about Cavan. It was too stressful.

"What are you thinking about?" Yocelin asked Aram. She needed to be distracted from her own dark thoughts.

"You don't need to be concerned with my thoughts," he answered in his classically blunt fashion.

"Oh! That means it's interesting! Please, won't you share with me?" Yocelin tipped herself to the side and bumped shoulders with him while giving him a pleading look.

Aram sighed. He supposed that she was just bored but didn't wish to divulge his exact thoughts with her. This was mainly because they were about her, so he opted for a different subject.

"What do you think about Eithne's fever? Do you think it will break soon?" he asked the question quietly in an attempt to be polite.

Darian glanced over when he heard them taking of it but said nothing. There was no privacy in the tiny shack.

"I don't know much about fevers. I've never really been sick. I suppose it's a demon thing to be healthy all the time. I hope it breaks soon, though," Yocelin responded in a low whisper.

"I don't know much either. I haven't been sick since before I was bitten. Even then, all I recall is staying in bed and my mother forcing me to drink a special kind of broth that tasted awful, but it was supposed to help be get better," Aram told his story absentmindedly. His eyes had drifted back to the fire.

Yocelin smiled as Aram shared his memory with her. It made her happy that he felt that he could talk about those things around her. For another person, it might have seemed like nothing, but for Aram, such glimpses into his personal life meant that he trusted her.

"So what do you think would have happened to us if we were caught tonight?" Yocelin asked.

"Nothing good," Aram answered matter-of-factly.

Yocelin sighed inwardly and rolled her eyes. He was being closed to conversation again. "Where do we go next?"

Aram shrugged. "Once Eithne is all right to travel, we will have to find the closest town that that we can restock on supplies and figure out exactly where we are. I guess we should just head for the most populated areas from there so the two of you can continue to collect god pieces."

"Or maybe just wherever Eithne and I feel the most drawn to? Tim said we should be able to sense the best direction," Yocelin said. "Restocking our supplies sounds good too. I could definitely use some decent winter clothing."

At the mention of clothing, Aram's eyes drifted over Yocelin's cloaked form that still leaned against him. He had almost forgotten that she only wore a thin nightdress and boots beneath her cloak.

It made him more understanding of her need to share body heat. It also made him feel uncomfortable again. He tried his best to push thoughts of Yocelin's curvaceous, scantily clad form and how close she was to him out of his mind. He changed the subject back to Eithne's health, and they continued to idly talk until dawn.

CHAPTER TWENTY-FOUR

*E*ITHNE'S FEVER BROKE just before dawn. Her eyes fluttered open as if waking from a bad dream. She saw Darian hovering over her. His expression was of great relief, and he gazed down at her softly. She smiled back up at him weakly.

"How long have I been out?" Eithne asked and tried to sit up.

Darian gently pressed down on her shoulder to keep her from getting up. It was too soon for that, and it would make her dizzy.

"You fainted while we fled the palace and were feverish the rest of the night. It is just now morning." Darian held the water skin to her lips, and she took it in her hands and drank deeply. She was so parched.

"You're awake!" Yocelin exclaimed excitedly and scrambled to her friend's side. She was elated that the fever had broken. She knew that fevers could be dangerous and was glad to see her friend out of danger. Yocelin clutched Eithne's hand and grinned at her. "How are you feeling?"

Yocelin's beaming grin made Eithne feel better just to know how much she cared. "Well, I'm aware of my surroundings now and not sweating so much." Eithne was suddenly distracted by her new surroundings. "Where are we?"

"In an abandoned shack in the forest," Darian answered.

"We were so lucky to find it. The snow was coming down so hard. It must be used by outlaws sometimes," Yocelin said, perhaps a little too fast. She was excited.

"Where's Aram?" Eithne was suddenly worried that one of them didn't make it.

"He's out looking for some breakfast. He'll be back soon," Yocelin assured promptly. "Just try to relax. Are you hungry?"

"Starved," Eithne answered.

Darian grinned at her reply. He was happy to know that she had a good appetite.

Aram returned a short while later with three squirrels in tow. It wasn't much, but hunting after a heavy snowfall was always more difficult. He too was happy to see Eithne awake and feeling better. Yocelin took half of one of the squirrels raw, and Aram set to skinning and cooking the rest over the fire. There was not as much meat on them as he would have liked, but they would do. The squirrels did not take long to cook on the positive side of things, so the companions could eat sooner. Yocelin politely waited for the other squirrels to be ready before eating her raw portion. Darian thought her habit of eating raw meat to be disgusting, but she was a demon after all. It was just easy to forget since Yocelin had been raised by elves, and so she acted in accordance with elvish behaviors. Eithne ate a few small bites of squirrel meat but mostly just wanted more water. Even though she had felt very hungry before, she found that her stomach filled quickly. Eithne knew that she would be ready to eat again sooner than the others, though.

"Do you feel better now?" Darian asked after Eithne had eaten and drank her fill.

Yocelin was back sitting with Aram. It seemed that, as usual, she was trying to get him to reveal something. Aram, of course, was trying very hard not to do so. He already knew that Yocelin was someone that he could trust, but revealing things to her would spoil the fun of the game.

Eithne looked at them for a moment then smiled back at Darian. "Yes, I feel much better, thank you. Do you think that they both understand that they're sort of flirting?" she whispered slyly.

Darian raised his eyebrows at her then looked at Aram and Yocelin. He supposed that they were flirting a little bit. Of course, Yocelin always seemed to be flirting when she talked with people, even Eithne. Darian did take note, however, that Aram might be returning the behavior in his own way. Usually, Darian wouldn't have cared for such a conversation, but he wanted to humor Eithne in her current state.

"I think Yocelin knows exactly what she is doing, and Aram is unaware of himself in this way, or at least he doesn't want to be," Darian replied analytically. He leaned into Eithne and spoke in a very low whisper.

"I think they look good together," Eithne stated. "Wouldn't it be lovely if they ended up together?" She whispered the last bit wistfully as she watched Aram and Yocelin carry on.

Darian recalled the wizard's warning to him and Aram. To think of it brought him down a bit, and he decided to clear his head of Tim for now. He gave Eithne a noncommittal shrug as an answer to her pondering.

Eithne rolled her eyes at him. She should have known better than to try and carry on such a girlish conversation with him. She let out a low sigh.

"I'm tired of sleeping, but I don't feel well enough for much else. So we need to keep talking." Eithne gave him an expectant look.

Darian was bemused by her behavior. She was still her feisty, slightly bossy self even when she was ill.

"Are you ordering me around? You know you wouldn't be in this nice, warm shack of safety if it weren't for me."

Eithne pouted and snuggled deeper into her bedroll. "Be nice to me. I'm sick."

Darian smiled at her and sighed. Somehow, it felt like she had won a small victory. "What do you want to talk about?"

He was rewarded with a pleased look from Eithne and a less girlish topic of conversation.

Most of the morning and early afternoon blurred together. Eithne went back and forth between sleeping and talking. It was a very quiet and fluid-feeling part of the day. Eithne learned of why they had to escape from Lupia in the middle of the night, and both she and Darian heard more from Yocelin and Aram about what had happened to the old elf.

Evening came upon them before any of them realized how much time had passed. Eithne decided that Darian should be the one to go find them some dinner, and he was hesitant to leave her side, but she insisted. Yocelin was more than happy to look after her friend in his place, and Eithne felt that she was keeping Darian cooped up in the shack. She wanted him to be able to get out of the cramped space for a little while. Darian was not gone for long and returned with the same sort of game as Aram. At least it was fresh, and they were able to hunt at all with several feet of snow covering the ground. It was no longer snowing actively, but the temperatures remained cold, and the two or more feet that had fallen were not melting away anytime soon.

After dinner, Eithne was still feeling unwell and couldn't really rest. Perhaps she just couldn't make herself sleep anymore, though she did try.

"I've come to a decision," Eithne announced to Darian, who was slightly perplexed at her statement. "You're going to say nice things to me to help me feel better and keep me entertained."

Darian blinked back at her. Then he glanced at Yocelin for help to find that she was busy prodding Aram for information again, which probably put Aram in about the same amount of emotional pain as Darian was currently feeling.

"They are not going to help you out of this," Eithne stated firmly. "Come on, you can lie if you want, but just make it believable."

Darian rolled his eyes. He supposed telling Eithne nice things was not the worst thing that could happen. Besides, she wasn't going to let it go, and he already knew what it was like to argue with her.

"I'm sure I won't have to lie in order to say nice things about you," Darian started. "Let's see . . . You are very good at demanding things from people."

Eithne chuckled at his comment and gestured for him to keep talking. Maybe this would make her headache go away.

Darian was encouraged by her chuckle. "You're actually a very talented fighter, just unpolished. With more practice, you may even give me a challenge."

"You're saying that I couldn't do that now?"

"No. No, you could not, particularly in your current condition. You have to remember that I'm still the captain of the guard," he answered with some comical finesse.

"Are you?" Eithne's question was honest. It suddenly occurred to her that they had been gone an awfully long time without contacting anyone back home. Did people think that they were dead? Did they still hold their places in Aranni society?

"I most certainly am," Darian confirmed with pride. "There is currently an interim captain of the guard taking care of things. You see, it's protocol that the current captain isn't presumed dead unless he's been gone for at least one year with no word." Darian was thoughtful for a moment. "I should send another letter at the next town we come to."

"My family probably thinks that I'm dead," Eithne said quietly. It made her sad to think about them. They loved her, and she just ran away without any real explanation.

"I'm sure they don't. Actually, I know they don't," Darian responded.

Eithne stared at him with wide eyes.

"I sent them a letter from Tomak explaining that you were with our party, and another letter from Duomo just two weeks ago. Also, I'm sure that Proithen told everyone in the village what happened at the caves and that you were still alive then. Your family knows that you are alive and with me, Eithne."

"Oh." She wasn't sure whether to feel relieved or annoyed.

At the time he had sent the letter, the last thing she would have wanted Darian to do was to notify her family of her whereabouts, though it did make her feel better now to know that they didn't think she was dead.

"A simple 'thank you' will suffice," Darian interrupted her thoughts. He could tell hat she was debating how to feel about his meddling.

Eithne smiled at him. "Thank you. So were they primarily letters for Rosalin?"

"Why?" Darian failed to see how that mattered one way or the other, nor was it any of her business.

The letters were not personally meant for Rosalin but had been addressed to her entire family. Come to think of it, Darian wondered if he were expected to be writing Rosalin letters since he had expressed an intention to court her for marriage. He sincerely doubted that Rosalin was waiting for him, and he did not find that idea at all bothersome. That all seemed so distant from him now.

Eithne shrugged. "I guess I'm just curious to know, though why wouldn't you be writing letters to Rosalin? After all, she is my practically perfect and far-more-lovely-than-I big sister."

Though Eithne dearly loved her older sister, she always had harbored some jealousy toward her. It was difficult to always stand in the shadow of someone so brilliant even if they were equally brilliant and kind to you.

"That's not true," Darian was quick to say with sure conviction, as if he were defending Eithne against herself. "I never thought that Rosalin was more beautiful than you. I've actually always seen you as the prettier one."

The words tumbled out of his mouth before he could stop himself from voicing them. Darian meant what he said, but Eithne did not need to know that about him. He clamped his mouth shut and looked away awkwardly.

At first, Eithne was caught off guard by his statement. He certainly sounded sincere, but it didn't seem to fit in her mind. Rosalin was the prettier sister. That's what everyone in the village said. Darian wanted to marry Rosalin, so he should definitely be of the same opinion as the rest of the village. He wasn't making any sense. Then Eithne understood.

"I appreciate you trying so hard to say nice things to me in order to make me feel better. I think that I do feel much better, actually. Anyway, I told you that you could lie so long as it was nice," Eithne rationalized as she snuggled down into her bedroll. She was feeling sleepy again.

Darian blinked in confusion. What had just happened? Eithne thought that he was simply humoring her? Well, he wasn't. He opened his mouth to correct her and let her know that it was not a lie but shut it quickly. He could see that she was starting to drift off to sleep again. Besides, she had just inadvertently saved him some degree of embarrassment. Why should he bother to correct her?

CHAPTER TWENTY-FIVE

*T*HE SUN HAD set a short time ago when there was a knock at the door of the little shack. The three companions inside that were awake started at the sound as they all looked to each other quizzically. Who could possibly be knocking? Furthermore, who would bother to knock at the door of a small, broken shack in the middle of the forest?

The knocking came again.

Yocelin shrugged at Aram and Darian as she got up to answer it. Aram quickly grabbed her arm and silently communicated that he would answer the door. She rolled her eyes at him but secretly appreciated his chivalry. Aram cautiously opened the door to find an elf man standing there with a broad smile.

"Good evening, fellow traveler," the elf man greeted warmly. "I was passing through and hoped that I could share your shelter for the night? My name is Giev."

Aram regarded Giev. He had white-blonde hair and deep-set green eyes. He was roughly average height and build for an elf and carried a sword under his cloak, though he did not look like a mercenary. He also had a way about him that made him appear very genuine. Perhaps it was because he truly was, or perhaps it was a well-practiced act. Aram wasn't sure what to make of him yet.

"Are you an outlaw?" Aram questioned bluntly.

"Me? No, I've never been in trouble with the law, unlike most people residing in these woods. I'm more of a drifter." Giev cocked his head to the side in confusion. "Aren't you outlaws? I just assumed with you staying in this place and all."

Aram hadn't really thought about it, but he supposed that they were outlaws now—at least as far as the guards in Lupia were concerned.

"You're the gutsy type, aren't you?" Yocelin squeezed her way into the doorway, forcing the door to open wider before Aram had the chance to object.

"Well, hello there!" Giev grinned broadly at the sight of such a pretty creature. She looked like she had a good amount of sass about her, and Giev liked that. "What's a gorgeous girl like you doing all the way out here?"

"Maybe if I get to know you better, I'll tell you," Yocelin flirted back with a wink.

Aram cleared his throat loudly and gave Yocelin a hard look that was meant to make her stop flirting with this stranger. He didn't think it was right that she act so friendly toward him. Yocelin reacted by giving Aram one of her knowing smiles and raising her eyebrows in a suggestive manner. Aram did not care for her at that moment.

"What sort of a drifter are you, Giev?" Darian's voice rang out in his authoritative tone from behind Aram and Yocelin. They stepped aside so that Darian could come forward to speak with Giev.

"You certainly seem like the leader. Just how many of you are in there?" Giev asked cordially but abandoned the question when Darian simply stared coldly at him. "I'm a shaman, actually. I know, I'm a rare breed these days, but that's also why I'm a drifter. I sort of just travel around, trying to make a living." Giev continued smiling at this leader fellow and tried to give the most positive impression of himself that he could.

Darian stared the drifter down for what seemed like forever. Finally, he came to a decision. He would permit Giev to stay with them for the night so long as he surrendered his weapons to them. It was no use telling him to leave. The little shack was the only place for miles, and Giev was not likely to go anywhere else. They were stuck with him for at least one night. Darian put out his hand.

"Hand over your weapons. You can stay with us for the night, but I will keep your weapons during that time."

"I completely understand," Giev answered happily.

He began taking off his sword and other weapons to give to Darian. He was just glad he wouldn't have to try and spend the night out in the snow. The company of other elves, particularly the lovely female, would be refreshing. After Giev had given all his weapons to Darian, he stepped aside to allow Giev to enter the tiny structure. Once inside, Giev was happy to see a small fire blazing, as well as surprised that there was a forth member of the group. Another beautiful young elf maiden lay asleep in a bedroll next to the fire. Of course, everything was next to the fire in the cramped place. It was a good thing that Giev was the sociable sort. At first, he was doubly pleased to be in the company of two lovely women, but his thoughts became less selfish when he realized that the woman in the bedroll was ill.

"What's the matter with her?" Giev asked in a quiet voice. Now that he knew someone was sleeping, he felt the need to talk in softer tones.

Darian was displeased with Giev's interest in Eithne and gave him another glare as he moved back to her side. Darian did not intend to give him an answer.

Yocelin failed to recognize Darian's intentions. She had already decided that she liked the newcomer very much.

"She had a fever all of last night. It broke this morning, so she's been resting since then."

"Oh, well, I don't want to intrude, but I am a shaman of some skill. I could probably help her to feel better much faster," Giev was genuinely trying to be helpful.

He really was a skilled shaman and already knew that he carried some herbs in his pack that could help the elf maiden.

"That's so sweet of you to offer!" Yocelin chortled gleefully. "Don't you think so, boys?"

She gave Darian and Aram a less sweet look as she addressed them. Yocelin felt that they were both being rude to their new friend with their hard stares and silence—especially since Giev was offering to help Eithne.

Aram ignored her completely. He did not like the way Giev's eyes drifted over Yocelin's body. Even under a thick cloak, it was obvious that it wasn't just her face that merited admiration. His lip curled slightly in a sneer as he poked at the fire to keep it going.

Darian had a bit of a stare down with Yocelin for her comment but eventually turned his attention back to Giev. Darian was wary, but he did seem like the honest type who wouldn't intentionally hurt others.

"What sort of treatment do you propose?" Darian asked warily.

Giev grinned at the social opening; even if it was strained, he was glad to be spoken to. "Well, I was thinking that I could use some of the medicines that I carry."

Giev went into his pack and pulled out a small linen pouch that had the pleasant aroma of lavender mixed with other herbs.

"A tea made with this will help her sleep more fitfully as well as speed her recovery." Giev handed the pouch to Darian and allowed him to investigate it thoroughly.

Darian sniffed at the pouch and decided to trust Giev in this situation. He handed the pouch back to him and nodded his permission to proceed with the treatment.

Giev set about making the tea. As he waited for the water to boil, he took a better look at his new companions. They did not have many belongings, but what they did have was of quality, so they were not poor. They also did not act or look like any sort of outlaw that Giev had ever seen. Well, maybe the darker male and bouncy, purple-haired female could pass as outlaws, but the leader was far too polished for that identity. He obviously was of military background. Giev could not tell much about the sick female other than she and the leader appeared to be tribal elves, while the other two had the look of city elves. He also noticed that there was a very good chance that they were two couples traveling together, which saddened Giev. He hoped that at least one of these lovely ladies was single.

"So if I may be so bold, I would be curious to know your names," Giev said after his ponderings.

"Oh! How rude of us!" Yocelin felt quite embarrassed. She so loved to be proper and cordial. "My name is Yocelin. This is Aram." She placed her hand on Aram's shoulder. "That's Darian, and the one in the bedroll is Eithne. I'm so sorry I forgot to tell you before." She cooed the last sentence and inclined her head in a slight bow.

"I'm pleased to know all of you," Giev responded. "So if you are not outlaws, who are you?"

"Just travelers," Darian answered bluntly. He waned to cut Yocelin off before she said anything the rest of them would regret.

Yocelin wrinkled her nose at Darian for treating her like a child. She knew what he was doing, and she was offended that he didn't trust her more.

"Begging your pardon, friend, but it's obvious that the four of you left some place in a hurry," Giev said slyly after watching the exchange.

"We were forced to flee the palace in Lupia. We were accused of doing something purposefully that was, in actuality, an accident," answered Aram.

All were shocked to hear Aram answer so fully. They stared at him in amazement.

Aram shrugged at them dismissively. "What's the point of keeping it from him? He's obviously not a Lupian guard."

Aram still did not like the way that Giev looked at Yocelin, but it occurred to him that this fellow could be a useful ally. Besides, the feelings for Yocelin that had recently stirred within him Aram found to be rather disquieting. Perhaps if Yocelin were flirting with Giev instead, his feelings would go away.

Giev was extremely pleased by Aram's sudden openness. "Well, that explains your current state."

The water was boiling now, so Giev carefully poured it into a cup with the tea leaves and set it aside for a moment to let it steep.

"What's going on?" Eithne was sitting up now and noticing that their group had grown by one. Of course, she found this newcomer's presence quite the surprise, as she hadn't a clue how he came to be here with them.

"This is Giev," Yocelin answered happily. "He was traveling in the forest and asked if he could share our shelter for the night. Darian and Aram were skeptical, but they still said yes. Now Giev is going to help you get better. He made tea." She took in a breath when she was finished speaking as it had all come out at once and very fast. There was a lot to explain after all, and Yocelin liked to be the one to do it.

Eithne blinked at her friend. It was a whirlwind of words to process. After a few seconds, she noticed that she was expected to respond. "Okay, thanks."

Then Eithne looked to Darian in hopes of an explanation that would be a less succinct and more clear. Darian's expression softened when Eithne looked to him, and he gave her a smile.

"What Yocelin says is all correct, of course. However, the slightly more detailed version is that Giev is a traveling shaman who was hoping or shelter from the cold tonight. As a shaman, he has offered his services to help speed along your recovery. Also, he knows that we have fled Lupia," Darian added the last sentence as an afterthought, but he thought it was worth mentioning so that Eithne would not feel the need to dance around that particular topic.

"Well, that makes a bit more sense. At least, it filled in the gaps." Eithne was thankful to Darian. She then turned to Giev. "Nice to meet you, Giev. I'm Eithne." She smiled politely at him, realized that he was rather handsome, and automatically made her smile more welcoming.

Giev grinned back at the pretty redhead and handed her the mug of tea without breaking eye contact. "It's a great pleasure, Eithne. This tea should help you feel better."

Eithne accepted the mug and sipped it gingerly. It smelled of lavender and other herbs and had a smooth, sweet flavor. She liked it. She also liked their new companion. Eithne glanced at Yocelin, who was watching Eithne with a glimmer in her eye. The two friends made eye contact and grinned devilishly at each other. Giev certainly seemed more open to flirtation than Darian or Aram. That made him more fun.

Neither of the girls bothered to look at Darian or Aram, who both wore dark expressions directed at Giev.

"So how long have you all been married?" Giev asked casually, but his question caused quite the reaction from his hosts.

Eithne almost spit out her tea. Darian immediately asked him to repeat the question as he couldn't believe what was just said. Aram looked up sharply in confusion, and Yocelin burst out laughing.

"You're kidding, right?" Yocelin asked as her laughter subsided. "I mean, you can't be serious!"

Giev could tell by their strong reactions that they were not only unwed but also all single. This gave him renewed hope regarding wooing one of the women.

"I'm sorry it seems so ridiculous to you all, but you do understand how I could assume that you are two married couples traveling together. So you're all single then?"

"Yes, we are indeed," Yocelin answered in her more womanly voice. "All of us." She illustrated her point further by leaning in closer to him, which Giev responded to by reciprocating her lean.

"That's good to know," Giev said with a sly expression.

He might want to try and travel with their group for a bit to see what possibilities could be explored.

CHAPTER TWENTY-SIX

THE NEXT DAY, Eithne felt much better and insisted that they make their way to the closest town. No one put up much of a fight as all were anxious to leave the cramped little shack behind. Giev continued to accompany them, much to Darian and Aram's disappointment. He did know the area very well, however, and he proved to be useful in helping them find their way. Darian and Aram were grateful for Giev showing them the way, but it was his shameless flirting with Eithne and Yocelin that they took issue with.

"Why does everything he say make them giggle like that?" Darian said in a low, irritable tone to Aram.

Giev and the girls were walking ahead of them, with Giev in between the two girls. The protectors kept a good distance behind them so that they could converse privately.

"Very annoying," Aram stated irritably. He agreed with Darian's sentiment.

"It's like we are traveling with teenagers. It's ridiculous," Darian continued to vent.

"Maybe he'll find some other pretty girls to distract him once we get to town," Aram suggested. The idea was very appealing to him.

"We can only hope," Darian muttered. "Giev is a big distraction to Eithne and Yocelin. I fear they may forget that they are on a sacred quest to save the world. It's part of our duty to make sure they stay on task."

Aram nodded. "Besides, I think that Giev's intentions with them are hardly honorable."

Darian's expression went darker as he thought about what Aram just said. He already knew what Giev's intentions were, but being reminded of it caused his mood to become even worse.

Aram's mood was already awful, as he couldn't stop thinking about what Giev wanted with Yocelin. Worse still was that she seemed receptive to the traveling shaman. It was not a good day.

The companions reached a small town just as night was beginning to fall. There wasn't much to see in the tiny place, but there was an inn that had vacancies. Eithne and Yocelin were quick to book a private room for just the two of them before their protectors could protest. The girls were feeling gossipy and wanted time away from the boys for a night. Thankfully, they still had most of the money that Tim had given them, which was a hefty sum, so they could afford the luxury of an extra room every once in a while.

Giev smiled at Darian and Aram after the girls had run upstairs. "Shall I room with the two of you then?"

"Get your own room," Aram snorted back. He did not try to hide his contempt.

Darian nodded in support of Aram. "I believe there are only two beds in each room."

That said, the protectors went upstairs to their room, which they confirmed was right next to Eithne and Yocelin's room. They left the shaman standing alone downstairs without a second glance.

Giev took the slight quite well. Honestly, he completely understood their position. Giev had done nothing but flirt with Eithne and Yocelin the whole time he'd known them, and it was easy to tell that Darian and Aram had a strong interest in each respective woman. There was no romantic relationship between them, so all was fair game in theory, but theories are very different from emotions. He understood their animosity toward him. Perhaps he should try a bit harder to win them over, for he did now intend to continue traveling with this group, even though they did not know it yet. Giev may be a womanizer, but he was still a shaman, and something told him to stick with this group of people.

Giev paid for his own room and went upstairs for the night. He made a mental note to get up especially early tomorrow to be sure the rest of them did not sneak away early without him.

The next morning, Giev was up before the sun and went downstairs for breakfast and to wait for his new companions to emerge. An hour later, Giev was beginning to feel nervous that perhaps they had gotten up even earlier and snuck away in the wee hours of the morning. Giev shook his head of the negative thoughts. They wouldn't have done that. The weather was far too bitter outside, and they were probably all just taking in more sleep while there were comfortable beds available. Besides, Giev had become aware that Eithne and Yocelin required new clothing, for they had both let it slip yesterday that they only wore nightdresses beneath their cloaks. Giev's lips curled into a sly smile as she sipped his coffee and imagined just how thin their nightdresses might be.

The sound of heavy boots coming down the stairs alerted Giev and took him from his less pure thoughts. Sure enough, the four of them emerged, still looking drowsy. Aram sensed Giev's presence and jerked his head in the proper direction. There he was, smiling and waving the companions over to his table as if they were friends. Aram growled low in his throat. He had hoped that they had seen the last of Giev, but it seemed that Giev was intent on sticking around. Aram glared at the shaman, but it did nothing to dampen his spirits to Aram's disappointment. Of course, Eithne and Yocelin joined Giev at his table gladly, which forced Darian and Aram to sit as well. Neither protector was especially happy all of a sudden.

"Did you all sleep well?" Giev asked politely.

"Great, in fact," Eithne answered. She was in especially good spirits this morning as she no longer felt at all ill. She found herself with the feeling of almost bursting with energy. "Also, I'm excited about today."

"Why?" Darian sounded sarcastic, but he didn't mean to sound that way. Giev's presence had caused him to feel a bit salty.

"Shopping, silly!" Yocelin beamed. "Eithne and I are buying new clothes today!"

"You two are excited about that? You do realize that we don't have a lot of money, you can't take all day shopping, and that there's probably only one shop in this little town, right?" Aram stated harshly.

"Getting new clothes is always exciting, no matter what the circumstances," Yocelin explained in a vindicated tone. "Maybe you should have something sweet for breakfast to balance out all your sourness." Yocelin knew full well that Aram was bitter about Giev still being here, but it was no reason for him to take it out on her and Eithne.

Aram simply growled grumpily in reply.

Giev cleared his throat. "Well, perhaps while you ladies are buying new clothes, Darian and Aram would like to join me for a drink and some conversation?"

"We'll be with the girls while they buy their new clothes," Darian stated. "We need to get moving again anyway. I'd like to be back on the trail by the early afternoon."

"Where are you headed?" Giev pried.

"That's not your business," Aram answered curtly.

Giev paused for a few seconds before replying. He considered Darian and Aram as he leaned back in his chair and sipped his coffee. "You haven't the slightest idea where you're going, do you?"

Darian shot him an icy glare, but Eithne and Yocelin's giggling ruined his intended affect.

"Giev, it seems you have found us out," Yocelin said with a shrewd smile. "We don't know where we are going exactly."

"We're figuring it out as we go. It's a process," Aram interjected.

He resented that Yocelin made it sound like they were lost. They were not lost. They had direction; it just wasn't geographic. The plan was to just keep traveling around until they had gathered all the god pieces. It didn't really matter which direction they took from here so long as they didn't go back to Lupia.

"I see," Giev drained the rest of his coffee and leaned forward on the table. "I would like to join you, wherever you're going."

"I'm afraid that's not possible," Darian stated in a final sort of tone.

"Why not?" Giev and Yocelin said this in unison, which would have been funnier if Darian and Aram weren't so irritated.

"Because what we are doing requires privacy, and I would prefer to keep our group as small as possible," Darian answered through gritted teeth while glaring at Giev.

Giev nodded at Darian. He fully understood his misgivings about allowing him to come along, but Giev just knew that he must join their group.

"I understand what you mean, Darian, but I'm afraid I must insist. How can I get you to agree to allow me along?"

"Why must you insist?" Aram snapped. He looked the shaman in the eyes and held his gaze. He was beginning to think that there was more to Giev's motives than pursuing Yocelin and Eithne.

Giev suddenly felt all eyes more intensely on him, but being the center of attention was not a problem for him.

"Well, as I mentioned before, I am a shaman and can, therefore, be of much use to your group. I've already helped Eithne to get well. Also, I have a very strong feeling that tells me to stay with your group, and I don't ignore my instincts. I believe it is like a higher power is guiding me to be with all of you."

"I'm still not convinced," Darian scoffed.

Giev took notice that as Darian spoke, his eyes flicked to Eithne and Yocelin. Perhaps their mission, whatever it was, required secrecy; but at the moment, the real reason he was being denied was because of his behavior toward the girls.

"I really do feel very strongly about coming with all of you. I can't explain it, but I know it's the right thing to do. I know my services will be of great help to you."

The protectors rolled their eyes. They were still unconvinced.

"Also, I will stop distracting Eithne and Yocelin from your mission if you allow me to come with you," Giev added.

Aram's eyebrows shot up at Giev's last statement. Perhaps he truly did feel that he must accompany them if he was willing to give up on trying to bed the girls. Aram and Darian looked at each other to see what the other's reaction was.

"Wait, what?" Yocelin blurted. "What do you mean you'll stop flirting? I like flirting!" She reached over and laid her hand on Giev's forearm. Yocelin did not like the thought of her amusement going away.

Giev was sympathetic. He enjoyed the flirtation as much as she did, but this was more important. Furthermore, Giev had the impression that, for all of his efforts, neither of these beautiful women would sleep with him. He could tell that they already had a certain attraction toward Darian and Aram that would prevent them from doing anything beyond flirting as long as they were around.

Yocelin pouted but did not put up much more argument. Her eyes drifted to Aram, and she removed her hand from Giev's arm. She realized now that her flirting had upset Aram, and she felt guilty for it. Aram looked back at her. His face was unreadable, though Yocelin felt ashamed of her behavior under his gaze. Her instinct was to go and hug him, but she knew that it was not the time or place to hug the presently surly werewolf. She would have to find a different way to compensate for her guilt.

Eithne had a different reaction to Giev's statement. She looked at Darian and stood from the table.

"Darian, could I speak to you privately for a moment?"

Darian was mildly put out by her request but stood and nodded affirmatively. They walked out of earshot (even for Aram and Yocelin). Darian turned to face Eithne with his arms crossed across his chest defensively. He had a feeling that she was going to try to convince him to let Giev come along.

Eithne could see that he knew what her intentions were, so she sighed and came right out with it. "I think Giev should come with us."

Darian's steel blue eyes narrowed. "What for?"

"It's not because he's handsome and flirtatious, if that's what you're thinking," she defended. "I actually have a feeling too. The same kind of feeling that told me which way to go to locate the Stone of Elissiyus. It's telling me to keep Giev around."

Darian didn't budge and continued his skeptical glare. "Really?"

Eithne could see that he was feeling rather defensive about this. Also, he didn't fully trust her motives. He needed to get out of that state of mind before he would listen to her.

"Would you relax and uncross your arms for a minute?" she pleaded.

"I'm fine, thanks." He didn't move a muscle.

"You're not," Eithne said flatly. "You're listening to me, but not really listening."

"That doesn't make any sense."

"Just humor me, please." Eithne reached over and tugged at his sleeve to suggest that he uncross his arms.

Darian grumbled as he released his arms and put his hands on his hips. "I seem to humor you a lot."

"And I appreciate that." Eithne stepped closer into him and looked up into his face. "I don't just want Giev along so that I can have a cute boy around to flirt with. You and Aram are plenty handsome, if that is what I was after. I really do believe that he is supposed to come with us, and I think that Yocelin feels it too. I know that you and Aram are extremely protective of us, but I'm asking you to trust me in this." She held eye contact with him as she spoke in order to try and let him see how sincere she was.

Darian held her gaze for a while after she finished speaking. He could tell that she was being honest with him. He didn't really want to give in, but if she felt that strongly about it, then he didn't feel like he had much choice either. How could he deny her?

"You've got to let me win someday," he said with resignation. "I'm all right with Giev coming as long as you all start taking this quest seriously."

Eithne smiled at him and had the urge to hug him, but resisted. "I'll do my best to make it all up to you one day."

Darian nodded and gestured that they should return to the table where the others were waiting.

"So you think I'm handsome?" Darian teased in a whisper as they went back.

Eithne tried to be nonchalant, but a slight pink flush in her cheeks gave her away. "You know you are, so it shouldn't come as a surprise."

Darian smirked satisfactorily and pulled out Eithne's chair for her to sit before seating himself. His expression hardened as he turned his attention to Giev, who was anxiously awaiting his words.

"All right, you can come with us, but no more funny business." Darian downed the rest of his coffee and sat back in his chair.

Aram's eyes narrowed menacingly at Giev. It was a silent warning.

"What did you say to him?" Yocelin quietly asked Eithne. She was shocked at the result of the short conversation.

"I was honest," Eithne replied with a smile.

The five of them ate a quiet breakfast together and set out to get Eithne and Yocelin some new clothes as well as stock up on supplies. It would have also been nice to get some horses, but it was more important to conserve what money they had. Tim had given them a good sum of money when they had left the mansion, but they also knew that this quest could take a very long time. They did not wish to squander it unnecessarily.

It did not take long before they were back on the road. Giev had suggested that they head for a town called Roos, which was northwest of their current position. It was a town that was along a major road, and many different kinds of people could be found there. Giev did not yet understand what their quest was, but he did understand that they wanted to be around larger populations. The shaman was the sort to catch on quickly.

Eithne and Yocelin were very pleased, and much warmer, in their new winter clothing. Both wore thick breeches, high leather boots, and woolen shirts beneath their cloaks. The styles were very similar, but the colors they wore were different. Yocelin had chosen mostly black garments with the exception of a gray shirt. Eithne wore varying shades of soft browns and a green shirt. Hopefully, these new clothes would last them through the winter without having to be left behind or replaced. The pair of women were keeping to themselves and chattering on endlessly. Aram could have eavesdropped with his superb hearing, but he assumed they were talking nonsense and didn't bother. If it were important, they would say something to the entire group.

The girls' conversation was not so flippant as Aram assumed. Yocelin had had another dream of Cavan, but she wasn't sure what it meant. It wasn't like the last time when she knew she was being watched. It was more like she was watching him. Just seeing him in a dream made her nervous. Did this mean that they would encounter him again soon? The thought of facing such a powerful brute sent shivers down her spine. How could they ever defeat him? Yocelin had told Eithne that in the dream, she saw Cavan in flashing images. One minute, he was pouring over a giant tome; the next, he was running someone through on a city street. It was a confusing sort of dream. Yocelin had no idea if she was seeing past, present, or future, but it was certainly real. Eithne was telling her to tell the boys about it, but she couldn't do that without telling Giev everything. Yocelin decided to wait until they stopped for the night to say anything. They had planned to press on to a small village where Giev said there was a decent inn. The snow fell on and off and lay in two-foot piles everywhere. It was bitterly cold and overcast, so an inn was definitely the preferred option for the night.

Luckily, the village was not far, and they arrived in time for supper. Once they all arranged their rooms, the five companions sat at one of the tables in the downstairs dining area to eat. All of them were tired from being in the cold, so the table was quiet for a few moments until Eithne nudged Yocelin to speak. The three men watched patiently as the girls exchanged looks and silently communicated while trying to be covert. Eventually, Eithne got her way, and Yocelin agreed to speak.

"I need to share something about a dream I had about Cavan, but before I do, I think we need to tell Giev what our quest is," Yocelin chimed clearly.

Darian and Aram became immediately alert at the mention of Cavan, but they were still unsure of Giev. They glanced at him and back at Yocelin.

"Why don't you just tell us what you know, and we'll fill Giev in as necessary," Aram said flatly.

"That's not fair to him!" Yocelin retorted. "If he's going to be traveling with us, he deserves to know what sort of trouble we may get into. Besides, Eithne and I trust him."

"I for one would very much appreciate a heads-up on trouble," Giev interjected in a cordial tone.

The protectors exchanged looks, seemed to understand each other, and looked back to the girls.

"You may inform him about Cavan, and nothing more," Darian stated in his authoritative voice.

Yocelin sighed in frustration. "But how do I tell him about Cavan without telling him why he's after me?"

"Simply leave that part out," Aram stared directly at Yocelin.

He held her gaze in silence for a few seconds. He looked very serious. Yocelin began to feel embarrassed and felt her face grow hot. It was unusual for her to feel embarrassed, but Aram had a way of doing that to her when she needed to be put in her place. He knew how to make her serious somehow.

Everyone else at the table felt the change of mood as well. It was time to stop act foolishly and concentrate on important matters. Eithne and Yocelin in particular had been acting more carefree than they should have lately. Now it was time to remember their quest, their new life's purpose, and focus on saving the world.

Eithne looked at Darian, and for the first time in a long time, she saw him as she used to. He had the energy of the captain of the guard whose orders were never disobeyed. Even the way he had said that they could tell Giev about only Cavan sounded like a command. Darian had a strange way of always making Eithne feel good and safe.

Giev sat quietly while the moment passed. It was almost as if there was a shift of power happening. Since he had joined the group, it had felt like Eithne and Yocelin were in charge, but now he saw that the real leaders were Darian and Aram. They were simply all right with the girls doing as they pleased. This decision rested more in the hands of the men. They were the ones entrusted with the safety of the group. It was an interesting dynamic. Giev enjoyed watching them all interact.

Yocelin let out a sigh, which broke the silence.

"Okay, Giev, so there's this guy named Cavan who is after us . . . Well, after me, specifically, for reasons that I'm not allowed to tell you." She gave Aram a sarcastic look as she mentioned the part about not being allowed to speak of certain things. She was further annoyed when Aram simply nodded at her to continue. "Anyway, Cavan is really evil and incredibly powerful. He even beat Aram and Darian at once during a fight!"

At the mention of being defeated in battle, both protectors shifted uncomfortably in their chairs but said nothing. Giev was very surprised to hear that. It was obvious that both Darian and Aram were formidable fighters. For someone to fight the two of them at once and win would be an incredible feat! Whoever this Cavan was, he must be supernatural.

"Cavan is out to kill me, unfortunately," Yocelin continued. "He and I also share a strange connection where I will sometimes have dreams or premonitions about him, which I recently have had such a dream. It usually means that he is close by, which is also very bad if he finds us. It will lead to a fight, and we all have to try out best to kill him or run away, which is basically what we did the last time we ran into him." Yocelin sighed when she finished and took a long drink of her wine.

Gieve didn't like the sound of this Cavan character at all. He sounded very dangerous, indeed. It was very curious that Yocelin had a connection with such an evil person.

"Why do you have dreams about him?" Giev asked.

"Oh, we know why," Yocelin answered confidently. "But that's one of those things that I'm not supposed to tell you yet."

"I see." Giev's eyes drifted to Darian and Aram, who were looking at him sternly.

"So what was your dream about?" Aram leaned forward on the table as he asked the question. He was anxious to know what she had seen.

Yocelin recounted the dream in vivid description of all the images she had seen. It all seemed jumbled, despite her clear memory, but a string of random images just didn't make much sense regardless. They all discussed it over their dinner and exhausted their minds trying to come up with all the possibilities of its meaning.

"Perhaps it simply means that we have to be on our guard because Cavan is close enough for Yocelin to be sensing his energy," Darian said as he leaned back in his chair and put his hands behind his head.

"Now that you mention it, I have been getting that feeling I get when certain energy is nearby," Eithne mused. "But I didn't think that I could sense the presence of Cavan."

Darian raised his eyebrows at her. Then she looked to Yocelin for confirmation.

Yocelin nodded. "Yes, I've been feeling it too, but I don't think it's Cavan. He feels different."

"Why didn't either of you mention this sooner? How long have you been feeling it?" Darian was annoyed that they had withheld information. Anything related to their quest should be immediately communicated.

Both girls shrugged in answer as to why they had not mentioned it earlier. They didn't have any real sort of answer for him. Darian's irritation made them feel sheepish.

"I started feeling it this afternoon, and the feeling got stronger as we got closer to town. Whatever is causing it isn't here in town, but it's close," Eithne defended meekly.

Darian was thoughtful for a few seconds. "All right, starting tomorrow, you and Yocelin will lead the group and follow the energy. We should all be extremely wary of Cavan as well. It could be that he is after whatever is causing the energy."

Aram, Yocelin, and Eithne all agreed with Darian and got up from the table to retire to their respective rooms for the night. They were all mentally exhausted and ready to sleep. They didn't even notice that Giev did not follow.

Giev was thoroughly confused. Just how normal was it for Yocelin and Eithne to be sensing strange magical energy? Who exactly was Cavan, and why was he so powerful? Why would Darian and Aram want to randomly follow a "feeling" the girls were having? Who, or what, were these new companions he had chosen to travel with? Darian and Eithne were certainly tribal elves, but Giev was beginning to wonder about Aram and Yocelin. Yocelin's eating habits were that of a demon, and even her appearance was somehow not really elven of human. Aram simply seemed strange, like he was hiding something. Giev's head started to hurt, and he realized that he was now alone at the table. He sighed and went to his room. He would do his best to banish all the questions in his mind so that he could get some sleep.

CHAPTER TWENTY-SEVEN

*T*HE NEXT MORNING, there was a blistering winter wind blowing that reddened their skin and made them all feel numb. They had left the inn later than initially planned. The companions had high hopes that the biting wind would calm before they started out, but after an hour of waiting, it became clear that they would have no such luck. It was now about midday, and they had made little progress. Eithne and Yocelin led the way, following the feeling of energy. The energy was steadily becoming stronger as they walked. Both women suspected that they were sensing the Stone of Elissiyus, which was well worth following, but they did not share the suspicion with each other. The feeling was such that they understood, and there was no point in talking about it. It also seemed as though they were not quite able to catch up with it. So if they were correct in believing it to be the stone, a traveler was carrying it.

Three days, it went on like this. The winter weather was harsh and unforgiving, but the small group of travelers pressed onward. They were headed northwest, which took them deep into the continent of Croissia. This part of the continent used to be a thick and hardy evergreen forest, but it no longer held its former splendor. Much of the once green forest was brown, brittle, and dead. Those trees that were still alive were sad imitations of what they once were. Animals had fled the dead forest or died, so hunting even small game was nearly impossible. Thankfully, there were still a few outposts of civilization in the depressing place. A handful of small communities where the people were too stubborn to leave their homes stayed behind. The companions were able to maintain a meager rations supply from these ghost towns. It was just enough to keep them going through the cold.

Late on the third day of travel, Eithne and Yocelin sensed something new—well, two new things to be more correct. Firstly, that they were much closer to the energy that they thought was the Stone of Elissiyus. The energy was finally staying in one place! Secondly, and much to their dismay, there was another very powerful energy approaching the other. It was dark and ominous, and Yocelin had no doubt as to what caused this energy: Cavan. Her heart gripped in fear as she realized that Cavan probably sensed that she was nearby as well. Should they run? Should they give up on following the other energy? In a short time, they would be too close to Cavan to get away. Yocelin stopped in her tracks and stood stiffly as if suddenly frozen.

"What's wrong?" Aram asked quietly as he came up next to her.

The other three stopped but stood back from the conversation.

"It's him. It's Cavan," Yocelin said flatly as she stared at the wet snow on the ground seeping through her leather boots.

"You mean the energy you've been following for the past three days is Cavan?" Aram asked. He did his best not to sound alarmed.

Yocelin shook her head. "No, Eithne and I believe that is the Stone of Elissiyus, but Cavan is close to it now and close to us." Yocelin paused then looked Aram in the face. "What should we do? If he finds us, he'll kill us."

Aram let out a slow breath and ran his hand through his dark tousled hair. He didn't know what to do. He certainly did not want to encounter Cavan again, but if what they had been following for the past few days actually was the stone, then it could be an invaluable tool on their quest. Aram turned to his friends.

"What do you guys think? Should we continue?"

There was a silence as they all pondered the question. The initial thought was to run, get as far away from Cavan as possible. However, if the other energy really was the stone, they couldn't let Cavan have it. If he possessed that sort of power, there would be no question that their quest to save the world would be over. Raashan would be forever plunged into a destructive darkness ruled by Muntros.

"Are the two energies together, or is it possible to reach the source of the other energy before Cavan does?" Darian asked, breaking the silence. His voice rang firm, which brought comfort to the others.

Yocelin closed her eyes and concentrated for a few seconds. "He is not upon it yet, but we would have to hurry if we want to evade him."

"Let's hurry then," Darian said definitively. His chiseled features were set hard and serious as he nodded at Yocelin to lead the way.

Yocelin looked to Eithne, who also felt the way to go. Yocelin felt rooted in place, but not from the cold. It was her fear of Cavan that held her. She could see that Eithne was scared too, but there was something else in her expression: resolve. Eithne took a deep breath in through her nose and let it out slowly. Then she nodded curtly at Yocelin. Yocelin nodded back. Both women broke into a run in the direction of the energy. The men all followed swiftly. The snowy ground seemed to blur and vanish beneath their feet. There was a sort of collective adrenaline rush that the companions experienced as they ran. Even Giev felt it surge through him with newfound energy. He could sense something powerful as they got closer as well. As a shaman, he had been trained to sense such energies. Whatever this thing was that they were following, it was very strong.

"Finnis!" Eithne exclaimed as she skidded to a halt in front of the elf that had been a part of the original party chosen by Darian to quest for the Stone of Elissiyus.

Finnis looked much worse for wear than she remembered. He was thinner, and his face had started to get a hollow appearance, which was only exaggerated by his eyes being as huge as saucers from the shock of five people bursting suddenly into his camp.

"Traitor!" Darian growled harshly through gritted teeth as he laid eyes on Finnis. Finnis tried to dart away, but Darian was too fast and snatched him up roughly by the front of his shirt. "You are a traitor to our people and a murderer!" Darian said with an angry, cold expression. His steel blue eyes were like ice, and they burned into Finnis.

Finnis was absolutely petrified. Captain Darian was a very imposing man, especially right now, and he felt certain that the captain was angry enough to kill him. After all, Finnis had committed terrible wrongs, but it was all wasted. All those bad deeds he did for the power of the stone, but he couldn't figure out how to use the blasted thing! He felt paranoid that he was being followed as long as he had the stone with him. So he had been on the move these past few months. Of course, given the sudden appearance of Captain Darian and Eithne, that paranoia did not seem so crazy now.

Darain stared back at Finnis with barely contained rage, but he was not altogether sure what to do with him now that the traitor was finally in his clutches. A rougher person may have wanted to just give him a good beating, and Darian had fantasized about doing that several times over the past months, but it somehow didn't feel like the right thing to do now. So he simply held him there giving him a cold, hard look. Darian was content to watch Finnis squirm in fear until he figured out what he was going to do with him.

Yocelin paid no attention to Darian's dilemma. Cavan was closing in, and she did not want to meet him again. It was rather convenient that Darian had a good hold on Finnis, though, because it enabled her to go through his belongings without interruption. The Stone of Elissiyus was not difficult to find. It was at the bottom of his pack, wrapped in cloth. It was fairly large and did not look so special, but it felt special. Yocelin partially undid the wrapping and looked upon the quartz rock in her hands. It felt mildly warm to the touch and seemed to pulsate with power in her hands. She was tempted to take a moment to stare at it and feel its power wash over her, but there would be time for that later. She threw the wrapping back over the stone and hurriedly tucked it into her pack.

"I've got the stone! Let's go!" Yocelin announced as she jumped up to run again.

Darian came out of his own thoughts and remembered what they were here for, as well as who else would be at the camp shortly. There was no time to properly punish Finnis. Darian locked eyes again with Finnis. He looked hard at him for another second then tossed him unto the frozen ground.

"Don't follow," Darian commanded coldly.

He then joined his companions in exiting the area. Cavan could deal with Finnis however he saw fit. Cavan would probably do much worse than whatever Darian could have done to him. Darian felt a bit guilty for leaving Finnis to Cavan, though Finnis had already given up on any courtesy when he betrayed their party and murdered Dal.

The five companions ran into the dead forest as fast as they could. The direction did not matter so long as they ran away from Cavan. They only hoped that he would be distracted enough by Finnis not to catch up with them.

Finnis lay on the hard, frozen ground in a state of shock. What had just happened? Were Captain Darian and Eithne really here just now? Aram was with them as well as two other people. Did the strange purple-haired woman take the stone? Finnis leaped up and grabbed his pack. He rummaged through it desperately, but it was gone. They had taken the stone and run off. He let out a pathetic moan of despair. How could this happen? He covered his face in his hands and knelt on the cold ground as he rocked back and forth. Now it was all truly for nothing. Betrayal, murder, alienation from his people, and he didn't even possess the stone anymore.

"Where is the stone of Elissiyus?" Ccme an almost inhuman and hard voice above Finnis.

Finnis came out of his self-loathing to find himself in the shadow of a huge, frightening human male. It was immediately obvious that this man had no care for Finnis's life, but he did want information. Finnis had been a weasel long enough to know what to do with this sort of person: give them exactly what they wanted and fast.

Finnis gulped down to moisten his throat enough to speak. "Three men and two women burst into my camp moments ago and stole it from me. They went that way."

Finnis pointed in the direction that the companions had run.

The dark man sniffed the air and kept his dead eyes on Finnis. "Did one of the women have purple hair and black curling horns?"

"Purple hair, yes, but I did not see any horns," Finnis stammered.

The man's lips curled up into an unnatural-looking smile. Before Finnis realized what was going on, the man plunged his sword through Finnis's neck as he knelt before him. Finnis fell wide-eyed and dead on the frozen ground. His blood seeped into the cold white snow.

Cavan turned and walked away without a second glance. He strode in the direction he was told the ones who took the Stone of Elissiyus had fled. The she-demon must have found a way to disguise her horns, but he had no doubt that it was she. He could smell all four of them in the air, as well as someone new. They were running fast, and already far ahead of him, but he would catch them soon enough. There was no wizard to shelter them this time. Cavan was surprised that he had not sensed the she-demon's presence earlier, but he reasoned that he was too focused on the stone's energy. Now the stone and the she-demon were together in a nice little package for Cavan to take.

CHAPTER TWENTY-EIGHT

*Y*OCELIN RAN FOR her life as they left the campsite. That they had a head start on Cavan made no difference at all. Being on the same continent as that monster was too close for comfort, and this time, they did not have a safe house to hide in. They would have to just keep running until there was enough distance between them that they could no longer sense each other. She could feel the burning in her chest over her heart where she had felt it before on the ship and wondered if it meant that Cavan was now following them. The pain was bad, but Yocelin's fear overrode the pain and kept her legs pumping beneath her.

Giev kept pace with the group, but he really wasn't sure why they had to keep on running so fast for so long. It seemed to him that there was no way this Cavan person could possibly catch them now; though if there was one thing he had learned about his new companions, it was that they did not act without reason. He kept up with them all and hoped for an explanation when they stopped running, whenever that may be.

Aram ran beside Yocelin. He glanced at her frequently to see if she was all right. He could tell by her expression that something was causing her pain. He wondered if she needed to be carried, but it was better if she did not need the help. Aram was strong and a good runner, but they would all be able to go farther more quickly if she did not need to be carried.

A few moments later, Yocelin let out a yelp and grasped her head in both hands. Aram's movements were fast and fluid. He barely broke his stride as he gathered her into his arms and kept running.

"What's wrong? Is it Cavan?" Aram questioned as he took her into his arms.

"I don't know," she moaned helplessly with her eyes squeezed shut.

Why was her head hurting so terribly all of a sudden? She felt something poke against her palms as she held her head. Yocelin's eyes flew open. Tim's potion was wearing off! Her horns were growing back! She groaned again at the realization. This was awful timing. Yocelin was so thankful to Aram for carrying her away from danger. He understood how important it was to keep running. She would be sure to thank him properly once they stopped. Another wave of intense pain hit her, and she surrendered to it. She trusted Aram to keep her safe.

Eithne was running in front of Yocelin when she heard her friend cry out in pain. She looked back to see Aram scooping her up into his arms. Eithne wanted to slow her pace and make sure Yocelin was okay. She began to fall back, but Darian reached back and grabbed her hand, pulling her back up to run next to him.

"Aram has her. Just keep running," Darian urged through heaving breathes.

Eithne resumed her faster pace. Darian was usually right about such things.

She and Darian ran at the front of the group followed by Aram, carrying Yocelin, and Giev. It felt to Giev that they must have been running for almost an hour, and he was feeling very tired. He imagined that the others must be tired too. How could this Cavan person still be after them anyway? Surely, he would have given up pursuit by now.

"Do you really think he's still following us?" Giev called out in between huffs of air.

Yocelin's horns had finished growing back, and they had put a good distance between themselves and Cavan, so she was feeling much better, though she still had an aching chest and splitting headache. Aram still carried her for the sake of not stopping to put her down. She could sense that Cavan was still following them. He was much farther off, however, as if he had just been walking after them this whole time. Perhaps he was less concerned with catching them at the moment, or he was simply that confident that they wouldn't get away. The feeling of him following them was chilling, but he was very far off now, and they were all tired.

"I think that we can walk for a while," Yocelin said. "But we need to keep moving."

They all slowed to a walking pace and caught their breath. All but Giev had been so driven that they didn't even feel the strain from the running until now. Aram set Yocelin down so that she could walk.

"It's a good thing you're so petite," Aram stated in a half-joking manner. "I always seem to end up carrying you when we need to run away."

Yocelin chuckled as she thought about it. He was right, but it wasn't as if she did it on purpose. "Well, it means a lot to me that you're always there. Thank you."

Yocelin accompanied her thanks with a hug, which, as usual, gave Aram a little surprise. He wondered if he would ever get used to her being so emotionally demonstrative. She released him, and they continued walking.

"You're a demon!" Giev suddenly shouted and pointed at Yocelin. He had stopped dead in his tracks.

Yocelin shrugged and nodded. There wasn't mush else to say about it. The other three had similar reactions to hers. Giev had simply made a factual statement.

"I drank a special potion to make my horns disappear while we were visiting the elves. They've grown back while we were running," Yocelin noticed that Giev needed more of an explanation.

"She's a good demon, though," Eithne interjected. "She was raised by elves and is much kinder than most people I know."

"Thanks, Eithne," Yocelin chimed with more of her characteristic pep.

There was a silence while Giev digested this new information. The other patiently waited.

"I knew there was something different about you," Giev said in a nonthreatening way. He sounded as if he had just won a game instead of being accusatory. "All right, I've come to a decision."

Darian crossed his arms defensively. It sounded like Giev thought that he could make decisions for the group now. He didn't like that. Eithne glanced up at Darian and smiled. She felt that she knew what he was thinking but said nothing. Giev would talk his way back into his good graces in a moment most likely.

"I need to know everything," Giev announced plainly.

"Why would we tell you everything?" Darian asked quizzically.

"Well, because I'm your companion and friend that you can trust," Giev answered with an open smile.

He could see that Eithne and Yocelin were content with that response, but Darian and Aram still needed convincing, which Giev wished was not necessary. He thought for a second about what he should say or do to convince them. He felt that he had already demonstrated behavior that showed that he could be trusted, but Darian and Aram were still very skeptical toward him. Giev needed to showcase his most useful talents and knowledge in order to somehow endear himself to them.

There was a long moment of silence as Darian waited for Giev to respond. Finally, Giev broke the silence.

"I know how to use the Stone of Elissiyus. I overheard you talking about it before, and I know that's what we took from that elf back there. I would venture an educated guess that none of you know how to work it. Also, I have other helpful knowledge, such as where certain artifacts are kept that can help you in whatever your quest is. If you let me in and tell me what is going on, then I will be happy to share the knowledge and skills that I possess with all of you."

Giev was half-bluffing about knowing how to use the stone. He did, however, have a very good idea of what to do as well as having a fair amount of experience using magical artifacts and items. He was sure he could figure it out. As far as his other knowledge was concerned, it was no bluff. Giev had taken his studies very seriously at an apprentice and knew a great deal about what magical artifacts still existed in this world.

Darian gave Giev his most scrutinizing glare. He was not at all sure that Giev was telling the whole truth about his value. Darian looked at Eithne in hopes of understanding her thoughts on the matter. He found that he desired her opinions more and more lately, especially when it came to the quest. He was disappointed to find that he could not figure what she was thinking at the moment. However, he did not want to ask her aloud; somehow it would spoil the moment. Darian sighed inwardly as he remembered Eithne's request to allow Giev to continue with them a few days ago. Her stand on the matter was probably unchanged. Also, she had mentioned then that Yocelin felt the same. Darian gave Giev a hard, thoughtful look for a few more seconds. He supposed that they didn't have much choice in the matter, anyway. Giev seemed like the type to follow them, even if he were told not to come along.

"Fine," Darian said with a heavy tone. "But before we sit to talk this all out, I propose we get to some place safer than the forest. Cavan is still on our trail, and we need more shelter than this to speak openly."

"Agreed, and thank you," Giev responded with a cordial smile. He was very pleased to finally be let in on their secrets and be part of the group.

Aram watched Giev as they resumed walking with a sour expression. He understood why Darian agreed to tell the shaman what they were doing, but he was still unsure of Giev's motives. Aram suspected that Darian felt the same, though Aram could not deny that Giev seemed to have a lot of value—especially if he really did know how to use the Stone of Elissiyus. Perhaps he would get used to Giev. Aram was not confident that he would learn to trust him. Aram glanced over at Yocelin walking beside him. She was rubbing her temples to try and alleviate her headache. He supposed now was not the best time to question her about Giev. Yocelin noticed him looking at her and made a pouty face. Aram gave her a small, sympathetic smile in return. She brightened at his compassion, and he turned his eyes forward again.

CHAPTER TWENTY-NINE

"*O*KAY," GIEV STATED the word with confidence as he sat in his chair at the small tavern. "We are in a village . . . sort of. We have some distance from the dreaded Cavan, as we have managed to find a table in the darkest, most private corner of the tavern. I say that circumstances are now all right to talk about your situation," he spoke in hushed tones, but he couldn't help but to look happy and energetic. He was excited to finally be let in on the secret.

Darian was much more somber, as were the rest of the companions at the table. Darian watched the barmaid bring their drinks and made sure that she was out of earshot before speaking. Giev considered this long moment torturous, but he tolerated it well.

"We are on a quest of the utmost importance," Darian began quietly and took a sip of his ale before continuing. "Have you ever heard of a wizard called Tim?"

Giev's brow wrinkled in mild confusion. "Do you mean the great wizard Timallyehoutsivycous, famous student of Elissiyus?"

The other four paused at the incredible name. Eithne leaned over to Yocelin and whispered, "No wonder he asked us to just call him Tim."

"Told us is more like it," Yocelin responded. She still held unto her unpleasant feelings for the old wizard, especially since she had another terrible headache that she could attribute to him.

"You know him?" Giev said in a voice that was too loud and rose slightly from his chair. He couldn't believe that his new friends knew the most famous and powerful wizard that lived!

Aram glared at Giev to let him know that he needed to control the volume of his voice.

Giev took the hint, sat back down, and calmed himself. "Please continue," he requested much more quietly, but they could all tell that he was barely able to control his excitement.

"Yes, that Tim. He was the one who charged us with the quest. You see, he seems to believe that the four of us were destined to, well, save the world," Darian felt so uncomfortable saying that. He had practically muttered the last part and took another sip of ale after speaking it to wash the strange taste out of his mouth.

"Save the world?" Giev whispered in awe. "How?"

Giev knew that Raashan did, indeed, need saving. Nothing had been right since the death of the gods. Giev, who was a few years older than his companions, could still remember how it felt to wield true magical power before everything went away. He had only been a novice at the time in the early years of his apprenticeship when it all happened. He remembered, though. Giev would give anything to feel the magic in that way again. He hoped that was part of saving the world.

"Well," Darian continued, "we are charged with collecting certain magical energy, for which Eithne and Yocelin are vessels. Once we collect enough of this energy, we are to perform some ceremony that will release it in a way that saves the world. Aram and I act as their protectors on this journey."

Eithne cocked her eyebrow at Darian and gave him a funny look. She thought that was a very lame way of explaining their quest. It almost didn't even make sense.

Giev was not stupid and knew that Darian was trying very hard to keep as much of the story from him as possible, though he would not push the matter at this time. He respected that Darian was not ready to reveal everything yet.

"So how does Cavan factor into all of this?" Giev asked.

"He's the bad guy in the story and a dangerous one," Darian answered shortly before taking a drink of ale.

Eithne sighed. Giev deserved more information than that. "Cavan is also a vessel that can hold the magical energy. There are others in the world that can do this. The problem is that Cavan is gathering this energy for his own selfish gain. He believes it will make him all-powerful. He is after Yocelin because he is able to steal the energy she has collected by killing her, which we really don't want to happen."

Giev nodded. "So gaining energy makes you stronger, and this Cavan has attained enough to be very scary, right?"

The others all nodded in unison.

"Why isn't he after you?" Giev addressed Eithne. "If you are also collecting energy, it only makes sense that he would try to kill you as well."

"Um, there are two different kinds of energy, light and dark. I am a vessel for the light, while Yocelin and Cavan are vessels for the dark. He cannot collect the light energy, though I'm sure he would be happy to kill me if he had the opportunity. He's happy to kill anyone really," Eithne explained.

"Ah, I see. So that is why two vessels are necessary. You must maintain the balance of good and evil. Thus, when you perform the ceremony, balance will be restored to Raashan."

"You're smart and cute," Yocelin smiled at Giev. She was impressed with how well he pieced everything together.

Giev grinned handsomely at her for the compliment.

"Is your curiosity satisfied now?" Aram asked bluntly.

Giev turned his grin to Aram, which irritated the werewolf. "No, never, but I have one more question before I will let you all relax. How do the two of you go around collecting that energy?"

"We don't kill anyone for it," Darian quickly interjected. He could tell what Giev's concern was.

"I didn't mean that! Well, all right, I wanted to clarify that part. How do you do it then?"

"Tim gave us charms to draw the energy out without killing the vessel. Usually, the person just feels temporarily weakened but are fine after a few hours," Eithne answered.

"Usually?"

"That's why we were fleeing Lupia when you first met us," Yocelin said guiltily. "One of the vessels I took the energy from was a very, very old elf who sort of accidently died when I took the energy from him. It was a complete accident, though! I just used the charm, and I thought he fell asleep, but that energy must have been the only thing keeping him alive because he was so old. He also happened to be a member of the royal family, so we had to get out of Lupia in a hurry." Yocelin dropped her head in shame as she spoke. She still felt very badly about having killed the old elf.

"Well, I'm sure it wasn't your fault if he were so old. I'm sorry." Giev didn't know how to respond and was admittedly surprised at how much remorse a demon was showing over the death of someone who probably should have been dead years ago. He knew that the reputation demons had was not reflected in all of them, but he hadn't supposed they could be so compassionate.

"Yocelin was raised by elves," Aram answered the confusion that was apparent on the shaman's face.

"What? How?" Giev was immediately more confused.

Yocelin told the story of her upbringing as the others had heard it a few months before. Her story led to the stories of Eithne and Darian. Aram shared very little about himself. He knew that he would eventually have to tell Giev what he was, but Aram was not ready to reveal himself yet. They all talked quietly into the night. When it became too late, the companions made camp just outside of the tiny village, for the village so rarely had visitors that there was no place to rent a room for the night.

Yocelin could still sense Cavan, but it felt as though he were keeping his distance. She couldn't imagine why. The feeling made her both relieved and nervous. Still she managed to sleep and alleviate her headache that night.

Cavan was keeping his distance for reasons he did not fully understand either. He continued to follow them but could not tell their exact location as he had been able to do before. It was like there was something scrambling his ability to hone in of the she-demon. He knew that they were within a three- or four-mile radius but had no idea exactly where within that space. Cavan tried to meditate to clear his senses that night. He realized that the she-demon was more powerful now, which meant that she had gained more of Muntros. His lip curled into a sadistic smile. It meant that there was all the more for him to gain when he killed her.

CHAPTER THIRTY

*L*IFE IN THE Aranni village had grown worse over the past months. The autumn harvest was meager at best, which meant that many in the village were starving over the winter. The people helped each other as much as possible. Those who were able to gather more food and hunt shared what they could with the community, but the surrounding forest offered very little even to the most experienced woodsmen. The people had become thin and sickly. It seemed that the consequences of the death of the gods had finally begun to take a more serious toll on the Aranni tribe. They could only imagine how the rest of the world was suffering if their small community, which had been very fortunate so far, was so affected.

Rosalin shivered under her cloak as she carried a basket of nuts that she had gathered in the forest home. It was a cold day with gray skies looming above. Rosalin could not remember the last time she had seen the sun. It depressed her horribly, as it did the rest of the tribal elves, for all elves revel in the sunlight. To be denied the joyous glow for so long was torturous to all who lived in the village. Rosalin's mother was among those who had grown ill recently, so she hurried home to check on her. She found that she missed Eithne desperately in these days. She wanted to tell her so much, and Eithne was always skilled with herbal remedies. Her little sister would be able to help her mother as well as many others in the village. Rosalin also yearned to share with her sister that Theryl had asked for her hand in marriage. Rosalin loved him dearly and proudly wore the symbol of his family around her neck to show that she was promised to him. It was a warm spot of joy to the Alfrey family in these harsh times. Rosalin and Theryl would wait until spring to marry, as all tribal elves married in the spring, preferably under a growing moon. It was a time of new beginnings and rebirth. To be married in any other season was believed to be bad luck. Once married, the tribal elf custom was that the husband and wife would have the symbol of the husband's family tattooed on the backs of each of their right hands to symbolize their union. Rosalin had girlishly drawn Theryl's family symbol on the back of her right hand using charcoal several times since becoming engaged. She liked the way it looked, and it made her happy to think about starting her new life as Theryl's wife.

Rosalin announced herself as she came inside the house and hung up her cloak. Her father called her into the bedroom. He had been by his wife's side since she fell ill a week ago. He sat in a chair next to the bed staring out the window.

"I'll heat up the broth," Rosalin whispered as she hugged her father in greeting and handed him the nuts she had collected. Her mother was sleeping soundly in the bed.

"It will do her well to eat something. I think that she has been better today," her father said meekly.

The skin on his face was pale and taunt with worry and lack of sleep. Also, like everyone else in the village, he had become thinner. He ignored the basket of nuts that Rosalin had left with him. He didn't feel like eating. It was best that his wife and daughter eat them instead.

"Was there any news today?" Rosalin inquired after she had lit the fire and put the pot of broth over it to heat. She came to sit next to her father and looked at him expectantly.

"Yes, Theryl was kind enough to deliver a letter," her father indicated the unopened envelope on the table. He noticed his daughter's worried expression and smiled kindly as he reached over and patted her hand. "Don't worry, he said that he would come back later since you were out. He didn't want to go a day without seeing you either. I haven't opened the letter yet. I waited for you to come home to read it. It looks like it came to us all the way from the continent of Croissia."

Rosalin's eyes grew wide. The letter had to be news from Darian. No one else could possibly be writing from so far away. It amazed her that they had traveled so far. Most tribal elves never even left their homeland, let alone journeying across the sea to a whole other continent! Rosalin hesitated to pick up the letter and open it. She and her family both hoped for and dreaded the arrival of such letters from Captain Darian. There was always an anxious fear that they would bear news that Eithne had been hurt or possibly even killed. Thankfully, no such news had come yet, but they never knew what each letter would bring. Rosalin swallowed her fears and boldly opened the letter for reading.

Father patiently allowed Rosalin to read the letter. She would tell him what it said once she was finished.

"They aren't coming back for a very long time," Rosalin squeaked as she put her hand to her mouth.

She was surprised at her own emotional reaction to the news. She wanted her sister to come home so badly, and to be told that Eithne would not be coming back for a long time was shockingly devastating.

"What do you mean?" her father anxiously leaned forward in his chair but tried not to let fear creep into his voice. He could see how upset his daughter was already.

Rosalin took a breath to calm herself and sniffed away her tears. "Darian writes that they are all well and staying with a wizard called Tim in the City of Duomo. He says that he cannot speak of everything that has transpired, but they have all been charged with an important quest. He said that Eithne is doing very well and, as always, that he will continue to protect and care for her, but then he says that the quest they are charged with will keep them away for a long time. He doesn't know how long. Darian only wrote that we should not expect their return for at least a year. He will continue to send letters at every opportunity."

Her father closed his eyes as he absorbed the new information. It was like being struck in the chest hearing that Eithne would not be coming home for at least a year. So much could happen to her in a year! Even though he loved both of his daughters dearly, he had always felt closer to Eithne. He wished she were here to lend her support to the family during these hard times. It was difficult knowing that she would not come home soon. Right now, though, his eldest daughter and wife needed him. Her father hugged Rosalin close and did his best to soothe her upset.

Her mother stirred in the bed. She was beginning to wake up.

"We won't tell your mother the part about Eithne not coming back anytime soon. Just that she is safe and with Darian still," her father whispered to Rosalin before releasing her.

Rosalin nodded her concurrence. There was no need to upset their mother further in her current state. She stood and went over to ladle the broth into a bowl for their mother to eat. She told herself that things would get better once spring came.

CHAPTER THIRTY-ONE

*G*IEV HAD BEEN feeling much more comfortable and yet with an overwhelming sense of responsibility the past two weeks. The group had managed to make it out of the dead forest and had been heading south toward more civilization and slightly warmer weather. Giev was comfortable because he felt more accepted by Aram and Darian. After the night that they had told him about their quest, they all felt that they knew more about each other. Also, he could tell that they were even starting to like him. Perhaps Giev would be able to call them his friends in another week or so. Giev felt a greater responsibility because now he found himself involved in a quest to save Raashan. It was quite a burden to bear. He hadn't really come to terms with the entire weight of it yet. He had spoken with the others about this, and they had all said the same thing. It takes a long time to process the idea that you are responsible for saving the world. They had all been doing so for months, and all admitted that none of them felt completely right about it yet. Such a thing is difficult to comprehend, logically or emotionally.

Giev had decided on taking a proactive approach to his newfound duty, and he had even thought of something that could help their progress. He had a chance to observe how they sought out those who carried the magical energy. They had been trained in a form of meditation to seek them out, but they had to be very close to a vessel in order to sense the energy. So the companions simply tried to travel to places of higher population density and hope to be lucky. It felt slow and random to Giev, and he happened to know of an artifact that would help a great deal, for it could be programmed to seek out the specific energies they needed from great distances. Therefore, less time would be wasted in the searching. Getting the object could prove difficult, however. How difficult it would be, would have to be seen.

The next night, they made camp near a crossroads. The companions all huddled around the fire to fight off the winter cold. There was snow on the ground as well as some large balls of hail that they had to take shelter from earlier that afternoon. It was so cold that nothing was melting away.

"So which direction shall we go tomorrow?" Eithne asked the group. "East is toward the City of Vei, which should have a lot of people."

The rest of them nodded their accord, except Giev who had another suggestion. "Why don't we go west?"

The others all looked at him as if he were daft. West led them into the mountains and far from civilization. It made no sense and would be rough travel.

"It seems that you know something we don't. Why not explain?" Aram said flatly.

"Well, I've noticed that the process of finding the energy pieces is a very lengthy, random one. I know of an artifact that could show us whether or not a city or town is even worth visiting. It would save us a lot of time and effort," Giev explained.

"Sounds too good to be true," Darian said thoughtfully, but the others could tell by his tone that he wanted to know more. "Why can't we just use the Stone of Elissiyus for that?"

"Well, I haven't quite figured how to operate the stone yet," Giev admitted sheepishly. He had been working with it and was able to get some small reactions from it, but harnessing its power would take much more time. Giev did not want to hold up the process of saving the world because of his inadequacies.

"Then what is the other artifact, and what do we have to do to get it? Is it pretty?" Yocelin chimed in her cheery way.

"It is pretty, actually. It's called the Gem of Amara. It is named for the maiden that legend says was the original owner. Now, the gem is kept by a race of monks in the mountains to the west. It was always intended as a locating charm for divine energy. The legend says one of the old demigods fell in love with the maiden Amara, who was of a nomadic race. As Amara and her demigod lover were both constantly on the move, finding one another often proved difficult. So the demigod created a gem that could be worn as a pendant on a necklace that would seek and locate divine energy over great distances. He gave it to Amara so that she could always find him." Giev smiled as he told the old legend. He always enjoyed such stories.

"That's very romantic," Eithne mused with a girlish sigh. "I like stories like that. What happened to them?"

Darian smiled at Eithne's feminine expression of emotion. Giev had noticed that Darian usually showed pleasure when Eithne acted this way. Giev did not think that Eithne took notice, though.

"The legend says that they were lovers until Amara died of old age. The demigod was immortal, and continued on until the death of the gods. As you know, the children of the gods, demigods, were also involved and subsequently killed during the Heavenly Wars."

"Oh, good," Yocelin said with a sign of relief. "I was so afraid that he was going to ditch her when she started getting old. So many of those old stories end up that way, but this one sounds like true love." She smiled wistfully, thinking of other romantic stories and notions. "I think we should go for it!"

"You're easily swayed by a nice story," Aram was trying to sound annoyed at her rashness, but the warmth in his voice gave away his true feelings. "Before we go off into the mountains, we need to know what is needed to acquire this Gem of Amara."

"There is good news and not so good news on that front," Giev replied. "The good news is that I know how to get to the mountain that the monks dwell upon and that the monks most definitely have the gem. The more gray area is that the mountain will be a difficult climb and that the monks will require a trade of service before handing it over to us."

"What sort of trade or service? I do not think that giving up the stone is a good idea," Darian stated thoughtfully.

"I agree," Aram confirmed.

"As do I," answered Giev. He held up his hands almost defensively to bar any idea of argument. "So we will exchange a service. It will probably be a sort of errand because the monks cannot leave their mountain. However, one of us will have to stay at the base of the mountain with the stone. If the monks sense its presence, then they may demand that we trade it."

Darian rubbed the growing stubble on his chin as he pondered on this new situation. He needed to shave. Facial hair was very slow to grow on elves, and so the clean-shaven look was largely preferred. Beards were not usually worth the time and effort for elves. "So how long will it take, and are you sure the monks will trade us for the gem?"

"I'm certain they will make a trade, yes. The monks themselves have no use for it. As far as time is concerned, it should only take us two or three days to reach the mountain from here, a day or more to climb it, and I don't know what sort of service they will ask of us. So I can't say how long we will be there," Giev answered as fully as he could.

"What if we got some horses?" Yocelin interjected. "That could cut the time in half, right?"

Darian nodded at Yocelin. Horses would make things better and faster overall. They had been conservative with the money Tim had given them, so he was certain that there would be enough to purchase a couple of horses.

Eithne clapped her hands together triumphantly. "It's decided then! We will get some horses and go after the Gem of Amara!"

"I never said that!" Darian protested.

"No, but you thought it. I've come to read you rather well, Darian MacAllow," Eithne responded in a smug, almost-flirtatious way. She leaned into him as she spoke in a distracting manner.

Darian realized he was grinning back at her when he heard Yocelin giggle. He immediately snapped to attention, as did Eithne, who blushed just a little pink from embarrassment.

"Keep getting to know him like that, and you'll make your sister jealous," Yocelin chided playfully at Eithne, who did not respond.

Even Aram was amused at the display. Usually, he was the one being embarrassed by Yocelin's extremely demonstrative ways. Even now, she was gently poking him with her elbow to make sure he was paying full attention to the humor of the situation.

Darian was surprised at Yocelin's mention of Rosalin. The last time he had thought of her was when Eithne mentioned her sister back when she had the fever. In fact, he realized he barely ever thought of her unless someone else spoke of her. His once-intended bride was obviously not the right woman for him. He had focused on Rosalin back in the village because she was considered to be highly desirable and very traditional. Darian had always wanted a family and thought that a beautiful traditional girl was his best choice for marriage. Rosalin fit this model exactly and even came from a good family, yet she did not appear to hold his interest. He turned and looked at Eithne. Perhaps he had simply been too preoccupied with Eithne and their quest to think about Rosalin.

Eithne's grass-green eyes flashed Darian's way when she realized he was looking at her again. Her blush, which had begun to ebb, deepened again.

"Will you stop that?" she whispered harshly at him. "You'll only make them keep teasing."

She was a little angry, as she sometimes expressed her embarrassment. Darian obliged her and looked back at the others. It seemed they were no longer paying attention to him and Eithne. Aram and Yocelin were having another one of their quiet battles. Yocelin was trying to snuggle up to him for warmth, and Aram was trying (not very hard) to get her to snuggle with Eithne instead. The she-demon expressed her refusal by staying firmly clamped to his side. She was always saying that Aram was the warmest one in the group and, therefore, the best one to be next to in the winter cold. As usual, Aram resigned himself to his fate. Darian did notice a softness come over his friend's face as he looked at Yocelin. It looked as though he enjoyed her affections more than he wanted her to know.

Aram looked up at Darian, and the two protectors locked eyes. They had the same thought, for they were both suddenly reminded of the wizard's warning.

Giev, who had been satisfied at Eithne's proclamation that they would be going west tomorrow, had already started dozing in his bedroll.

CHAPTER THIRTY-TWO

*T*RUE TO GIEV'S estimation, they arrived at the base of the monk's mountain at the end of the second day of traveling since the crossroads. They had purchased three horses and some warm gloves in a town that they had passed through the day before. The mountain was not very high, and it did not fit with the rest of the proud rocky peaks jutting up around them. This mountain had a craggy, twisted apprearance with little to no vegetation growing on it. It was not a friendly looking thing.

"You expect us to climb that?" Yocelin scoffed as she dismounted.

Giev chuckled to try and make light of the situation and ease any tensions. "It's not as bad as it seems. There are plenty of hand- and footholds on the climb, so don't worry."

"Too late for that," Yocelin grumbled as she continued to regard the monk's mountain.

The peak seemed to have a dense cloud resting on top of it. The cloud made it impossible to see the summit. At first, Yocelin dismissed it as just a low resting winter cloud but realized it was more sinister when she saw that all the other clouds in the sky were much higher in the sky and not nearly as heavy and gray. Now it wasn't the climb that bothered her so much as reaching the top.

"So what do we do when we get to the top? Will these monks be easy to find?" Aram asked Giev as he tethered the horses.

"You don't have to think about that. The monks will find you, probably before you reach the top," Giev responded. "They know when someone is on their mountain and will come to retrieve you."

"So they like having guests then?"

"You could say that, but they like doing business more," Giev started unsaddling the horses. There was no need to burden the animals with their tack while they weren't being ridden.

Aram nodded affirmatively. He hoped this would be an easy transaction. Having the Gem of Amara would be well worth their detour.

It had already been decided that Giev would be the one to stay with the horses and Stone of Elissiyus at the base of the mountain. The terrain of this mountain was not suitable for horses. They made camp, since it was already late. Darian, Aram, Eithne, and Yocelin would begin their climb early tomorrow morning.

The climb started off all right at the base of the mountain, but as they climbed higher, things became progressively worse. Bitter winter winds tore into them at high force and numbed their aching fingers. The face of the mountain was so steep that they were almost vertical the entire time. The trial completely exhausted their bodies to the point that the girls did not even have strength enough to voice complaint. All efforts were directed upward. They stopped to rest whenever it was possible. Any outcropping large enough to sit and rest a while was a welcome relief. A little over a third of the way up, they were lucky enough to find a cave to shelter in. It was not the deepest of caves, but it protected them from the horrible wind, and there was enough space for the four of them to lie down to sleep for the night. The sun was starting to set already. Progress had been slow today, but none of it could be attributed to a lack of effort. No one spoke as they tore into their rations of dried meat and bread. Then they laid out their bedrolls and went to sleep. There was no need to keep watch as any of them saw it. There were no animals to fear, and the only other people on the mountain were the monks they had not yet reached.

A soft blue light illuminated the cave from the pitch-black of the winter night. From the light emerged a hooded figure in a tattered brown robe. The figure was humanoid in shape, but its face was completely obscured by a hood. It stood over the four figures sleeping on the cave floor and regarded them for a moment in silence. It seemed it was waiting for something to happen.

Eithne awoke suddenly with the feeling that someone else was in the cave. She was startled to find that she was right upon waking, for there was a robed figure standing in front of her. Eithne did not utter a sound. Rather, she promptly hit Darian's shoulder, who was sleeping next to her, without taking her eyes off the robed figure. Darian's reaction was similar. He shook Aram awake, and Aram did the same to Yocelin. Once they were all awake and alert, the figure— who had remained completely still and silent until now—nodded slowly and spoke, "Welcome, travelers. You have come to barter with us, yes?"

Its voice wasn't quite human and had a strange hissing quality to it.

"Are you one of the monks that live on this mountain?" Darian asked.

The robed figure gave another slow nod.

"Then, yes, we seek to barter with you," Darian answered cautiously.

"Follow me," the monk stated. Then he slowly began to walk down a long corridor that had not been there before, taking the dim blue light with it.

The four companions quickly snatched up their bedrolls and followed. It seemed as though they walked for hours going slightly uphill the entire time. The walk was easy enough, but they were still very tired at the end, having had exerted themselves so much that day then not getting proper sleep to refresh. Finally, they were at an end when there was a spot of faint daylight after turning a final corner in the corridor. Eithne and Yocelin exchanged looks of great relief when they saw this. Hopefully, the monks were the hospitable sort and there would be some form of refreshment offered once the emerged. The monk that led them had not spoken at all during the walk and had kept a steady, almost-hypnotizing pace the whole way. None of the companions had been able to glimpse his face, though not for lack of trying. The hood completely obstructed the view. Even the monk's hands had remained perfectly folded into the sleeves of his robe. They were all extremely curious to see what the monks looked like. So this behavior was disappointing. Giev had described the monks as being a different race altogether with a very strange appearance to elf and human eyes. Hopefully, the monks would not be so prudent the entire time that they were here.

The tunnel opened into a cloudy forum. The monk that led them went to stand with two other monks in the center of a large circular platform. The platform was clear, but the mist fell everywhere around it. This was the top of the mountain that was forever veiled in the gray cloud. It was strangely warm and humid in the cloud. It must have been some sort of magic. The four of them stood on the clear platform just outside the entrance to the tunnel for several long, awkward moments. The monks were still and silent.

Finally, Darian realized that they were expected to start the dealings.

"We come to barter for the Gem of Amara," he stated with his military confidence.

"We have the Gem of Amara," the monk in the center hissed. "What do you bring to barter?"

"Our services. We have no items that would be of interest to you. What do you wish us to do in exchange for the gem?" Darian answered plainly.

The monks stood silent for a couple of minutes. As they did, there seemed to be a strange humming sound in the air, and the monks themselves appeared to almost be vibrating.

"Do you think they are communicating telepathically?" Eithne whispered to Yocelin. She was afraid to speak at full volume and possibly upset the monks.

"It looks that way," Yocelin answered, but she wasn't really certain what was happening. The humming in the air made her body feel slightly tingly all over.

The humming ceased.

"Yes," the monk to the right said, "there is an errand we require. Some time ago, we lent one of our treasures to Sir Orson Smyls. We will accept the retrieval and delivery of our treasure as payment for the Gem of Amara."

That seemed simple enough—so long as Sir Orson Smyls was expecting to return the treasure and he didn't live halfway around the world. Those two possible hurdles were rather worrisome.

"Where does Sir Orson live?" Aram asked skeptically.

"Not far," the monk hissed. "One week's ride south from here, you will find his manor. He will be expecting you."

The companions all looked at each other and shrugged. That didn't sound bad at all.

"Do we have a deal?" the monk to the left, who had led them to this place, asked in a voice that sounded almost as if it were salivating over the prospect of the deal.

"Yes, we have a deal," Darian confirmed.

"Excellent!" all three monks spoke the word in unison, and the air seemed to hum with pleasure for an instant.

"A guide will take the two males back down the mountain and provide you with directions to the manor," the monk in the center directed.

"Wait. Aren't we going too?" Yocelin didn't like the feeling she was getting. It made her certain that she wasn't going to like whatever would happen next.

"The two females will remain here as collateral," the one on the right said with what sounded like it would have been a mocking chuckle.

"That wasn't part of the deal!" Darian stated his words so boldly that it was practically a shout. His straight, chiseled features were set in an angry expression.

Aram growled and bristled. He was not as vocal as his friend, but it was apparent that he was just as angered by the sudden surprise.

The monks showed no signs of fear or upset. They had no reason to worry over two mortals, for their power was not gifted from the magic of the old gods. They themselves were the source and, as such, were possibly the most powerful beings left on the miserable, dying planet. Perhaps they even possessed the power to save Raashan, but the monks had no care for such grand schemes. The threat of death did not cause them any dismay.

"If you all go, then we have no assurance that you will bring our treasure back to us. The females will be well cared for in your absence. No harm will come to them," the monk hissed in its reptilian voice. Its tone was patronizing.

"How can we be sure they will be safe?" Darian demanded, still angry at the situation.

He felt as though he never wanted Eithne to leave his sight. Was he failing her as her protector if he left her here with these things?

Aram stepped in front of Yocelin. He didn't like the feeling of this place or the monks. There was something eerily wrong here. Aram could see into the thick mist with his keen eyes, and there were many other brown robed figures moving there all around them. There were perhaps a hundred of these creatures up here. It was not a good situation.

"You have our word," the monk answered Darian coolly.

"In that case," Eithne chimed in, "you have our word that we will return the treasure to you in two weeks' time, maximum. We'll just all go together to fetch it."

She didn't really think her childish rebuttal would be accepted, but she thought it was a good idea to at least try. The look Darian gave her told her just how ridiculous she sounded, unfortunately.

The monks paid no mind to Eithne's offer and stood silently, waiting for the reaction from Darian, with whom they had struck the deal initially.

"We will take a moment to discuss this," Darian stated firmly. It was not a request.

The monks nodded their accord in perfect unison.

"Do we have any choice here?" Eithne started when they all turned to face each other in a small huddle. "I thought that Giev said you couldn't renege on the deal once it was struck. The deal is struck!"

"Well, how bad could it be?" Yocelin replied, trying to sound positive. "It would only be a few days, and Eithne and I are capable. I don't think these monks have any interest in harming us."

"Not physically, no," Aram said. "But they seem sadistic in nature. I wouldn't doubt that they would do something to upset you."

"Thanks for that," Yocelin said sarcastically.

"This decision lies with you two," Darian addressed Eithne and Yocelin. "If you absolutely feel that you cannot stay on the mountain, then we will try to cancel the deal. If you want to try it their way, I'll respect that, but I won't like it."

Darian would have preferred the former option, but it really wasn't his or Aram's decision. He too felt that the monks were cruel in nature, but he believed that they would also keep their word.

Eithne and Yocelin stared at each other. What should they do?

"I'll stay here while you go," Eithne tried to sound completely resolved. The truth was that she didn't really see any other options. She shuddered to think what might happen to them if they tried to go back on the deal.

"Ditto," Yocelin followed Eithne's lead and resigned herself to the deal.

"You're certain?" Aram asked, hopeful that they would have second thoughts.

Both women nodded that they were certain of their decision.

"Just double check the whole no-harm-will-come-to-the-females part, okay? Make sure that covers all definitions of harm," Yocelin requested anxiously.

"I was just about to do that," Darian said as he looked at Eithne. She gave him a little smile to let him know she would be okay.

Darian took a deep breath in and gave Aram a curt nod, which was returned, before turning back to answer the monks.

"Eithne and Yocelin have agreed to stay on the mountain while Aram and I fetch the item back for you, so long as no harm comes to them whatsoever, physical, emotional, or otherwise." Darian held his head high as he spoke. His voice seemed to resound all around as he answered, which made his statement all the more impactful.

"Agreed," all three monks hissed with pleasure.

"The two of you will be led back to the base of the mountain and given directions," the middle one stated, and the same monk that had led them through the underground tunnel stepped forward.

The monk nodded at Darian and Aram to follow and walked toward another tunnel, which seemed to appear from nothing.

Aram briefly turned to Yocelin and rested his hand on her shoulder. Before he could even speak, she hugged her arms around him and gave him a good squeeze. Aram felt a pang of regret as she did so. He already hated this decision and knew something bad would come of Yocelin staying on the mountain. Awkwardly, he returned her squeeze and held on until she released him. The brave smile she gave him did little to settle his nerves as he followed the monk into the tunnel.

Darian did not immediately follow the monk but stood staring at Eithne with a concerned expression. Eithne looked back with the bravest face she could muster. He was taking too long, and she couldn't look brave forever. He wasn't wavering. Eithne took a step forward and clasped his hand in hers.

"Go now, and come back soon," she whispered then released his hand. Darian held her eyes as he gave her a slow nod. Then he turned and left.

Eithne and Yocelin stood together as they watched Darian and Aram disappear down the tunnel. Both women hoped that they would return as quickly as possible. The monk's mountain was not a happy place to be, and no good could come of their brief stay here.

Darian and Aram found themselves in a state of haste. Walking back down the tunnels to the base of the mountain took far too long. They felt like running past the monk leading them to get to the horses as fast as possible, but they both knew they couldn't do that. Whatever magic operated these tunnels, the monks controlled it. So they probably wouldn't get to where they needed to be if they ran past their guide with its irritatingly slow gait. Finally, the tunnel opened into daylight at the base of the twisted mountain. Without a second glance, Darian and Aram pushed out of the tunnel and began looking for Giev and the horses.

"Wait," the monk hissed.

The protectors turned back with mighty impatience and glared at the monk.

The monk made a noise that sounded like a mocking chuckle, but it did have something important to tell them.

"When you return, come to this exact spot and announce your-selves. Someone will be along shortly to guide you back up."

Darian gave a curt nod and turned his attention back to locat-ing the camp. Aram did not even offer the courtesy of a nod.

They managed to locate the campsite within a few minutes. They explained the situation in as few words as possible to Giev. Thankfully, Giev understood their haste and did not question them. He simply cautioned them against riding the horses to death while he helped to saddle them and let the protectors be on their way. Giev stayed at the camp with the remaining horse and the Stone of Elissiyus. He gazed up to the stormy peak of the twisted mountain and prayed for Eithne and Yocelin's safety. Giev only knew that they were with the monk's collateral and should not be harmed, but the monks did not inspire trust. He feared, as the protectors did, that the monks would do something unpleasant to his friends.

Darian and Aram were still running on pure adrenaline when they arrived at the gates of Sir Orson Smyls's manor. Their horses were run ragged and were slathered with white foaming sweat. Even at an easy walk, the animals labored for breath. Darian felt badly for riding the horses to such exhaustion, but as he and Aram saw it, there was no other way. They had made it to the manor in just over four days. They greeted the guard at the gate and told him that they wished to speak to the master of the house because they had urgent news for him. The guard led them into the reception hall of the manor and gave them refreshments. A groom came to tend to their horses. Both men knew they would not be long at the manor, but the horses could certainly use some food, water, and perhaps some basic grooming to ease their overworked muscles.

The protectors were not kept waiting long. Sir Orson Smyls appeared with a lady, who was apparently his wife, on his arm. He was human, in his late middle age of life, with thick silver hair at his temples contrasting sharply with the jet-black hair covering the rest of his head. He had a strong, rugged appearance. The lady he escorted was of the same age, blond and statuesque.

"Welcome to my home, travelers," Sir Orson greeted cordially. "My wife and I would welcome you more formally, but we were told that your news is urgent."

"Thank you, Sir Orson. I am Captain Darian, and this is my friend, Aram. We have been sent by the monks to retrieve the artifact you borrowed some time ago," Darian rarely introduced himself with his military rank these days, but since they were greeting a lord, he thought it best to reveal himself.

Sir Orson's wife paled at the mention of the monks, and Sir Orson's expression darkened. He cleared his throat before speaking again. "I can understand your haste if you have been sent by them. Ronald!" he called out for the servant so suddenly that it startled the other three present.

A servant, who was probably Ronald, hurried into the reception hall and bowed to his master.

"Please fetch me the small wooden box on the bookshelf in my study and bring it to me," Sir Orson commanded. Ronald bowed a second time and went off to retrieve the box.

"We appreciate your understanding," Aram thanked him for hurrying.

"I wish I didn't understand it so well," Sir Orson replied with a heavy sigh as he guided his wife to sit in a nearby chair. "So whom did you two have to leave with those monsters?"

Darian and Aram were both struck by the way he referred to the monks and the hatred in his voice as he spoke to them.

"Our . . . friends," Darian stammered worriedly. "Did you have a similar deal with them?"

Sir Orson nodded slowly. "Yes, I did. Some thirty-five years ago, when I was a young man, too ambitious, and sought an artifact from the monks that would make me a superhuman warrior. My dear wife and I had just been married. She accompanied me on the journey." He looked down at his wife and squeezed her hand. She held his hand in both of hers and gave him a weak smile. "In order to get the artifact, I had to leave my wife with them as 'collateral' while I ran an errand for them. I hated it, but she assured me she would be fine, and my ambitions outweighed my good judgment. I was gone for seven days. When I returned for her and the artifact, the monks gave me the artifact readily, but Juliana . . ." He looked to his wife again. "Juliana was changed, not herself. She had been drugged somehow and no longer recognized me, nor did she want to leave the mountain."

Juliana cast her eyes downward, embarrassed still of what happened all those years ago. Her husband continued his story in a darker tone.

"It was as if the monks were playing a cruel joke on us for their own sick amusement. They told me that I could take her back if she would go with me. She would not. In desperation, I forcibly removed Juliana from the mountain and tied her to her horse for two days to keep her from returning to the mountain. I can still hear their infernal hissing laughter in my ears."

Both Sir Orson and his wife were quiet for a few seconds. Neither one of them liked thinking about that time.

"What happened after the two days had gone by?" Aram asked very seriously.

"The drugs or whatever they had given me wore off, and I once again remembered who I was and who Orson was," Juliana answered meekly.

"What happened to you on the mountain?" Darian understood that he was prying, but he was desperate to know what might be happening to Eithne and Yocelin.

Juliana shook her head and pursed her lips tightly. She was becoming upset by stirring up the old memories.

"She doesn't really remember," Sir Orson responded for her when he saw that his wife was not going to answer the question. "After the effects of the drugs wore off, she claimed that she couldn't remember what had transpired those days she was on the mountain."

He looked at his wife as he spoke with pain in his eyes. There was a deep emotional wound there.

"I didn't remember," Juliana defended. "Sometimes I have nightmares that I think must be my memories of what happened there, I try my best to forget them."

A long pause hung heavily in the air. Darian and Aram exchanged looks. Both were even more scared for Eithne and Yocelin now. What was happening to them on that cursed mountain?

Ronald came back into the hall carrying the wooden box. It was a simple box with no carvings or adornments, but the protectors could actually feel the energy coming from what was inside that non-descript box. Sir Orson indicated that Ronald was to give the box to Darian, which the servant did readily. Darian accepted it and tucked it into his pack without bothering to see what was inside. It did not matter.

"I will not keep you as you must be even more anxious to get back to your friends now," Sir Orson stated. "I have had rations provided for you and fresh horses brought around. You will get back faster that way. I will simply keep the ones you rode in on, and you may keep the new ones."

Darian and Aram thanked him for his great generosity and empathy of their situation. Then they turned to follow the servant to their new mounts.

Darian stopped just before exiting the hall and turned back to Sir Orson and Juliana. "Was it worth it?"

A pained expression crossed the lord's face at the question. He had realized the answer to that question thirty-five years ago.

"No, the artifact delivered supreme fighting capabilities and strength, as promised. As a result, I advanced quickly in the knighthood and gained much wealth and admiration. When I think about it, however, none of that really matters. Juliana and I could have easily led a full, happy life together with less extravagance. We probably would have even been happier without that dark memory in our minds. I hope you two do not come to regret your deal with the monks as we do."

Darian did not trouble them further. He simply thanked Sir Orson again and hurried out to the horses. He already regretted leaving Eithne and Yocelin with the monks. His only solace was that their quest was not for personal gain as Sir Orson's had been.

Aram was already on his horse and ready to leave. Darian quickly mounted the other animal, and the two rode out at a gallop without a second glance.

CHAPTER THIRTY-THREE

ARIAN AND ARAM arrived back at the monk's mountain in another four days' time. The exhausted horses skidded to a halt at the campsite where Giev and the third horse were. Giev immediately jumped to his feet to help however he could.

"How did it go?" Giev asked apprehensively.

"We have the artifact," Aram answered bluntly.

He and Darian were already dismounted and headed to the spot that the magical tunnel had opened out to before. Under normal circumstances, their behavior would have been very rude, but Giev barely took notice. He was nearly as anxious as they were to have Eithne and Yocelin back. The faster they got the item back to the monks, the sooner this would all be over. Giev tended to the horses, which he noticed were not the same ones they had departed on, and kept looking to the stormy summit of the mountain, hoping everything was all right.

Darian and Aram announced themselves at the proper spot, and the tunnel promptly appeared with a monk at its entrance. Once again, they were forced to endure what felt like a snail's pace as they were led to the forum at the top of the mountain. Once again, there were the two monks waiting for them on the clear platform, and the guide joined them and faced the protectors.

Darian immediately took the wooden box from his pack and presented it to the monks. "Here is the item you asked us to retrieve. Now where are Eithne and Yocelin?"

The monk in the center glided over to them. It unfolded its hands from inside the robes to take the wooden box. Darian noted a mild foul odor when the monk was close to him and saw that its hands were scaly, yellow, absent of any fingernails, and only had four digits. The sight was disturbing to him, but he managed to maintain his stoic demeanor. The monk glided back and stood in its place, holding the box. There was a soft flare of light, and on the ground at Darian and Aram's feet, a necklace appeared with a large emerald pendant that was set in ornately designed gold.

"The Gem of Amara, as promised," the three monks hissed in unison.

Darian bent down and picked up the necklace. He stowed it in his pocket.

"Where are our women?" Aram growled. He wanted them back right this instant.

There was a vibration that swept through the air followed by an even brighter flash of light. Eithne and Yocelin appeared off to the right of the monks. They stood still with dazed expressions on their faces but otherwise looked unharmed. Darian and Aram were so relieved to see the girls again! They immediately started toward them but suddenly stopped as they hit an invisible barrier. The monks chuckled in unison at Darian and Aram's anger.

"You will stop these games now!" Darian bellowed angrily. "Let us take our friends back!"

"Ah! But they are more than that!" the center monk's mood suddenly changed as he hissed the words venomously. "These are no ordinary women. It seems you left us more than mere collateral, for we now have new treasures to keep."

"No! You can't do that! We had a deal!" Aram shouted. He could feel himself wanting to change. He could always feel the wolf rising within whenever he became very angry.

"The deal was for the Gem of Amara, which we have provided," the monk on the left stated smugly. "As for the women, we promised that no harm would come to them. We never said you would get them back. There is a great magical power in each of them. That makes them valuable to us."

The protectors were so infuriated that they both tried to physically attack the monks, only to find another invisible wall in their way. This was beyond bad. What could they do? The men paced like hungry wolves and eyed the monks, trying to gauge a weakness in them. As they paced, the monks were tranquil. They remained still and silent, awaiting the next offer.

Aram stopped his pacing and stared at the monks. That was it! They would have to make another trade, and for the first time, Aram was glad a werewolf had bitten him.

"I have another offer for you!" Aram shouted violently.

The monks nodded, indicating that he should tell them his offer.

"The trade will be for both of our women, completely intact, with all of the energy within that each currently possesses, both of them, exactly as they are now," Aram wanted to be absolutely clear on the terms.

"What are you doing?" Darian whispered harshly in Aram's ear. He trusted his friend but did not wish to barter further with the ignoble monks.

"I'm getting the girls back the best way I can think of. Just let me try this, and go along with what I ask," Aram answered coolly.

Darian nodded curtly. He still didn't like the idea of making a second deal, but he didn't have a plan at the moment, and Aram clearly did.

The monks were practically salivating at the prospect of another deal. The one thing that they had a true passion for was bargaining, and they so rarely got to do it. To make two bargains in such a short time was most exciting.

"What do you offer in exchange for the women?" they hissed in anticipation.

"The fang of a werewolf," Aram answered confidently.

He knew that werewolf fangs were actually quite valuable. They were used for making deadly poisons, could make someone a werewolf, and wizards could work very powerful spells with the aid of a werewolf tooth. Aram wished he thought of it before to bargain for the Gem of Amara. His entire mouth was full of these precious teeth! This whole situation could have been avoided if he had only realized his value before. He tried not to think too much about that.

Darian's eyebrows shot up. He had never heard of using werewolf teeth for bartering. Then again, Darian was not the type to have black market dealings in his past, so he would not know about the value of such things.

The air all around hummed intensely. The monks seemed quite intrigued with Aram's offer. The tooth of a werewolf was rare and valuable, indeed.

"Is it fresh?" the center monk hissed with a sort of hunger.

"Not even a day old," Aram answered. He shifted his eyes to Darian and gave him a look when he spoke.

Darian was confused for a second about what Aram was trying to communicate. Then it dawned on him: Aram needed him to pull the tooth from his mouth! Usually, this would not be a daunting task, but if Darian even accidently scratched his hand on one of Aram's teeth, he too would be become a werewolf. It was very frightening indeed. He looked over to Eithne and Yocelin. They seemed to be in a state of suspended animation—just still with blank expressions. They had to get them back. Darian returned his gaze to meet Aram's and nodded his assent. He would pull out the tooth.

"The fresh tooth of a werewolf, and both Yocelin and Eithne are returned to us, completely intact with the magical energies. Do we have a deal?" Aram prompted impatiently. This could all be over quickly, and he intended to make it happen that way.

The monks paused a moment more before responding. "We wish to see that you have the tooth before we commit to the deal," the one of the left hissed skeptically.

"Very well," Aram growled.

Without hesitation, his body began to change as Aram allowed the wolf within to show itself. Coarse black hair sprouted from his body; an ugly snout emerged from his delicately handsome face, and his teeth elongated and grew sharp in his mouth.

Darian watched as his friend transformed. It was a disturbing sight, but he calmly watched with his stoic expression. He knew Aram hated the wolf within him and hated exposing it even more. He would do anything to get Yocelin back.

The monks stood quietly, without indication of emotion, as Aram changed. When he stood before them in his complete beastly guise, the monks simply made a unified nod to indicate they were satisfied that Aram had the werewolf tooth.

"Do we have a deal?" Aram growled again in a voice that lacked humanity and was full of barely controlled rage.

"Yes!" the monks answered altogether with enthusiasm.

Aram turned to Darian.

"Do it now," he growled.

Outwardly, Darian didn't even flinch as he donned his gloves to protect his hands and approached the wolf monster that was his best friend. His expression remained stoic and his hands steady as he reached inside the werewolf's mouth and took a firm grip on one of the larger fangs. Before pulling, Darian looked into the wolf's eyes to be sure everything was all right. There, he did not see the eyes of a murderous beast but the eyes of Aram. Darian's insides had been a completely different story than his exterior. He was tense and terrified with every bit of himself jumbled into knots, but seeing his friend's eyes made the knots loosen and the tension release. Darian knew that nothing would happen to him because he could trust that Aram was in complete control.

Darian gave a hard, swift yank that pulled the tooth free in one movement.

Aram winced mildly as Darian took his tooth but showed no other signs of pain or discomfort. In truth, it was much more difficult for Aram to keep himself from sinking his fangs into his friend's sweet flesh than it was to deal with the pain of having his tooth pulled.

As soon as the tooth was out, Aram changed back into his true self. Then he took the tooth from Darian and presented it to the monks. They could tell the monks were pleased and excited with the bargain as the air hummed wildly around them. The center monk reached out its yellow hand and accepted the tooth. It folded the precious item into its robes for safekeeping. While the one accepted the tooth, the other two clapped twice, and there was a popping sound, like a bubble bursting.

"You may take your women now," the center monk hissed with grotesque pleasure.

Darian and Aram rushed to the girls. This time, they were not stopped by the invisible force field. Both protectors hugged their respective woman close only to find that there was no response. They were still in a state of suspended animation with glazed, vacant expressions on their faces.

"What have you bastards done?" Darian turned back on the monks with a strong vengeance. To his great frustration, he found another invisible barrier between him and the accursed monks.

"It will wear off in a day or so. No need to fret," the monks answered cynically. "You will be shown the way of the mountain now." The three monks gestured at once to a tunnel that appeared with another figure in brown robes standing at its mouth to guide them.

Neither Darian nor Aram knew what else they could do, so they each gathered Eithne and Yocelin into their arms and followed the monks' guide down the tunnel. If the monks were lying about the girls coming back to their senses, then perhaps Giev could help the situation. If not the shaman, then they knew that they could journey back to Duomo and ask for Tim's help. Right now, it was most important to just get off of this cursed mountain.

CHAPTER THIRTY-FOUR

*W*HEN GIEV FIRST spied his companions coming toward the camp, he jumped to his feet to greet them and grinned broadly. Then he took note of their faces. Darian and Aram were extremely angry, while Eithne and Yocelin looked vacant, as if their minds had been wiped clean and they no longer possessed the faculty of thought.

"What happened? What's wrong with them?" Giev questioned anxiously. He was very concerned for his friends' welfare.

"Let's just get far away from this accursed mountain for now," Darian stated with finality.

Aram had already set about readying the horses and packing up the small camp.

Giev nodded dumbly and quickly began helping Aram.

The companions rode until after nightfall and stopped in a small valley between foothills to make camp. Eithne and Yocelin had changed very little, but the boys were encouraged that they had begun having slight reactions to things. Both women had made groaning noises, as if waking from a deep sleep. Yocelin's fingers had even closed around the reins once while riding with Aram. These were all very encouraging signs.

"Were they drugged?" Giev regarded Eithne and Yocelin while he chewed on some dried meat for his supper. They had made a fire, and the three men were sitting around it.

The girls had been laid in their bedrolls near where the boys sat, enjoying their evening meals. They seemed to be recovering faster now. The girls rolled and groaned in their bedrolls as if suffering from nightmares. Darian and Aram had tried to give them water, but they still were not aware enough of the world around them to drink properly.

"We assume something like that," Aram answered, watching Yocelin. Even though she was not acting in a pleasant manner, he was happy to see her acting alive at all. It was a small comfort.

"Perhaps they drugged them to keep them from any trouble while on the mountain. The monks said it would wear off in a while, but I'm still worried. Those monsters don't inspire trust," Darian added as he tore into his dried meat ration. He was still quite upset.

Giev chewed his food while he thought for a moment before saying more. "What did Sir Orson's wife say about her experience on the mountain?"

Darian and Aram had briefly related the story of their errand to Giev as they had traveled away from the monks' mountain.

The protectors exchanged a sad look before responding.

"She said that she didn't remember what happened to her on the mountain, at first. She mentioned she sometimes had nightmares about what happened but wouldn't speak of them." Darian paused, and his eyes drifted to Eithne. "Sir Orson also mentioned that when he first took her from the mountain, she fought against him and wanted to return. After the spell or drug had worn off, she was herself again, but I believe that the experience left a deep wound in both of them." He looked away from Eithne and focused on the brown winter grass at his feet.

Aram was staring at the food in his hand that he had not bitten into yet and probably wouldn't eat.

A silence fell over the camp. None of them felt like talking anymore. Perhaps Giev would be the exception, but he could tell that his friends were not in the mood for talking. Besides, they had already related what they cared to say. The silence stayed over the camp for some time, save for Eithne and Yocelin's noises and the crackling of the fire. The men became comfortable in it and settled quietly.

A piercing scream abruptly disturbed the pleasant hush of the camp! Yocelin had bolted upright from her bedroll. It was as if she had suddenly been awakened from a terrible dream. Her deep blue eyes were as wide as the full moon, and her skin was drained of all color in her face.

Aram was at her side in an instant. He gripped her by the shoulders and stared into her face. She was still for a few seconds, then she blinked, and her eyes focused on Aram.

"Where am I?" Yocelin asked in a faraway voice.

"Yocelin, are you all right? How do you feel?" Aram was most concerned for her welfare and, therefore, did not answer her question.

Yocelin's brow furrowed in familiar annoyance at Aram's passiveness. She turned her head from side to side to take in her surroundings.

"We're not on the mountain anymore?" her voice sounded strange, as if she were verging on panic.

"No," Aram replied cautiously. "We are far from it now," he tried to sound soothing, but his words did not have the effect he hoped they would.

Yocelin became panicked when she knew she was no longer on the mountain. She shook her head violently and started screaming: "No! No! No!" over and over again! She was fighting against Aram to get up and away. Yocelin was strong in her own right, especially for her size; but even in a crazed panic, she was no match for Aram. For all her hysterics, he held her down. Yocelin was irrationally desperate to get back to the mountain.

Giev watched in shock as Yocelin fought and screamed at Aram to let her go back to the mountain. He had not been expecting such a reaction when Darian had said that the girls might try to get back there. He had no idea what he could do to help the stressful situation.

Suddenly, a second nightmarish scream pierced through the air! Eithne was awake now too. Darian, like Aram, was immediately at her side. However, he was better prepared for her reaction to realizing that she was no longer on the mountain. She also began to scream and fight like an enraged cat! Darian did not have a problem holding Eithne down either, but the women were not calming down, and their protectors were quite stuck where they were.

Giev realized the best way he could help the situation, though he was not sure how well this aid would be received by Darian and Aram. Giev went to his pack and took out some rope.

Both Darian and Aram were surprisingly agreeable to tying the girls up and gagging them until the effects of the drugs, or whatever it was, wore off. It took a good amount of time and effort to get both women bound and gagged without hurting them. Aram took extra care to make the knots of Yocelin's bindings particularly difficult. He had not forgotten what she had told him the first night they met. The boys also managed to get them each to drink some water. The girls may have been hysterical to get back to the mountain, but they did not seem to think that the boys would poison them.

"We'll have to take turns watching them throughout the night," Darian stated as he surveyed Eithne and Yocelin struggling against their bonds. "I can take the first shift."

Giev and Aram nodded and went about laying out their bed-rolls to get some rest before their shifts.

The next day, the men decided to stay at their current campsite. Eithne and Yocelin were still too belligerent to be untied and would have only caused trouble if they tried to travel. It was decided that it was best to wait for the effects of the drug to wear off before trying to travel. Besides, if they were far from civilization, it was convenient in their current predicament. Entering a town with two bound and gagged women just did not look very good. Staying away from civilization was also for Aram's benefit. The full moon was tomorrow night, and it was easier for him to venture off into the forest for the night so the others did not have to witness his transformation.

Giev had already learned of Aram being a werewolf, so he understood, but it still caused him to lose sleep on the night of the full moon. Darian assured him that Aram was in full control of his condition and would not come close to the camp while in his wolf form. However, this did not help the shaman to stop imagining that a black hairy beast was lurking just beyond the firelight with its jaws salivating. Even once Giev's watch was over, he lay wide awake, scanning the tree line around the camp.

The next morning was better than the day before had been for Eithne and Yocelin. They were struggling less against their bonds and were more complacent about being away from the mountain. Darian and Aram believed this meant that the drug was wearing off. The girls remained tied up, but the boys changed the positioning of their bonds to make them more comfortable and removed their gags. Neither of the girls was willing to have a real conversation yet. Whenever spoken to, they simply asked to be taken back to the mountain. They were much less adamant now, though, and even seemed confused when one of the boys would ask why they wanted to go back so badly. The day before, they had simply screamed that it was where they needed to be. This morning was better.

Aram had come back early, looking tired. Giev reasoned that he didn't get much sleep as a wolf. He was probably running about the forest all night. Giev found that he caught himself staring at Aram on several occasions that morning. He couldn't help it. He kept looking for patches of hair or something else wolflike. That, or the shaman was imagining what he might look like as a wolf.

Aram realized that Giev was staring but ignored him. Darian had acted in a similar way after learning what he was. It was a normal reaction, and one that Aram greatly preferred over being persecuted or feared.

The day continued with promise as Eithne and Yocelin were much calmer and took food and drink without coaxing. That evening, when Aram went to Yocelin to give her something to eat, she appeared completely lucid.

"I'm ready to be untied," Yocelin stated wearily and with some shame.

Aram lifted his eyebrows. "Really? How do you feel about that mountain?"

"I never want to talk about it or see it again," her voice was low but earnest. It was obvious she felt very ashamed of how she had behaved.

Aram nodded and began untying her. He glanced at her face a couple of times, but she didn't look at him. After she was free, Aram sat back, facing her. Yocelin rubbed her wrists and stretched a bit before picking up the food he had brought for her to eat. Aram watched her in silence for several moments, observing her polite mannerisms while she ate. Yocelin was much more somber than usual, but she appeared to be herself again. The gestures and expressions he had come to know as being unique to her were present once again. Aram relaxed and enjoyed watching her be herself.

"Are you expecting me to do something special?" Yocelin asked with a hint of her usual sass.

She wasn't used to Aram watching her like that. Did he think she was going to try and run off to the mountain still?

Aram blinked at her then realized he had been staring. "No, sorry. It's just nice to have you back."

With that, Aram stood up and went to get himself some food. He felt a little embarrassed.

Yocelin watched him go and was sorry he had walked away. His comment and behavior had left her with a tingle of pleasure she was not accustomed to feeling.

Darian was also pleasantly surprised to find Eithne being more like herself when he brought her some dinner. "You're looking much better."

Eithne nodded. "I feel like I can think for myself again. The past few days have been a blur." She did not meet his gaze but looked at the ground.

"How do you feel about going back to the mountain?" Darian asked.

A visible shudder ran through Eithne's body. "Please, don't even joke about that place. I want to forget it exists at all."

Darian felt a slight pang at upsetting her, but he had to see her reaction to that question. He found her answer satisfactory, so he reached over and began untying her. When he was done, he looked at her wrists to be sure she didn't have rope burn.

"Better?"

"Much, thank you," Eithne responded.

She still kept her eyes cast downward. She couldn't fully remember what she did or said over the past few days, but she had an idea of it, and that made her feel shame.

"You can look at me, you know," Darian's tone was gentle. He wanted her to look him in the eyes so that he could really see that she was all right.

"I'm too embarrassed. The way I must have been behaving these last couple of days . . . It's embarrassing," she replied meekly, keeping her eyes averted.

"Don't worry about that." Darian reached over and gently tilted her face with his hand so that she would look at him. "That wasn't you saying those things. You and Yocelin were drugged or had an evil spell cast on you by those wretched monks. I know the real Eithne would have never acted that way. You have nothing to be embarrassed about." He held her eyes with his own for several long seconds after he finished speaking.

Eithne nodded that she understood, and Darian released her. She still felt guilty for the way she had behaved, but Darian's little pep talk had helped to alleviate the guilt somewhat. She liked that he always seemed to be there with encouraging words and an impactful stare (just to be sure his words sank in).

Darian continued to sit with her while she ate. The rest of the evening was uneventful. The companions chatted idly and went to sleep early. It was good to have Eithne and Yocelin back to normal. The girls were also pleased to learn that they had the Gem of Amara. Giev had already learned how to use it, so they could begin seeking out the god pieces, with greater efficiency, again soon. The companions planned to head out the next day after a good night's rest.

CHAPTER THIRTY-FIVE

*T*HE NEXT COUPLE of months were dedicated to searching for the god pieces. The Gem of Amara was incredibly helpful in this task. Both Eithne and Yocelin felt very accomplished in the amount of god pieces they had each collected. Eithne found more of Anut than Yocelin did of Muntros, but the explanation for that was simple: Cavan. Cavan had already collected much of Muntros. The companions all dreaded the day that they would be forced to face him again, but it would have to come, and Yocelin would have to deliver a killing blow. Sometimes, Yocelin would sense that Cavan was nearby, but never close enough to cause alarm. It was as if Cavan was not able to come any closer for some unknown reason. Giev theorized that perhaps it had to do with the magical artifacts they carried. The other four accepted this happily enough. So long as Cavan was not interfering with them, they were glad.

Eithne and Yocelin had returned to their former selves despite their experience with the monks. Both claimed to not remember a thing form their time on the mountain, and neither wished to talk about it. It was generally realized by the men that, whatever had transpired on the monk's mountain, the girls were repressing any memories they may have, and that was exactly how they liked it. Eithne and Yocelin did suffer from nightmares occasionally, but they also claimed not to remember those once awake. Thankfully, this seemed to be at least mostly true, as the girls did not appear to be plagued with dark thoughts while awake.

The mood of the entire group was very positive. This was, of course, greatly attributed to their success in gathering god pieces. Another factor was that the bitter winter had finally subsided. It was now early spring, and it was delightful. The air was getting warmer and carried sweet fragrances as it gently rolled over the cheeks of the five travelers. Birds sang in the treetops, and animals everywhere were awakening from their winter slumbers to discover the blooming world around them. Even Aram was less broody than usual. Of course, even the most glorious season was tainted with days of extreme heat and sudden descents back into winter. One day in particular, there was heavy snowfall, with about two feet of snow, but it remained terribly hot and humid as the puffy white flakes fell down. It was confounding and made no sense whatsoever, but such seemingly impossible things had become much more commonplace in recent years, so they were accepted.

Giev had always enjoyed watching the world around him reawaken each year to spring. He took much joy in observing the goings on of nature as it bustled back to life. Giev found that he was observing some new, and very interesting, behavior this year. He could not help but notice some subtle changes in the way Aram and Yocelin, and Darian and Eithne interacted. It had always been clear to the shaman that each pair liked each other, but recently, they had become more familiar and obvious about it. They were always finding excuses to touch and stand, or sit, very close to each other. Yocelin had forgotten all pretense of saying she was cold and now simply hugged onto Aram at every opportunity. The werewolf frequently forgot to feign annoyance at her affection and even seemed to enjoy it. Darian was constantly teasing or complimenting Eithne to make her blush. It was clear that Darian thought Eithne very sweet and pretty when she blushed, so he did his best to make her do it regularly. He was quite successful. Eithne would have probably gotten upset with someone else teasing her so much, but for Darian, she laughed and blushed prettily while halfheartedly telling him to stop. The flirting of the two couples was only expounded by the fact that they only had three horses. Giev rode on one horse with most of the supplies, while each respective pair rode the other two. This situation caused endless opportunity for sexual tensions to rise, and they were rising fast! Giev found the romantic displays all around him to be very amusing and sweet. He liked all his friends and thought that each pair would do well together. The frustrating part was that they weren't actually together. He couldn't understand it. Eithne and Yocelin were more than receptive to Darian and Aram, so why weren't they making any moves? Giev was the sort who pretended to himself that he did not like to meddle in others' personal affairs, but he could bear it no longer! He had to know why their relationships were not progressing, so he would find out.

One evening, they found themselves staying at an inn in a town called Crinlock. They had all eaten together, and after some pleasant conversation, Eithne and Yocelin decided to retire to their room for the night. Darian, Aram, and Giev stayed downstairs to have a couple more drinks. It was the perfect opportunity for Giev to ask after his curiosities, and so he seized it.

"So why haven't either of you done anything about your romantic relationships with Eithne and Yocelin?" Giev plainly asked. He looked at Darian and Aram politely as he waited for their response.

Darian and Aram both froze at the question and stared right back at the shaman. Darian held his mug of ale at the halfway point between the table and his mouth. Neither of the protectors were fools; they knew exactly why Giev would ask that question. They just didn't know how to react to it. After a long moment of staring, Aram passively looked away and pretended that he never heard the question at all. Darian finished bringing his mug to his lips and took a long drink while still maintaining eye contact with Giev.

Giev's face fell to an expression of annoyance. Were they really going to act this way? Well, he simply wouldn't let that happen. He didn't care if the conversation was completely one-sided. They were going to have this talk, whether they liked it or not.

Giev sighed and began the conversation without them.

"Look, it's blatant how much you all like each other. As a spectator, it's become painful to watch. It was cute at first, but now I'm just among the four of you, in pain, over your inadequacy to move in on two beautiful women that clearly want you. Seriously, is there something wrong with the two of you?"

Darian and Aram regarded Giev, obviously still considering not answering at all. Then they looked at each other, seemed to have a nonverbal agreement as they exchanged resolved nods, and then both began chugging their mugs of ale.

"You're both pathetic," Giev stated in a despondent tone after watching them chug ale for a few seconds.

The protectors slowly lowered their mugs and gathered their thoughts.

Darian tried first, "Just because we're attracted to each other doesn't mean th—"

"I think we all know that this is more than simple attraction," Giev cut Darian off. He wasn't in the mood for lame excuses.

Darian cleared his throat and tried again, "I'm to begin courtship of Eithne's sister wh—"

"Try again. We all know which sister you want," Giev stated firmly.

"We're not allowed to be with them like that," Aram blurted out. He figured they should just tell Giev the real reason so that he would leave them alone.

"What? Are you secretly married to other women, or something?" Giev didn't understand Aram's reasoning at all.

"No," Aram answered flatly. "Tim disallowed it."

"Tim? The great and powerful wizard, who sent the four of you on a quest to save the world, disallowed you from being with Eithne and Yocelin?" Giev's tone was sarcastic. He failed to see why Tim should be concerned with such things.

"Yes," Aram answered again. He was annoyed with Giev's tone and suddenly didn't feel like volunteering information anymore. Besides, if you thought about it, it wasn't so far-fetched that Tim wouldn't want the four of them being distracted by each other.

"Well, I can't wait to hear the reasoning behind that," Giev leaned back in his chair and put his hands behind his head in a relaxed fashion.

"He didn't give us a specific reason. Tim just told us that we could not be with Eithne or Yocelin like that. He said that it was simply a bad idea," Darian replied straightforwardly, though now that he said it out loud, it sounded flimsy.

Giev lifted his eyebrows and regarded his friends from across the table. Darian looked a little defeated for having given up the information. Aram just stared back at Giev with an unreadable expression. Giev gazed at them and pondered for several long moments. He didn't know if the wizard had a greater reason for disallowing romantic relations between them, but Tim should have said something about it if it were so important. Besides, the damage was already done, as far as Giev was concerned.

"If you ask me," Giev began slowly as he leaned forward on the table, "the four of you are more distracted by flirting without going anywhere than you would be if you just had at each other and were happy." He drained the rest of his ale in one long gulp and stood to leave. "The feelings are already present. It's too late to try and ignore them."

Giev then left some coins on the table to pay for his drinks and went up to his room. He felt rather pleased with himself and hoped that his words would have a positive effect on the group as a whole.

Darian and Aram sat quietly, letting Giev's words marinate in their minds.

After a long moment, Darian spoke, "I don't want to talk about it. Let's just drink."

"Agreed," Aram replied affirmatively.

They called on the barmaid to bring them more ale and tried very hard not to think about Giev's words for the rest of the evening, hoping that copious amounts of alcohol would wash them away.

Eithne and Yocelin sat on the bed in their room together, chattering away like excited birds. They had excused themselves from the boys' company and scurried upstairs where they could talk as femininely as possible. After all, they both had so many wonderful feelings to share with one another, and it was rare to have privacy from the rest of the group.

"You're not a bad sister!" Yocelin defended Eithne against her own guilt that she had just professed.

"I just feel badly about it. Rosalin was pretty excited about Darian courting her, and I knew that. Now I find myself shamelessly

312

flirting with him every day! Why can't I help it?" Eithne was feeling very torn between her budding feelings for Darian and loyalty to her sister.

"It's not like the flirting is one-sided. He starts it most of the time, trust me. Besides, wasn't Rosalin the most popular girl in your village? Chances are that at least five other suitors popped up as soon as you and Darian left. She's probably having a lovely time, being courted by someone else, and forgotten all about Darian." Even though Yocelin did not know Rosalin, she had heard enough about her to feel that this was an accurate assumption. "Anyway, it's obvious who Darian wants," Yocelin said the last statement like a sly fox and gave Eithne a knowing look.

Eithne's cheeks pinked slightly, and she looked down at her hands clasped in her lap. Until recently, Eithne had been a bit dumb regarding how she felt about Darian. She realized now that her respect for him had grown into much more. Yocelin assured her that it was completely obvious that Darian felt the same way, which made Eithne very happy.

"I guess I shouldn't let Rosalin get in the way of my own feelings," Eithne answered hesitantly. "Besides, she and Darian were never officially anything together."

"That's the spirit!" Yocelin encouraged heartily and swung her arm in a reinforcing gesture.

"So what are you going to do about Aram?" Eithne shifted to the other topic they had been discussing that night.

There were no issues of guilt between Yocelin and Aram, just a certain degree of social awkwardness on Aram's part. The two women had already surmised that Aram probably had never had any kind of serious relationship with a woman, so he simply didn't know what to do about it.

Yocelin grinned saucily at her friend's question. "I'm going to make it impossible for him to ignore the sexual tension between us."

"Really?" Eithne leaned forward and smiled with anticipation. "How will you do that?"

"I will break said tension with a kiss," Yocelin proclaimed with pride. She greatly enjoyed her simple, yet dramatic plan.

Eithne clapped her hands together and let out a noise of surprise. "You're so bold! You don't even know how he will react!"

"Well, that's part of the fun!" Yocelin answered confidently. She felt she had a good idea of how Aram would react, anyway.

The pair laughed merrily at the joke and continued to talk about Darian and Aram into the night. Little did they know that their happy mood upstairs was in direct contrast with Darian and Aram's mood of denial downstairs about the very same topic.

CHAPTER THIRTY-SIX

TWO WEEKS HAD gone by since the night that Yocelin had proclaimed that she would kiss Aram, and she had not yet acted on her plan. Eithne sometimes asked her why she hadn't done it yet, to which Yocelin would reply that she had not found the right moment yet. Apparently, the she-demon had greatly miscalculated the availability of such moments and was perturbed that the proper opportunity did not seem to come.

One evening, the companions all sat about the campfire, enjoying a pleasant spring evening. Giev sat working with the Stone of Elissiyus, trying to figure how to use it. He had made some progress in his time with the stone. Giev could make it glow and vibrate but was still working toward understanding it. Darian and Aram sat by the fire, discussing where to travel to next while eating their dinner, leaving Eithne and Yocelin to their own devices.

"Why don't you just create the right moment to kiss him?" Eithne whispered in mild exasperation.

"What? Like, just get him alone and kiss him?" Yocelin responded with sarcasm.

"Well, why not?" Eithne replied smartly. "The way you're putting it off, I think you might be afraid to do it."

"I am not!" Yocelin retorted at full speaking volume, which caused the three men to stop what they were doing for a second and look to the women.

Eithne and Yocelin grinned innocently at them, then they scooted so that their backs were to the boys and went back to speaking in low whispers.

"Well, prove that you're not afraid and kiss him already!" Eithne persisted.

Yocelin crossed her arms in a stubborn huff. "I don't have to prove anything to you. I'll kiss him at the first opportunity that feels right and we're alone. I can't have our first kiss happen in front of a whole group of people. It's an intimate and very private matter."

"Fine," Eithne put a conniving and upbeat tone on such a small word.

Yocelin sensed what she was going to do next, but she wasn't fast enough to stop her friend.

"Aram?" Eithne called out for his attention, and he obliged by looking at her. "Would you mind going with Yocelin to gather some more firewood?"

Aram shrugged affirmatively and stood to leave. He didn't know why they would want more firewood, but it weren't as if he were working on anything important at the moment. The Gem of Amara really dictated where they went these days, so pouring over maps with Darian was just something they did to help pass the time.

Yocelin gave Eithne an angry look but did not hesitate to stand and go with Aram. There was no harm in going to gather firewood. Besides, she would only kiss him if the moment were right.

Eithne could not hide her pleasure as she smiled and playfully waved to Yocelin. She got up from her spot and went to join Darian next to the fire. He was eating some of the rabbit they had managed to catch for dinner.

"What are you so smug about?" Darian asked as he took note of Eithne's demeanor.

"Oh, nothing," Eithne chimed, still looking very pleased.

"It's clearly something. Did I ever tell you how awful you are at hiding your emotions?"

Now Darian was being playful. He had told her many times how her feelings were always on the surface. It was something that he quite liked about Eithne. It made knowing what to say and do around her easier.

Eithne was unfazed by his comment. She maintained her smugness as she straightened up and gave him a smart look.

"Well, it doesn't matter if you can see how I feel because I'm not going to tell you why I feel this way."

Darian was no fool when it came to Eithne. He knew exactly how to get what he wanted from her. He studied her for a few seconds then gave her a dashing grin.

"You're so cute."

Eithne stiffened. He was going to fluster her into talking! In recent weeks, Eithne had discovered a very different side to Darian. One would not suspect it from his usually cold and stoic demeanor, but he could be downright charming when he wanted to be. Unfortunately for her, she found herself very affected by his charms.

"That's not going to work," Eithne tried to sound confident, but he had caught her off guard when he called her cute.

Darian's grin deepened, and he casually leaned closer to her. "I don't know what you are talking about."

Eithne's heart skipped a beat. It was more out of anxiety that Darian would make her talk than anything else. She knew it must be completely obvious to him that she was becoming nervous.

"I'm not going to let you fluster me with your handsomeness!" Eithne suddenly blurted too loudly and crossed her arms stubbornly. It was ridiculous.

Darian blinked at her then started chuckling. Then came the flat-out laughter! He couldn't stop for a few minutes. It was just too funny to him.

Eithne maintained her seated position with her arms crossed while Darian laughed, but her cheeks definitely took on an annoyed pinkish hue. Just what did he find so funny, anyway?

Giev looked up and smiled knowingly. He could see an opportunity forming, so he quietly scooted off to the edge of the campsite to give them more privacy. Perhaps Darian would finally make a move with enough space. Knowing that Aram and Yocelin were off alone somewhere was also a good sign, as far as the young shaman was concerned.

"Oh, stop it! What's so funny, anyway?" Eithne leaned over and smacked Darian in his shoulder to emphasize her point. She had grown tired of his guffaws.

"You are so feisty," Darian stated defensively, still chuckling a little. "Did you not hear what you said just then? Now that really was very cute." He grinned again, but not because he was trying to charm her this time.

Eithne wasn't exactly sure what she said to make him laugh so hard, but she was still determined not to let him get to her. On the other hand, he had said that she was cute, twice. This made her feel very happy inside. With her own emotions conflicted, Eithne did not know how to respond to him. So she sat and tried to look imposing.

Darian could see that if their conversation were to continue at this point, he would have to be the one to keep it going. "So do you often feel flustered by my handsomeness, as you so eloquently put it?"

Eithne suddenly heard how silly her statement sounded and felt herself relax. She let out a slow breath and turned her face toward his. "Seems I get flustered by you more often of late."

They were so close, and there was an electricity sparking in the air between them. Before Darian even knew what he was doing, he reached over to her, ran his fingers through her red hair, and pulled her to him. Darian kissed her. Eithne put up no resistance. Everything about it felt right to her. His lips were strong, yet gentle. Eithne let out a sigh and slipped her arms around him. Darian deepened the kiss. He wanted her so much and had ached to kiss her for much longer than she knew.

It was a long while before they separated. When they did, they maintained the physical closeness and gazed at each other for a moment. It had actually happened. They both felt as though they had just stepped into a dream. They had each imagined that kiss so many times over the past few weeks; now it had really happened. It had been so much more than either had imagined it would be. Now, what happened next?

An unwelcome thought pierced through the dreamy haze of Darian's thoughts: the wizard's warning. He shouldn't have given into his desire for Eithne. He didn't understand why Tim was so insistent, but he knew that it wasn't without reason. The soldier in him had failed to stay disciplined, but nothing about kissing Eithne had felt wrong. In fact, nothing he had ever done before had felt so right! His brow furrowed in conflict as he looked upon Eithne. His hand was still gently stroking her hair. He dropped his hand and slowly stood up. Darian held Eithne's gaze as he did. She looked so confused, and it pained him deeply. How could he have done this to her?

"Eithne, I . . . Forgive my indiscretion," Darian stammered quietly, then he walked away into the forest. He needed to be alone.

Eithne was speechless. At first, she felt as though the most wonderful moment of her life had happened, and she had wanted it to happen. Then Darian became cold and walked away! Did he not enjoy the kiss? She felt utterly rejected. It hurt her heart in a way she had never known before, and she wanted to cry all of a sudden. Eithne sat still where Darian had left her, hopelessly wrestling with the tears welling up in her throat.

Aram and Yocelin wandered about the woods around the campsite collecting firewood. It was nice to walk around for a bit. Aram was relaxed and peaceful as he picked up branches that made good kindling here and there. He did not feel the need to speak; he rarely did and was comfortable enough with Yocelin to know that she didn't expect him to. She always did the talking anyway.

Yocelin was not feeling like her usual self. She was anxious and awkward. Now, the pressure was on for her to make good on her mission to kiss Aram. She very much wanted to do it, but she also wanted it to be right. An awkwardly forced first kiss was not what she wanted at all. Also, she had been hopeful in the beginning that Aram would make the first move. She soon realized that it was ludicrous of her to expect that of him. He probably didn't even notice that she was nervous. No, it was all up to her and her repertoire of womanly wiles.

Yocelin cleared her throat to get his attention before she spoke. "Say, Aram?"

Aram had been walking just ahead of Yocelin, so he stopped and turned to look at her to show that he was listening. He had learned long ago to give her his full attention when she requested it. She would be certain to take it regardless.

"Have you ever had a girlfriend?" Yocelin asked inquisitively. She thought this was a good start to getting on the proper topic.

It was apparent from his reaction that Aram thought her question to be ridiculous. "Why?"

"I just want to know, is all," Yocelin chimed back innocently.

"You already know the answer to that," Aram said dismissively and turned back to collecting firewood.

Yocelin pretended to look thoughtful and shook her head slowly. "Nope, you've never mentioned if you have had a girlfriend or not."

Aram sighed. "Not directly, no, but you definitely know the answer to that question."

That was true. Yocelin knew enough about Aram and his lone wolf ways to assume that he had never had a girlfriend. She took a breath in and let it out as she thought up her next brilliant question.

"Well, you're not a virgin, are you?" the words tumbled out of her mouth before she had time to stop herself. She immediately regretted asking that. She just made herself sound like a blundering idiot!

Aram stopped, half-turned, and gave her a perplexed look. What was wrong with her tonight?

"Okay, okay! Stupid question. I know you're not a virgin. I guess what I'm getting at here is, how long has it been since you kissed a girl?" She knew she sound completely clumsy, but she couldn't find her way back to being suave at the moment.

Aram shook his head in befuddlement. "Why?"

Yocelin trotted over to him and latched onto his arm. "I'm just curious. Please tell me." She smiled and batted her eyes at him trying to look precious.

"It's been since before we met," he answered flatly. She was asking some bizarre questions tonight.

Yocelin's expression fell. She knew that much already! "Come on," she cooed. "Give me a number of months or something."

Aram sighed again in annoyance. She was clearly trying to get at something, but he didn't know what. He wished she would just say what she was thinking and stop dancing around the subject.

"I don't keep track of the time between kissing girls. It's been a while, all right?"

"Do you miss it?" her rebuttal came so quickly that Aram had barely finished speaking his last syllable.

He gave her a strange look. "Why are you asking me all these goofy questions?"

Yocelin gave a nervous giggle. She couldn't believe how horrible she was at this. She was usually so good at flirting. "Sorry, that was another stupid question. Everyone enjoys kissing! Why wouldn't you miss it? I know, I miss it. It's been a long time since I was kissed, which seems strange since I've been traveling with such handsome men lately. Ha-ha! It's almost ironic, really—"

"Stop babbling," Aram cut her off. He didn't want to let that nonsense continue.

"There are nicer way to get me to be quiet, you know," Yocelin managed to sound more like her sultry self. She stayed clasped onto Aram's muscular arm. "Certain tricks to stop superfluous speech." She leaned up into him more, so that if he were not taking her hint already, he would have further reminder that there was a beautiful and receptive woman on his arm.

Even Aram wasn't that thick. He knew what she was hinting at, and he wanted to oblige her. Aram hesitated only because of Tim's warning. He had no other reason to avoid being with Yocelin. In fact, she was a perfect match for him, when he thought about it. Tim was the only thing standing between him and happiness with Yocelin. He looked down at her, considering the consequences of giving into their mutual desires. It may complicate the quest, but Giev had rightly pointed out that the emotions were already present; therefore, things were already complicated in that manner. Of course, what Aram felt most cautious about were the consequences of acting on that desire. Tim had never said why to stay uninvolved with Yocelin.

Yocelin was in the moment. She sensed that he wanted her and wanted to act on his feelings. She had made herself completely available, so what was he waiting for? She could wait no longer. Before Aram knew what she was doing, Yocelin grabbed the front of his shirt in both her hands, pushed up onto the tips of her toes, and kissed him on the mouth.

At first, Aram was too surprised to react, then his instincts took over, and he gathered her up into his arms and kissed her back hard. He took full control of the kiss, which sent Yocelin into a dizzying spin. She loved it and surrendered to him absolutely. He gave her exactly what she had hoped for. Yocelin had no idea how long the kiss lasted. She did not realize how passionate Aram would be! She had never been kissed so well in her life!

Suddenly, Aram stopped and pushed away from Yocelin. She found that her back was now up against a tree. She had no idea when that happened. Aram had not gone far. His hands still rested on her shoulders; their bodies were only about a foot apart.

"We can't do this," Aram sounded as though he were in turmoil.

"What? What are you talking about?" Yocelin was still gathering her composure and feeling a bit out of sorts.

"You and I can't act on our feelings for each other. We're not supposed to." Aram was beginning to calm down from the emotional release and regain his somewhat cold demeanor.

"Why not?" Yocelin was quicker to anger than even she anticipated.

She was feeling such an upheaval of emotion at the moment. How dare he tell her that it was wrong when it was clearly right! Aram had better explain himself and fast.

Aram tightened his grip on her shoulders and looked at her straight on.

"I wasn't supposed to tell you this, but right before we left Tim's mansion, he took Darian and I aside to specifically warn us against getting romantically involved with either you or Eithne. Tim basically forbade us from having any kind of romantic or sexual relationship."

Aram watched Yocelin as she digested this information. He was unhappy to see her looking angrier. She seemed to be taking in bigger breaths through her nose and pursing her lips. She aggressively tossed his hands away from her shoulders. He took a couple steps back from her and stood waiting for the pending out lash of her anger.

"*I hate Tim*!" Yocelin shouted and stamped her foot. "Tim is always finding ways to ruin things! I hate him!"

Aram let out a sigh of relief that she was not directing her anger at him. He was definitely all right with letting the wizard take the blame for this. Yocelin was absolutely fuming.

"At the time that Tim told us that, I didn't perceive it becoming a problem," Aram half-mumbled. He felt that he needed to say something but didn't know what.

Yocelin pretended not to hear what he just said. She was angry enough already, and acknowledging that statement would only make both of them feel worse.

"So what wise reason did stupid Tim have for saying we couldn't be together?"

Aram awkwardly cleared his throat. "He didn't say."

"Excuse me?" Yocelin sounded more than a little sarcastic. "Tim didn't tell you why? You just shrugged your shoulders and accepted it without question?"

"No," Aram was quick to answer. He needed to defuse her. "Darian and I asked why, but Tim said that he couldn't tell us and to just keep out hands to ourselves."

Yocelin huffed, bit her lip, and crossed her arms while she thought of what to say next. After a few seconds, she had worked out what she really wanted to know.

"Do you want me?"

"You know I do," Aram was entirely genuine in his reply.

"If it weren't for Tim's stupid rule, would you have taken me in a manly fashion a long time ago?" she continued.

Aram raised an eyebrow at her phrasing but affirmatively confirmed her query.

Yocelin held his eyes for a moment to be sure that he wasn't just placating her. Then she released a long breath and slumped up against the tree. As much as she hated Tim, she had to admit that he did not do things without reason. If he had warned Aram and Darian not to become romantically involved with her or Eithne, there had to be a good reason behind it. It was just so infuriating! She wished that she at least knew why.

"I wish I had known that before I kissed you," Yocelin sighed in a defeated tone. "Now what do we do? Are we just supposed to remain in some suspended platonic state?"

Aram rubbed his forehead. "I don't know, something like that. We can't keep kissing. That only leads to more."

Yocelin shook her head and stood up straight. "Well, I guess we'll have to live by a new, very irritating, code: Timulous."

"Timulous?"

"Yes, Timulous. The way of life forced upon us by the stupid wizard Tim. The motto is, If it feels good, stop."

Now she was really being sarcastic, but Aram had to admit that it was somewhat relieving to hear her make light of the situation. Even though he was outwardly cool and collected, he still burned to gather Yocelin up into his arms and continue that kiss. He was harder to resist the urges now that he had finally tasted her.

Yocelin continued to go on about Timulous while they walked back to camp. He wondered what Darian would say when he found out what happened and that Aram had told Yocelin about the wizard's warning. He believed that it was better that Yocelin and Eithne know about it, anyway. It would help to keep things less complicated.

Upon arriving back at camp, Yocelin and Aram were shocked to find that Eithne was in tears and Darian was nowhere to be seen. Giev was quietly comforting Eithne. It seemed that they weren't the only ones with a story to tell tonight. Naturally, Yocelin immediately asked what was wrong and went to console her friend. Eithne confided what had happened with Darian. Thankfully, Giev had not allowed her to remain lost for an explanation. As soon as Darian had walked away, Giev went to Eithne and told her what Darian and Aram had told him two weeks ago at the inn in Crinlock. It had clarified things for her greatly; she could even understand why Darian would simply walk away from her after they kissed, but it hadn't made her feel any better.

"So where is Darian now?" Yocelin asked.

Eithne shrugged. "Just out walking, I suppose. He needed to be alone with his guilt."

Aram thought her statement to be a little mean, considering what he knew of Darian's feelings for Eithne, but she was probably just venting. It was best that she do that now while Darian wasn't around to hear it.

There was a long, silent pause while unspoken thoughts and emotions hung in the air.

"I kind of hate Tim too now," Eithne said quietly.

"What did I tell you? Tim is the ruiner of all things good. I even made up a new word tonight in reference to his dumb rules," Yocelin was anxious to share her new coping mechanism.

Eithne looked at her friend with interest. Giev was also very keen on hearing this. There was still a big part of him that was astonished that his companions got to meet and be under the tutelage of such an amazingly powerful wizard. It made it all the more surprising that they were all so cavalier about him.

Yocelin decided to share what had happened to her tonight in order to fully explain her new word.

"Aram and I finally kissed tonight too." She paused as she saw Eithne and Giev's eyes grow wide, but they did not say anything, so she continued, "Then much like you and Darian, Aram pushed me away and said that we couldn't do that. I got super mad, Aram explained about Tim, then I was super mad at Tim. You see, he wants us to all live by the most stifling of codes: Timulous."

"What does that mean?" Giev asked inquisitively.

"Timulous is a way of life in which the four of us aren't allowed to have any adult fun together because he says we just can't. It's so frustrating. I don't understand it, but I can name it." Yocelin was happy to explain. It helped her to further vent her upset over the predicament.

Giev's face hid nothing of his thoughts. That was one of the most ridiculous things he had ever heard, and he loved it. There was never a shortage of entertainment in this group; that was for sure. Giev was so amused by the new concept of Timulous that he had almost forgotten that Yocelin had glazed over the part about her and Aram kissing. The shaman looked around for Aram so that he could talk to him about it. Where had he gone?

"Where's Aram?" Giev asked.

Eithne and Yocelin looked at Giev quizzically. They had been carrying on about Timulous while Giev was lost in his thoughts. Eithne very much liked the new concept. It helped her to have something to blame without being angry with Darian. She did not wish to be angry with Darian.

"He walked off like Darian did when Yocelin started talking about their kiss," Eithne informed the shaman.

Giev studied the two women, and they regarded him in turn.

"So both Darian and Aram just left to be alone with their guilt over having finally kissed the women they love," Giev stated after some thoughtful pondering. "Honestly, do the four of you try to do things in pairs all the time?"

Eithne and Yocelin blinked, then looked at each other, then back at Giev.

"Well, not on purpose," Eithne responded hesitantly.

"They're in love with us?" Yocelin interjected, anxiously hopeful for more information.

Giev sighed.

CHAPTER THIRTY-SEVEN

HE FOLLOWING MONTHS were spent very focused on the quest. Where things used to be all flirting and teasing, they had now turned somewhat awkward. The two couples still very much wanted each other, and there was much time devoted to longing looks and lingering caresses. However, they were now all painfully aware that they were not to indulge their feelings, so they refrained. All the excess energy was devoted to the business of finding god pieces. The companions had found many god pieces and were all pleased with the progress. Also, no one else had died on account of having a god piece taken from them, which was excellent for group morale.

One hot summer night, Giev broached the topic of Cavan. They would have to track him down and kill him in order for Yocelin to receive all the pieces of Muntros. Eithne's success in finding pieces of Anut vastly outweighed Yocelin's progress since there was no one else that they knew of searching for pieces of the sun god. As scary as it was, they would have to seek out Cavan and find some way to defeat him. Giev had learned how to better manipulate the Stone of Elissiyus. He did not believe that he would ever be able to unlock the stone's full potential, but the shaman had learned to do some things with it. He believed he could stun Cavan with the stone's power long enough for Yocelin to simply run him through. Naturally, this plan was quite agreeable to the rest of the group. Had Cavan been a man of honor, and not a downright evil bastard, then there would have been some objections, but Cavan did not possess honor or mercy. So it was the belief of the group that he deserved none.

The companions began seeking out Cavan the very next day. Chances were that they would find more god pieces along the way to him anyway. Giev used the Gem of Amara for focus more on the energy of Muntros, and they all set out in that direction. It also happened to be taking them closer to Duomo, where the wizard Tim resided. It seemed like a lifetime ago that they had stayed in the mansion and first learned of their quest. In reality, it had been about six months, but it felt much longer. They had traveled so far and done so much since the time they had left Tim's mansion. Giev was anxious to stop and meet the great wizard, and the others agreed that it was probably best to check in, but the other four had mixed feelings about seeing Tim again. Having been completely focused on their romantic frustrations, none—except the shaman—were feeling particularly excited about seeing the old wizard again.

"Do you think Tim can see where we are as we travel?" Eithne asked while riding with Darian one day.

They were still about ten days away from Duomo. The companions planned on stopping in a small human town called Walb, which was along the way.

Darian shrugged his shoulders. "I assume that he can use his powers to see what we are doing or where we are whenever he decides to check in on us."

"Hmmm," Eithne was thoughtful for a moment, before she said what she was really thinking about. "So do you think he knows?"

Darian frowned at the idea of Tim knowing about their indiscretion a couple of months previously. That very question was always lurking in the back of his mind coupled with the constant urge to kiss Eithne again. He was in a constant state of turmoil beneath his stoic exterior.

"I suppose that he doesn't keep watch on us all the time. I would guess not, as it was just the one time."

"A part of me hopes that he does know about it," Eithne responded in a small voice.

She knew Darian hoped the exact opposite, but she would feel relief if Tim just knew already. Besides, even if Tim didn't know it yet, he would probably sense that something happened as soon as he saw them again. Tim was no fool.

Darian did not wish to continue the conversation. Thinking about it now, with Eithne so close, was only inspiring feelings of guilt and frustration. They both fell into a silence that they had grown more accustomed to of late.

The companions arrived in Walb in the late afternoon a couple of days later. It was not difficult to find an inn to stay at for the night. Upon arrival, they also could not help but notice that the entire town was abuzz with festivities. There were people running past in garish clothing, and lively music was being played in the streets. It was a very pleasant and fun to see it all.

"What's going on around here?" Yocelin excitedly asked of the innkeeper as they reserved a room for the night.

"It's the Midsummer Festival!" The innkeeper replied jovially. "Every year, about this time, we celebrate for three days and three nights. Around here, it is a time to find your special someone and dance in the streets without a care for who might see you."

Clearly, the old innkeeper had a great affection for the Midsummer Festival, probably born of many good times past.

Yocelin clapped her hands together gleefully and made a little squeaking noise. "I love it! Let's go to the festival!" She bounced happily as she addressed her friends.

"I welcome that idea!" Giev grinned broadly and gave Aram an encouraging clap on the back.

Aram looked at the shaman with mild annoyance. He felt that Giev might try to encourage certain behavior between he and Yocelin, for it seemed that Giev still did not see why the two couples shouldn't just be together. Regardless, Aram felt himself nodding his accord to the idea of attending the festival, practically against his own will. When he looked at Yocelin bouncing in place with pleading eyes, he could not help but to agree. Somehow, she always managed to sway him.

Eithne grinned brightly and looked to Darian. "Well, I think it's perfect."

Darian raised an eyebrow at her. Eithne seemed genuinely pleased, which he had not seen for a while.

"Don't give me that look," Eithne commanded playfully while placing her hands on her hips. "We could all use the opportunity to relax and have a little fun. We need this."

Darian changed his expression by lifting both eyebrows when he caught her meaning and gave a confident nod. It made Eithne feel warm inside to have his approval, and she gazed at him smiling, for perhaps too long. Darian did not seem to mind.

"Well, come on then." Yocelin hooked her arm with Eithne and started leading her away. "Let's go buy something to wear to the festival. We can't dance in these dirty travel clothes."

The two women marched off together to go shopping and called out that they would see the boys later. A moment after they left, Darian realized he had not given them any money. He was generally the one in charge of their money so he carried the majority of it. He put his hand to the purse on his belt and looked as though he would go after the girls.

"Don't worry about it, Captain." Giev held up his hand to stop him. "You're not the only one with money around here. The dresses are on me today. You two just show up at the festival and have a nice time." Giev then swung his pack onto his shoulder and began heading upstairs. "I hope you don't mind that I got my own room tonight. I plan on enjoying the festival in my own way."

Darian and Aram knew very well what Giev meant to do tonight. They even admired his candor in a masculine sort of way. The two protectors went to the room they had reserved for themselves and the girls. They would relax until it was time to attend the festival.

Hours later, Darian awoke from his nap and swung his legs over the side of the bed to pull his boots on. Aram was sitting in a chair across the room, cleaning his weapons. Darian looked out the window. The sun was just beginning to set.

"Any sign of Eithne and Yocelin?" Darian asked.

Aram shook his head. "Giev stopped by to tell us that the girls said they would meet us in the town square."

"Well, I guess we should be getting to the square," Darian stood and stretched. "Ready?"

Aram put aside his weapons and stood to leave.

Neither of them knew exactly what to expect. Tonight was supposed to be about letting loose and having fun, and they really ought to enjoy themselves, though there was some anxiety. What would happen if they became too relaxed around Eithne and Yocelin? Furthermore, was it even such a terrible thing to allow themselves one night free of Tim and his warnings?

"I'm going to need a few drinks tonight," Aram plainly stated as they walked to the square.

"Agreed," said Darian with a resolved nod.

Walb was not a large town, so finding the main square was not a difficult task. The square itself was decorated with lights, and colorful garlands strung overhead. The many attendants of the festival celebrated in the streets all around them. There was almost a euphoric feeling to all of it. As Darian and Aram approached the square, the atmosphere helped to relax them. Perhaps they should just stop worrying and enjoy themselves for a change.

Upon entering the square, they did not see Eithne or Yocelin at first. Then Aram heard the all too familiar chime of Yocelin's flirtatious laughter. He turned and saw Yocelin and Eithne talking to a young human boy who looked to be about ten years old. Aram and Darian headed over to them.

Eithne saw the boys approaching and waved happily to them. As she lifted her arm, Darian noticed how exposed her midriff was in her new attire. Eithne wore a long yellow skirt that sat low on her hips, with a shortly cropped cream shirt. The shirt was loose fitting with short sleeves. All in all, it left her rather more exposed than what was considered appropriate by tribal elf standards. Seeing a woman's bare midriff in public was very taboo, but that was not what struck Darian the most. With her midriff exposed, he could see Eithne's tattoo of her spirit animal. Well, a portion of it, at least. He had never glimpsed it before. Darian knew she had one; everyone in their tribe did. He had a rearing horse tattooed down the backside of his right shoulder. Darian could not tell what animal was tattooed unto

Eithne, but it was huge. He surmised that it must go down almost the entire length of her body on the left side. He cursed inwardly as his imagination began to visualize being able to see all her tattoo. Suddenly, he felt like he needed that drink again.

Aram too felt himself uncomfortably enticed by Yocelin's dress. Yocelin wore a simple white linen dress that fell off her shoulders. It was very low cut and her ample bosom was only exaggerated by the neckline. It also did not help that she was currently bent forward to better speak with the young boy. Aram took a breath in and released it slowly as Yocelin glanced up at him with a flutter of her lashes. She knew exactly what she was doing, and Aram knew it. It was too bad that didn't prevent her ploys from being effective. He shook his head to clear it of impure thoughts and tried to look somewhere besides her chest. He smirked as he took note that Yocelin had concealed her horns by wrapping her thick purple hair around them in two elongated buns. They hairstyle was whimsical, and it suited her well.

"So who is this young man?" Darian asked warmly as he and Aram approached.

The boy seemed very pleased to be spoken to and grinned broadly. "I'm Jacob."

Darian knelt down on one knee in front of Jacob to better relate to him. "Nice to meet you, Jacob. My name is Darian. Are you keeping these two ladies company?"

"Yes, sir!" Jacob responded enthusiastically. "I was telling them about the Midsummer Festival."

"Well, you must be an expert," Darian replied with a confidence that made the boy puff out his chest with pride. "I bet you know all the best things to do."

"That's what I was telling them about!" Jacob replied happily.

"He was. Jacob here is very knowledgeable," Yocelin chimed in sweetly.

"Oh, yes, he's been a big help," Eithne confirmed.

Darian nodded and rubbed his chin in a thoughtful gesture. "Hmm, well it seems the two of you are in very capable hands. Wouldn't you agree, Aram?"

Aram was not used to children, nor did he understand what Darian was trying to accomplish with his strange statement. How could a young boy possibly be capable of taking care of two women like Yocelin and Eithne? Still, he realized that Darian meant for him to agree, so Aram gave a curt, affirmative nod.

Darian stood and addressed Eithne and Yocelin, "Well, ladies, I can see that you are well cared for by Jacob here. So Aram and I will leave you with the more experienced festival-goer." He then turned and pretended to start leaving.

Aram stood still, feeling confused.

"Wait! Mr. Darian!" Jacob called out desperately. Darian turned back and regarded the boy. "My mom is waiting for me, so I have to go."

Darian pretended to be thoughtful again. "Aram and I will be a poor substitute, but I suppose we will have to do in your absence. Thank you for telling them about the festival, Jacob."

The boy beamed with pride again. "I always like helping others!"

"An excellent quality!" Darian declared and patted Jacob on the back. "Now, your mother is waiting. Aram and I will do our best."

Jacob continued to beam with pride as he quickly said good-bye and hurried home.

Eithne smiled at Darian with a certain softness he had never seen before. He liked it.

"What is it?" Darian asked.

"You're so good with children. It's very sweet." She continued to look on him with the same soft smile for a moment then gave her head a little shake. "Anyway, what would you like to do? There's dancing, games, vendors, all sorts of things."

Darian wasn't paying attention to her question. His eyes drifted up and down her body as she spoke, taking her in. He truly enjoyed looking at her, and he never got tired of it.

"What is your spirit animal?" Darian asked as his gaze lingered on her torso.

Eithne blinked as she was caught off guard by his question. She realized where he was looking, and her cheeks became slightly pink. "It's unusual. I am guided by the phoenix."

It was Darian's turn to be caught off guard. "Really? I have never heard of anyone receiving a magical creature as their spirit animal. That's quite special."

"As far as I know, I'm the only one in our tribe with such an animal. Maybe it has something to do with this whole quest." She tried to sound casual, but she could feel the butterflies in her stomach fluttering wildly.

Darian came closer and touched the exposed skin where her tattoo was visible. "The magical bird that is reborn in flames. Rather fitting for the vessel of the sun god."

Eithne tingled all over from his touch. She wished that she had the courage to simply act on her feelings for Darian. Tim be damned. Little did she know, Darian was having the same thought.

Eithne cleared her throat to break the tension. "So what is your spirit animal?"

Darian did not move away, nor take his hand from her waist. It seemed as though he leaned in closer as he let his fingers trace the lines of her tattoo. "I am guided by the horse. It is on my back and shoulder."

"Strong and noble. It suits you well." Eithne allowed herself to make eye contact with him. She could see what he wanted. She wanted it too. Neither of them could act on it, so they stood and stared.

"Hey, you two!" Yocelin interrupted. "Are we going to see this festival or not?"

"Of course!" Eithne stuttered awkwardly. "Darian, shall we go play a game?"

Eithne walked past Darian toward their friends. He let his hand drop away from her as she passed. He let out a heavy sigh of frustration. It felt like they were already playing a game.

As the four friends began walking to see the festival, Aram touched Yocelin on her arm to get her attention. "Do you like children?"

"For dinner? No, they don't have a good flavor," Yocelin grinned at him devilishly.

Aram grinned back at her, which made Yocelin beam all the brighter. He thought her joke was very funny. It was rare that Aram smiled like that.

The festival was indeed a treat for the weary travelers. They spent the entire evening playing games, dancing, eating sweet treats, and laughing. It was wonderful to be free of responsibility for one night. All the companions were in a joyous mood. Once or twice, they even spotted Giev, who was very distracted by some beautiful young maidens. The maidens, in turn, looked very enamored of Giev. It was obvious that he had good reason for having his own room tonight. The merriment continued on for hours into the night. Eithne and Yocelin had allowed themselves to get tipsy. They didn't care. Tonight was a night to be irresponsible. While Aram and Darian had also been drinking, they still had more of their wits about them than the girls.

"Aram, you must dance with me again!" Yocelin demanded with her fists placed firmly on her hips. She stood in front of him as she addressed him. He was comfortably seated on a bench.

"I have already danced with you twice, and I am very bad at it. I believe I've suffered enough embarrassment for one night," Aram remarked plainly.

Yocelin was undeterred. "The third dance is the charm! You can't give up now! Please dance again. It makes me happy." She fluttered her long lashes at him and did her best to look persuasive.

Unfortunately, in Yocelin's inebriated state, the charming posture she was trying to hold caused her to sway. Then she began to topple. Aram caught her easily. He stood up as she pitched forward and cushioned her fall into his chest. Yocelin did not get her feet back under her. Instead, she continued to depend on him to stay upright. She felt that he might let go if she regained her balance. This was what she had wanted all along, to be held in Aram's arms. It was why she kept pushing him to dance with her. Now, Yocelin was exactly where she wanted to be, and he was playing his part perfectly by not letting go. She lifted her head and looked into his face. He had a caring, protective expression as he looked back at her. Yocelin loved that, the way he looked at her. He never looked at anyone else that way. It made her want to break the rules and kiss him. Had she been sober, she might have stopped herself, but she was drunk enough to throw her inhibitions away and simply act on instinct. She caught Aram by surprise again by taking his face in both her hand and kissing him on the mouth.

Had Aram been completely sober, he may have at least hesitated to respond, but there was no such hesitation tonight. He wanted Yocelin and had waited long enough to show it. His arms tightened around her petite frame and drew her in closer to him. The lights and sounds of the festival blurred around them.

A horrified shriek pierced through the air! People everywhere began running for cover. Aram and Yocelin stopped their kissing but still held each other close as they looked skyward. A large wyvern glided overhead, surveying the town of Walb. People were running inside the nearest buildings and ducking under tables, anything to keep from being seen from above. In spite of all the panic, the wyvern did not attack. It simply flew lazily over the town and then headed east and out of sight.

The pair remained in their embrace, looking up at the sky for a few minutes until they were certain the creature was gone. It had been a shock to have their intimate moment interrupted that way. They looked to each other, considering what to do next. Aram came to his conclusion first. Tomorrow morning, he could blame his inappropriate behavior on the alcohol. He did not know when he would have another opportunity to act on his feelings for Yocelin. This time was not to be wasted. Aram kissed her again, and she accepted willingly. Somehow, they found their way to sit on the nearby bench without coming apart. They did not separate for a long while, for they were so hungry for each other.

No one else present noticed the pair passionately kissing on the bench. Everyone around was either too intoxicated or too distracted by the wyvern's sudden appearance to notice.

CHAPTER THIRTY-EIGHT

HE NEXT MORNING, everything was blurry. Yocelin sat up and rubbed her aching head. Somehow she had managed to make it back to the inn and into bed. Someone stirred next to her. It was Aram! Yocelin did an immediate check of herself to find that she was still fully clothed in the white dress; only her shoes were off. Aram was awake and watching her patiently. He was also fully clothed in what he had been wearing the night before. Suddenly, it all flooded back to Yocelin's mind: they had kissed last night, and they had done an awful lot of it!

"We didn't have sex. Just a lot of kissing and heavy petting," Aram assured her. He could see from the look on her face that the memories of last night were coming back to her in bits and pieces. He swung his legs over the side of the bed so that his back was now to her. "We got a little too drunk, I'm afraid."

Yocelin regarded his back. Did Aram think that she was upset about anything that happened last night? Well, she wasn't! She wouldn't even be upset if they did have sex. Actually, she would be mad if they did and she didn't remember it, but she would not regret it if it had happened. Yocelin had feelings for Aram. Strong feelings. She loved him, and she believed that he felt the same for her. To be together every day, wanting each other so much and not acting on it was sheer torture. She was downright glad she got drunk last night and smothered Aram with kisses. He was still sitting with his back to her. Yocelin knew he didn't regret anything either. He just wasn't sure how she was taking it.

Yocelin sighed. "You know, it's a shame." She slowly got out of bed and went to fix her hair by the small oval mirror on the wall.

Aram's shoulders fell, and his hands gripped the side of the bed as the emotional hurt of her words struck him. "I'm sorry. I lost control. It won't happen again."

"Oh, no, quite the opposite," Yocelin responded quickly in her saucy voice. "It's a shame we didn't go further. Now that was a waste of a perfectly good drunken opportunity."

Aram stiffened and sharply turned his head to stare at her. "What? You're not mad at me for taking advantage of you?"

Yocelin smiled at him in her womanly way. "On the contrary, I would like to suggest that we get drunk and irresponsible much more often."

Aram swallowed hard. Heeding the wizard's warning just became even more difficult. Damn Tim.

Eithne and Darian had had a rather different sort of evening. They too had enjoyed dancing and the like, and even had a few moments where they forgot that they weren't supposed to be a couple. Unfortunately for them, Eithne was not the type to take initiative romantically, and Darian considered giving into his temptation for Eithne a personal failure of his discipline. There was one moment in particular where it seemed they would give into their base emotions, then the wyvern flew overhead. Darian was prepared to ignore it as it didn't seem to be a threat, but Eithne had a different reaction. What had become a familiar sensation came over her when the wyvern flew over Walb. The creature carried a piece of Anut. Eithne would have to kill it. She told Darian what she sensed, and he had simply nodded affirmatively. They both shifted back into the mind-set of completing the quest. They had resolved to speak to the innkeeper about where to find the wyvern the next morning and went to bed.

Darian and Eithne had heard Yocelin and Aram come in late. It wasn't until the morning that Eithne and Darian saw that their counterparts had fallen asleep in the same bed. It seemed that they had enjoyed their evening very much, indeed. Darian and Eithne let them sleep and went downstairs for breakfast.

"The innkeeper said that we can find the wyvern in some caves east of town," Darian informed Eithne as he sat back down at the table next to her. She was picking at her breakfast. "Apparently, the beast eats their livestock and occasionally takes a person. They will be happy to be rid of it."

Eithne heard him but did not care. At the moment, she had other things on her mind. She continued to pick at her food and did not respond.

Darian was confused. "Eithne, did you hear me?"

She sighed and put her fork down. "I'm so jealous."

"What?"

"I said I'm jealous," Eithne repeated in a tone that told Darian that she could easily become unpleasant if he wasn't careful.

"Jealous of what?"

"Why couldn't you take advantage of the situation last night? I was drunk, and you had a few yourself," she pouted.

Darian's eyebrows shot straight up. She was jealous that Aram and Yocelin had obviously been enjoying each other last night, and they had not. He smirked automatically. It pleased him very much that Eithne wanted to have such contact with him. His smirk quickly faded when he remembered why they weren't doing such things, though. He rubbed his face with his hand.

"So you're saying that you would want me to take advantage of you when you're intoxicated? I thought that was generally considered a dishonorable thing." Darian needed some clarification. Her words had enticed a notion that was always lingering in his mind and caused Tim's warning to quiet.

"Not if I want to be taken advantage of, you dummy!" Eithne shot back in her feisty voice. "I admire how noble you are, but do you have to be that way all the time?"

Darian felt very confused. He sat, silently looking at her since he didn't know how to answer, or if she even wanted him to answer her.

She continued to glare at him with expectation. She wanted an answer.

"I'm sorry," Darian replied awkwardly after Eithne didn't say anything for a while. This did not have the calming effect he was going for.

"Furthermore, I still wonder how you feel about my sister!" Eithne went on hotly. "You wanted to court her for marriage not so long ago. Now it seems like you don't want her anymore, but I'm really not sure. It upsets me when I think about it, and my head hurts!"

She was in full swing now. It wasn't good. She was continuing on with hot-tempered babble about her emotions, and it was all just sounding like nonsense. Darian had to find a way to calm and reassure her quickly before she got any worse. Anything he said would probably only make her angrier. He could see in her face that she was displeased with his lack of reaction, and so she would probably start directing her rant at him soon.

Darian quickly pulled her to him and kissed her on the mouth. He felt her relax into him after a few seconds, and she slipped her arms around his neck. Darian hugged her closer and allowed himself to have this moment with her. Just now, he finally felt the constant, burning ache that was his desire for Eithne ebb.

The kiss ended, but they remained together with only a breath between their lips.

"Eithne, it's always been you. I don't even think about your sister. Now stop being such a handful," Darian whispered then gave her a couple more small kisses.

"I'm less jealous now," Eithne purred with a dreamy smile.

"Hey, are you two still drunk? Technically, you're not allowed to do that unless you're drunk. It's the code of Timulous," Yocelin's voice pierced through the moment.

She and Aram had just arrived at the table to join them for breakfast.

Darian groaned inwardly and begrudgingly released Eithne. She slid off of Darian's lap and back onto her onto her chair, feeling a little embarrassed, but mostly perturbed.

"So," Yocelin cooed as she leaned over the table toward Darian and Eithne, "what did you two do last night?"

Darian regarded her irritably and crossed his arms. "A lot less than the two of you."

Yocelin laughed.

Aram shifted uncomfortably. "We were drunk."

Eithne was a little too embarrassed to be speaking about all this. It felt strange to have it all out in the open like it was normal.

"We have to kill the wyvern," Eithne blurted out loudly. "We should probably get going because we have to kill it."

Darian smirked at her. He felt proud that she was so flustered.

"The wyvern? You mean the one that flew over town last night?" Aram asked.

"You noticed that, huh?" Darian teased his friend.

"Just barely," Yocelin smiled smugly. "Why do we need to kill it?"

"It carries a piece of Anut. Also, sometimes it kills the people who live here and their livestock," Eithne responded. "It lives in some caves east of here."

"That's enough reason for me. Let's go!" Yocelin hopped up then she looked at each of her companions. "Oh, wait, we're missing Giev." She sat back down.

"I thought we'd let Giev sit this one out," Darian said. "We can take care of the wyvern and come back here to get him after. I'm sure he would be hard pressed to leave his bed this morning."

"Good point," Aram concurred.

"I'll just leave a message with the innkeeper to tell Giev that we'll be back and he should wait here for us." Eithne got up and walked over to the innkeeper to leave the message.

The four companions had a light breakfast and got on the road from there. They were all hoping that killing the wyvern would be a relatively easy task. The creatures were generally nocturnal, so if they came upon it while it slept, killing it could be very simple. It was nice to have something different to do along their journey. This little side trip was a welcome change of pace.

They got the proper directions to the cave and set out on the small journey. The townspeople that heard that they were off to kill the wyvern were very enthusiastic. Several of them approached the foursome as they left Walb to offer encouragement and gratitude. It was pleasing to be so appreciated, even if just for a moment. Aram did not know how to respond to any of it, but it was pleasant for him all the same.

The caves were not very far at all. In fact, it only took a couple of hours on foot to reach them. They had opted to allow the horses to rest as well as Giev. They came upon a large gaping entrance to a cave-in the forest, and all stopped to take stock of the situation.

"Well, it certainly smells like a wyvern lives in there. I think this is the place," Yocelin said.

"Right. Do we just walk in? It's sleeping now, right?" Eithne did not have a great fear of the creature in the cave, but she felt hesitant. This all seemed too easy, and something could go wrong.

"Yes, let's just go in quietly so we don't wake it. I'm sure our noses will lead us to it easily enough," Darian confirmed. He drew his sword and chopped off a couple of nearby tree branches. He then went about makes some torches.

"Do we really need those?" Aram asked, watching Darian.

Darian chuckled. "I just like to be prepared. Besides, I don't see so well in the dark as demons and werewolves."

Aram nodded. He sometimes forgot that his senses were heightened in comparison to regular elves. Being around his friends made him feel normal again. He knew was different, and somewhat awkward due to his self-inflicted years of solitude. His companions treated him as normal, as someone who wasn't damned. It warmed Aram's heart.

As they entered the cave, it was immediately clear that following the stench was the best way to find the wyvern. The beast stank up the whole place terribly. Thankfully, they all had relatively strong stomachs, though it did make breathing unpleasant. As they came around a corner, they could hear the heavy breathing of the sleeping beast. Darian and Eithne went forward first, continuing with their stealth. After turning another corner, they came upon the wyvern's lair. The torch illuminated the cavern to reveal that the wyvern was not the sole source of the awful smell. Strewn all about were the half-eaten and decaying carcasses of livestock and even a couple of people. The wyvern slept in the center of the gruesome display, snoring peacefully. Eithne could feel the spark of Anut within it. She was ready to get this over with and go back outside where the air was fresh. She silently approached the wyvern with her sword drawn. Darian was right behind her. Yocelin and Aram hung back but remained at the ready in case something went wrong. Eithne came to stand beside the head of the creature, which was resting on the half-eaten carcass of a cow. Gripping it with both hands, she raised her sword high and drove it straight down through the wyvern's brain, killing it instantly. She then felt the warm tingling sensation of another piece of Anut coming into her body.

Darian waited until after the transfer of Anut was complete, then he squeezed her shoulder and told her that she had done well.

Eithne half-turned and smiled at him.

"Whoo-hoo!" Yocelin cheered loudly. "You killed that wyvern!"

Immediately after Yocelin's supportive declaration, a piercing inhuman scream filled the cavern! Darian threw his torch in the direction of the horrible noise, illuminating a second, fully-grown wyvern! Eithne had just killed its mate. Clearly, it was angry.

Aram and Yocelin rushed forward with weapons drawn to stand with their friends. The wyvern surveyed the intruders and what they had done to its mate, then the creature let out another piercing scream that shook the walls around them and caused the companions to cover their ears with their hands. Since the wyvern did not have the space to fly inside the cavern, it charged. The four companions scattered and tried to surround the beast. Wyverns were not as big as their dragon cousins. This one looked large at roughly fourteen feet from nose to tail. Their skin was leathery and lacked the scaly armor that dragons possessed. Other than those main physical differences and a distinct lack of intelligence, wyverns were basically small dragons, which made them formidable opponents. The beast began spitting acid at its foes. The four companions all raced and tumbled to get out of the way of the fatal liquid.

Somehow, Aram found himself behind the wyvern, which was concentrated on Eithne at the moment. Using his supernatural speed and agility, he dodged around its lashing tail and ran up unto the back of the beast. He drove his sword in between its shoulder blades, severing the spine. The wyvern screamed again, this time out of pain and collapsed. It was not dead but immobilized. Darian finished the job by running his sword through its brain, killing it quickly and humanely.

The friends were about to relax when an unpleasant rumbling sound rolled through the air, and everything around them shook violently! Aram and Darian sprung into action, each grabbing Eithne and Yocelin respectively and finding the nearest exits out of the collapsing cavern. Consequently, each couple had been at opposite ends of the cavern, so they went through different tunnels. There was no time to properly coordinate an exit strategy as the cave-in occurred.

CHAPTER THIRTY-NINE

❧

THE DUST AROUND Aram and Yocelin was still settling. He had thrown himself over her as a shield against the falling rocks. Aram pushed himself up and inspected Yocelin beneath him. "Are you injured?" he asked.

She coughed the dust from her lungs and shook her head. "I'm fine. Just a little rattled. Thank you, Aram."

He rolled off of her and coughed. "I'm your protector. No need to thank me. It's what I'm here for."

Yocelin propped herself up on her elbows and gave him a quirky look. "You just saved my life. Protector or not, you're getting thanks, so just accept it."

Aram nodded and got to his feet. It was pitch-dark, but he could see well enough to survey their situation. They appeared to be in a tunnel, but it was not the same one they initially approached the cavern from. He had no idea whether they would be lucky enough to find an exit. There was a strong possibility that they may have to dig their way out before they ran out of air.

"Where are Eithne and Darian?" Yocelin's voice had a tinge of panic in it. She feared the worst might have happened to her friends.

"Darian grabbed Eithne and ran into the tunnel that we originally entered from. We were too far away to make it to that tunnel in time. They are probably fine. Right now, I'm more worried about us," Aram answered.

Yocelin's eyes got wide as the seriousness of their situation dawned on her. They could be buried alive! They needed to find a way out of the cave before they ran out of air.

Aram was already looking at the rubble to try and figure out the safest way to begin moving the rocks. The chances of the tunnel they were in leading outside were slim to none, but Yocelin decided it was a good idea to try anyway.

"I'm going to see where this tunnel leads," she announced and started walking into the blackness.

Aram nodded and let her go. They had just killed the most dangerous things in the cave, so he felt she would be safe. It was also worth being certain that they had to dig themselves out. On the off chance that this tunnel actually led outside, it was best not to waste energy digging. In the meantime, Aram would get started on moving the rocks out of the way, so that nothing was wasted. The chances of this tunnel being an exit were very small.

Yocelin's trip down the tunnel was not a long one. She was walking for about ten minutes when she came to a dead end. She sighed unhappily. She knew that the tunnel probably wasn't going to lead outside, but she had been hopeful, nonetheless. Yocelin inspected the area thoroughly to be sure it really was a dead end then turned back to go help Aram.

When Yocelin returned, they didn't speak but simply nodded at each other. Aram could tell from her demeanor that they had not gotten lucky. She set about helping him dig. Speaking would only use up valuable air. The mood between them was very somber. Both realized that they might not survive this.

Darian had fallen on top of Eithne to shield her in a similar way that Aram had shielded Yocelin. After making sure that Eithne was not seriously hurt, he took stock of the situation. They were in the tunnel they had entered from originally, so that was very good. They had a way out. Aram and Yocelin, however, were nowhere around.

"Where are Aram and Yocelin?" Eithne asked hurriedly. She already knew the answer but looked for them anyway.

"Damn it!" Darian swore quietly. "They must have taken shelter in another tunnel."

"Are you sure they were able to take shelter?" Eithne's voice quivered with fear.

Darian nodded decisively as he replayed what had happened in his mind. He had definitely seen Aram grab Yocelin and duck into another tunnel. They did not get caught in the cavern. "They got out of the cavern in time. I'm sure of it."

"But they're probably trapped!" Eithne persisted anxiously.

Darian nodded solemnly.

Eithne went to the pile of rocks where the tunnel entrance was and began to dig. Darian joined her. They would dig their friends out if it took a week.

Aram and Yocelin had been digging for a very long time—hours maybe. Yocelin felt weak and a little dizzy. She knew that it was due to exhaustion coupled with the air running out. She tried not to think about it. They had made good progress, but the cavern had been very large. They knew that they had worked their way into the main cavern. It was obvious by the crushed bones and carcasses they kept uncovering. If only they could be certain that they were digging in the right direction. Both of them had heightened senses, but unfortunately, a super sense of direction was not one of them. They just had to guess as best they could and hope it was correct. Their lives depended on it.

Yocelin stopped digging and took a moment to rest. She and Aram had been taking rest breaks every once in a while, so Aram did not think anything of it. He continued to dig. Yocelin watched him. Her demon eyes allowed her to see him in the inky darkness. She admired his diligence and will to survive. He was a great comfort to her in this situation. Aram did not panic, nor did he talk about the bad things that could happen. He simply focused on solving the problem. Yocelin smiled as she thought on him. At his core, Aram was an optimist, though most people would never know it. She loved that about him. She blinked and stiffened as she realized that he may never hear her tell him that. Well, she couldn't live with that! They might die in this cave, and Aram should know that he had her love. She needed him to know that.

Yocelin reached out and lightly touched Aram's hands to stop him from digging. He stilled and faced her.

"Aram, I need to tell you something, just in case . . ." Yocelin spoke softly, almost in a whisper. It didn't feel right to speak at full volume after having been quiet for so long.

Aram's expression softened. He had a good idea of what she wanted to tell him. He had been tempted to say the same thing to her, but saying it now made him feel like they weren't going to get out of this cave. Aram was in no mood to think like that. He refused to accept the possibility of them not getting out of here alive.

Yocelin took in a slow breath to begin speaking again. Aram gently placed two fingers on her lips to quiet her.

"Don't tell me," he said in a low voice.

He watched her expression sadden as if she suddenly thought that he didn't feel the same way as she did.

"Wait until after," Aram continued hopefully. "Tell me after we get out of here."

Yocelin relaxed again but felt like crying bittersweet tears. She went into him, and Aram held her close for a while.

A few hours later, Aram and Yocelin were starting to feel quite desperate. They were still digging but were beginning to think that they would not get out alive. They were so tired and dizzy. Yocelin felt that she was dangerously close to blacking out. Then it would be over. Their lives and their quest to save Raashan would end here.

There was a low rumble all around, and their hearts dropped simultaneously. All their digging to get out must have caused another cave-in. It was truly over.

The stones to the left of them began to shift, but only those stones. They shifted like a moving puzzle, and small beams of bluish white light peeked through the crevices. Aram and Yocelin watched with renewed hope and amazement as a doorway full of light formed. Fresh air rushed their faces, and they breathed it in greedily. For a moment, Yocelin thought they were dead, that this was a doorway to the afterlife. Then through the light stepped Giev, Eithne, and Darian. Eithne rushed forward and hugged onto Yocelin tightly. She was so thankful to find her friends alive!

"Are you dead too?" Yocelin asked in the tiniest hush. She still did not understand if she were alive or not.

"What?" Eithne held Yocelin's shoulders at arm's length and looked her in the eyes. "Yocelin, you're alive! We're all alive! Giev used the Stone of Elissiyus to rescue you and Aram. You're safe now."

Yocelin stood quiet for a few seconds while she absorbed what Eithne told her. Tears welled up in her eyes and streaked down her dirty cheeks.

"We're alive!" Yocelin cried and embraced Eithne warmly as she sobbed with relief.

"Let's get you two out of here," Darian stated as he helped support Aram. He was not sure how long Giev could continue what he was doing with the stone.

With Eithne helping Yocelin and Darian helping Aram, Giev led them back out of the caves efficiently. Once outside, Giev exhaled deeply and collapsed against a nearby boulder. Using the stone's power was exhausting. There was immensely powerful magic there, and it was very difficult for him to channel it properly.

Darian and Eithne made certain that their friends got plenty of water and rested for a while. Their bodies had been through a lot of stress and needed some time to recuperate.

"How did you find us?" Aram asked after about fifteen minutes had passed.

"It was Giev, really," Darian replied. "He heard from the innkeeper where we had gone and decided to come after us. Thank goodness, he did, or we may have lost you both!"

Aram nodded. Then he looked to Giev. "Sincerely, thank you, for both of us."

Giev nodded back gladly. "Anything for my friends."

Yocelin went over to Giev and hugged him. It did not make Aram jealous. He rather felt like hugging Giev himself. It was an extremely profound gratitude that he felt for Giev, Darian, and Eithne. He knew he had true friends. Aram felt pleasantly warm inside.

"So how did you do it? How did you find us?" Yocelin asked after the long hug.

"I used the Stone of Elissiyus's power to find you. I never leave it behind, as it is too precious, and when I realized the situation, I had to try to use it. I've learned quite a bit about the stone these past months. One of the things I've found is that if you properly channel your energy, the stone will sort of sense your needs and work with you to resolve the situation. You do not need specific spells to work it," Giev explained.

Yocelin blinked at Giev's long explanation. It was interesting how the stone worked. "Well, I just can't tell you how happy I am that Aram and I are alive! I never want to be so close to death again!"

The companions all laughed good-naturedly. They all wanted the same thing.

"I have a rule for everyone," Eithne announced. They all gave her their attention. "No one is to exclaim congratulations for me, or anyone else, when in a dark cave. That's the second time I have seen horrible consequences from such an exclamation, so they are now outlawed. Congratulations on a job well done are to be held until safely out of the cave."

It sounded like a silly thing to say, but Eithne was quite serious. The incident had reminded her of what had happened all those months ago when Roth was crushed to death by the giant cave worm. She could not bear losing anyone else because of such circumstances. It made her feel guilt that she did not wish to bear.

Darian smiled sympathetically at Eithne and hugged her around her shoulders. He understood her intentions perfectly.

The rest all agreed to the new rule. They did not understand it, but it was a good rule, and it was important to Eithne.

CHAPTER FORTY

---

*T*HE HAPPY COMPANIONS returned to Walb as heroes. The
townspeople rejoiced over the news that the wyverns were
dead. It had always been assumed that there was only one, so
to know that two had been slain made the companions seem even
more heroic. The people of Walb wanted to throw a great party in
their honor and give them all sorts of rewards, but almost all were
declined. The companions were too conscientious of getting back
on the road to continue their quest. They only took enough from
the people of Walb to restock their rations and some new clothing.
They refused any money. After all, killing the wyverns had helped to
further their goal as well. It did not feel right to take compensation
under the circumstances.

They were on their way out of Walb by the next day. At first,
they simply continued on toward Duomo, where they would recon-
nect with the wizard Tim. Giev was extremely excited to meet the
famous wizard. The rest were much less enthusiastic. They continued
for a while in the direction of Duomo with the intention of seeing
Tim again. Then one morning, Yocelin woke Aram up early.

"What's wrong?" Aram asked as he was awakened. He knew
that she wouldn't bother him so early if it weren't important.

"I feel him. Cavan is very close," Yocelin answered.

Aram became fully awake at this news. "So what do you want
to do?"

Yocelin was hesitant. Her first instinct was to run away, but Giev
said that he could stun Cavan with the Stone of Elissiyus. If Cavan
could truly be stunned long enough for her to run him through, killing him should be simple.

"I think we should find him," she answered quietly.

Aram held her eyes for a moment then gave a slow nod. "You sure you're ready for that?"

She sighed. "As I'll ever be."

Aram nodded again and cupped the back of her head with his hand to draw her forehead to his lips. He kissed her there and hugged her supportively.

Aram and Yocelin awoke the others and told them that this might be the best time to go after Cavan. It was a prospect that made everyone anxious, but the task needed to be done. The general feeling was that it would be now or never. The companions were on their way within the hour with Yocelin leading. Cavan was very close. In fact, Yocelin felt that they should find him by the afternoon. There were no towns nearby, so Cavan was obviously on the road. The feeling of him drew closer and closer. They would face Cavan again soon.

Yocelin felt almost as if she were walking through a thick fog. The ominous feeling was so stifling. She almost didn't even see the fields and trees around her. She just kept following Cavan's energy. She was barely aware that she was still on the road at all. Suddenly, Yocelin pulled back on the reins and halted the horse. Aram, who rode with her, sat patiently and waited to see what she was doing. Then he glanced to the left. There he saw a small dirt path marked by an old, faded sign. Aram squinted as he struggled to make out the weathered writing. It read: "Velden the Necromancer." Aram's eyebrows shot up. He did not have a fear of necromancers, but he was very surprised and cautious about seeing one out here.

"Which way, Yocelin?" he whispered gently into her ear.

Yocelin twitched a little. "Left. We go left."

Aram nodded, took the reins, and guided their horse down the dirt path to the left. He silently looked back at the others as they turned down the path. It seemed that they had all read the faded sign as well, but their faces shown stern resolve. Who knew what they were walking into? Cavan and a necromancer together? It seemed a horrific combination. They were here now, however, so they would simply have to deal with whatever was at the end of the road.

The little dirt path was not long, but it seemed to take forever. No birds chirped. The air was still and stiflingly hot. There was also a faint, unpleasant odor of decay that steadily grew stronger as they continued. It spooked the horses, so they decided to dismount and lead the animals with their weapons drawn. Yocelin led, still entranced, while the others followed.

Eithne had read the sign, as the others had, but she was not sure what a necromancer was. It was a subject that she had never come across in her studies. She looked at Giev, who was walking next to her; the shaman could probably explain it best.

"Giev, what is a necromancer?" Eithne whispered. She was afraid to speak at full volume.

Giev looked to her and leaned over closer to answer. "A sorcerer of sorts. Necromancers deal in death. They are best known for reanimating corpses with their magic and using the corpses as mindless minions."

"Oh." Eithne looked straight ahead again. That sounded extremely unpleasant. Also, to be going toward Cavan at the same time was even worse. She gripped the hilt of her sword tighter and took a deep breath. They had to be prepared for anything.

The road dead-ended at a faded wooden house. Wind chimes made of various types of bones hung still in the stagnant air, and a dead, partially decomposed cat sat on the front steps flicking its crooked tail. Flies buzzed all around the place, and the smell of death and decay was so strong that it was difficult to stomach. It was a horrible place. None of them wanted to continue, but they had to.

Aram reached over and gave Yocelin's shoulder a squeeze. Yocelin blinked out of her daze and nodded to show that she was aware of where they were. The companions all held their weapons at the ready as they hesitated for a moment. The air was hot and static around them. They were about to approach the house when the undead cat let out a gurgled howl. It was the worst noise Eithne thought she had ever heard in her life. The companions all froze where they stood. Then they heard some shuffling from inside the house. The front door creaked open, and out stepped a wrinkled old man in torn, dirty sorcerer's robes. This must be Velden.

"Are you customers?" Velden asked with a withered voice. He seemed completely unfazed by the fact that there were five people in front of his house with their weapons drawn.

"I suppose that depends," Darian answered. "We came here seeking someone we believe to be in your house."

Velden nodded slowly and absentmindedly scratched his rough chin whiskers. "Ah, well, say, there is another customer inside. What is it that you want with them?"

"We plan to kill him," Darian decided to be frank. It was clear that the necromancer had no loyalties to speak of, so there was no use in beating around the bush.

Velden's eyebrows rose with interest. He was both a necromancer and a businessman, and dead things were useful to him. Also, perhaps these people would be in need of his services. He was always happy to accommodate new customers. Being a necromancer wasn't terribly lucrative.

"Perhaps we can strike up a deal?" Velden suggested slyly.

Darian lowered his sword but did not sheath it. "What did you have in mind?"

"It occurs to me that all of you may also be interested in some of my services. If we can do business, then maybe I can let you see if the person you want to kill is inside my house. If they happen to be the one you are looking for, I will not stop you from killing them." Velden gave an almost toothless smile that was meant to be friendly and reassuring but was mostly disturbing.

Darian heard Aram scoff. It sounded like a bad deal. What services could they possibly need from a necromancer?

"Can you perform the guided veil?" Giev surprised everyone present with his question. None of his companions had any idea what the "guided veil" was, let alone asking about it.

Velden's scraggly gray eyebrows shot up in amazement, but he quickly recovered. "You know something of my art?"

Giev nodded affirmatively.

Velden continued, "Yes, I can perform the guided veil."

"Can you do more than one person at a time?" Giev countered.

Again, the necromancer looked impressed with Giev's question. "Yes, but I cannot be an anchor for more than one person."

"Give us a moment, please," Giev indicated that his companions should huddle so that they could speak privately.

"I think that we should have him perform the guided veil on Eithne and Yocelin," Giev said. He clearly didn't realize that the rest of them had no idea what he was talking about.

"What is the guided veil, and why should we have the girls experience it?" Aram asked plainly. It was exactly what everyone else wanted to understand.

Giev smiled sheepishly at his mistake in assuming that his friends would know he was talking about. He explained, "The guided veil is a sort of trance that an experienced necromancer can put people under. Basically, the person simulates death—"

"What? I don't want to die!" Yocelin interjected, feeling very concerned over Eithne and her welfare. She had recently survived one brush with death and was not keen on experiencing another.

Giev held up his hands, signifying that they needed to hear him out. "Calm down. I certainly don't want anyone to die either. You won't be dead. You will just be in a sort of trance that simulates death and allows the two of you to see the 'other side.'"

Darian reached down and took Eithne's hand in his. This talk was making him uneasy.

"Why do we want to see the realm of the dead?" Eithne asked, feeling morbid.

"Because there are those whom god pieces were placed in that are already dead. Humans are not as long lived as elves and demons. It's been fifty years since the death of the gods. Surely, many god piece carriers are dead. You will need to find their souls in the afterlife in order to recover them," Giev explained.

"Then that's why Cavan is here, to gather god pieces of Muntros from the dead," Yocelin made a statement. She did not need to guess. She knew that was why Cavan had come here as soon as Giev said it.

Giev nodded excitedly, happy to have his friends understanding what he was saying. "That's good news, in a way. If you can kill him while he is entranced, then that task is completed with minimal risk! We won't even need to use the stone."

The others all stared at the shaman with wide eyes while his statement sunk in. Could it be true? Could they dispose of Cavan so easily?

Darian held up his hand. "What are the risks to Eithne and Yocelin if they do this? Is there any chance of harm to them?"

Giev's excitement faded a little. "There is always a risk. In the case of the guided veil, the responsibility lies mostly on the anchor. As long as the anchor does their job properly, there is very little risk involved."

"Darian and I will act as their anchors then," Aram stated firmly. Yocelin hugged onto his arm as he spoke. She adored how protective he was over her.

Giev nodded his agreement. "I think that is best for all concerned."

The companions all nodded together in agreement. Their minds were made up. They turned back to Velden, who was standing patiently on his porch.

"We would like you to perform the guided veil on Eithne and Yocelin," Giev indicated the proper people as he spoke. "Aram and Darian will act as their anchors."

Velden's wrinkled mouth curled upward in a smile. "The price for that would be around two hundred coin." Velden scratched the rough whiskers on his chin while he pretended to ponder something. "However, I could be persuaded to lessen the price if you have something else to offer besides money."

"In a way, we do have something else to offer," Giev answered.

"I'm listening," Velden folded his hands into his tattered sleeves and waited to hear what Giev had to say.

"Your other customer. We are nearly certain that he is the man we wish to kill. As you are a necromancer, dead bodies are of use to you, particularly fresh ones," Giev replied.

Eithne and Yocelin exchanged a look. It was so morbid and strange to hear Giev talking like that.

"Though it would be unscrupulous of you to harm your own client for personal gain, perhaps it isn't so bad if another client kills him? Not only would you have a fresh body, but we would also be happy to let you have any money or valuables that he is carrying," Giev stated shrewdly.

Velden's eyebrows went up in great interest. The man inside certainly looked as though he carried a good deal of money. Not to mention the worth of the fresh corpse alone was of great value to him. It was highly unusual for him to have access to humanoid corpses at all, especially one so young and strong as the man inside. It was true that any upstanding necromancer would not kill their clients to have use of fresh corpses, no matter how tempting. However, if someone else were to kill a client inside his house, there was nothing ethically wrong with taking advantage of the situation.

"I must ask why you want this man dead?" Velden asked cautiously.

"He is an evil man," Aram answered plainly. "He will hunt us down and kill us as well as countless others if we do not kill him."

Velden nodded. He had certainly gotten that sort of impression from the man inside. In fact, the necromancer was half-wondering if he meant to run him through once he had gotten what he wanted. Velden knew he was old, but he was not ready to die yet. All in all, this sounded like an excellent deal.

"I will only charge you seventy-five coin if the man inside is the one you seek. Of course, the resulting corpse and all its possessions will remain with me. In the event that it is not the one you want, then my price remains two hundred coin."

The companions nodded their acceptance of the terms to the necromancer.

Velden then led them inside to inspect his other client. The companions gave the undead cat a wide berth as they stepped past it. The house was creaky, dusty, and reeked of death. Taxidermy animals of various species were everywhere. It appeared that Velden was completely obsessed with death in all aspects, not just as a necromancer. It was unsettling to think that someone would desire to be so surrounded by dead things. Velden led them into a room where they found a teenaged boy, probably no more than sixteen, kneeling next to Cavan, who lay flat on his back with his eyes closed. He appeared to be dead, but they all knew that he was not. Yocelin gripped her chest as her heat burned with white-hot agony. Aram slipped his arm around her waist in case she needed the support. Yocelin bore the pain well and kept her eyes locked on Cavan.

"Is this the man you are looking for?" Velden asked politely, though he could tell that it was the right person.

"Yes," Yocelin said through clenched teeth and drew her sword. She was ready to be rid of Cavan once and for all.

"Please wait a moment," Velden asked calmly. "My apprentice needs to be detached from him before you can kill him."

Yocelin looked to the boy, who must be acting as Cavan's anchor in the guided veil. He would probably be harmed in some way if Yocelin were to kill Cavan without warning.

"Will the detachment awaken Cavan?" Darian asked before Velden could act.

The necromancer nodded. "Yes, but there will be a moment between the detachment and his awakening. I assume that you are capable of acting without hesitation."

Yocelin gave a resolved nod. Then she stood over Cavan with her sword ready to be thrust down into his wicked heart.

"Signal me as soon as your apprentice is detached," the she-demon stated coldly.

Velden quickly went about detaching his apprentice from Cavan. It only took a moment, but it seemed like an hour to Yocelin as she stood poised to strike. She couldn't believe how easy it was going to be to finally be rid of Cavan. They had feared him and run from him for so long; now she was going to just snuff him out without a fight. She did not have any complaints about her good fortune, mind you. It was just such an odd feeling to kill Cavan so easily.

The young apprentice slumped and blinked his eyes open. Velden whipped around and greedily hissed, "Now!"

Yocelin forcefully plunged her sword into Cavan's chest! Cavan's eyes flew open, and horrible rage burned in them as his gasped his last breath. His last vision in life was of the purple-haired she-demon stabbing him through the heart. Then his whole body went limp and still. His raging eyes became vacant. Cavan was dead.

Suddenly, a mass of dark orbs of blackish light rose from Cavan's body and violently dove into Yocelin! She jerked her head skyward and screamed as the pieces of Muntros entered her. It was not a scream of pain but of overwhelming power. To have so much of the god of destruction rushing into her all at once was a very profound and passionate experience.

All went silent. Yocelin stood rooted in place, her hands still clutching her sword that was imbedded in Cavan's lifeless body. She remained looking skyward, huffing from exertion. To say that the experience had been intense seemed a vast understatement.

"What is going on?" Velden's apprentice squeaked out. The poor boy had no idea what had just transpired or why.

"I will explain everything later, but now is not the time," Velden assured in a comforting voice. "Now go prepare enough mixture for two more guided veils."

The boy nodded dumbly. As he left to do his master's bidding, he looked over the whole scene of the room again. It was a very strange and interesting day.

"How long will it take him to prepare the mixture?" Giev asked.

"Not long," Velden answered. He was already going through Cavan's pockets. "Enough time for me to explain the ritual to all of you and what you will need to do for it to be properly executed."

CHAPTER FORTY-ONE

❧

*A*LL WAS READY. Eithne and Yocelin lay flat on their backs on the floor. Darian sat by Eithne's head and Aram by Yocelin's head. Necromancer symbols had been drawn on each of their foreheads in ashes. None wanted to know where the ashes came from, through they all strongly suspected that they were humanoid. Each knew how to play their roles. Giev sat as an observer in the corner of the room. Velden stood by Eithne and Yocelin's feet, ready to instruct. It was time to begin.

Velden began to chant an incantation. As he did, Darian and Aram fed the girls a milky potion. After they drank the potion, both of them laid back, and their eyelids fluttered rapidly as they entered the trance. Eithne and Yocelin felt light and dizzy. The room around them seemed to melt away and blur. For long moments, there was nothing but dizziness and swirling colors. They were not sure if they were stationary or moving.

Finally, their surroundings settled into a pale orange-yellow color. Eithne and Yocelin stood together on what appeared to be a blank plane. Eithne looked at her hand and saw a delicate red thread tied to her left pinky finger. She followed the path of the thread with her eyes. It went very far, beyond her sight. Yocelin also had a red thread tied to her left pinky finger. The threads must be the visual representation of their connection to Darian and Aram. Velden had told them there would be something like this to show the connection to their anchors.

"What are we supposed to do now?" Yocelin whispered. It didn't feel right to speak at full volume. "Velden said we would understand what to do once we got here."

Eithne nodded slowly. Velden had said that, but there was nothing here.

Just before Eithne could respond, they felt a surge of energy. Suddenly, they were surrounded by hundreds of gray ghostly forms. After the immediate shock wore off, they took a closer look at the figures milling all around them.

"Look there!" Eithne whispered excitedly and pointed at a figure in the crowd. At the center of the ghostly figure, there was a white glowing orb. It was a piece of Anut. Eithne knew it.

"I see them now," Yocelin answered. She was beginning to notice the black orbs in the centers of other figures.

Eithne moved toward one of the figures with a piece of Anut. She was not sure how, but she knew that she just needed to get close enough and the god piece would go into her. The faceless figures all around were listless and seemed completely unaware of Eithne and Yocelin's presence. As the women pushed through the crowd, and subsequently came into contact with them, they felt a cold, moist sensation, as if they were made of heavy mist. The feeling made them shiver. Eithne came to stand in front of the ghostly figure, took a deep breath, and as she inhaled, the god piece floated away from its original host and went into her. She closed her eyes and felt the welling of energy as she received Anut. When she opened her eyes again, the faceless gray figure was standing languidly in front of her. Eithne blinked, feeling stunned, and moved on to the next piece of the sun god.

Yocelin watched her friend and began doing the same. They wandered among the uncaring ghostly crowd for what felt likes hours, gathering god pieces. The work became somewhat tedious after a while.

Yocelin caught some movement among the milling masses out of the corner of her eye. At first, she dismissed it, but then she felt a chill down her spine, as if she were being followed. An eerily familiar pain gripped in her heart, and her eyes grew wide. She whirled around to see a large gray figure moving directly toward her. Suddenly, it dawned on her: it was Cavan! He had just died, so his soul still retained some intent and memory lingering in it from life, and he remembered whom he had been hunting.

Yocelin gasped in horror and scurried to Eithne as Cavan plowed toward her. Yocelin had no idea if she or Eithne could actually be harmed by the souls of the dead, but she was not about to find out.

The commotion caught Eithne's attention. She realized immediately what was going on. The panic in her friend's face said it all. Just once, Eithne wished something could go as planned. It seemed that the business of saving the world was not meant to run smoothly. Yocelin reached Eithne, and the friends ran together away from Cavan. They had no weapons, nor any idea of how to possibly fight on this plane. How could they defend themselves against an angry ghost? So they ran as fast as their legs would carry them, deeper and deeper into the crowd of languid souls. Neither could remember what to do if they got into trouble on this plane. It was as if their minds had been wiped of the precious information. They knew that Velden had very briefly gone over it, but he had said that the chances of them getting into trouble on this plane were so slim that it wasn't worth spending much time going over it. Why hadn't they paid closer attention? They should have known that if anyone would get into trouble on this plane, it would be them! Cavan was gaining fast, and they could only run. There was nowhere to hide.

Giev grew concerned as he watched his companions during the guided veil. Eithne and Yocelin's eyes rolled and fluttered rapidly, and their appendages twitched as if they were experiencing nightmares. Darian and Aram also twitched and clenched and unclenched their fists. They had all looked so peaceful until a few moments ago. Giev met eyes with Velden, silently asking the obvious question. Velden nodded in recognition of his concern.

"Do not fret," the necromancer said soothingly. "Their anchors will know what to do."

Giev took a deep breath in and released it slowly. He knew that the protectors would do everything they could, but this was not their area of expertise. Giev worried that, as capable as they were, they would not realize how to help Eithne and Yocelin out of whatever otherworldly troubles they were facing.

Darian knew that something was wrong. He could feel Eithne's anxiety and knew that he had to bring her back. In his own trance, all was dark around him. All he could sense was Eithne's turmoil. Then he felt a tug on the pinky finger of his left hand. This was his connection to her. He would get her out of the unknown danger. Without fully understanding how he knew it was the right thing to do, Darian began to draw in the string that connected them. It was thin and delicate, but somehow it held strong. It would not break.

Giev watched as both Darian and Aram made hand-over-fist motions as if they were pulling something in by a rope. He also noticed that Eithne and Yocelin's twitching began to calm.

Velden smiled knowingly and nodded with silent encouragement as he watched. They were doing exactly what they were supposed to do. They would probably even come out of the trance on their own.

It seemed a long moment to Giev as he watched his friends. Then Eithne inhaled sharply and awakened. Darian also opened his eyes and looked upon Eithne lying in front of him. He had done it. He had brought her back safely from whatever danger she was facing on the other plane. Without words, Eithne sat up and embraced her protector, burying her head into his chest. It was a long time before they let go of each other.

Seconds after Eithne awakened, Yocelin did as well in a similar fashion. Aram gathered her close to him and breathed a great sigh of relief.

CHAPTER FORTY-TWO

*T*HE DAYS FOLLOWING the companions' experience with Velden the necromancer felt rather surreal and light. Cavan, the shadow that had loomed over their thoughts and dreams for months, was simply no more. Yocelin had killed him. She and Eithne had then further escaped his angered soul on the ghostly plane. It was a tremendous relief to have Cavan gone, but it almost didn't feel real—as if they had collectively dreamed his demise. There had not been much verbal communication since leaving the necromancer. Even Yocelin was uncharacteristically quiet, but it was a good sort of quiet. It was peaceful. They all exchanged meaningful looks and related to each other in more physical ways. Giev took note of how the two couples simply allowed themselves to relax into each other. He found it to be very pleasing to have them behave so naturally together. Neither couple was copulating, as far as Giev knew—though they seemed to have come to terms with their feelings for each other. The shaman suspected that Tim's warning still lingered enough for them to refrain from expressing the full extent of their physical affections. The weight of Tim's warning was also made stronger since the companions would arrive in the City of Duomo and see the great wizard within the next couple days.

"Tristin, are the rooms ready?" the old wizard called from his study.

He was standing in front of one of his tall bookcases and had been looking for a certain volume, when it occurred to him that they would soon have guests.

Tristin hurried to his master and stood straight as he answered, "Yes, Master, the rooms are fit for guests. I can go and freshen them up if you would like?"

Tim nodded and smiled kindly at his apprentice. The boy then rushed upstairs to do his master's bidding. Tim turned back to his wall of worn volumes. He knew that the companions would be arriving either this evening, or perhaps tomorrow morning, depending on whether or not they decided to come to his mansion directly upon arriving in Duomo. The old wizard was no fool. He understood that the companions all had a certain amount of apprehension when it came to seeing him again—even outright disdain in Yocelin's case. However, they all also realized that Tim ultimately had good intentions for all those concerned. His old white eyebrows furrowed. He wondered if Darian and Aram had even allowed themselves to properly analyze why he had warned them not to fall in love with Eithne and Yocelin. He guessed not. They were intelligent men and would have possibly abandoned the quest if they had come to the proper conclusion. That they were all still working so hard to complete the quest gave credence to the wizard's guess. However, he very strongly suspected that their shaman friend, Giev, had reasoned out the truth. As someone who understood the workings of magic, knowing that all magic comes at a cost, surely Giev realized the tremendous price the companions would have to pay. Tim sighed. He had not met this Giev person, but he was terribly grateful to him for his role in the quest as well as his discretion. He was very much looking forward to meeting the young shaman.

Tim sighed again, more heavily this time. There would be much to discuss and reveal when they arrived. Perhaps he would also prefer for them to wait until the morning. Besides, they were not the only guests the old wizard was expecting. The others would be here in two days' time. There was much to do, indeed.

Now, where was that book he had been searching for?

CHAPTER FORTY-THREE

*T*HE FIVE COMPANIONS stood sweating in the swelteringly hot morning sun before the front door of the wizard's mansion. Much to Giev's disappointment, the group had opted to stay the first night in Duomo at a nearby inn. Giev understood their reservations better than his friends suspected, but he also could not contain his excitement at actually coming face-to-face with the second most powerful wizard that had ever lived! The anticipation was very nearly killing him as they stood in front of the mansion. Darian hadn't even rung the bell yet! Why did they continue to put it off? They had to face him eventually.

Giev was about to take matters into his own hands and ring the bell himself when the tall double doors slowly opened, revealing an old man in long purple robes and a floppy cap to match.

"I think you've procrastinated long enough, don't you? Now come in, my friends, or you will make me feel as though you're not happy to see me," Tim welcomed with thinly veiled sarcasm, but his tone remained light and welcoming all the same.

Tim smiled pleasantly at his guests as he awaited their reaction.

"Hello, Tim. Nice to see you again." Eithne stated in a reserved and cordial tone as she stepped inside. She was the first to accept the wizard's welcome. Enough was enough, no point in being rude just because they were all nervous as far as she saw it.

The rest of the group mumbled their helloes and went inside. The mansion was graciously cool inside. They were guided to the sitting parlor, and they all made themselves comfortable. Tim sent Tristin to fetch refreshments. The air in the room felt heavy with context, but no one spoke for long moments. No one really knew what to say.

Finally, Giev found his words. "I am so pleased and honored to meet you, Lord Timallyehoutsivycous! I have long admired you and your art!" Giev blurted this perhaps with too much zeal.

Tim took Giev's outburst in stride. "Well, it's not often I come across someone who can properly pronounce my full name. How nice!" Tim smiled kindly at the shaman. "In fact, I am rather pleased to make your acquaintance as well. I hope that you and I can have some good conversations, Giev."

Giev, who had been immediately shameful of his outburst in the presence of such a great wizard, forgot his embarrassment as soon as Tim said that he wanted to converse with him.

"Really? I would be so honored, Lord Timallyehoutsivycous! Thank you!"

Yocelin rolled her eyes at Giev's excitement over Tim. She told herself that once Giev got to know the old wizard better, he may not be so anxious to speak with him.

Eithne saw her friend's expression and patted Yocelin's hand sympathetically.

"Now, now, just Tim will suffice. No need to continue saying that mouthful," Tim corrected cordially to the shaman.

Giev nodded his understanding happily. Not only did this great wizard want to speak with him, but now Giev had permission to call him by a nickname! Truly, he could not have imagined such gifts would be bestowed upon him!

Tristin returned with six glasses of wine and served them to the guests. Once everyone was served, Tim dismissed his apprentice and waited until Tristin had left the room before speaking again.

"All right, let's just get down to business, shall we? I know that you lot don't like it very much when I dwell on small talk."

Tim sipped his wine while the others waited for him to continue. The companions would not have minded a bit of small talk, actually. It would allow more time to relax, but that was not the wizard's way.

"So you have done an excellent job of collecting god pieces thus far, with some good help from Giev, of course. There was a bit of a slipup with King Reimus's uncle back in Lupia, and make no mistake, I had to do a fair amount of damage control to make things right again. I know it was an accident, but I do hope that you are all much more discreet with such situations now. Other than that problem, I am quite impressed, but there is a something that you have overlooked."

Darian blinked. It perplexed him that Tim would say this. They had traveled far and wide the past few months and gotten much accomplished. They had even traveled across the sea and back!

"What have we overlooked? We have been extremely thorough."

Eithne could tell from his tone that Darian was not pleased to hear that they had not performed as well as he hoped. She took his hand in hers and gave it a little squeeze of supportive reassurance. Darian's stoic demeanor betrayed nothing, but his return of the squeeze let her know it was appreciated.

Tim held up his hand as a sign of peace. "You have all done a wonderful job. Truly, I thought your task would take much longer than it has." Tim's eyes drifted to Darian and Eithne's clasped hands, and he released a small sigh of disappointment. "However, elves and humans are not the only races that can hold god pieces. You have overlooked the demon demographic." He took another slow sip of wine and allowed his words to sink in.

"Why didn't I think of that?" Yocelin exclaimed at a volume that expressed a fair amount of frustration on her part. "I'm a demon, so it only makes sense that we should have looked there too!" Yocelin groaned and rested her head on Aram's shoulder. Then in a much smaller voice she stated, "I feel dumb."

Aram put his arm around her and rubbed her shoulder with his thumb. "None of us realized it either."

Once again, Tim took notice of the affectionate display and did not approve.

"Not to worry," Tim continued. "I have already arranged to have Yocelin and Eithne travel to the demon cities in order to collect the remaining god pieces. Their escorts will be here in a day or so."

Darian's brow furrowed, and he instinctively drew Eithne closer to him. "What do you mean 'their escorts'? We are Eithne and Yocelin's protectors. Aram and I will escort them."

"Actually, you won't be, for this part of the journey. As protectors, the two of you have other duties you must be trained for," Tim sounded nonchalant, yet very final. Neither Darian nor Aram took his statement kindly.

Giev felt rather uncomfortable sitting in the tension-filled room. He drank his wine and tried his best to become one with the large leather armchair he was sitting in. He was beginning to better understand why his friends were not terribly fond of the great wizard. It seemed that Tim had a blunt habit of telling them things they did not wish to hear.

"My place is with Eithne," Darian stated firmly. "I will not leave her side."

Aram nodded that he felt the same about Yocelin.

Tim regarded them coolly. "I'm afraid that you don't have a choice in the matter. Heroic as your intentions are, it simply isn't going to work that way."

Tim watched as the protectors' expressions grew very dark and cold as he spoke, but he did not mind. They could not touch him, and they knew it. Of course, he would have to give a small morsel of concession to be sure that they would work with him while the girls were away.

"Do not fret over their safety. I am very confident that both of you will approve of the escorts I have arranged. Besides, it will be a few short weeks, and you all can be together again." Tim smiled pleasantly to try and ease the tension.

They all silently stared daggers at the wizard—except Giev, who was concentrating on being invisible.

Seeing that his minor attempt to make them all accept the circumstances had failed, Tim relaxed into his cushioned armchair and let out a sigh of exasperation. "You see? This is why I didn't want you all falling in love with each other. Well, the circumstances are inevitable, so you will all have to suffer the pain of separation for a short while."

At the mention of why Tim didn't want them falling in love, Giev made eye contact with the wizard, who gave him the slightest of nods. Giev downed the rest of his wine in one gulp.

"Well, I just don't accept your circumstances," Yocelin said with a huff and crossed her arms.

Eithne hugged unto Darian's arm in a more silent protest.

Tim took a good look at each of the couples. Then let out a long breath as he thought of what to say next. He slowly rose from his armchair and stroked his long white beard.

"I can see that you all require some time to absorb this new information. Very well, you shall have it. I will leave you all be until you are ready to speak to me or until the escorts arrive, whichever comes first. Your rooms are upstairs, as before. Please feel free to eat what you like and make yourselves at home in the meantime." Tim then addressed Giev, "If you would like to join me in my study, perhaps we can have that talk?"

Giev nodded vigorously and followed Tim into the study.

The two couples sat silently seething for a moment. Eithne and Darian stood and went upstairs. Yocelin made some frustrated noises, grumbled about how much she hated Tim, and stalked into the courtyard for some fresh air. Aram went into the kitchen. He decided it would make him feel better to put a dent in the wizard's food supply.

CHAPTER FORTY-FOUR

"*I* DON'T LIKE IT, not one bit," Darian grumbled as he paced up and down the bedroom floor.

Eithne sat on one of the beds and watched him. She agreed with Darian, of course, but she also knew that they didn't have a choice in the matter. It frustrated her horribly. The thought of being parted from Darian at all made her feel sick. She loved him.

Darian continued his pacing.

"We will simply find another way to do whatever Tim wants or needs us to do, a way that doesn't require you going off with some stranger." He went on talking like that for a while, formulating plans and different ways to keep them together.

It made Eithne's heart ache for both good and bad reasons. Watching him toil made her wish that they could just forget about the quest—forget everything but each other and what they wanted in that moment.

Eithne stood briskly, walked to the door, then shut and locked it. Darian stopped scheming and looked at her. Eithne faced him, her grass-green eyes flashed with intent. Darian regarded her and waited for her to act. His heart was pounding, but his demeanor did not betray him. Eithne slipped off her boots. Then she tugged her hair loose from its bun, and her fiery locks fell about her face and shoulders.

Darian felt mesmerized by her graceful movements. She was beautiful. She continued to remove her accessories and clothing until all she wore was her white linen shirt, which had a few buttons undone, and her brown breeches. Darian swallowed hard as she walked over to him. He loved the way her hips rocked as she moved, and her willowy frame almost seemed to float. Eithne slid her arms around his neck as she reached him. Darian could not help but to wrap his arms around her and press her body against his. He felt aroused. He had never desired anyone the way he desired Eithne. Darian felt as though he were on fire and that he would go crazy if he weren't touching her. He kissed her deeply, forgetting all his troubles and surrendering to his body's urges. His hands roamed over her body, and she explored his in return. They never allowed themselves to do this, always conscious that they are not supposed to do these things, but nothing had ever felt more perfect.

Darian picked Eithne up and carried her to the bed. He pulled his shirt off over his head before lying down on top of her and claiming her mouth. Eithne was truly excited by the sight of his body. She could not have imagined a more perfect man with his strong frame and firm muscles. She delighted in letting her fingers discover every inch of him.

Somewhere along the way, Eithne had lost her shirt and breeches, and Darian no longer wore his trousers or boots. Both only had their thin undergarments to separate them. They had been in a spiral of passion, finally allowing themselves to physically express how they felt for each other.

"Wait." Darian pushed himself up with his arms and hovered over Eithne. Seeing the woman he loved practically naked and breathless beneath him, Darian almost completely forgot himself again, but he shook his head to clear his intoxicated mind and spoke, "Eithne, what are we doing? We are not supposed to be—"

"Shhh." Eithne put a finger to his lips to quiet him. "This is what I know, Captain Darian MacAllow. I know that I love you more dearly than I can express. I know that you love me too, and I know that right now is only for us. Take me. I am yours."

Darian stared into her eyes and knew that she was resolved about every word she had spoken.

"And I am at your command," he replied. "I belong to you, my dear."

They spent the rest of the day and night locked in a lover's embrace, discovering each other in ways that they had only dared to dream about before without care for what happened beyond the locked door. This time was theirs.

"So I assume you have worked out the price by now. You're an intelligent fellow," Tim spoke the words to Giev rather abruptly.

They had been making small talk and going on about magic for the last twenty minutes. The sudden shift in conversation caught Giev by surprise. Tim sat at his large mahogany desk, looking at the shaman and patiently awaiting a response. Giev wished he didn't know exactly what Tim was referring to.

Giev sighed. "Well, you certainly are not afraid to approach your point."

The wizard simply looked at him silently.

Giev ran a hand over his face and responded in a low voice. He suddenly felt very tired. "Yes, I worked it out awhile ago, almost as soon as I fully understood the quest."

Tim nodded slowly then leaned forward. "So then, why did you encourage them to be together romantically?"

"I could ask you why you tried to keep them apart," Giev replied with some of his characteristic playfulness returning to his voice.

"To spare them the pain, of course," Tim answered matter-of-factly.

Giev nodded. He understood that. "It was too late for that, though, at least by the time I encountered them. They were already head over heels for each other, past the point of no return. So all I could wonder was why they weren't making the most of the time they had together? As lovesick as they all are, I just kept thinking how much Darian and Aram would regret never really being with them. As the old saying goes, 'It is better to have loved and lost than to have never loved at all.'"

Tim leaned back into his leather armchair and stroked his long beard. "Hmmm . . . Are you suggesting that I was wrong to discourage them?"

"I believe that they took it more like you forbade it, and yes. In my humble opinion, it was wrong to discourage them," the shaman spoke bravely, but his face shown how nervous he felt speaking out in direct opposition to the great wizard.

Tim stilled his hand from his beard and raised his bushy eyebrows at Giev. He regarded him thoughtfully for a long, painstaking moment while Giev held his breath. Then Tim smiled at him.

"That's what I like about you, Giev. You are not afraid to be true to you convictions. It's not often you find someone who is strong enough to tell Raashan's most powerful wizard that he's wrong about something. Just because I've been around for almost a thousand years doesn't mean that I am infallible." The wizard winked and smiled at the shaman.

Giev let out his breath with relief. "Thank you, Lord Tim. I can't tell you how relieved I am that you are not turning me into some sort of vermin right now."

Tim chuckled at the notion that he would be so petty.

Giev saw a good opportunity to talk about what he had been hoping to discuss since he heard they would be coming to see the wizard. "Since you seem so open to suggestions, I have a bit of a scheme involving the Stone of Elissiyus."

"Ah, yes! You all managed to find my old master's magic rock. I am quite impressed by the progress you have made in using it."

"Thank you, again, but I believe I will require your guidance for what I am planning. I want to use the stone to bring Eithne and Yocelin back after the ceremony."

Tim's expression became furrowed with concern. "You must be aware that the prophecy dictates that they must die. It is the sacrifice that is demanded in order to restore the proper balance of the world."

"I understand, and I don't wish to change the prophecy. I know that cannot be done. I just want to amend it. After they have died, I want to use the power of the stone to bring them back immediately. I want my friends to have the happy ending that they all deserve," Giev implored.

Tim looked up at the domed ceiling of his study thoughtfully for a while before returning his attention to Giev. When he did, the wizard's expression was warm with pride. "Yes, I do think I like you a good deal, Giev. It may be possible, what you are suggesting. Let's see if Elissiyus's magic rock is worth its salt."

CHAPTER FORTY-FIVE

THE NEXT MORNING, everyone in the mansion gathered in the kitchen for breakfast. There was a sort of comfortable silence as they all ate their food. Darian and Eithne both ate hungrily and were more openly affectionate toward each other than usual. Yocelin leaned over the island countertop with both hands clasped around her clay coffee mug. Aram stood next to her, casually eating and allowing his eyes to subtly drift over Yocelin's petite and curvaceous form. Usually, Yocelin would have taken advantage of his mood, but her attention was focused on Darian and Eithne this morning.

"So you two certainly had an eventful day yesterday," Yocelin grinned shamelessly at her friends.

Eithne flushed pink and stopped eating. Darian regarded the she-demon nonchalantly.

"I don't see how it's any of your business," Darian tried to deflect the topic.

He was not put off by her nosiness; that was just Yocelin. However, he was certainly not the type of man who discussed such things. Besides, it really wasn't any of her business, or anyone else's, for that matter. Darian's eyes flicked to Tim sitting at the other end of the table and felt nervous.

Tim rolled his eyes. "I'm not daft yet. I was aware of what was going on upstairs. We all were, frankly."

Yocelin giggled then immediately ceased laughing when she realized that it made Tim happy that she enjoyed his comment.

"I'm really not comfortable with this conversation," Eithne said firmly. "Like Darian said, it's none of any of your business."

Yocelin playfully stuck her tongue out at Eithne. "Well, all right. I will leave the two of you alone, for now."

Eithne smirked back at her friend.

A long, uncomfortable moment passed. The happy silence could not be retrieved.

"I must say," Tim began, "that I do not appreciate the complete disregard for my instructions. You all deliberately disobeyed them."

The companions all regarded Tim with mixed emotions. Honestly, none of them were sorry about being in love, far from it—though the wizard was sort of their unofficial master, and they were all slightly worried that they had somehow monopolized the quest. None of them knew Tim's reasons behind forbidding them to fall in love.

"Well, technically, Aram and Yocelin haven't disobeyed your instructions," Eithne didn't know why, but she thought it seemed helpful to point out that Aram and Yocelin had not been intimate.

"The physical act of intercourse doesn't make much difference once the emotions are there," Tim countered haughtily.

"Aram and I have definitely been disobedient on all counts, regardless. We've been at it for a while," Yocelin sipped her coffee as if she had just talked about the weather.

Aram abruptly shot her a sharp look. "Really? We work so hard to be secretive, and you just decide to tell everyone all of a sudden?"

Yocelin looked at him sheepishly. Her intention was not to upset him. "The words just spilled out. I'm sorry."

Aram sighed in exasperation. He was upset at how cavalier she was about everything. Now was not the time to discuss that aspect of their relationship, however. "I guess it doesn't matter."

"What do you mean you've been at it for a while? How did the rest of us not know about this?" Giev protested in utter surprise. Neither he nor anyone else had the slightest idea that they were doing anything, except Tim perhaps.

"None of your business," Aram growled. As an extremely private person, he was unhappy that this information had been brought to light at all.

Tim sighed and shook his head as he sipped his morning tea. "I suppose I never had any real hope of sparing any of you from falling in love." He sipped his tea again. "Oh, and to make things a little more even, Aram and Yocelin started having coitus almost immediately after the cave-in nearly killed them."

All eyes went to Tim, wide and stunned. Yocelin and Aram in particular looked upset.

"Don't be so appalled," Tim said with a dismissive wave. "You all knew that I would be keeping tabs on you."

Another awkward moment went by.

"What do you mean 'sparing us'? Spare us from what?" Darian asked seriously in his military tone. As he asked the question, he noticed Giev and Tim exchange a look. Giev knew something that Darian did not.

"Spare you from the folly of your own feelings, of course," Tim replied very convincingly. "Falling in love only complicates things."

Despite Tim's cool answer, Darian knew that wasn't the real reason. He gave the wizard his stoic, steel blue stare.

"You'll get more details on the matter while I train the two of you in preparation for the ceremony." Tim returned in an authoritative voice that meant the discussion on this topic was now closed.

Darian continued to stare for a few seconds, unhappy with the answer, but he knew better than to try and push the conversation. He didn't like it, but he and Aram would have to wait.

Eithne sensed that another tension filled moment was coming, and she couldn't take another one. "So tell us about these escorts that are arriving in a day or so."

"Oh, no," Tim replied with a mischievous glint in his eye. "I want them to be a surprise."

The next day was stormy and thunderous. The rain poured down heavily, flooding the streets, and the usually bustling City of Duomo was stilled by the onslaught of weather. Though it was late morning, the sky was so dark that it seemed like night. Two large lone figures walked through the deserted streets. Being heavily cloaked, it was impossible to tell who or what they were, but they walked with purpose. Those citizens of Duomo who happened to glance out their windows as the two figures passed found themselves alarmed by their sheer size and promptly checked to be certain their doors were securely locked.

The two hulking figures found their way to the large mansion in the center of the city and rang the bell.

"My dear friends! Please, please, come in out of the storm," Tim prompted cheerfully as he swung open the double doors and greeted his enormous guests.

The pair greeted the wizard in turn with gravely voices and ducked their heads as they walked into the foyer. Neither of them wished to track water all over the floors, so they did not venture further inside.

"Tristin!" Tim called, and the boy appeared with an armload of fresh towels. "Please take off your cloaks and dry off. How was your journey?"

"All is well. It was lucky we have the storm today as it made it easier to get through the city without being detected," the one on the right responded as he removed his cloak, revealing a great horned head, orange-red skin, and piercing golden eyes with slit pupils.

His companion looked exactly the same except skin was more of a sooty black color. Both had sharp black fangs that jutted upward from their bottom teeth over their upper lips. They were thickly muscled with black razorlike fingernails. Each stood at nearly eight feet tall. If it weren't for the difference in skin color, one would not be able to tell them apart.

"I thought a little bad weather might be convenient for you," Tim responded with a wink. He was completely nonchalant about having a couple of behemoth demons in his foyer.

Tristin was shaken, but he trusted his master and tried his best to be polite as he offered them towels and took their sodden cloaks; though when Tim dismissed his apprentice to fetch some food for his guests, Tristin left with more speed than usual.

Tim invited his guests to adjourn to the sitting parlor, which they did. The furniture creaked in protest as the giants sat down, but it held beneath them.

"So where are the ones we are meant to escort?" the orange demon inquired as he chewed some raw meat that had been brought out for them and placed on the table.

"I'm certain they will realize you're here in a short while and appear. To be honest, I can't wait to see the looks on their faces when they see the two of you," Tim stated with a boyish glint of mischief in his clear blue eyes. Old as he may be, Tim maintained a young spirit.

His guests chuckled roughly at the wizard's excitement. They had already guessed that he had not told these people who was coming to escort them into demon territory.

"So are you both clear on your duties?" Tim asked.

"It's simple enough," the sooty one replied. "Just take the girls around to the demon cities so they can collect god pieces. In a few weeks, bring them back here. By the way, how will they be disguised?"

Tim waved his hand dismissively. "I've got that all handled. They will be extremely convincing."

"Good," the orange one replied. "We don't want any trouble."

There was the sound of a cup breaking. All eyes turned to the source of the noise. Eithne, who was just coming out of the kitchen, stood frozen and looking pale. Her teacup lay broken at her feet in a puddle of hot tea.

"Ah, right on time!" Tim jeered with delight. "Eithne, I would like you to meet your new escorts, Cassius and Xerksys."

The moments that followed were scrambled with a mixture of fear and confusion, much to Tim's chagrin. Darian, Aram, Yocelin, and Giev came rushing out of the kitchen after hearing the cup break. All were extremely shocked and concerned that there were two behemoth demons in the sitting parlor! Naturally, the boys' first instinct was to put the girls behind them and get ready to fight. Behemoth demons were not known as the peaceful sort. After some explaining from Tim, they all calmed down. It also helped a great deal that the two demons didn't make any threatening moves. In fact, they sat on the sofa the entire time, leisurely chewing on meat and generally acting indifferent to the drama their sudden appearance had caused.

Once everyone was settled and assured that they were not in danger, all sat together in the parlor and listened while Tim explained that Cassius and Xerksys were the escorts he had told them about. They would be responsible or taking Eithne and Yocelin to the demon cities to collect more god pieces while Darian and Aram trained with Tim in preparation for the ceremony of resurrection for Anut and Muntros.

"So you just expect us to trust them?" Darian asked after Tim had stopped talking. He was already uncomfortable with the idea of strangers escorting Eithne and Yocelin. That Tim expected him to trust two formidable demons seemed absolutely ludicrous.

"I would entrust Cassius and Xerksys with my own life," Tim replied while sipping some spiced wine.

"We really don't have any choice in the matter," Aram was not asking a question. He already knew the answer. He didn't like it either, but arguing with the wizard was fruitless.

Tim gave a simple nod.

"I think I like them," Yocelin piped up happily, and much unexpectedly.

"You're comfortable with the situation?" Aram asked her quietly with mild surprise.

Yocelin rolled her eyes. "Do you all just forget that I myself am a demon? Of course, I'm comfortable with other demons. In fact, I'm sure that Cassius, Xerksys, and I will become great friends." She beamed her best smile at the demon brothers.

Cassius and Xerksys both wrinkled their noses in return. The she-demon acted very strangely.

Eithne sighed. She suddenly felt guilty for reacting to Cassius and Xerksys the way she had. "Well, if Tim and Yocelin trust you, then I trust you too."

Darian jerked his head to look at her. Why was she just giving in like this? Didn't she want to stay with him?

Eithne squeezed his hand comfortingly. "It will only be a few weeks, and I will be safe the entire time. Besides," Eithne lowered her voice to a soft whisper, "we don't have a choice. It's best to accept it. I would never be parted from you if I could help it."

Darian softened a little, but his mouth was set in a firm line. "I promised to never leave your side again," Darian argued. He was referring to the promise he had made to her after what happened at the monk's mountain.

Overhearing this, Aram put his hand on Yocelin's knee and looked at her meaningfully. He had made the same promise to her. Yocelin put her hand over his and smiled reassuringly.

"Given the circumstances," Tim interjected after an appropriate pause, "the two of you can take a break from your promises with the ladies' permission. Anyway, you aren't leaving them with a group of soulless, sadistic monks this time."

A visible strain of grief went across the companions' faces, including Giev, at Tim's comment. It hurt that he was not wrong about that.

All went quiet.

Cassius cleared his throat, feeling uncomfortable. "When do we leave?"

"Tomorrow, in the late morning should be fine. No use delaying anything," Tim responded. He then looked to the girls. "Eithne and Yocelin, I will need to see you after breakfast tomorrow morning to get you properly disguised to visit demon territory. I will allow you this night without the disguises." Tim glanced meaningfully at Darian and Aram. Then he stood from his chair and addressed Giev, "Won't you join me in my study so we can work on our project?"

Giev brightened considerably and jumped up to follow Tim. "Of course."

"Cassius, Xerksys, please feel free to do what you like for the rest of the day. Tristin will show you where your rooms are located."

Each pair in the mansion kept to themselves for the rest of the stormy day.

CHAPTER FORTY-SIX

*T*HE NEXT MORNING, after making breakfast last as long as possible, Eithne and Yocelin finally went to meet Tim in his study.

"Good morning," Tim greeted cordially.

The women muttered their greetings much less cordially. They were both anxious about how they were to be disguised.

"Have you already said your good-byes to Darian and Aram?" Tim asked.

Yocelin blinked. "Not yet. Were we supposed to?"

"Well, after you are both disguised, you will not look like yourselves. They will probably find it unsettling to kiss you," Tim replied somewhat patronizingly.

"What exactly are we going to look like?" Eithne was skeptical.

"Like demons, of course."

"But I already am a demon. I don't need a disguise," Yocelin protested.

"Yes, but you are the sort of demon that attracts a lot of unwanted attention. You need to look more classically demon," Time explained patiently.

Yocelin crossed her arms and made a little huffing sound. "So we're going to look grotesque."

"Precisely."

Eithne looked very sad.

Both girls looked at each other in silent resignation and walked out of the study to say their good-byes.

Eithne and Yocelin came back a while later looking rather solemn, like they had been crying. Tim smiled kindly at them. He wasn't a coldhearted old man. He didn't like making them separate either, but their fate was a harsh one. He only hoped that Giev's plan would work and they would be able to live long, happy lives with Darian and Aram. They all deserved to have that compensation after sacrificing so much. Fate could be a very cruel mistress, Tim knew.

"So as the two of you are already aware, you are going to be transformed into grotesque-looking demons. I will cast a spell on you for the initial effect. However, you will both need to drink a special tea every three to five days to keep up appearances." Tim then handed each of them a box of dried tea leaves with proper brewing instructions written on the lid of each box.

Yocelin gingerly lifted the lid of her box and sniffed the contents. She immediately scrunched her face in disgust and slammed the box shut. "It smells horrible!"

Tim shrugged. "Yes, well magic rarely smells pleasant. You'll get used to it."

"Not for long, we won't," Eithne grumbled with a wrinkled nose as she too had decided to smell the tea leaves.

"Yes, well, are you ready? Who wants to go first?" Tim stood and rolled up his voluminous sleeves.

"I guess I'll go first." Eithne unenthusiastically volunteered.

"Wonderful. Now, just put your tea down and stand just in front of me. Good. Now hold still."

Tim then began chanting an incantation of magic. The entire room seemed to darken. He threw metallic sand over Eithne, which swirled around her in a funnel. She closed her eyes as she was feeling nauseated and tingly all over. Several long moments later, she heard Tim tell her to open her eyes.

Eithne looked around the room. She still felt nauseated. She also felt like she were several inches taller. Hesitantly, she looked down at her hands. They were a sickly green color, webbed, covered in warts, and had brittle yellow fingernails. She felt even sicker as her stomach turned over at the sight. How ugly the rest of her must look! Eithne had never been vain, so she didn't realize how upsetting it would be to be so ugly all of a sudden. She couldn't even bring herself to touch her face or approach a mirror. Eithne dropped her head in sat back down in her chair, which creaked under her newly increased weight.

"It's only temporary, dear," Tim tried to comfort her.

"You're very pretty for a swamp demon. Really, you are," Yocelin offered and patted Eithne's warty hand.

Eithne sighed sadly.

Then it was Yocelin's turn. She too felt very sick as the spell was cast. When she looked at her hands, she discovered that she now only had three thick fingers on each dark-blue hand. Her arms felt much longer and gangly. Shakily, Yocelin reached up to touch her face. She let out a piglike squeal when she discovered a snout. She now appeared to be a swine demon. She gave Tim a disdainful look. Did he have to choose two of the ugliest demon breeds to turn them into?

"I hate you," Yocelin croaked.

Tim looked sad. "Please understand it's only temporary. Besides, both of these forms will provide their benefits as you travel. Think of how happy you'll be to look like yourselves again in a few weeks." He offered a sympathetic smile, but it did nothing to console them.

Eithne and Yocelin left with their new escorts not long after their transformations. It was still pouring rain, so it made it easier to exit the city without incident. All were very quiet as they left Duomo. Cassius and Xerksys were not much for conversation, and Eithne and Yocelin were still very upset at looking so horrid. They had taken care not to be seen by Darian or Aram as they left. The last thing either of them wanted was for the boys' last vision of them to be so grotesque. It was painful enough being forced to be apart for such a long time without imagining that they would be remembering wretched demons instead of the women they loved.

"So then, shall we begin your training?" Tim announced as he walked into the kitchen where Darian, Aram, and Giev had gathered.

For a moment, there was no answer. Both protectors were still seething over the forced separation. Already they felt anxious and lost with Eithne and Yocelin being gone. Giev awkwardly drank some coffee and waited for someone to do something. It didn't happen.

Tim was standing patiently, awaiting a response. It appeared that it fell on the shaman again to create a reaction.

Giev downed the rest of his coffee and stood up forcefully. "If it's time for you to begin your training, then I will get out of your way. If anyone wants me, I'll be in my room." Before exiting, Giev leaned over the table close to Darian and Aram. "Try to go easy on the old man. He's not actually trying to make you miserable. It's just bad luck that fate chose you and the girls to save the world." He tapped his fist on the table twice to emphasize his point and left.

Tim nodded at Giev in silent gratitude as he walked out of the kitchen. When he looked back to Darian and Aram, he smiled to see that they had both stood to begin their training. They regarded the wizard coldly, but they were being corporative, which was the most important thing.

Tim led them into the meditation room. They would have to first learn proper focus and mental control over their emotions before getting into the actual workings of the ceremony. A few weeks was a short time to train two people with no real experience in magical practices, but it needed to be done. Tim was also concerned over telling them of Eithne and Yocelin's fate. It needed to be told, and soon. He would confer more with Giev first about the likelihood of his scheme being feasible first. Tim had to be certain about it before offering that hope.

CHAPTER FORTY-SEVEN

*D*ARIAN HAD ALWAYS considered himself to be a dedicated and steadfast soldier. He had always come through, did as he was told, and performed above expectations. It was a personal point of pride for him and an important element of his self-worth. However, having heard what had just been told to him, he was immediately ready to forsake it all. Damn being a good soldier, and damn his pride to hell! He would not see Eithne die! He could feel his body shaking with anger as he dug his fingers into the armrests of the leather chair in Tim's sitting parlor. He wanted to leave, go find Eithne, and forget all responsibility to the rest of Rashaan. The world might end, but he couldn't care less so long as she was saved. A world without Eithne, even a better one, was not worth living in as far as Darian was concerned.

Aram let out an inhuman, beastly growl as the outcome of the ceremony sunk in. How dare Tim put them through this ridiculous quest without telling them the end result! How dare he forbid them from falling in love! How dare he expect that they would simply accept their fate! Aram felt his blood boiling. The wolf within him wanted out. It wanted to tear the old wizard into fleshy threads and howl victoriously over his demise. Yocelin was the only person who brought light to his tortured existence—the only one who could bring warmth to his spirit. He would not kill the one soul who brought him pure joy.

Giev felt absolute terror as he stared at Darian and Aram, livid with rage. He felt as though they would spring up and rip Tim apart at any second. Tim had delivered the news of Eithne and Yocelin's end to the protectors rather frankly, as he was prone to do, but Giev could not help but to think that the wizard should have exercised more tact in this case. Tim sat confidently and calmly in his favorite chair, not at all perturbed by the two powerful warriors who clearly wanted his blood. Giev supposed that it was the peace of mind that comes with being the most powerful wizard in the world. The shaman gulped down hard as he reminded himself that Darian and Aram would have no such barriers in their way if they decided to attack him instead. When it came to protecting the women they loved, Giev knew they were capable of most anything.

"But they don't have to stay dead!" Giev blurted out, his voice cracking.

Tim shot Giev a harsh look. He had specifically told Giev to wait to tell them about that possibility. It seemed that Giev's fear got the better of him. Tim looked back to Darian and Aram in their quiet rage. He supposed he couldn't blame the young shaman for his own self-preservation instinct.

"Well, keep talking," Darian ordered through gritted teeth.

"Of course! I think I can use the Stone of Elissiyus to bring them both back as soon as the ceremony is complete. They would only be dead for a few minutes, and they would be just as they were before. No funny stuff or weird new tendencies," Giev obliged hurriedly.

"Are you certain this can be done?" Aram asked, still growling.

"Yes! Yes, with Tim's help, I was able to confirm that I could use the magic of the stone in that way."

Darian's steel blue eyes shot back to Tim. "Why didn't you lead with that instead of angering Aram and me so much?"

Tim casually sipped a cup of tea before answering. "Two reasons, the girls still must die before they can be resurrected, so you need to accept that. Secondly, like all powerful magic, there is a chance it may not work as we expect or at all. Also, we would only get one chance at the spell. Channeling that much magic through the stone will drain it. It will most likely be nothing more than a useless rock afterward." Tim sipped his tea again.

Giev could see danger levels rising again within the protectors at the mention that the magic might not work. He needed to try and defuse this delicate situation. "But the chances of it not working at all are almost nonexistent."

"True," Tim interjected. "The chances of it not working as anticipated are much higher."

"What does that mean?" Darian demanded.

"It means that things may not happen exactly as planned," Tim answered calmly. "The girls may take longer to come back to life, or they might come back at different times. There are mostly timing kinks in this sort of magic."

"But there's no chance of them coming back without an arm, different coloring, or something of that nature. That part of the spell is sound," Giev insisted energetically. He wanted to be very clear about that.

"So the main risks are that they won't come back in a timely fashion or at the same time?" Darian asked.

"Or that the spell won't work. A very minute possibility, but it is still part of the risk," Tim replied.

"When you say that they may not come back in a timely fashion, what sort of time frame are we talking about here?" Aram asked.

"They may be delayed by an hour, or perhaps a couple of weeks. We really can't say," Tim answered vaguely.

Darian rubbed his temples and wrung his hands with a heavy sigh. He stood up and started pacing. "No. I don't want to do this at all. I cannot risk Eithne."

Aram stared daggers at Tim but kept his thoughts to himself, though Giev and Tim correctly assumed that they paralleled Darian's sentiments.

All was quiet and tense for a moment except for the sound of Darian's pacing.

"You know, it's not your decision to make," Tim stated coolly and sipped his tea.

Darian stopped his pacing and looked at the wizard.

Aram blinked in mild confusion.

"Eithne and Yocelin have a say in this as well, more say than the two of you. It's their lives at risk, after all, and they are just as invested in this quest as you two," Tim explained.

Darian and Aram both felt a tinge of sheepishness and irritation. Tim was right, though they hated to admit it. The choice ultimately was not theirs but Eithne and Yocelin's decision.

Giev blinked. He too was feeling a bit sheepish. This decision was none of theirs. They were simply the informed parties.

Tim sighed and stood up from his chair. The cup of tea disappeared, as he no longer wanted it. "I will make this suggestion to you. We continue your training for the ceremony as planned. When Eithne and Yocelin return in three weeks' time, you may speak to them first about what we have spoken of today. They will make their own decision about what they want to do, and all of us, myself included, will accept whatever they decide."

The strained tension in the room remained, but Darian and Aram seemed to settle. The protectors looked at each other for a moment, silently communicating, then both looked back to Tim and nodded curtly. They had a deal.

Giev sighed in relief and relaxed into his chair. Then he felt all eyes on him, and he knew why. The shaman popped up promptly from his seat. "I will perfect the spell to the most precise and practiced I can be."

Giev hurried to Tim's study where he and the wizard had been working with the stone.

Tim nodded at the protectors and went after Giev to aid him in practicing the spell. He also viewed it as his responsibility.

Darian and Aram grabbed their swords and went out into the courtyard to spar. They needed to expel this negative energy. They were both already very upset that the girls had been gone for longer than originally estimated, and what they had heard today was really more than they should be made to bear.

Yocelin sniffed the mug of foul-smelling tea she held in her blue three-fingered hands. She and Eithne had dubbed the horrible beverage "stinky tea." Even Cassius and Xerksys agreed with them. She usually chugged the stinky tea as quickly as possible, but tonight she hesitated. Yocelin couldn't help but to take a moment to relish the thought that this was the last mug she would ever have to drink.

After this dose wore off, she would be able to return to her true form and be reunited with Aram. Just this one last time, and it would be nearly done.

The past couple of months had been a blur. They had all pushed themselves very hard to cover as much territory as possible, and they had succeeded. They had even managed to go to the Southern Continent and back. They had visited all the major demon cities, and now there was only one place left to visit. The Gem of Amara was directing them to a demon town north of Lupia. After that, they would make their way back to Duomo.

Yocelin looked to the swamp demon, who was Eithne, who sat next to her. Eithne was also hesitating to drink her stinky tea. It was tempting not to drink it at all, but they both knew better.

"Doesn't that muck taste even worse when it's cold?" Cassius urged from across the campfire. He was tired of smelling it already.

"Sorry," Eithne grumbled then she held her nose and downed the tea as quickly as possible. As always, she had to fight to keep it down.

Yocelin followed her friend's example.

Cassius and Xerksys apathetically watched their usual display of fighting the gag reflex and scrunching of faces.

"We will be in Heeds the day after tomorrow," Xerksys stated as the display calmed. "After that, we will continue on to Duomo."

"Sounds good," Yocelin croaked through strained coughs.

Eithne handed her some mint leaves to chew on. She had taken to carrying mint leaves with her everywhere to help with the aftertaste of the stinky tea. It helped considerably but still did not make the putrid flavor go away completely.

Cassius and Xerksys went back to eating their raw meat. Traveling on the road was easier for demons when it came to food rations. Since they ate raw meat, so long as animals were active in the forest, demons could simply snatch their meals off the land and eat them fresh. No need to burden themselves with the extra packing of food stuffs as other races must do. Many demons had a mild superiority complex about this particular trait. In fact, Cassius and Xerksys had a habit of just snatching little animals and birds right out of the trees and biting their heads off. Eithne and Yocelin found this habit to be extremely distasteful. Eithne particularly did. She had grown accustomed to Yocelin eating raw meat, but she did it so politely that one barely noticed what she was eating. Watching how other demons ate was certainly a cultural eye-opener for Eithne. It helped her to better understand how Yocelin was such an outcast among her own people.

They made it to Heeds in the late morning. It was a sunny day, but the chill of autumn was in the air. The leaves were just beginning to change in the trees. The season was very late this year. The unrelenting heat of summer had lasted much longer than it should have. Most of the fall harvest had wilted and died. Famine was rampant all over Raashan, and thousands had died from hunger alone. Demon cities and towns were doing slightly better simply because of the carnivorous nature of demons, but that did not mean that they were not also suffering. With so many other animals and races dying, meat supplies were beginning to dwindle as well.

If Heeds had been an elven or human town, the travelers would have been smelling freshly baked pies and spiced nuts in the air and watching children run by happily in the streets, but this was a demon city. The coppery smells of rotting meat and blood filled their nostrils, and the demons went about their business without smiling. This was yet another reason that Yocelin did not fit in with her own kind. Demons were not cheerful. She may have been born a demon, but she was raised as an elf.

Eithne could feel that they were close to their target as they moved closer into the center of town. She felt drawn to the local tavern. This was good and bad. It was good because the raucous atmosphere and presence of strong drink made it easy to get close to the target and take the god piece without being detected. It was bad because it meant that Eithne, who was still an elf on the inside, would probably be forced to choke down the thick, syrupy demon ale and maybe even some raw meat. Eithne found it wholly unpleasant. The last time she had to do this, the demon she was taking the piece from aggressively flirted with her and tried to coax her into the alley for a seedy encounter. This disturbed her on several levels; not only did she find the demon utterly repulsive, but she was completely disturbed that he wanted her with her current appearance. It made Eithne's skin crawl. Yocelin had told her that she really was attractive for a swamp demon, but that just didn't help her feel better. She couldn't wait to be rid of this disguise.

The four of them pushed their way to an empty table once inside the crowded tavern. The whole place was dirty, rancid, and stank of unwashed bodies. Xerksys bellowed to have four ales brought over. Eithne just closed her eyes and tried to focus on who in the tavern held the piece of Anut. As she had become well practiced at this, she was able to single out the demon quickly. It was a stout red demon two tables over. He already appeared to be pretty drunk, so that was good. Eithne didn't feel like wasting any time today. She was ready to be finished with this part of the quest and get back to Darian. So it was only a couple of minutes before she stood and made her way over to the little red demon. Her three companions pretended to ignore her and continued speaking among themselves. Eithne spent a short while making small talk in the common tongue. Language was the only real advantage Eithne had been able to figure from Yocelin and her particular demon forms. Since both swamp and swine demons are very rare, it was less likely that anyone would speak to them in a foreign language they were supposed to know. Thankfully, the common tongue transcended all races and locations. Eithne patiently socialized until she felt that her target was drunk enough to perhaps fall asleep. Feigning sleepiness herself, she slumped while she concentrated on drawing out the piece of Anut. Within a moment, the red demon weakened and lost consciousness with a loud thump as his head hit the table. Eithne pretended to jolt awake at the noise then clumsily made her way back to her companions while the demons at the other table erupted in laughter.

They spent the appropriate amount of time at the tavern before leaving and making camp outside of town. They had preferred to stay out of town for Eithne and Yocelin's comfort. Demon inns could be very rough places and usually very filthy. Camping outdoors was generally more sanitary. Tomorrow morning, they would start making their way back to Duomo. The girls dreamed that night of getting their true forms back and reuniting with Darian and Aram.

CHAPTER FORTY-EIGHT

*A*NOTHER STORM WAS pouring over Duomo. Today was the day that Eithne and Yocelin were to return. Darian and Aram were both exhilarated and tense about seeing them again. Naturally, they yearned to be reunited, but they were also in turmoil over telling them about the ceremony and what happened at the end. What was even more worrisome was the thought that the girls would opt to go through with the ceremony and let Giev try his spell. Both of the protectors not so secretly wished that they would save themselves and damn Raashan. It was a selfish hope, but they could not deny it.

Darian paced the parlor anxiously while Aram sat on the sofa with a distant expression. They had both been on pins and needles all morning, waiting for Eithne and Yocelin to return.

Giev walked into the parlor and observed his stressed friends. He hated that their joy of reunion was dampened by what they had learned about their loves' fates.

Giev cleared his throat to make his presence known. "May I make a suggestion?"

Both protectors looked at him. They were listening.

"For now, for today, don't even think about the conversation you have to have with them. Just let that go and allow yourselves to completely enjoy being together again. Allow yourselves the luxury of a few hours of untainted joy," the shaman offered kindly.

The protectors stared dumbly at Giev for a moment. His words seemed like an unexpected gift.

Darian strode briskly up to Giev, which startled the shaman as Darian's stoic expression betrayed nothing of his intentions, but Giev held his ground. Darian embraced his friend warmly.

"I don't know how I can properly thank you for all that you have done for us, Giev," Darian said. He then released him but still gripped him firmly by one shoulder as he looked into his face. "You are a true friend, one that I could not do without."

Giev felt overwhelmed by Darian's sudden display. He felt the same about him. In truth, Giev had never felt such a bond of friendship before as he did with Darian and Aram.

Before Giev could respond, Aram was suddenly hugging him as well. He held on for a bit longer than Darian had. In fact, he wasn't letting go. Darian hugged them both again. Words simply could not express the appreciation they had for Giev and all he had done to help them in their quest as well as in their relationships.

"I hate to intrude on such a touching moment, but I am not willing to wait another second for my hug," Yocelin's voice rang through the parlor. She and Eithne stood together, soaked through by the rain, with Cassius and Xerksys behind them.

The protectors abruptly broke their embrace and immediately rushed to the women they loved. The moments that followed were a gorgeous display of hugging, kissing, and tears of joy. As Giev watched his friends all being reunited, he felt tears of joy welling up in his eyes. He went to them and joined in their embracing and happiness. Today was a good day.

The behemoth demon brothers quietly went to their rooms. They did not wish to intrude upon the reunion, and frankly, it made them slightly uncomfortable. They would rest here for the night and leave early tomorrow morning.

Tim also felt tears in his old eyes as he silently watched the reunion from his study. He dared not make himself known while the companions bathed in the warm glow of being together again. Tim did not wish to ruin any of it. He had deliberately allowed them to see him as the bearer of bad news. Someone had to do it, and the wizard was willing to accept that responsibility. He took no pleasure in being the one who caused them emotional grief. That was why he was always so blunt about it. Tim just wanted to get it over with. He held a great affection for the companions, more than they realized, and he couldn't help but to feel his old heart expand as he watched them embrace. Tim blotted away his tears with a handkerchief he kept in his voluminous sleeve and smiled openly. Today there would be no talk of ceremonies or cruel fate. Today would be pure in its happiness. Even though the dark storm raged outside, it felt as though it were a bright summer's day within the walls of the wizard's mansion.

"A truly beautiful day! Wouldn't you all agree?" Tim greeted merrily as he stepped out into the courtyard where the companions had gathered.

The storm from the day before had left a refreshing scent in the air. The late autumn sun shone brightly in the blue sky, and birds happily sung their songs of the season. Such days were incredibly rare since the death of the gods, and anyone who was able on Raashan would spend the day outdoors to fully take in the wonderful anomaly.

"Yes, it is a beautiful day," Eithne responded with a smile.

Tim returned her smile kindly. Somehow, Eithne always seemed to appreciate Tim's position and did not hold a grudge against him. Her acceptance made the wizard happy.

The companions had all gathered after breakfast on the benches in the mansion's courtyard. The weather was so pleasant that they had been there for hours, talking of their adventures during their time apart. It was clear that neither Darian nor Aram had spoken to Eithne or Yocelin about the choice they faced. Unfortunately, that was one of the reasons Tim had joined them.

The wizard settled into one of the empty chairs and smiled at the companions. A mug of hot cider suddenly appeared in his hands. "So I trust you all had a pleasant reunion?"

"Pleasant doesn't begin to describe the feeling," Yocelin purred happily. She lounged up against Aram on one of the benches like a cat. Aram comfortably had his arm around her shoulders. His fingers absentmindedly played with her long violet tresses.

Darian and Eithne were cuddled together on an adjacent bench, looking equally euphoric. Giev had chosen to lie on the soft grass to look at the sky. He had propped himself up on his elbows when Tim approached.

Tim could not stand to shatter this perfect moment just yet. Selfishly, he wanted to be able to enjoy this time with the companions. After all, one never does outgrow the need to feel wanted among friends.

"Well, ladies, do tell me of your time with Cassius and Xerksys. I'd love to hear all about it." Tim had already gotten a thorough report from the demon brothers, who had departed before sunrise this morning, but he needed to prolong this happy time.

"Only if you promise to never, ever give us a horrible potion to drink ever again," Eithne teased, though she was really only half-kidding. She and Yocelin had drunk enough stinky tea to last a lifetime.

Tim chuckled. "I promise that I am out of bad-tasting potions." He sipped his cider and raised his eyebrows as though a thought had just occurred to him. "Ah, does it help you to know that I have had to ingest a great many terrible things during my long life?"

"A little, however you willingly chose the path of stinky tea and Timulous. You brought that upon yourself," Eithne chided back with a grin.

The wizard laughed openly, as did everyone else, at Eithne's joke. "You have me there!"

The hours that followed were lovely. All forgot their responsibilities of the quest and that the world of Raashan, while bright on this day, was slowly dying all around them. They spoke of the little things that happened along the way. Like when Yocelin, unaccustomed to having a tail as a swine demon, got her tail pinched between a couple of floorboards at a crowded pub and squealed like a real pig at the unexpected pain. It was quite a scene! Then when Darian, who is usually very graceful, knocked over the incense during meditations twice in the same session. He was still embarrassed at his clumsiness. There were many of these stories told as well as some childhood tales from each of them. Tim in particular had some exciting and fascinating stories from his youth. His tales helped the companions to see him more as a person instead of a master.

They continued on this way over lunch, and it wasn't until the late afternoon waned into evening that Tim remembered that the magic of this day must be broken.

"May I suggest that we adjourn to my sitting parlor?" Tim asked as he pushed himself up from the wooden chair. "This body is no longer built to sit on hard surfaces for so long. Besides, it seemed that the insects are coming out."

As if to emphasize Tim's point, Aram swatted at a mosquito that had landed on his arm. "Yes, it seems it is time to go inside."

The group all found their way to the sitting parlor and made themselves comfortable on the leather sofa and armchairs. Tristin hurried in with a tray of mugs filled with hot apple cider for everyone.

Once all were settled, Tim spoke, "I have had a truly delightful afternoon with all of you." He smiled gratefully, wrinkling the skin around his bright blue eyes. "That said, I'm afraid I do have a small bit of business to attend to with you all."

A tense stillness descended over the group. They had thoroughly enjoyed getting to know Tim better today but were still wary of them he announced that there was business to attend to.

Tim held up his hand to calm them. "Don't worry, I am happy to report that this time you will not mind what must be done." His eyes drifted to the protectors, and his jovial expression fell a little. "The unwelcome conversation to be had must come from your protectors this time."

Darian and Aram shifted uncomfortably and nodded. They had been putting off the talk about Eithne and Yocelin's choice for obvious reasons, but they would have to do it tonight. Further procrastination was a luxury that could not afford. If they chose to go through with the ceremony, it would take place in three days' time.

The girls glanced at their protectors and Giev inquisitively. Tim's statement had confused them, so they hoped for answers from the boys. All three simply looked solemn and would not make eye contact. The girls both shrugged it off and waited to see what would happen next. Whatever Tim was referring to, they were bound to find out about it soon. There was no point on dwelling on it at the moment.

"Right, that aside, we will take care of the easier task first. Ladies, if you will both please stand in the center of the room?" Tim stood and hurriedly gestured to the space where his large coffee table had suddenly disappeared from.

Eithne and Yocelin complied. They were not thrown off by the disappearing table. When you stay at the wizard's mansion, you get used to things vanishing and reappearing at his will.

"Good, good, stand just a little further apart. Excellent. Now, stand still for a moment."

Tim then took out two bottles of different colored sand from his robe pockets. One contained shimmering white sand, the other coal black sand. He poured the white sand in a circle around Eithne, and the black sand in a circle around Yocelin. Then he unceremoniously shook whatever was left in each bottle out over the tops of their heads. Tim then stood in front of them and clapped his hands together.

"Good, are you ready? Now, hone!" the wizard commanded.

Eithne and Yocelin blinked at him. They were blinking partially because of loose grains of sand that had fallen into their eyes. Neither of them understood exactly what they were supposed to be doing at the moment.

"You're going to have to be a bit clearer on your instructions," Yocelin said flatly.

Tim rolled his eyes. "Oh, you've been doing this for nearly a year now. There are still a few god pieces out there, but each of you have gathered enough to simply call the rest of them to you. Just close your eyes and hone in on them like you've been taught. The remaining pieces will come to you. Was that a sufficient explanation?" his tone was mildly impatient.

Eithne rolled her eyes, and Yocelin stuck out her tongue in protest, but the two of them did close their eyes and began concentrating on seeking out the remaining god pieces of Anut and Muntros. The other in the room held their collective breaths while the girls concentrated. After a while, the sand circles around each of them began to vibrate. Then several grains of sand in each circle glowed brightly and floated up. The grains hovered briefly before rushing into Eithne and

Yocelin. The girls sharply took in air and arched their backs as they received the god pieces. The sand circles ceased their vibrating, and the girls opened their eyes.

"Well done, both of you!" Tim applauded once the girls were finished. "Okay, now you have both collected all of the god pieces. You may sit back down."

"That was an experience," Eithne breathed as she sat back down. She could still feel the warm magic pulsating within her. She felt powerful, very powerful, and complete in a way she had not known before.

"I got more of a thrill from killing Cavan," Yocelin said with a wink. Killing Cavan had been much more thrilling, but she could not deny that there was a completeness within her now that absorbing the pieces from Cavan did not.

Tim muttered and waved his hands. The sand circles disappeared, and his coffee table had returned to its proper place.

"That was it for me, I'm afraid. I will leave the rest of you to talk." The wizard gave Darian and Aram a serious look. "Giev, won't you join me in my study?"

"Gladly." The shaman got up and followed Tim, leaving the two couples alone in the sitting parlor.

"So what is going on that Eithne and I don't know about?" Yocelin asked playfully.

She kissed Aram on the cheek and rested her chin on his shoulder, her eyes glittering merrily. Aram turned his head to meet her eyes. He kissed her forehead and sighed sadly.

"What's wrong? Tell me right now!" Yocelin demanded, her playfulness diminished.

"Don't worry, we are telling you now, but you're not going to like it," Aram answered in a resigned voice.

"I think this would be easier said if we could face both of you," Darian stated.

He stood from the sofa and sat on the coffee table, directly facing Eithne. Aram sat next to him, facing Yocelin. The girls scooted closer together and hooked their arms together. They both had the feeling that they would need some extra support for whatever was coming.

Darian spoke first, "I'm going to ask a favor of you both before we tell you. Aram and I would ask that you let us completely finish before you interject. We are certain that you will feel a strong urge to interrupt, but please let us get the whole story out first."

The girls looked at each other and their protectors with concern. Keeping their mouths shut was difficult under normal circumstances, but it was clearly important that they exercise restraint this time. They both nodded earnestly that they understood.

"Okay, good. Thanks," Aram said nervously. "I don't even know how to start." He raked his fingers through his dark, wild hair.

Darian rubbed his face and temples. "Me neither." He took a deep breath and looked at Eithne. "Have either of you ever given any thought to what happens to you during the ceremony?"

Eithne pursed her lips. Of course, she had thought about it. She had thought of many different outcomes to the ceremony. She had imagined that all would be well, and she had imagined that she and Yocelin would die. The possibilities were frightening. Eithne did not want to violate the no-talking rule, so she simply nodded affirmatively.

"Well, Aram and I know what happens now. What must happen if you choose to go through with the ceremony . . ." Darian paused for a long time. He reached over and took Eithne's hands in his own. He was having a hard time forming the words. His tongue suddenly felt too big for his mouth.

"You have to die. For Anut and Muntros to be reborn, both of you must die," Aram whispered softly.

His words seemed to echo in the parlor. A deep, debilitating sadness shown in his dark eyes as he gazed upon Yocelin.

It felt as though all the air went out of the room. They all sat frozen in place, as if they all had the childish notion that if they just stayed very still for a while, all the bad things would go away. Minutes passed by, and they were very still and quiet, but the words remained hanging heavily in the air. They did not go away.

Eithne drew in a shuddering breath. Her shoulders were shaking slightly as she squeezed Darian's hands firmly and looked into his eyes. "Finish."

"What?" Darian was not sure what she meant. For an instant, his heart dropped to the floor, as he thought that she meant that she was finished with something else.

"You said that you wanted to completely finish telling us everything before we responded. I refuse to believe that telling us that we are going to die is the end, so finish!" Eithne's voice was growing angry, and her eyes glinted with fire. Her fire picked Darian's heart up off the floor and lifted it back into his chest.

"Giev has concocted a spell to bring you both back after the ceremony. You will have to die first, but he is very confident that he can bring both of you back, just as you are now," Darian answered with as much confidence as he could muster. "He swears it can be done."

"But?" Yocelin prompted cautiously. She swallowed to try and moisten her dry mouth. There was always a "but" in cases such as this.

"But the timing of the spell is apparently tricky. You may come back right away, or it could take awhile longer. It is something that cannot be controlled," Aram answered.

"What do you mean by a while longer?" Yocelin asked.

"Tim said that it could be hours, or possibly weeks before you come back. The magic will only work on its own schedule," Darian stated with some thinly veiled irritation. The whole thing just upset him.

"You know we would wait for you, as long as it takes," Aram said quietly, but with great conviction.

"What if the spell doesn't work at all, and we never come back?" Eithne asked in a very small voice. She felt like crying, but the tears were not coming.

Darian reached over and cupped her cheek in his hand. "Then we will have a long wait."

The tears came then. Eithne squeezed her eyes shut as the salty drops silently rolled down her cheeks. Next to her, Yocelin was in a static state. She felt numb and did not move. Being of such a positive disposition, it had not previously occurred to her that she may have to die for Raashan. It left Yocelin in a state of mild shock.

Darian and Aram allowed this information to marinate for a few seconds before putting forth what they had wanted to say all along.

"You do still have a choice. Neither of you have to die, and we can all be together." Darian looked at the stone floor as he said this. He felt cowardly to even suggest it, but the thought of keeping Eithne safe from harm overrode all other senses of duty.

Eithne opened her eyes. Her tears continued to flow freely. She knew what Darian meant. They could all just forget their quest and not go through with the ceremony. The prophecy would not be fulfilled, and Raashan would not be saved. Their world would continue to slowly plummet into chaos until all was dead. She stared at Darian and selfishly imagined how wonderful it would be to just live out the rest of her existence wrapped in his strong arms, not caring if everything else was dying around them. They would have each other. They could be happy, at least for a little while.

"I couldn't do that," Yocelin peeped.

She had also taken Darian's meaning, and when she looked at Aram, she knew that he almost wished her to deny her fate. It was extremely tempting. After all, the world had not been particularly kind to her, so why should she be kind to the world? However, Yocelin just wasn't the type to see the world from that perspective. The guilt would crush her, and she knew it.

"I couldn't either," Eithne sighed sadly.

She hated to admit it, but she wouldn't be able to live with herself knowing that Raashan could have been saved but she was simply too selfish to save it. Yocelin was right.

Both Darian and Aram felt a surge of great pride coupled with despair. They had always known in their hearts what the girls' answer would be, and it was incredibly admirable that they were willing to sacrifice themselves for the sake of others. However, the crushing despair and anxiety that came with having to watch them die. That they could not be completely confident in the spell to resurrect them only made matters worse.

"Are you certain? Tim will accept whatever you choose to do," Darian had to ask just one last time, though he already knew the answer.

Eithne nodded and leaned into him. Darian still clasped her hands in his.

"Darian, I cannot run away from something that must be done. I can't save myself only to spend the rest of my life looking into the faces of countless strangers knowing that I have sentenced them all to a slow and painful death. I think it would drive me mad."

Aram rested his hand on Yocelin's knee. "And you feel the same way?"

Yocelin nodded curtly. "Exactly the same." She then cleared her throat and forced a cheerful smile to her face. "You know you can't get rid of me, anyway. I'm like one of those unlucky coins, or a cat that refuses to go away. There is no way Giev's spell won't work because my tenacity knows no bounds."

Aram didn't smile at her attempt to relieve the tension and terrible sadness with her humor, but he appreciated it all the same. He reached across for her and pulled her into him. He just held unto her. Yocelin made no protest.

CHAPTER FORTY-NINE

HE DAYS LEADING up to the ceremony were subdued. The weather seemed to reflect the moods of the companions within the mansion, as it was dark and somber with a damp chill in the air. The one glorious day of the reunion seemed a distant memory. One of the trees in the wizard's courtyard, which only a couple of days before was healthy and robust with bright-orange leaves, had shriveled and died without explanation. Tim would have usually used his magic to take away the eyesore, but he let the dead tree remain. It was somehow more appropriate.

Mostly, the couples kept to their own rooms, trying to absorb as much of each other as possible before the ceremony. Giev and Tim spent countless hours working tirelessly on perfecting the resurrection spell. There was barely any speaking outside of each pair's designated rooms. There was a general hush that fell over the entire mansion. The three days were certainly hardest of all on the two couples. At least, Giev and Tim had a task to busy themselves with. The lovers couldn't help but to dread the clock as the space between the present and the ceremony slowly closed.

The evening before the ceremony, Eithne and Yocelin took a cleansing bath to prepare themselves. The horribly anticipated ceremony would take place at dawn the next morning. It would perhaps be the last sunrise they ever witnessed.

Eithne absentmindedly rubbed the washcloth over the same spot on her forearm. She was lost in thought, or rather, she was lost in all absence of thought. Yocelin sat in the porcelain soaking tub across from Eithne with her knees clutched up to her chest. She was very much in the same mental state as her friend.

"You're getting red," Yocelin distantly mentioned as she looked at Eithne's forearm. The spot she had been rubbing had become raw and irritated.

Eithne stopped the repetitive motion. She just stayed seated on the same bath stool, staring out into nothingness.

All was still and quiet in the small, tiled bathing room. The sound of dripping water seemed loud, and each drop echoed in the stillness.

A small sob broke the silence.

Eithne came out of her reverie and looked to her best friend. Yocelin sat in the soaking tub, hugging her knees, with tears streaming from her large blue eyes and down her cheeks.

"It's not fair!" Yocelin sobbed.

Eithne felt a large lump in her throat; her lip quivered, then she was freely crying too.

"Why did it have to be us?" Eithne wailed in commiseration.

"I never asked for this. I never wanted to be special. I just wanted to be normal, and to have friends, not even a lot of friends—just one or two that I could really count on. Now that I finally have friends, and even someone to love, I have to die. It's not fair!" Yocelin cried out the last sentence then buried her face in her knees, sobbing uncontrollably.

"I never wanted to be special either," Eithne sniffed. "I just wanted to have the freedom to live as I pleased. I didn't want to bother anyone at all. I just wanted to find a small space in the world to call my own, where I could read books and practice with the sword. No one would have ever had to pay any attention to me. I just wanted freedom, and now I'm trapped by a stupid prophecy and guilt." She sniffed again and wiped her eyes with the washcloth. "I guess I'm just not meant to be happy."

"Maybe none of us are meant for happiness. We're all a bunch of outcasts who never belonged. So who better to fulfill the stupid prophecy but a couple of nobodies that no one will miss," Yocelin whined with self-pity.

Eithne sobbed and took in a breath. "Maybe you're right."

A quiet moment passed. The water drips echoed.

"I don't want to be right about that," Yocelin stated meekly.

Eithne pursed her lips. "I don't want you to be right about that either." She sniffed again and took a deep breath. "I'm tired of not complaining about being chosen to fulfill the prophecy, though. I don't complain to Darian because it would only make him feel worse about everything."

"Me too. I hate the guilt and hurt that I see on Aram's face when he thinks about tomorrow. I can't make him feel any more terrible than he already does by complaining about it," Yocelin responded.

"I guess we just needed to say it to each other then." Eithne looked at her friend's red, tear-stained face and knew that she must look just as awful. "It's not easy being us."

Yocelin took in a cleansing breath and almost started to giggle. "No, it's not."

There was a calming silence as the two friends quietly stopped their crying. The outburst had felt good. It was therapeutic to express the negativity they had both been bottling up over the past three days. They were thankful that they had not learned of their predetermined end earlier. Neither of them could imagine carrying the emotional weight of it for more than a couple of days. It was good that Tim had not revealed it to them in the beginning.

"You're turning into a prune in there," Eithne tried to lighten the mood by referring to her waterlogged friend sitting in the soaking tub.

Yocelin laughed. It started out small and giggly, then it grew into full, musical laughter. Eithne laughed too. They laughed together in great guffaws. The merry crescendo slowly died down into little giggles again.

"We're nothing but a mess!" Eithne declared. She stood from her stool and went to help Yocelin out of the tub. It was time that they dried off and left the bath.

"I know. We're crying, we're laughing—we just can't keep ourselves straight. We don't know what to feel anymore. It's all jumbled up inside," Yocelin said as she stepped out of the tub and began to dry off with a towel.

Eithne looked ponderous for a few seconds. "You know, I think I just figured it out."

"What?"

"Hope. We are supposed to feel hopeful," Eithne answered.

CHAPTER FIFTY

❧

*T*HE TIME OF the ceremony had come. The companions all stood on a hilltop just outside of Duomo. The early morning journey there had felt like a death march. It was still dark outside, as the sun had not yet peeked out over the horizon. The sky was just beginning to fade from black to gray in anticipation of the dawn. The time was close now. A cold, bitter wind blew over the hilltop. Today the air all around them felt as though it was colder than the previous day. The first blush of the season autumn season was over. Soon winter would grip them. The bitter chill in the air only reminded them of the morbid circumstances of this morning. None of the five gathered had slept the night before. They simply could not have done it with their nerves turning their stomachs.

The wizard Tim did not accompany them to the hilltop. The great wizard had simply stated that he could not be present and gave them directions and a reassuring vote of confidence. It was the first time that it had occurred to any of the companions that Tim never seemed to leave the mansion. It was something they would have all been more curious about if they didn't have much more pressing issues on their minds.

The five companions stood on the top of the barren hill. The grass was brown and dead beneath their feet. Eithne and Yocelin both wore simple gray woolen gowns and slippers. Their backs faced away from the east. Darian and Aram stood facing the women. They too wore simple gray clothing. The color represented neutrality, for even though each pair represented the alignment of good or evil, as individuals they must all be neutral. It was the divine balance of the whole world that they were concerned with, not the prevalence of one god over the other. They were all silently waiting with heavy hearts for the sunrise. The couples stood, each clasping hands for emotional support. Darian and Aram kept their eyes on the eastern horizon, watching for the orange orb to peek out. Eithne and Yocelin looked down at the ground, just waiting.

Giev sat apart from his four best friends. He would have no part in the ceremony. His part would come immediately following its completion. His mouth was dry. Giev clutched the Stone of Elissiyus to his chest. The magical stone felt warm through his wool shirt, and he could feel its magic pulsating reassuringly. Giev had done little else the past weeks but work on the spell. He was certain that it was going to work. He refused to believe that he could let down his friends now in their greatest time of need. His eyes stared at the four of them. His body was still like a deer, not wishing to be seen in the forest. Giev would be ready to act when his time came.

The bright-orange spot sizzled on the horizon and began its slow creep upward. Darian and Aram saw it. It was time. They each shared one last kiss with the women they loved then began. The protectors chanted the words of magic that had been taught to them as they both took their thumbs and smeared a vermillion paste on the foreheads of Eithne and Yocelin. The vessels stood still and closed their eyes. Tim had instructed them to only do this. Darian and Aram would take care of the rest. As their eyes were closed, they could not see the tears running down the faces of their protectors. It was for the best. The chanting grew louder, more intense. Sunlight poured over the hilltop as the fiery orb rose higher. The vessels felt a strong wind beneath them, and they could no longer feel anything. Temperature and touch had no meaning, as if their bodies had gone numb. They could still hear the chanting growing louder all around them. It seemed to fill them like their very blood and course through their veins.

Giev gaped, and his eyes grew wide as he watched Eithne and Yocelin float upward. They both glowed with divine light, which was intensified by the rising sun behind them. Darian and Aram continued to chant strongly. Giev admired their strength of will and resolve. Even though both men had tears streaming down their cheeks, not so much as a tremor crept into their voices. The protectors knew how important it was to get the spell absolutely right. If one mistake was made, it could put Giev's plan to resurrect the girls in jeopardy. They both spoke the words in such perfect unison that it seemed as thought they were one voice. The light became brighter, and the chanting more fevered. It hurt Giev's eyes, and he had to turn away. He could no longer see Eithne or Yocelin through the painful glare. The chanting ceased abruptly and a deafening clap of thunder filled the air. Giev opened his eyes just in time to see two beams of light rush into the heavens. Ashes floated down to the ground where Eithne and Yocelin had stood moments before. The ashes seemed to glint in the sunlight as they made their slow descent and settled at the protectors' feet. Their bodies had been burned up by the divine energy, as Anut and Muntros were reborn from them. Both Darian and Aram had fallen to their knees, openly weeping and staring at the sun rising over the horizon. It was done.

A bolt of energy ripped through Giev as he sprung into action. Holding the Stone of Elissiyus out in front of his chest, he began to chant the words of magic. A loud humming filled the air, and Giev could feel the stone vibrating and heating up in his hands. He continued to chant the practiced words with determination. The stone grew hotter. The shaman could feel the flesh of his palms burning, but he would not let go. The spell was working! He could feel it in his bones. It must be completed! The ashy remnants of Eithne and Yocelin seemed magnetized to the stone and rushed through the air to fuse with it. The stone glowed intensely with bright purple light. The burning became worse. The searing pain that Giev felt did not matter. He continued to chant. The intense purple light flared as he spoke the final words. Then the stone darkened. Giev pitched forward from the sudden weight of the stone and fell to his knees. The once great Stone of Elissiyus was now a cold, dull lump of quartz. All its powers had been drained. Elissiyus's legacy was no more.

Cold winter wind howled over the hilltop. The three elves knelt still and quiet as it chilled through them. Long minutes passed as they all held their breath, hopeful for immediate results, but nothing happened. None of them really knew how much time had passed by the time they finally spoke, but the sun had risen high above the horizon. Two hours, at least, must have gone by.

Aram's fingers twitched as the wind blew again. He felt cold, but he didn't care. He had a horrible deadness consuming his insides.

"Where is Yocelin?" he croaked out the question. His mouth had gone completely dry.

"And Eithne?" Darian interjected in a similar croaking voice.

The protectors seemed lost and dazed, as if they did not fully comprehend what had happened. Giev was also feeling dazed. Spell-casting had left him physically and mentally drained. He barely noticed that his hands had fused to the Stone of Elissiyus and were stuck clutching it. Perhaps he didn't feel it simply because the burns were that severe. Slowly, Giev realized that Darian and Aram were looking to him for the answer to their question.

"It worked. I felt that the spell had worked. I know it did."

Giev was still stunned, but he spoke with as much confidence as he could muster. There was doubt in his mind regarding Eithne and Yocelin's return, but he refused to share those doubts with his friends. He could not torture them further. When magic courses through a caster's body, the caster almost always knows whether or not the magic had worked. However, casting that spell had left Giev so drained of his senses that he could not tap into that righteous clarity. He was determined to keep his doubts to himself. He had done the best he could.

"They will come back."

"We just don't know when," Darian stated quietly, but his words seemed to echo across the barren hilltop.

Aram sniffed and took a deep breath as he stood and put his hands on his hips. "Fine. Then we will wait here until they return."

Darian concurred matter-of-factly. In the mind of the protectors, it was the only thing to do.

Giev nodded numbly. There would be no moving either of them. He, however, was realizing that he needed some medical attention. Also, someone would have to report back to Tim. Giev still felt too tired from spell-casting and wasn't sure if he could make it back to the mansion on his own. Darian and Aram had settled into waiting. Giev would not consider asking them to help. They deserved to do as they pleased without interruption. So the shaman sat and tried to rest until he felt well enough to walk back on his own.

While he waited, Giev couldn't help but to let his mind wander to what had been accomplished this day. Raashan had been saved! Anut and Muntros had been reborn, and balance restored to the world. It was too soon to see any changes, but Giev could feel it. Somehow the air on the hilltop seemed fresher. Change was abuzz all around. He turned his head and gazed upon the City of Duomo. All the people who lived there had no idea what had happened here today. They had all been saved! All of them had just been given a new world. New life had been breathed into the dying world. Soon, crops would again be plentiful; weather would not be so frequently extreme because the gods had been reborn to maintain what they had helped to create long ago. Things would never be as they were in the times before the Heavenly Wars, but now there was an opportunity for something better than chaos and slow death. Of course, none of those people would ever be aware of the magnitude of the personal sacrifice that had been made by his friends. The rest of Raashan would most likely assume that Anut and Muntros had simply not died in the Heavenly Wars and had waited until now to resurface, for whatever reason. Most mortals were content to shrug such complications off as something they would never understand because they didn't need to understand it. It was the natural way of things, and so it was for the best.

Giev squinted as he saw someone in the distance coming up the hill. It was a young man in wizard's apprentice robes. Giev breathed a sigh of relief as he realized that Tim had sent Tristin to check on them. Tristin would be able to help him back to the mansion.

CHAPTER FIFTY-ONE

❦

*T*HE WORLD OF Raashan had been revived! Over the months following the ascension of Anut and Muntros, there had been very distinguishable changes to the entire planet. At first, there was a definite struggle between the two old gods as they fought for supremacy over one another. There were violent storms, a plague of disease, and even a week of scorching summer heat in the middle of winter. However, this all died down as the gods realized that they were evenly matched and that one could not gain control over the other. There was even a rumor that all their fighting had somehow birthed a new neutral god who acted as a nonpartisan mediator between the two extremes. It was strongly suspected by those that knew of the wizard Tim that the great wizard actually knew the whole truth of that rumor, but whenever he was asked about it, Tim only winked and asked why people were concerning themselves with such nonsense.

The spring that followed that winter brought the most successful planting season in over fifty years. Naturally, the summer and fall harvests that followed were the most bountiful the world had seen in just as many years. Even the great northern forest that had died years before was coming back to life. There had been a great wildfire that burned through all the dead, brittle trees. It was most likely the doing of Muntros, but the fire had enriched the long infertile soil with much-needed nutrients. Now a whole new forest was growing in its place.

Back in the Aranni village, the tribal elves were also experiencing a great boom of prosperity. The population was growing again, and the people were overjoyed to have good hunting and harvests. Rosalin and Theryl had been married the spring before in a small ceremony under the growing moon, as was their tradition. Rosalin had become pregnant soon after the wedding and gave birth to their first child, a son, the following year. She was blissfully happy with her husband and child, and that the world suddenly became bountiful and rich again only deepened her happiness. Rosalin and Eithne's mother had become well again, and their father was also doing much better. The harmony of life in the Aranni village had returned. However, there was one dark spot in all the light for Eithne's family. Their youngest daughter had still not returned. Darian's letters had given the Alfrey family much hope and peace of mind, but the letters had stopped coming about one year ago. The family feared the worst. They feared that both Eithne and Darian were dead. They tried to stay positive. Rosalin especially had taken up the habit of concocting possible circumstances where both her sister and Darian were alive and happy. Her favorite scenario was that Eithne and Darian had fallen in love, married, and that they had become so wrapped up in their own lives that they had forgotten to write. Rosalin had suspected from the letters Darian had sent that he and Eithne had sparked a romance, so it seemed to her to be a likely explanation for the lack of communication. Her parents also very much enjoyed the romantic notion and liked to tell themselves that it was the truth. One day, Darian and Eithne would remember their old home and return.

The past year had been one of perfect harmony and prosperity for all of Raashan. None could deny it. The whole world rejoiced in the good fortune that was the return of the gods—all but two elves, who waited on a hilltop just outside of the City of Duomo on the continent of Croissia.

A full year had passed since Darian and Aram had performed the ceremony that killed the women they loved. They had not left the hilltop for fear of missing Eithne and Yocelin's return. They had promised that they would wait, and so they waited patiently. They had built a small log cabin to live in with the help of Giev and Tristin. Tim made the construction of the cabin go more smoothly and quickly from the comfort of his mansion with magic. It was a small two-room cabin that was cozy and suited Darian and Aram's needs.

They filled their days with swordplay, hunting, and conversation. Giev came by almost every day to see his friends and to bring them food and supplies. The shaman had taken up residence at Tim's mansion. It was a wonderful learning opportunity for him. Also, Giev and the great wizard truly enjoyed each other's company. Tim rather liked having another person around, who was not his apprentice. Giev also bonded well with Tristin and taught the boy some important social skills that he was perhaps lacking. Tristin was no longer Tim's only apprentice. Since the return of the gods, magic had once again become more prevalent. More and more people were finding that they had magical gifts, and so prospective apprentices arrived at the wizard's mansion to request the privilege of his tutelage almost every week. Tim could not accept them all, of course, but he took in those that he felt were most promising. The large mansion that had echoed with emptiness for so long once again bustled with young people from all backgrounds striving to perfect the magical arts. Giev was a great help in managing and teaching the young apprentices. Sometimes Tim worried that the handsome elf was perhaps too popular with the female, and some of the male, apprentices. However, Giev remained professional and took care not to dip his quill in the apprentice inkwell, so to speak. He knew that it was wrong and that Tim would always find out if he strayed. There were plenty of beautiful women in Duomo to keep him busy, regardless.

Giev hiked up the hill that Darian and Aram resided upon in the late morning with a sack of potatoes and vegetables slung over his shoulder. He breathed in the crisp autumn air as he reached the top and surveyed the view. A brilliant symphony of fiery hues greeted him against the clear blue sky. It was another beautiful day over Duomo. There had been so many beautiful days this past year.

"Nice to see you finally made it back up here." Darian came up behind Giev and clapped him on the back welcomingly.

"What do you mean 'finally'?" Aram said jokingly as he approached. "He was just here yesterday."

"What can I say? I like the view." Giev countered with a grin.

It was good to see his friends again, though the visits were always tinged with unspoken sadness and disappointment. When the shaman mentioned the view, Darian and Aram both let their eyes drift to the spot where the ceremony had taken place a year earlier. They often stared at that spot, constantly hopeful that Eithne and Yocelin would appear.

Giev cleared his throat to help pass the awkwardness. "Not to mention that someone has to keep you two properly fed."

He handed the sack of food to Aram, who nodded his thanks. The three friends walked over to the small cabin to sit in some chairs just in front of it. They spent some time catching up on the goings-on at the mansion and talked of other news. Even though they all saw each other frequently, they never seemed to be at a los for good conversation. The hours drifted by, and the sun moved across the sky into the afternoon.

"You know, I almost forgot to tell you what the latest rumor is about you two," Giev said as he puffed on his pipe. He had taken up pipe smoking several months ago and found that it suited him very well.

"Ah, yes, the ever-popular gossip. What was the last rumor? That we are brothers who were raised by wolves and can't bring ourselves to join civilized society?" Darian chuckled.

Since they never left the hilltop, the good people of Duomo had let their imaginations run wild with creative explanations for their seclusion. Occasionally, adolescent or teenaged citizens of the city would dare to venture up to the cabin on the hill to spy the two elves that lived there. Sometimes Darian and Aram would play innocent pranks on them, and other times they would just ignore them entirely. Any attempts they made to have a normal conversation with the intruders never seemed to work out. It provided a welcome distraction to their routine.

"I liked that one," Giev stated as he reclined with his pipe. "Little do they know that the occasional howling they hear at the full moon is really just the friendly neighborhood werewolf."

"I do what I can." Aram smiled.

He found that he was amused with the stories he heard about himself and Darian. Aram often wondered if they would ever realize that the truth of their presence on the hill was just as far-fetched as the fantasies. His smile faded, and he looked at the ground as his thoughts drifted to Yocelin. If the people of Duomo knew the truth, they would probably revere it as a great love story—he and Darian just patiently waiting for the return of their true loves. To someone on the outside, it would seem like such an amazing and beautiful story, but Aram had trouble seeing it that way. All he knew was that he lived with a debilitating pain in his heart every second of every day. He put on a brave face and learned to live with the pain, but every morning when he woke from his dreams of Yocelin, the wound was fresh and stinging. Until she returned to him, he would not be whole.

"Stop holding us in suspense. What is our new persona?" Darian's words interrupted Aram's depressing thoughts.

Aram was thankful. Such gossip was a welcome distraction.

"Well, apparently, you are both priests of the new gods and are currently on a holy hermitage on this very hilltop," Giev answered with great satisfaction. This new rumor did seem to have a bit of the actual truth in it.

Darian and Aram both chuckled at the latest story. They never seemed to laugh out loud anymore, even when presented with the most ridiculous stories. They simply couldn't bring themselves to laugh out loud. It wouldn't come.

"Are we to be expecting pilgrims?" Darian asked, anxious to keep his mind from drifting to the more depressing thoughts that filled him most of the time.

"It's too soon to tell, but I'll let you know if I see people heading your way bearing offerings," Giev replied slyly.

"Well, don't stop them if they are going to be bringing us gifts. Just let us know their coming so Aram and I can pretend to be holy hermits," Darian joked.

"And that holy men are partial to roasted lamb and potatoes," Aram offered pointedly.

Giev laughed out loud at their jokes. He could just imagine the people of Duomo making regular pilgrimages to the hilltop, carrying roasted lamb and potatoes on great platters. Darian and Aram smiled warmly but did not join in their friend's raucous laughter. They did enjoy his mirth, though. Giev's visits always brought them laughter, which they very much needed these days.

The friends spoke for a while longer about rumors and amusing stories. Giev noticed that the sun was dipping low over the horizon. It was early evening and time that he left. It was rare that he had the opportunity to spend the entire day up on the hill, and he had greatly enjoyed his time here today. He liked to think that Darian and Aram benefited from his visits as well, and he was right. Giev was really the only social contact they had. Every once in a while, Tristin would come to visit, but mostly they relied on Giev. Tim often expressed a wish to visit, but he never did make the trip. This did further curiosity among the friends about why Tim never left the mansion, but they never asked the old wizard about it. The topic was fun to theorize about when they ran out of other conversation, so knowing the answer would spoil the fun.

"Well, I'm afraid that I must be going." Giev tapped out his pipe off the arm of his chair and pushed himself up from it.

The friends said their good-byes, and Giev went back down the hill into Duomo. He always felt the weight in his heart as he walked back to the mansion, knowing that his best friends wished he could stay longer. Giev was painfully aware that he was a distraction from the emotional turmoil that Darian and Aram endured every minute of the day as they waited, hopeful for the return of Eithne and Yocelin. He knew that his friends did not blame him for the pain and long wait, but Giev felt guilty all the same. Often, his sleep was interrupted by the thoughts of how he could have done the spell better somehow, how he could have possibly been more accurate with the timing. Unfortunately for the shaman's guilty feelings, constant review of his performance, as well as many conversations with Tim, had all told him that there was nothing more he could have done. The magic would work when the magic chose to work. Tim had even said that he could not have done any better himself. Even with all this affirmation, Giev still could not sleep soundly. Until Eithne and Yocelin returned, he would also be waiting anxiously.

Things were quiet at the cabin on the hill after Giev left. Darian and Aram rarely spoke, for when they did, it only led to further depression. The only thing on both their minds was the return of Eithne and Yocelin. It only hurt to speak of it and led to deeper despair. Hope was the most important thing for them as they remained on their isolated hilltop. That quiet hope was all they lived for.

A cold autumn wind blew as Darian and Aram settled in for the night. Winter was on its way again. To them, the cold did not matter. They recognized that the world around them changed over the course of a year with the seasons in all their glory, but life on the hilltop seemed a perpetual, numbing winter.

CHAPTER FIFTY-TWO

A HEAVY LATE SPRING rainstorm fell over Duomo in large splashing drops. The sound of it was pleasant and musical. The city was quiet as residents stayed indoors and peacefully enjoyed the melody of the warm spring rain.

The great wizard Tim was sitting in his study gazing out the large window in quiet reverie. A hot mug of tea accompanied his peaceful thoughts as he happily watched the rain pour down into his courtyard. The summer was approaching, and the humidity in the air caused a steamy mist to hover low over the ground. It was a beautiful and tranquil experience. Raashan had become a delightful place again since the return of the gods. The companions had done a fine job.

As Tim took a long drink of the honeyed brew, a sort of epiphany shot into his mind. It startled him so much that he froze in midsip with wide eyes and raised eyebrows. Then as if to exaggerate Tim's epiphany, a loud clap of thunder sounded! Though the rain was heavy, it was not a storm, and there had been no thunder before the single clap. The wizard sat frozen in place for a very long moment, as if he had suddenly turned into a statue. As the minutes passed, a slow grin of elation spread wide across his face and wrinkled the skin around his bright blue eyes. He could not remember the last time he had felt such overwhelming joy! Moving with the sudden spring of a young man, the old wizard popped up and ran to find Giev. Today Tim got to be the bearer of the most wonderful news!

Up on the hilltop, Darian and Aram were having yet another quiet day of no consequence. As it was raining outside, they knew that Giev would not visit today. They both sat inside the cabin, silently passing the time. Darian sat in his favorite chair, carving a piece of wood into a small figure of a phoenix. It was one of the many hobbies he had picked up over the past two and a half years. He did not know what possessed him to try carving a phoenix today. It was not something he had attempted previously, and it was much more intricate than he was accustomed to, but he thought it was coming along all right, anyway. Aram sat across the small room at the table. He was playing a solitary card game. Aram felt bored with it. He seemed to keep drawing the suit of hearts, and it was making it difficult for him to complete the game.

A loud clap of thunder sounded and caused both men to look up from their activities.

"I didn't think it would turn into a storm," Aram stated suspiciously.

"Neither did I," Darian responded with equal skepticism.

The thunderclap seemed very much out of place. They paused for a long time, waiting for another clap to sound, or for the lightning to flash, but neither happened. The melody of the raindrops had resumed as it had played all day long. It seemed that the thunder was an isolated incident. They shrugged at each other and resumed their activities.

An instant later, Aram's head shot up, intently listening. He could have sworn he had heard Yocelin's voice just then. Both he and Darian had gone through a phase in the first few months of waiting where they could have sworn that they had heard the voices of Eithne or Yocelin outside. Every time, they would bolt out of the cabin only to have their hopes miserably dashed when they realized the voices were only in their heads. This time was different, though. Aram had not heard Yocelin's chiming laughter, or her calling his name. This time he thought he had heard her sneeze in her distinctive, and very cute, little squeaking *a-choo*. Even more unusually, he thought he heard Eithne say, "Bless you." Aram had never imagined hearing Eithne's voice before.

He heard the sneeze again!

Aram strained his ears. He could swear that he could hear both girls exclaiming over being so wet and out of sorts. He stood up so fast that he knocked his chair to the floor. Darian stared at him with wide eyes. He too was on his feet and tense with energy. The heavy rain made it hard for them to hear, and both feared that the voices were merely phantoms of overzealous hope, but there was something different this time. A certain tingle spread throughout their bodies, telling them that it was real this time. This time there were no phantoms and dashed hopes outside. This time they would find the women they loved in the flesh! Darian and Aram went to the door so quickly that they almost got stuck trying to run through the narrow space at the same time. Bursting out into the rain, they frantically looked around. At first, everything was so blurry. The rain and mist made visibility poor.

"Eithne!" Darian cried.

"Yocelin!" Aram shouted.

"*A-choo*! Over here!" Yocelin's voice called back cheerfully.

"Darian, where are you?" Eithne responded.

Their voices were coming from around the back of the cabin. They had responded! They had truly returned! Hearts pounding in their ears, and still afraid that this was all imagined, Darian and Aram skidded around to the back of the cabin, practically tripping over each other, to see two naked women huddled together in the rain: one, a tall, willowy red-haired elf with a phoenix tattoo down the entire left side of her body, and the other, a petite, curvy demon with purple hair and curling black horns. Eithne and Yocelin had finally returned.

Darian and Aram needed no words. They each rushed to the women they loved and gathered them tightly into their arms with no intentions of ever letting go again. Both men openly wept from the sheer joy of finally being reunited.

Neither Eithne nor Yocelin had any concept of how long it had taken for them to return. To them, the ceremony had only taken place a moment ago. However, they realized that they were gone much longer than a moment. The warm rain told them it was at least spring now, not to mention the degree to which they were both being smothered with hugs and kisses from their loves spoke of a much longer absence. Not that Eithne or Yocelin minded the attention in the least. Though the separation had felt fleeting to them, it did nothing to dampen the elation of being alive and with their protectors. The couples basked in the pure happiness of being reunited for a very long time, not caring that they were all getting soaked to the bone.

"*A-choo*!" Yocelin sneezed again. "Could we perhaps get out of the rain?" she requested between kisses.

"Also, we could use some clothes," Eithne said with a good amount of chagrin.

Aram stopped smothering Yocelin briefly and blinked at her as he pushed her wet hair away from her deep blue eyes. She couldn't stop smiling at him with her rosy cheeks and twinkling eyes. As far as he was concerned, she would get exactly everything she wanted for the rest of her life. He would make it so. Yocelin forgot her request as Aram looked at her. She could have forgotten her own name as she looked into his dark-brown eyes. She barely noticed as he scooped her up and carried her into the cabin.

Darian had not really noticed the naked state of Eithne. He had been so focused on having her back in his arms that all else was secondary, including being dry and comfortable. He cupped her face in his hands and kissed her again.

"Whatever you wish so long, as you don't wish me to let go."

Eithne shook her head. "I will be very cross with you if you release me."

"Then we understand each other." Darian nuzzled her neck and pressed Eithne up against him in a bear hug.

He shuffled her into the cabin in a very silly manner that made her laugh her tinkling laughter. Darian felt whole again for the first time in years.

"I believe that I have found what is different about you," Darian announced with a satisfied smirk.

He and Eithne were lying on some blankets on the floor in the main room of the little cabin at the foot of the crackling fire in the hearth. Darian's clothing had long been tossed aside. It had to have been hours since Eithne had returned to him, but neither of them had any concept of time. Eithne lay on her right side. Darian lay behind her tracing the lines of her tattoo with his fingertips.

"You're being silly," Eithne chided nervously. "There's nothing different about me." As she spoke, she stretched in a catlike way to better allow him to trace along her skin. She was enjoying the sensation of his touch, but talk of her coming back different made her feel uncomfortable.

"No, I found it. At first, I couldn't quite place what it was, but now that I have thoroughly explored you, I figured it out." Darian grinned shamelessly when she flushed pink at the mention of being so explored. He thought it was very endearing that she could still get embarrassed after what they had been doing for the past few hours. "You're phoenix is brighter."

"What?"

"The color of the phoenix used to be more brownish red, rusty, like everyone else in our tribe. Now it is brighter and seems more detailed. It's like your spirit guide was reborn with you," Darian continued tracing as he spoke, following the lines and taking in the new flaming colors of her tattoo.

"Really? That's interesting."

Eithne propped herself up on one elbow to get a better view of her left side. It looked like Darian was right. The phoenix did appear to be brighter and more colorful. It settled her nerves to know that this was the difference he had been referring to. She smiled and ran her hand over one of the wings. She rather liked the change.

"You waited that long for me to come back?" Yocelin asked in the smallest of voices.

Aram had just told her how long it had been since she and Eithne were burned up in the ceremony. She and Aram were in the bedroom of the cabin, both on what Yocelin assumed was Aram's bed. He lay on his back with her on top of him, looking into her face. They had taken a break to talk after rejoicing in each other. It was dark outside now, and it seemed that the rain fell more lightly.

Aram nodded in response to her question. "I told you I would wait for as long as it took. I may have never left this hilltop."

Yocelin bent her head and kissed his bare chest over his heart. "I'm so sorry I made you wait."

Aram smoothed her hair. "You didn't make me do anything. I knew you would come back. I wasn't going to leave this spot until it happened. You're worth every long second it took and much longer."

Yocelin felt her eyes moisten with tears. It had happened a lot since she had blinked back into existence. She could not help how touched she was by almost everything Aram did and said. She didn't know what she had done to deserve such a man.

Aram smiled at her happy tears. She looked beautiful when she let herself cry. He could not believe that Yocelin was back. His beacon of light had returned to keep his heart safe and warm.

CHAPTER FIFTY-THREE

*T*HE MONTHS FOLLOWING the return of Eithne and Yocelin were filled with joy and changes. Darian and Aram were all too happy to move out of the cabin on the hill. Giev took it over as a part-time residence for himself. As much as he enjoyed living at Tim's mansion, Giev was the type who needed to retreat in solitude every once in a while. The little cabin suited his needs perfectly.

Darian and Eithne traveled back to their village at last. Their families were overjoyed to see them again, and there was so much news to share. They were married in the village that summer under a growing moon. Their families tried to urge them to wait until the following spring, as was traditional, but Darian and Eithne had no care for such things anymore. They respected the traditions of their tribe, but their view of the world was different now, and such things did not concern them. After they were married, they stayed and enjoyed the company of their loved ones for several weeks. Eithne delighted in meeting her nephew and getting to know Rosalin's husband. Rosalin was thrilled that she had been right, in a way, about the fate of her sister. She had so much to share with Eithne and spent as much time as she could with her little sister. However, Eithne and Darian grew tired of retelling the stories of their adventures much more often than they liked. You can never really go home again after you have had a great adventure. It was so good to see everyone, but something within Darian and Eithne had changed. They could no longer accept a simple village life, especially Eithne, as she had never felt that a limited existence in the village was for her. So they said good-bye to their families and to a life in the Aranni village and moved back to Duomo. They built a house on the outskirts of the

426

city, with the help of their friends, so that they could still be close to nature. Tribal elves did not do well behind city walls.

Aram and Yocelin had also made their home in the outskirts of Duomo. Both would have preferred to be closer into the city center, but since Aram turned into a werewolf once a month, they thought it was better to be a little more removed from society. Aram and Yocelin never properly married. They did not feel the need to do so. They referred to each other as a spouse, and so, in their hearts, they were married. That was enough, though Yocelin was known to occasionally lament that she never did get to wear a beautiful wedding gown. It was a fleeting complaint that didn't really matter.

Tim was extremely pleased that all the companions had chosen to remain close to his mansion. The companions all came around to visit regularly, which made the old wizard very happy. He had grown to think of them as his family, and so their visits were greatly appreciated. Tim had never had children of his own, and his own family had all died long ago. He came to regard the companions as his children in a way, and so he had a fatherly sort of love for all of them. He was so proud. Occasionally, during visits the companions would jokingly ask Tim if any new prophecies involving them had come to him. The wizard knew that they were partly serious when they asked. They lived with an anxiety that they would be called upon again to fulfill a prophecy. Tim would always chuckle and say that he was sure that saving the world once was quite enough for one lifetime. However, Tim could never set their minds completely at ease. After all, the gods and magic had a funny way of depending on the same people to accomplish tasks when they needed doing. Of course, the old wizard did not mention this to the companions. He had a great hope that they would have the luxury of living out the rest of their lives in peace.

THE END

For Now...

ABOUT THE AUTHOR

 Hollis enjoys expressing herself through many different creative mediums—including writing, cosplay, drawing, and dance. She loves animals and helping others, so when she isn't working on her next creative project, she is working with animals and volunteering. Stricken with a terrible case of wanderlust, traveling is her happy place, and she will not stop until she's seen everything . . . twice. Having been raised a Navy brat and spent seven years as an immigration officer in the world of higher education, much of the world has already been seen, but it's never enough!

CPSIA information can be obtained
at www.ICGtesting.com
Printed in the USA
FFOW03n2115100717
37558FF